Guerrillas in our Midst

Also by Claire Peate and available from Honno

The Floristry Commission
Big Cats and Kitten Heels
Head Hunters

Guerrillas in our Midst

by

Claire Peate

HONNO MODERN FICTION

Published by Honno

'Ailsa Craig', Heol y Cawl, Dinas Powys,

South Glamorgan, Wales, CF64 4AH

The author would like to stress that this is a work of fiction and
no resemblance to any actual individual or institution is
intended or implied.

ISBN: 978-1-906784-25-6

Published with the financial support of the Welsh Books Council.

Cover design: G Preston
Cover photograph: © Getty Images
Printed in Wales by Gomer Press

For EJP and MJP. When you're older…

With thanks to David, as always. Also a big thank you to Elizabeth McWilliams for the detailed stuff: sorry I called you Barry Manilow's daughter at school, that was very wrong. Thanks to Bo and Alison who helped me with book-polishing. Thanks also to Hugh and Jane – supporters extraordinaire. And, lastly, thank you to my editor, Caroline Oakley, who gets inside my head and tells me what I'm thinking. Spooky.

Edda Mackenzie
189 Geoffrey Road
Brockley
LONDON
SE4 1NT

13th May

Dear Ms Mackenzie

Thank you for your letters regarding the abandoned skip. We appreciate that you are *not one to complain* (letter number two) and *are being driven to breaking point by the unsightliness of it* (letter four), but I regret to inform you that the Council will be unable to move the said waste receptacle on health and safety grounds: we suggest that you continue in your endeavours to contact Invinci-Skips who are legally obliged to remove their own property.

I sincerely wish you the best of luck for your *forthcoming papal visit* (letter seven) and feel confident that despite your concerns his Eminence will be in no way offended by the unsightly waste receptacle, during his luncheon at your house, should it not be removed in time.

Best wishes

Adrian Jag
Senior Assistant Sub Manager
Waste and Recycling, Lewisham Council
LEWISHAM COUNCIL: TOGETHER WE CAN MAKE A DIFFERENCE

failure notice

From: "MAILER-
DAEMON@n21.bullet.mail.ukl.com" <MAILER-
DAEMON@n21.bullet.mail.ukl.com>
Add
To: Eddamackenzie@yahoo.co.uk

Sorry, we were unable to deliver your message to the
following address.

ENQUIRIES@INVINCI-SKIPS.CO.UK

No MX or A records for htmali.cmo

--- Below this line is a copy of the message.

Received: from [217.146.182.177] by
n21.bullet.mail.ukl.com with NNFMP; 14May
19:18:45 -0000
Content-Type: multipart/alternative; boundary="0-
1083190294-1269458324=:33052"

<html><head><style type=3D"Text/css"><!— DIV
{margin:0px;} —></style></he=
ad><body><div style=3D

//returned content //

Subject: DUMPED SKIP

2

Dear Sir/ Madam

After repeated attempts to telephone you (is your phone cut off?) and writing to you I hope email will get through. One of your skips has been dumped on vacant land in front of my house and has not been collected for FIVE MONTHS. It is now overflowing with household waste, including a filthy mattress that smells of dead dogs. I imagine. Please can you move it immediately otherwise I will have to take legal action.
Yours sincerely

Edda Mackenzie
189 Geoffrey Road, Brockley, SE4 1NT

One

"Where's the goddamn trowel, Edda, I need it right now!" Beth called from inside the skip.

"Shhh!" I was on the pavement below and looked up from my cork-wrangling. "I haven't got the trowel," I hissed as loudly as I dared. "You were going to bring it." I turned back to the bottle of Cava. Why I'd bought Cava I don't know: the deafening POP! was going to wake the neighbourhood and blow our cover. We should have brought something silent like a box of wine – although how much we would actually have achieved if we'd brought an entire box of wine with us was another matter. I also should have brought night-vision goggles: who would have thought it would be so dark? Only every other street light was working.

"*Edda we talked about this!*" A stern-voiced Beth peered over the top of the skip. "I mean, for God's sake Eds, the plan was that *you* would bring the trowels and *I* would bring – the – oh pants – no no, it was me bringing trowels wasn't it? Oh, hon, I'm sorry!" She sank back into the skip again, out of view. "I don't know what's got into me lately," her voice wobbled into the night, "I'm all over the place! I'd swear I'm going completely mad. I am! I'm going mad…"

Shpfut-thhhhhhhh. The cork greasily slid out of the Cava bottle. It was obvious from the wet noise that the drink inside the bottle was not destined for greatness.

But who cared about greatness? It was Cava – probably – and it was needed. I clambered up onto a rickety dumped chair I'd found inside the skip and got into the skip itself beside my best friend. "It's fine that we don't have trowels," I said, sniffing the neck of the bottle. "We can trowel with our hands. I bunged two spades in the shopping trolley, so we'll be OK for the big stuff. Here – try this!" I drank from the bottle and passed it to her.

And nearly threw up. "Urgh!"

"Bloody hell, Eds!" Beth angled the label to the faint orange street light to read what she'd just imbibed. "It's like … it's like … *white wine vinegar*. Carbonated." She gamely took another swig and passed it back. "Dear God! But hey it's probably really good for my teeth though. How are they – are they Hollywood white now?"

"I can't see, Beth. It's dark."

"So it is." She laughed, took another mouthful, gasped and passed the bottle back to me.

"Shall we have a fag before we start?" I said, hunting in my pockets. Anything to delay the start of the actual manual labour.

Beside us were two shopping trolleys, merely borrowed – and in no way stolen – from the local Sainsbury's in New Cross Gate. They were filled to the brim with bags of topsoil, shrubs and flowers. Mr Iqbal from the corner shop had lent us vast empty water bottles refilled with tap water – *For a party is it girls? I*

6

don't know – you two girls are forever on the town. You need to get yourselves good husbands and you know my two sons are very successful in the City. Did I tell you about my Ali who is forty and a very good looking boy…

The water bottles were much too heavy to lift so to transport the water from the bottles in the trolleys to the garden we had the tiny watering can that I'd had as a child. Beth had scoffed when she saw it, but I loved my watering can. Around the body of the can was a picture of Zippy and Bungle holding an enormous marrow which, even at an early age, had struck me as inappropriate: something to do with the look in Zippy's eyes.

It had been 1am on Saturday morning when we had finally sneaked out of my house after many fortifying bottles of beer. We'd each pushed a squeaky trolley the few metres across the road to the *offending waste receptacle*, which for all the complaining in the world had proved immovable. An hour of settling, stamping and pushing later, and the dumped waste only came three-quarters of the way up the abandoned skip, leaving us the top to cover in soil and plant up. My plan was coming together.

Beth knocked back the Cava. "Let's save the fags for when we've put the soil in… This skip stinks! Do you think there really is a dead dog or something in the bottom?"

"*Get down!*" I hissed, and as one we ducked.

"What is it?" came a tiny voice beside me.

7

"It's Babs. I think I see her watching from her bedroom window," I whispered.

"Babs? Babs from next door? God I hate that old crone!"

"Don't be so rude. I like Babs."

In the dark I could just make out that Beth had turned in my direction and was staring incredulously at me. "Seriously Eds, you don't really like her do you? She's just a miserable old rumourmonger. Here," she reached over the side of the skip to the trolley and passed me an enormous sombrero, which I donned while she put on her own. Our disguise was now complete. No one, not even my neighbour Babs with her beady eyes, would know who was gardening the skip. Unless of course Babs had noticed the shopping trolleys in my front garden, which for the last week had been piled with bags of topsoil…

It was my job to heft the bags of topsoil from the trolleys up to the skip and it was Beth's job – on account of feeling under the weather – to open them and distribute the soil over the dumped waste. A quarter of an hour of hefting and carbonated-white-wine-vinegaring and we were done: the aroma of dead dog was sealed off for good. A mini garden was being born. I clambered up onto the cool earth and together we enjoyed our Marlboro Lights – no easy task when sporting a one-metre sombrero – and the rest of the Cava, leaning back against the rusty metal of the skip.

"You know this is such a cool idea of yours honey – it's going to look *ace!*" Beth gave me a one-armed hug and we clashed hat brims. "And I just can't believe that *you* actually came up with it! Of all the people!" She laughed, quietly, and tipped back the Cava bottle.

"Ha!" I said. And then added, "Me of all people? You're surprised?"

"Well a bit. Do you want any more of this by the way?"

I took the bottle from her. "Surprised by what?" I asked, as lightly as I could.

"What? Oh. Well. I suppose it's just that you're usually so … I don't know … you're usually quite reserved?"

"*Reserved?*"

"OK, *quiet* then." Beth contemplated her cigarette. "I mean, illegally planting up a skip in the dead of night seems a bit extreme. For you. That's all. Cracking idea, though, my love. Brilliant."

"I can be extreme," I said, in a small voice. "You know I can." After spending half our life together Beth must surely have up her sleeve one or two examples of when I'd been extreme.

Beth lifted up her sombrero and looked me in the eye. "Darling you've never been extreme in all your life. Not ever. And that's no bad thing." She managed to find me in the dark and plant a hat-dislodging kiss on my forehead. "I guess you just snapped when no one listened to your complaints. Did you call the newspapers by the way? They're usually pretty good for stories like this and once the papers get hold of it then the Council will have to do something."

"They weren't interested. Unless there was a body in the skip and then they said they'd send someone round."

"What about the dog?"

"I think they meant a human body. Anyway there might not actually be a dead dog beneath us: it just smells like there's one there."

"I hope there isn't. It'd be kind of freaky if we were sitting above a dead dog. Now pass the bottle over and— It's empty! Edda you've finished it all!"

"I think you had more than half actually," I said.

"I think not! You've pigged the goddamn lot! How am I supposed to carry on with this illicit manual labour without any more Cava? Since you finished it you should go and get some more."

"Beth! You could go too – you had just as much as I had. If not more."

"Yes but that's *your* house, right there. That is *your* living room window. I can see *your* cat sleeping on *your* bedroom windowsill."

"You boss me about too much." I said but nevertheless stood up and made to exit the skip. Not such an easy thing to do in the dark with a sombrero and after drinking half – well, maybe three-quarters – of a bottle of Cava.

"I do not boss you around too much," Beth waved my comment away. "You love me telling you what's what. If you didn't have me to boss you around you'd be— "

"I'd still be up in a skip with a trowel, but on my own. And I'd have had a bottle of Cava all to myself."

"Shut up, woman, and do as I say and get more supplies!" and she threw a handful of topsoil at me.

SKIP SKIP HOORAY!
FROM ABANDONED SKIP TO CHELSEA
FLOWER SHOW CONTENDER

Something beautiful is happening in Brockley. On Saturday night, an abandoned skip was transformed into a miniature Garden of Eden fit for the Chelsea Flower Show itself. The skip, situated in the conservation area of up-and-coming Brockley, had been left there when local firm Invinci-Skips went into receivership. It had become a dumping ground for the community but one enterprising individual – or individuals – has turned it into something quite remarkable, as our picture attests. Painted in Farrow and Ball's Saxon Green, the skip features trailing variegated ivies, scented rosemary bushes and striking scarlet geraniums that brighten the street.

"Brockley is on the rise," says Eustace Fox, proprietor of Fox Estates of Brockley. "Once the suburb of choice for the wealthy Victorian industrialist, Brockley is being reclaimed by wealthy urban families appreciative of its beautiful early Victorian houses, large gardens and proximity to Central London. We're just seven minutes away from London Bridge. I'm not surprised people are taking responsibility for their area, there's a lot of love for the neighbourhood and the new Brockleyites are a force to be reckoned with."

So, for now Brockleyites are enjoying their new garden. But can a leopard really change its spots? Is Brockley ready for gentrification and a move towards becoming the new Greenwich? Perhaps not just yet: already the vandals have paid a visit to the skip and left their mark. "It's such a shame," Eustace Fox had to concede, "that disgraceful youths have thrown several empty Cava bottles and fag ends into the new skip garden. Some people have no respect."

Two

Something really odd was happening. Since the skip escapade, I'd hardly seen Beth at all. In fact, I *hadn't* seen her at all: all I'd had was a couple of text messages about the cheapness of the Cava, the cheapness of me for having bought it, and having sore muscles after the digging. Apart from that: silence. I'd left messages and had even wandered down the road to her flat, earlier in the week, to see how she was doing, but both she and Jack had been out. Or hiding.

It was strange: horrible and strange, because I usually saw her or spoke to her if not every day then every other day. But it had been nearly a week and I was getting concerned. And lonely: the weekend was looming and it was going to be a long and barren one after the text on Friday night:

sorry hon feeling dreadful. resched Saturday? B x

I'd texted back but there had been no more replies. Just what was going on with Beth?

So, on Saturday morning, with no raging hangover to battle and no partying to look forward to, I ran out of excuses to put off doing something I should have done a year ago or more. I decided to Clean My House. Since Beth had moved out two years ago, the place had begun to resemble the set of a gothic horror film: cobwebs, dust and dusty cobwebs – it was all there. And it did bother me and I did fully intend to clean, but there was always that nagging argument *well who else will see it but me, why bother?* That morning, however, buoyed up by my new-found activism post skip-gardening and with my enforced Bethlessness I'd got as far as finding the Dyson. And then the phone rang.

"Oh!" said the person on the other end of the phone:, at least I thought it was a person. "Eh! Eh! Eep eep eep eep eep eep eep eep eep eep eep…" I held the phone away from my ear. Who on earth was calling me – a mouse? I put it back to my ear. "Eep eep eep eep eep eep!"

My cat, Finley, could clearly hear the caller and was looking particularly interested. Most mice restricted themselves to the garden but I could tell that he was thinking that one bold enough to phone up was surely going to be fantastic sport.

"Hello?" I said when there was a break in the squeaking. "Who is this? Is this a sales call?"

There was a pause and then I heard a wobbly intake of breath, "Edda…!"

"Beth? Beth, is it you?" My chest tightened.

There was heavy sobbing followed by more squeaking.

"Beth, are you OK? Is everything OK? Are you in your flat? Shall I come round?" I felt sick to my core. Was she ill, was she *dying*? Had something awful happened to her boyfriend, Jack?

14

"Oh! Eds! Oh!"

"What's wrong?" I was almost crying myself, gripping the phone.

"Oh, Edda," Beth had a moment of squeakless clarity, "it's *awful!*"

"You're at your flat aren't you? I'm on my way! Stay there! Don't die! OK? *Don't die Beth!*"

I have never sprinted as fast as I did between my house and Beth and Jack's flat as I did just then. And in those three minutes scenes of horrific images filled my head: Beth with a kitchen knife plunged between her bloodied ribs, Beth on her bathroom floor with a bottle of pills spilling from her cold grey hand, Beth cradling an unconscious Jack in her arms at the bottom of her staircase…

I pummelled her front door and, thank God, she opened it. Clutching the door frame and panting like a sex fiend, I quickly scanned her for misplaced knives and mangled limbs. All looked in order.

She threw herself into my arms and wailed, "Oh, Edda, I am so bad! So bad!"

"Why? Why are you so bad?" I stroked her hair. "You're not bad, Beth!"

"No I am bad! I'm a really bad person."

"No honey you're not!" I held her close.

"I am! I'm so bad because I'm going to have a BABY Edda! I'm bloody well PREGNANT and I was DRUNK and I SMOKED and I was DRUNK…"

I held her to me, stroking her hair and saying nothing

because my throat was tight and my heart was pounding and my eyes were prickling with tears. In a single second my whole world had just fallen apart.

Bethan was going to be a mum.

And there was no one to stroke my hair and hold me.

"Oh Edda!" An exhausted cried-out Beth stared at me across the kitchen table with swollen red eyes.

I held her hands. "It will be OK you know…"

"No it won't!" She wailed.

"Well, how were you to know—"

"What kind of a mother am I going to be if I get pissed out of my head on cheap Cava and smoke a pack of fags a night?"

"They were *Lights* you know."

"Edda, for God's sake, this is serious!" she dropped my hands and started wailing again.

Fine. Fine then. There was no arguing with her. Beth – as always – was the boss.

After an hour of hand holding, hair stroking, hugging and generally hushing, Beth still hadn't progressed from the crying. Jack had hovered nervously in the background: I'd only noticed him after fifteen minutes; he was pacing the kitchen looking worried, an unlit fag in his mouth. He'd left soon after I'd noticed him; escaping to Surrey to tell his parents the good news and leaving me to sort out his pregnant girlfriend.

"Women do this, don't they Edda?" He'd whispered at me, wide-eyed, ramming on his shoes in the hallway while Beth, still wailing, had disappeared into the kitchen to get more kitchen towel. "They get all hormonal, don't they, when they're up the duff. That's right isn't it Edda? This is normal yeah?"

"Oh yes," I said, wondering why just being a woman gave him the impression that I had insight into this kind of stuff. "Beth is acting completely normally and rationally for a pregnant woman."

Back with Beth, there was a glint of hope as she surfaced from her wailing and took a sip of water. "I could have caused my little baby permanent harm though, couldn't I? That Cava was so bloody awful and I had so much of it! Do you think I've mutated my baby?"

"I'm—"

"Oh I would never have got so hammered on cheap alcohol and smoked if I'd have known!" she wailed. "When I think of the harm that I—"

"IT. IS. FINE," I shouted at her.

And for the first time that morning she stopped giving it the full Lady Macbeth and looked up at me.

I never shouted. Beth shouted. But I never did.

"Look, Beth," I filled the uncomfortable post-shout silence. "I don't know much about babies, but right now I imagine that your baby is probably no more than some dividing cells. You will have just mellowed out the cell division: eight cells probably didn't become sixteen cells quite as quickly as they might have done. That's all. You haven't given it a weird nose or anything…"

"*Given it a weird nose?*"

Damn. The second I'd said the bit about the weird nose Beth started up again, wailing about foetal alcohol syndrome and sobbing the word *mutation* over and over, so I sat in silence with my head resting on my hands and contemplated the lonely road ahead.

Three

The day after finding out about The Baby, and still in shock, I was on my way into work when I found myself standing beside a street light on Wickham Road, open mouthed and agog. More strange stuff. *What was going on with my world?* Wrapped around the base of the street light beside me, winding upwards, was a giant yellow and purple *knitted snake*. And there wasn't just one of the things, there were lots of them, twirled around all the street lights that ran along the length of the road, their heads drooping and tiny black wool tongues poking out at the pedestrians beneath them.

I hadn't noticed them straightaway, I'd been in my usual head-down if-I-don't-think-about-work-then-it-might-not-actually-happen mood, trudging down to the Council offices for another day filing paper in Beigedom. And then, for no real reason, I'd looked up and there was this giant woolly snake, looking down at me with white bobble eyes.

And I'd yipped, actually yipped like a poodle.

Fortunately there hadn't been anyone around at the time. Just me and the woolly snakes.

I raised a cautious hand up to the snake and touched it. Yes, it was definitely knitted. I started walking again, slowly, looking up at each of the snakes as I passed them: green and yellow, black and white, orange and blue, round and round the street lights, some of them boss-eyed, some of them winking, some of them looking straight down at me…

I turned the corner into Ashby Road with the same trepidation that a hunter might enter the jungle: what would be lurking *here*?

Hearts! Hundreds and hundreds of knitted hearts, hanging on woollen threads from the branches of the trees along the road. Pink and red and scarlet and raspberry, and every shade in between. I found it beautiful but also unnerving at the same time: like Sushi.

On Lewisham Way there were leg warmers on the parking meters and cutesy knitted animals, in fluffy pink and blue yarn, on the road signs. But by Lewisham it was all over – I found myself staring hard at the landscape around me, half expecting to see a giant tea-cosy over the entrance to the station. But no – the mass of knitted things appeared to be just limited to Brockley.

I continued my journey, still spooked.

The world was going mad.

Because not only had Brockley been attacked by grannies – which was odd enough – but last week I had made it into the national newspapers. It turned out that in the Big Society 'everyone doing their bit' was hot news and gardening an abandoned skip was very *now*. The *Telegraph* had taken a photo of my skip and hailed the new generation of do-gooders. OK so *I* wasn't mentioned per se (there was talk of residents seeing 'two men in large straw hats, clearly inebriated'), but at least someone had noticed my efforts, and even better than that was the fact that Alan Titchmarsh had classed it, "a bold and imaginative use of colour and texture."

"Do you realise Edda," Amanda jumped on to the edge of my desk and flashed her knickers at me, "that that's like the fiftieth time, or something, you've sighed since you got into work this morning?"

"Is it?" I said, weirdly drawn to gaze at her knickers, which were right there on display in front of me as they were most days. Today they were blue and had white hearts printed on them. They must have been her favourite pair: she wore them a lot.

"And you've just done it again." Amanda laughed.

"Done what?"

"Sigh."

"Oh." I bit my lip and managed to turn my attention to her face. "Yes. Maybe you're right…"

"So, what's up?"

I sighed. "I don't know … it's … well …" I threw my hands up. "It's because I've had my heart broken."

"Oh … no way! Boyfriend troubles?"

"You know I haven't got one."

"*Girlfriend* troubles?" her eyes widened with interest: Boring Old Colleague in Lesbian Shocker.

"Yes, but *not* in the way you're thinking."

"Oh. Go on then…" She leant back and, faced with the blue with white hearts again, I struggled to regain my train of thought.

21

"Is this the friend you're like *always* going on about? The one called Bethan?"

"Yes it is. But I don't always go on about her." I bristled.

"Yes you do. Seriously, you like never talk about anyone else; it's like *oh my God she's talking about that girl Bethan again already*."

Amanda watched too much American TV. She spent hours in front of the TV dramas because it was her sole ambition in life to be an actress: she studied American soaps like she was cramming for an audition.

"Well, I go on about Bethan because she's special to me," I said.

"But like not gay?" Amanda looked on unmoved.

"No." I said. And then because Amanda was completely impassive and, ridiculously, I wanted her to be moved by my tragic abandoned circumstances, I added, "Because when I was fourteen and I suddenly had no one, Beth and her family took me in and loved me, and she's been like a sister to me." Still nothing. "Beth is all the family I've got. We went to university together, we lived together in London, up until she moved in with her boyfriend…"

"Oh, OK." Happily, Amanda looked slightly more moved now she was beginning to understand the full extent of my relationship with Beth. "So, like, why have you two split up?" She winked and then added, "In like a totally non-gay way, of course."

"We haven't 'split up'. She's far too lovely to split up from anyone. My friend's having a baby. Her life is going in one direction—"

"And yours is going in the other."

"Yes. Sort of. Actually, mine's staying the same. Mine has no other direction to go in."

"But she's, like, old, right?"

"She's twenty-eight. The same as me."

"Yeah. Exactly. So you must have seen it coming, yeah? I mean if someone's going to start a family they ought to do it before thirty, right?"

I winced. The single biggest mistake I have probably ever made was to tell nineteen–year-old Amanda that I was twenty-eight. To Amanda, someone 'staring thirty in the arse' (her words) had enjoyed a *good innings*. To Amanda I was ancient and wizened, I had lived out a distant childhood in sepia and had experienced the Industrial Revolution first hand. Last week she'd asked me if I had all my own teeth.

"Anyway, that explains the sighing," I said, hoping she'd push off and take her blue knickers with her. Because I realised that I didn't want to talk to her about it. Apart from feeling sad and abandoned I didn't really have any other coherent thoughts to discuss or plans to move on.

"I read about this." Amanda was wagging her adolescent finger at me. "And do you know why you're so destroyed?"

"I am not *destroyed*."

"Well, whatever, but you're so *cut up* about this because you're, like, getting 'platonically divorced' from your friend."

"I am?"

"Totally. I read it in a magazine. Like, I *so* did," she added, seeing my scepticism, "You guys have been like a husband and wife…"

"I'm still not gay."

"No. So … you and Beth have been living so close for all those years and, like, your lives have been so bound up together – that's what the magazine said – and now she's cheated on you."

"With her boyfriend?"

"With her baby! So now there's going to be no room for you in her life. You're cast aside like an empty vessel."

I sat back and contemplated what Amanda had said. "You really think I'm an empty vessel?"

"Do *you* think you are?"

"Nooo…?"

"Good for you!" Amanda enthused. "Because it's still not too late for you, you know that. Even, like, near thirty. You have to treat it like a proper divorce, you know? Move on and everything. Go out with someone else, see your other friends when you would have seen her. You can come out with me and my friends if you want," she said. "There's older people in our group. My mate Rebecca is twenty-three. So you'd be OK, you'd have someone to talk to and everything."

I couldn't have been more tight-lipped if I'd caught my mouth in a vice. "Mmm. Great. Thanks."

"But the article said, in situations like this it's, like, absolutely over between the two of you. You aren't going back. You *can't* go back to how you were because she's having a baby and doesn't want you any more. So you have to start afresh. It's the start of a whole new you," she enthused.

"Well, that's just ridiculous," I said with a lump in my throat at the thought that Beth didn't want me any more. "We can pick up with something new. Just because she's having a baby doesn't mean it's the end. We can adapt: we've been friends for fourteen years." And then mentally added, *since you were five*. OK. Sometimes maybe I did seem quite old.

But the blue-knickered harbinger of doom was shaking her head. "It's, like, *so over* Edda. Accept it. You should like totally go wild and stuff, let your hair down. Hey – do you share a mortgage or something? Because that's, like, really bad if you do."

"No. I live on my own."

"You have your own flat?"

"House."

"You have your own *house*?" Amanda squeaked.

"It's an inheritance." I said lightly. And then stopped there. I was absolutely not going to get caught up in a conversation with Amanda about my dead parents. God knows what improving magazine article she would thrust at me.

"Well you could get a lodger, couldn't you? Like, a really hot guy…"

I considered it for a moment. "Ye-es. Or a nice girl, for company and not in a gay way…"

"Or a really hot guy." Amanda corrected me.

"I don't know. I'm really out of practice with socialising. It's been me and Beth practically forever and

I think I must have lost the knack of meeting new people."

"So you've, like, put all your social eggs in one friend's basket?" Amanda said.

"Erm. What?"

A man politely cleared his throat behind me. "*Excuse me…*"

Amanda and I spun round and together we saw the Head of Planning looming up behind us. Just two steps down from the Chief Executive at Lewisham Council, Peter Shaw was definitely classed as a Person To Stop a Conversation For.

"I am very sorry to interrupt you two young ladies but I wondered if I could have a word with Edda Mackenzie."

"I'll be off, then," Amanda jumped down in a flurry of pale blue pants.

Peter Shaw politely looked away and, once she was gone, drew up a chair beside me.

"I don't think we've met." He offered me his hand and I shook it. "I head up Planning at the Council."

"Hi."

I knew who he was. Everybody at Lewisham Council knew who he was. He wasn't the God of Lewisham Council – that was the Chief Executive – but he was definitely around the Moses level. He certainly parted the queues at the on-site shop when he paid it a visit.

"I'm here," he dropped his voice and leant in towards me, all silver grey hair and affable M&S jumper stretched over a paunch, "in a non-work-related capacity."

I had no idea how to react to that. None. Was the Head of Planning going to ask me out on a date? Weirder things had happened: Beth was up the duff, I was in the papers (ish) and Brockley had been covered in knitting. Why shouldn't he ask me out? I braced myself.

"Edda, I have reason to believe," he looked left and right like a spy in an old espionage film, "That *you* are responsible for planting up the infamous Brockley skip. Am I right?"

"*What?*" I nearly jumped out of my seat. "How do you know?"

"Ahh!" He leant back. "So you are! Well, let me tell you how I worked it out. I was intrigued by the story of the gardened skip in the papers, so I did some investigating. I wanted to track down the person who planted that garden, so I thought to myself that the person who took it upon themselves to deal with the skip of their own volition had probably complained about it beforehand. And lo – there were *seven* written complaints about the skip in the Environmental Office's files. And all of them were from you."

"Oh."

"And one of the letters mentioned the fact that you worked for the Council."

"Did it? I—"

Peter Shaw, Head of Planning, *Moses*, pulled out papers, which I instantly recognised as being my letters, from a maroon leather folder he'd been carrying under his arm. He sifted through them, cleared his throat and looking around in case anyone was listening he read, "*I work for the Council: can't you pull your goddamn finger out for one of your own?"*

"Ah." I said clammily, "Actually, I'm not really that rude. I sort of snapped. It had been months and the dumped rubbish smelled really, really bad."

"I quite understand. So, you see, it wasn't very hard to locate you as you'd said yourself that you worked for the Council. When I looked your details up in the Payroll Department I found that your house just happens to be directly opposite said skip, *would you believe?* And so I assembled the facts and I worked out that you are in a particularly unique position to have benefited from such a philanthropic act."

I shivered. I had been investigated. I had been investigated by the Lewisham Moses and he had put together a file on me. Was this it? Was I going to get the sack because of my rude letters and my illegal gardening? As much as I hated my job – and I really did – I didn't want to be sacked from it.

"Don't worry – in a way I'm just doing my job: we planners can be meticulous investigators. I wanted to find the skip-planter for a very *particular* reason, however..." He let the words hang in the air.

He was going to serve an Order on me. He was going to prosecute me, caution me, repossess my house and throw me out onto the South London streets ... the Planning team at the Council were notorious, power-crazed, workaholics who liked nothing better than breaking the spirits of residents who flouted their regulations by so much as a millimetre.

28

Loft conversion too high? Five thousand pound fine!
Garage extension too large? Go to jail for six months!

"You don't need to look quite so alarmed, Edda." He laughed quietly.

"I'm fine." I laughed lightly, ungripping the table and dropping my shoulders by half a metre.

"No, no, no, no." He leant forward and placed a hand on my own. He *was* going to ask me out. Eugh. "I *admire* what you did. And so does my partner, Eustace Fox." OK. He wasn't going to ask me out. "And it's on his behalf that I came round here to see you. Do you know Eustace? He owns Fox Estates … at the corner of your road."

Hadn't I bought my house from a man called Eustace Fox a few years ago? A plump man with chequered trousers was all I could recall…

"Anyway," Peter continued, "Eustace very much wants to meet the infamous Brockley skip planter and he's throwing a party, a soirée if you like, at his Tresillian Road house, on Saturday night. He would be absolutely delighted if you were able to come along; plus guest, of course. There'll be lots of like-minded Brockleyites there and I'm sure you'd enjoy it." He leant close, waiting for a response.

Oh God. Amanda's magazine-style advice was ringing in my ears: I should get out more and socialise. But, *really*, did this offer count as socialising? A soirée with Lewisham Council's Moses and his middle-aged, check-trousered partner? I realised too late that my expression was answering the question for me: *DEAR*

GOD NO! so I tried to smile politely. But Peter Shaw was already laughing.

"I can see you're not convinced, Edda. But I really think someone with your attitude would fit right in…"

"You've got the wrong impression of me. I was really flipping out when I did what I did to the skip," I explained. "It's so out of character for me. Usually I'm a very calm and quiet person. I—"

He stopped me in my self-deprecating tracks. "Did you see the *yarnstorming* in Brockley this morning?"

"Pardon?"

"Yarnstorming. Knitted graffiti."

"Oh!" I remembered the knitted street light snakes and the tree branch knitted hearts. "Yes, yes I did! That's 'yarnstorming'?"

"Yup. And that's *us*! You see, we're a radical bunch and someone who plants up a skip is going to fit in just perfectly. Here's an invitation." He placed a small card onto my desk with an address on Tresillian Road. "Come at around nine. And good work with the skip, young lady!"

I sat at my desk, unmoving, for the next ten minutes until the trembling stopped. And then I called Beth.

Four

It would have been easier to have persuaded Madonna to *cover up a bit love and put a cardigan on* but – finally – I convinced Beth to come with me to the soirée. There was no way I would go on my own: I was hopeless in social situations without my Beth as a prop.

"You don't have to be so nervous, little Eds!" Beth gave me a hug as we walked down the widening roads towards the party. "Eustace seems like a really nice person."

"What?" I said. "You *know* Eustace Fox? You know the bloke whose party we're going to? Why didn't you say before?"

"Well I forgot, darling. Of course I know him – he's selling our flat."

"*What?*" This time I stopped dead in my tracks.

Beth slapped her forehead. "Oh, shit, I'm sorry Eds. I didn't tell you, did I? Honestly, they weren't making it up when they say that motherhood completely messes with your head. I don't know if I'm coming or going. Anyway, yes, sorry honey, I should have told you. Jack and I are selling the flat and moving to Surrey."

"Oh."

"I know. It's a shock. I'm so sorry you found out like this."

"Oh."

"It makes sense, though. We'll be near his parents, so that'll be really helpful. His mum's already said she'll babysit for us, bless her, and – well – you know. It's just nicer out there isn't it? South London's so, well … gritty, isn't it? Not the sort of place you want to bring up a little life. I can't believe I didn't tell you we were moving! I'm so sorry, honey."

I took a deep breath. "'s fine."

"I knew you'd be OK about it. It's just so exciting! Jack's going to view this tiny cottage just outside Guildford tonight and it has a little nursery on the top floor; how perfect is that? It's pastel yellow and—"

Instantly, I tuned out. Pastel yellow now had that effect on me: it was like a sort of hypnotic trigger, putting me into a state where I could cope with being talked to about the baby. I could go under for minutes, or even hours, as I had done at the weekend when I'd finally managed to drag her out to V-2 and she'd talked solidly about baby-stuff all morning. The hypnotic release was always *Edda, Edda are you even listening to me?* at which point I would come round and say something like *that sounds like a great idea,* which usually worked well.

The further Beth and I walked from my house the grander the properties had become, until we reached Tresillian Road where Eustace Fox, friend to Beth, lived. The street was lined with palatial white villas, set back behind perfectly planted front gardens. And Eustace's house was the most palatial of all. It sported a turret, a balcony, gargoyles, gables and pretty much every

Victorian whimsy except a drawbridge and a bronze of Bouddica in a chariot.

Beth stopped her stream of consciousness baby-talk – something about cribs versus cots – and gaped at the villa. "Eustace Fox lives here? He lives here and he runs an *estate agency*? Urgh, my flat sale is funding his amazing lifestyle. *I* am paying for this."

"Do you think we should turn back?" I said, ever the one to chicken out and seek the quiet life in these strange and disappointing times.

"Oh, don't be so bloody stupid," Beth grabbed my arm and frogmarched me up the mosaic-tiled pathway. "It was your skip and it's you they want to see. Stop being such a wuss. And you look great – see, I told you to wear the blue dress with the silver shoes."

Beth rapped on the vast glossy black front door, like a debt collector on a mission, while I cowered behind. Within a moment it was opened and a portly, jolly-faced man was ushering us in.

"Ahh, Miss Smedley," he said, seeing only Beth – on account of me cowering behind her. "How lovely to see you again! Do you know, your perfectly lovely flat has had quite a bit of interest. Expect great things in the next few days, but I must say that I am exceedingly sorry that you will be moving out of the neighbourhood: Brockley needs people like you and your charming fiancé in order to thrive. If you change your mind I can put a couple of very exciting properties your way. And you," he fixed his eyes on me when Beth stepped inside and left me exposed on the door step, "You must be the Lady of the Skip!"

"She is."

"I am." I shook the hand that was held out to me.

"Well, I'm delighted to meet you of course! Edda isn't it? Jolly good. Come in, come in!"

"What an absolutely amazing home you have," Beth gushed as she walked in, while I mumbled something vaguely similar but was too overawed by the place to fully commit to talking sense. It was *incredible*. It was, in fact, like stepping into a Victorian period drama so real that at any moment Sherlock Holmes might leap out of a doorway with an opium-addled *ha ha!* and toss off a tune on his violin. There were animal heads on dark-papered walls, etched lanterns, candelabra and a giant marble fireplace. And all of it in *a hallway*.

I turned back to the host, who now I realised looked every bit as Victorian as his house. Dressed in tweeds, he sported white whiskers and red cheeks with an air of joviality that gave him the look of a Dickens character: the jolly sort who went about saving East London orphans and handing out hot pies, as opposed to the evil sort who made hot pies out of East London orphans.

The next guests arrived almost immediately after us, so we were shown into a sitting room and the direction of an ample bar pointed out. "I'll catch up with you soon, ladies," Eustace Fox said. "Excuse me."

"Well," I collected a gin and tonic and handed Beth a mineral water, "he's not what I was expecting."

"No – the whole thing is quite odd isn't it?" We took in our surroundings as we sipped our drinks. There were vast gilt-framed oil paintings, velvet wallpapers, exotic button-eyed stuffed birds in glass jars; the place was a living museum. In fact, apart from the mass of party-goers with drinks in hand, and the flat-screen TV, it could have been the National Trust-preserved house of a wealthy Victorian industrialist. All it needed was some roped-off areas and *don't you even think about sitting on this you common peasant* notices on the chairs.

"Glad you came?" Beth asked.

"I think so. Aren't I?"

"Yes, you are. We should mingle."

"I don't think I really feel like mingling," I looked at the various groups of trendy slick-haired types, dreadlocked cool sorts and serious barrister types. There weren't many Council pen-pusher types amongst them. "I wouldn't know what to say to anyone. Why don't you mingle and I'll tag along!"

"Oh come on – don't be so shy! Look at them all looking at you – I think they know who you are! How cool is that Eds? Eds! Come out from there. I'm not having you hiding yourself away. Mingle woman! Mingle! Do you think all these people live in Brockley? I don't recall seeing this sort of person in and around Brockley, much. Greenwich maybe..."

"This place is so weird – there's a giant stuffed bear holding umbrellas at the end of the hallway. A real stuffed bear with teeth and claws and umbrellas."

"Well, the people look pretty normal. Trendy. But normal."

"I still wouldn't know what to say to them." I said.

"You could tell them you're here because of the skip?"

"I suppose so ... oh my God ... Beth, look at that man!"

"I am!" As one we had focused on the spot where the partygoers had parted and there, newly revealed, was the most gorgeous dark-haired arty type leaning louchely against the far wall. A Milk Tray man. A man with jet black ringlets, stubble, an open-necked shirt and an utterly, fantastically, beautiful bod.

"I am carrying my fiancé's baby and I am lusting after that man," Beth mused. "Is that bad? Does that make me a bad person?"

"Yes it does."

"Ah ha, I find you again at last!" The cheerful voice of Eustace Fox boomed behind us.

"We were just – ah – admiring your place," Beth peeled her eyes away from the very particular place she'd been admiring. "It must have taken you years to get it like this."

"Oh you'd be surprised," he said. "When I bought the villa it was almost entirely unmodernised: there was very little work needed to renovate it. I'm glad you like it. What say you, Edda? Is it to your taste?"

"Oh," I said, focusing for no good reason on the wall of stuffed animal heads opposite, "absolutely."

Eustace laughed and to my surprise he lent down to me and said in a low voice, "I don't like the animal trophies either but some bugger shot them a century ago and it seems sacrilegious to throw them away. Makes their shooting seem all the more pointless, don't you think? Might as well have 'em up. So," he stood up,

"*Edda*. That *is* an unusual name."

"It's Old Norse." I replied, taking a liking to him. There was something fun about him, in a jolly-uncle sort of a way. "It means *poem*."

"Does it? Does it really? Well, how unique. I don't think I've ever met anyone with an Old Norse name before. You're of Scandinavian origin I take it? Although your beautiful red hair and those hazel eyes are quite Celtic…"

"Her parents were Viking fanatics. Totally mad for it all weren't they, Eds?" Beth spoke up for me.

"Well, there's a lot to be said for the Vikings," Eustace contemplated his vast tumbler of whisky. "Lot of bad press in the last decades but everyone's so damn touchy-feely these days. You see, I admire them: they did a lot of good. Yes they might have been a bit eager with the broad sword and a touch boisterous with the women, but in doing so they gave England its backbone. Wouldn't you say so, eh? Otherwise where would we be? Overly Norman with a fondness for heavily stylised tapestries… No – we owe our fighting British spirit to those men from across the sea! So, do your parents take part in re-enactments Edda? Hog roasts and sword fights? Eh?"

"I…"

What I wanted to say was a breezy *Oh they're no longer with us, sadly,* but experience told me that no matter how breezy I tried to be I would actually end up saying something along the lines of *They're dead. Dead and gone. I'm an orphan!* because I'd never mastered the art of unemotively telling people my parents had died. So, I tried to compose myself before I responded. In the composing-silence that followed Beth, love her, stepped in to save me.

"Edda's parents died."

"Oh, I'm sorry to hear that." Eustace put a hand on my shoulder and patted it, which was surprisingly comforting.

"It's fine. Fine." I waved the tragedy away with the breezy tone I'd been composing myself for. "It was a long time ago."

"It was quite bizarre, actually. How they died. Wasn't it, Eds?" Beth laughed. "Plain freaky, really. It made the national papers at the time didn't it, Eds?"

"I—"

"Well, this is no place for maudlin talk," Eustace cut in, "Although I mean no disrespect to your late parents, of course, my dear Edda, however they passed into the next life. Now then, I wanted to talk to you, Edda, about your planting of the skip – if you don't mind my talking openly about your little secret."

"Oh no. Not at all," I said, suddenly wondering whether I *should* actually worry about talking about it. After all wasn't it illegal, or at the least unauthorised?

"Well, then, I think it shows enormous spunk to do what you did."

I could feel Beth stiffen beside me, stifling a giggle.

"Eustace! Darling!" A thin, blonde forty-something flew at him with a kiss. While he obliged I looked over at Beth who was pointing to me and mouthing the word *spunky*. "So sorry to interrupt," the blonde woman was saying, "but I just wanted to say hello!" she beamed at him. "By the way, Eust – there's another one of those signs right outside your house. Timing couldn't be more off could it, darling? Ciao!" and she headed off to the drinks table.

Eustace, frowning, turned to us. "Excuse me, ladies," and without another word he marched to the front door.

Beth and I stared after him.

"What was all that about?" Beth said.

"I have no idea."

"What was she talking about? Did you see a sign right outside his house?"

"No. Did you?" I said.

"No—"

"Shall we follow him?" I surprised myself.

"Of course!"

Together, like the contingent of the Famous Five we had always been BB (before baby), Beth and I speed-walked through the house in the direction that Eustace had taken. Taking up a position screened behind the bear with the umbrellas we watched as, a moment later, the man himself crashed back in through the front doorway, purple-faced, staggering heavily and with an enormous yellow metal rectangle on legs wedged under his arm.

"Is that a *police* sign?" Beth hissed in my ear.

"I think so. Can you read what it says?"

"No, darling. There's a giant stuffed bear in the way."

Eustace had now rested the sign on the floor and was busy jabbing a key into the lock of an understairs cupboard door.

The sign was facing us and I could see the words quite clearly.

Woman fatally stabbed here between 1 and 2am, Friday 6th. Witnesses in the vicinity at the time should contact Lewisham Police on the numbers below.

A woman had died outside Eustace Fox's house in the early hours of this morning. And Eustace had just removed the police sign.

Beth clamped a hand on my arm.

We watched in a troubled silence as he opened the cupboard and disappeared into it.

"Go on," Beth was pushing me out past the bear. "See what's inside the cupboard."

"Bethan! Bloody hell!" Feeling horribly exposed in the bear-free open space of the hallway, I dithered.

"Oh, for God's sake I thought you were supposed to have spunk? Isn't that what Eustace Fox said?" Beth came out from behind the bear and took a step towards the cupboard. Empowered, now I had my friend beside me, I stood beside her and we looked into the darkness.

I could see shelves, pegs, coats and hats and…

I gasped. It was an Aladdin's cave of crime signs! There were yellow and black metal signs leaning up against the walls, piled on top of one another, hanging from the walls, shouting doom and gloom like a week's worth of *Daily Mail* headlines: *man attacked here, spate of bags snatched here, woman fatally shot here, man stabbed here, five cars set alight here…*

Several men knifed
Man shot
Youth assaulted
Here
Here
Here…

There was a noise from the cupboard. Eustace was coming out.

Beth and I shot back into the sitting room and threw ourselves onto a vacant Chesterfield: she staring dumbfounded at me and me opening the hatch and sinking the rest of my gin and tonic in a single gulp.

"So… That was normal, then," I said, pulling the slice of lemon out of my throat and hoping that by saying things were normal they suddenly would be.

"No." Beth said. "That was quite far from normal, I'd say." She was frowning and stroking her slight bump of a stomach.

"Are you OK?"

"Yes. Yes, of course. Just a twinge." She waved my concern away and fixed a smile on her face. "I probably shouldn't run that fast."

"Do you think he's hiding those police signs because he's the one that did all that stuff?" I said, after a moment's reflection.

"Edda!"

"Well – the sign said someone was stabbed *right outside his house.*"

"Eds, don't be so melodramatic!" Beth was laughing at me, "Eustace is a portly estate agent. He's probably worried that all the bad publicity will affect house prices, that's all. He's not built to be a bag-snatching, gang-raping arsonist and besides, it wouldn't be good for business."

I considered it for a moment. "Yes. You're probably right—"

Beth yawned and sank back onto the sofa.

"You're tired." I said.

"I am."

"Do you want to go? I don't mind. I mean – Mr Sign-hoarder doesn't really do it for me and it's not like we've mingled or anything. This is all pretty weird…" My focus went back to the wall of glassy-eyed animal heads.

Beth yawned again. "Do you mind? I am outrageously tired all of a sudden. I'm so sorry, Eds. I must be the crappiest friend ever."

"No," I said as I hauled her off the sofa. "No, you're not and you know it. Damn you. I wish you were crappy then I wouldn't mind half as much that you're running off to Surrey without me."

"Oh, you say the sweetest things, honey."

"I wonder who the good-looking man was?"

"Listen, darling," Beth put a hand on my shoulder, "you stay here and enjoy yourself. Go meet the Romeo with the dark hair and then call me tomorrow and tell me every single thing that happened. OK?"

"I don't want to stay without you." I said. "I'd just wander around the party fretting: I don't know any people here except for that balding bloke over by the window."

"Who?"

"That one," I pointed out Peter Shaw to her as discreetly as I could. "He's Eustace Fox's partner and he's high up in the Council – so I don't particularly want to talk to the only person I know here, bar Eustace Fox himself. No, come on, let's go."

I took her hand and gently pulled her forwards. "Oh thank you, darling," she said, leaning against me as we slowly left the party. "You have so much *spunk*, you know that?" She was laughing again, holding her sides. "Oh God, I so have to grow up with baby on the way."

"Oh, come on," I said, walking her slowly to the front door, "You can be rude, can't you? It can't hear you."

"Yes but no big laughs and no blue cheese…"

"Pregnant Woman Caught Laughing With Spunky Sidekick Here. Any witnesses call Lewisham Police…"

"Edda! Bloody well stop it!"

Five

Like a true divorcee I was finding the weekends tough. In fact, it was probably worse than divorce because I didn't have the benefit of a lawyer to focus my anger on. I just had long stretches of time when I felt I ought to be making some sort of effort to be sociable but, actually, doing nothing about it, still clinging to the fantasy that *hey everything will just fall back into place with Beth, and the baby is a temporary blip.*

But, in the mean time, I was in danger of turning into a modern day Miss Havisham, holed up in my large empty Victorian house with dust bunnies rolling across the landings like tumbleweed. I could see why people living on their own went mad. I could totally understand the Miss Havisham thing: what a rational and misunderstood woman she must have been.

Friendless and alone I was slowly descending into some dark and terrible place: I would end up dressed in faded and rotting Boden loungewear, surveying the boxed remains of KFC family feasts arranged on a long table being nibbled by rats. I hadn't quite got round to stopping the clocks in the house at the point when Beth had announced her pregnancy, but I hadn't had the heart to throw out her collection of mouldering pestos from the fridge. She loved pesto and having the jars there made it seem, almost, like she still lived with me. A little bit of our past that still existed in our fridge. Thrived actually. Bloomed…

Over the last couple of weeks Amanda's suggestion of getting a lodger cropped up more and more in my thoughts: I had just enough perspective to realise that living on my own was not working out too well and besides there was the financial incentive: my bank manager was now entering an almost weekly correspondence with me – like a one man postal blog – about the benefits of *coming in for a chat about your finances*. So maybe a lodger would address the pressing financial issue as well as my pressing mental issue. Maybe if Miss Havisham had had a lodger she would have felt obliged to clear up the wedding cake and dust down her rats every so often. With the idea of a lodger now in my mind I realised I would have to tackle the house and the garden. No one would want to live in a place like this: even Finley would look disdainfully at our surroundings. Things would have to be done.

And at least I now had plenty of time to do them.

"Gardenin' is it darlin'?" my elderly neighbour, Babs, shouted across the garden wall. She was sitting on the top step of her raised front door, smoking a cheap fag, and watching the world go by. Between daybreak and dusk it was odds on that Babs would be on the step with a fag in, watching the goings on in South East London. "Lovely day ain't it? It's gonna be a good summer, or so they're sayin'. Although 'ow a warm April means it's gonna be 'ot in August I don't know. It's all bollocks, ain't it? You all right, Edda, love?" She was eyeing me suspiciously over the rims of her dirty pink glasses.

"I'm fine," I said, coming nearer to the wall so that I didn't have to shout my part of the conversation to all of Brockley.

"Yer don't look it. Yer look ill."

Great: I was divorced, I was becoming Miss Havisham, I was looking ill. I ticked *all* the boxes.

"I haven't got much sleep the last few weeks." I rubbed a hand across my face.

"Shaggin' was yer?"

"No I was not!" Babs never failed to horrify me.

"What then?" she continued, refusing to be put off.

"My best friend's having a baby."

"Ahh … a little baby! One of them long labours?"

"She wasn't in labour. I only found out she was pregnant a month ago."

"An' that's it? So wotchu losin' sleep over your best friend being up the duff for, then?"

I shrugged. "It's been a shock. That's all. I didn't think we were ready for a baby."

Babs gave a loud phlegmy snort. "You sound like the bleedin' father of it! Not ready for it aren't yer? You ain't got a lot of choice my darlin', 'cause it's comin' whether you wants it or not."

"I know. Anyway … how are you?" If in doubt, with Babs, change the subject.

"Can't complain." She took a long drag of her fag. "Helluva week for old Reg at the launderette, though."

"Why?"

"He 'ad a sheet in last week what 'ad gun shot holes in it, an' blood all over it."

"And someone wanted it *cleaned*?" I stared at her.

"You'd be surprised," Babs said nonchalantly. "Anyhow, them police came in an' questioned Reg for hours about why he cleaned it, why he got rid o' evidence from the scene of a crime an' that. Got into big trouble for just doin' his job. How'd 'e know the bloke with the laundry was a triple murderer?"

"Exactly. Who would know?" I tried to sound as reasonable and unshocked as possible.

Beth was so wrong about my neighbour Babs: the woman was *great*. Since Beth had moved out, and increasingly now, with so much time on my hands, I was getting to know Babs a lot more, swapping brunch at V-2 with Beth for a cuppa on the front step with Babs. And I enjoyed our conversations very much. Beth was always horrified that I even talked to the woman – *she lives in the gutter Eds!* – but Babs gave me a real and mostly terrifying insight into the 'other' Brockley. The authentic South London place it was before all the gentrification and the *Guardian* readers started moving in and making everything *'nice'*. Babs' world was filled with gin-soaked criminals and infamous rogues, a world with a direct line back to Dickens' criminal world. Yes, sometimes I came away from talking to Babs in fear for my life and not wanting to ever leave the house again, but mostly I just enjoyed the vicarious thrill of knowing what the criminal underclass were up to in and around SE4.

Fella got shot right outside our Tyrone's on Tuesday. Bullet missed me by inches.

Found a rock of heroin in the street when I was on me way to bingo that was as big as me fist.

The owner of The Greasy Finger Café tried to hang 'imself last week by 'is wife's bra…

"Babs…?" I'd walked a few steps down the garden path but stopped and faced my neighbour again, "You know everything about everyone in Brockley…"

"I can't deny it," Babs drew on her cheap fag. "The stories I could tell you…"

"You do tell me Babs."

"Not some of 'em," she laughed and broke into a filterless fag coughing fit. "Yer as dainty as a doily, Edda, an' there are some things that ain't for your fine ears."

"Right. Well. I'm sure. But I was going to ask – what do you know about Fox Estates, just around the corner, and the man who owns it – Eustace Fox?" Since the party I'd been thinking about him and his sign-hoarding. Who *was* the man who had wanted to have me at his party because I'd gardened the skip? What sort of man wears such loud trousers and keeps a stuffed bear in the hallway?

Babs scratched beneath her wig and thought for a moment, looking down the street in the direction of the estate agency. "Been open a couple of years, ain't it? Posh place. Bay trees outside. Bay trees in South East London, I bloody ask yer! It's a dirty place South East London, no matter 'ow them estate agents try to dress it up with their fancy trees. It ain't no *Blackheath Borders* or *Greenwich Envy Rons* round 'ere. Round 'ere it's the arse end of the Old Kent Road and yer can't change that. Bay trees! Good job 'e's chained the last lot of 'em down, otherwise they'd be down Catford Market inside an hour if 'e didn't. You get a good price for 'em." She pointed her fag at me to make her point. "I'd imagine."

"So what *do* you know about Eustace Fox?" I tried to refocus my neighbour.

There followed a short silence and I realised, shocked, that Babs was actually exercising caution before speaking. The queen of gossip and dirt-dishing was chewing her lip and frowning, clearly not sure what she should or shouldn't tell me about this man. I was shocked to my core. This was the first time she'd ever, in the five years I'd been her neighbour, and the last few weeks I'd really got to know her, felt unable to instantly dish the gossip.

To say I was intrigued was an understatement. What could she possibly know about Eustace Fox that she couldn't speak to me about?

"Lives over Tresillian Road, don't he? Why'd you ask?"

"Oh. I just wondered…" I said, playing it cool and picking up my hatchet. I turned to survey the rambling wasteland that was my neglected front garden.

"Don't know much about 'im," she muttered. "Anyway, I'll leave yer to it, darlin'." And off she went inside.

Odd. Very odd. But Babs was someone who lived for gossip and I was pretty sure I'd hear more about Eustace Fox from her very soon.

So … the garden. Here was a place I could take out all my pent-up rage and anger.

There was an inner fire burning … inside me. An anger at my empty weekend, my Bethless abandonment. Anger that I had been made into a victim.

The hatchet felt good in my hands. It was heavy, sharp and – once I'd cleaned the reddish brown marks from it – it glinted dangerously in the sunshine. I'd found the hatchet in the skip when Beth and I had spent the night gardening and I knew I'd find a use for it.

"Right then," I said, and then I set to work.

"Feelin' better now, are yer?"

"Hello again, Babs." I'd smelt her fags on the air, so it was no surprise to see my neighbour hanging over the garden again. Panting slightly I put down my hatchet and joined her at the wall. Wiping my hair off my wet forehead I stood back to admire my day's work for the first time.

Oh.

"Got carried away did yer, darlin'?" Babs broke into my long stunned silence.

"Erm." I said, looking out over a wasteland of devastation. "I might have done."

From the house right up to the hedge bordering the pavement there was bare, savaged earth, hacked and mutilated plants in disarray and the most epic weed mountain that even the keenest gardener at Kew would not have been able to top.

"Well, I can't say it didn't need it." Babs continued.

"Shame about them stocks though. I would'a had 'em off you. Beautiful they were – late white flowers an' a fancy smell to 'em."

"Oh." I turned back to my weed mountain that stretched up towards the first floor window. "So they might not all be weeds in the weed pile, then?"

"Bloody 'ell, Edda. Didn't yer mum an' dad never tell yer about gardenin'?"

"Not very much," I said. *Because my parents are dead!* Yes it was impossible for me to ever slip that fact into a conversation. Maybe if I'd had proper counselling at the time, then I would have learnt how to calmly and rationally express their deceasification. But instead all I'd been given was a plump lady, with a moustache and a powerful baritone voice, who nodded a lot and said, "Do you cry? It's good to cry," every ten minutes.

"Well, by my reckonin' you've got strawberry trees, fuchsia, stocks and some lovely forsythia in there." Babs pointed to the towering pile.

"Ri-ight."

"An' parsley, rosemary, chive, sage, a whole bush full o' mint an' some lavender an' all."

"Oh." That explained the pot pourri period of gardening nearer the house.

"Not to worry though darlin', it's good to have a clear out ain't it?" She blew a smoke ring up into the air. "And you did rip out one or two nettles an' all."

"Yes, well, I feel like I've really achieved something today," I said, "Even if it is devastation. At least it's a start."

"So, what are yer gonna do with it now?"

I looked back to my new bleak wilderness. "I hadn't really thought that far ahead. I've got some gardening books, so now that I've cleared everything away I can draw up some plans for my new garden."

"Well, I don't blame yer for leavin' the garden for a bit. You got better things to do than dig 'aven't yer? All that clubbin' an' shaggin' you kids get up to these days. You ain't got time for gardens."

"That's what it is," I said, trying to block out the image in my head. There were always inappropriate noises wafting down from Babs' open bedroom window at night.

"An' yer got some gardenin' practice when you 'ad a good go at that skip didn't yer?" Babs broke into my thoughts.

I leant in to the wall in shock. "You know it was me? You saw me?"

"Course I bleedin' did, Edda! You an' that mate o' yours were making enough noise to wake the dead in Nunhead Cemetery."

"Really? I thought we'd been pretty discreet."

Babs snorted and took a long drag of her fag.

"Anyway," I went for the distraction tactic again, "I have to tidy up the place – I'm thinking of getting a lodger in."

"Makes sense darlin'. Big old 'ouses like ours need fillin'. That friend, the one in the skip, didn't she used to live with yer a while back? I seem to remember seein' a lot of 'er. Not that she ever spoke to me."

"She moved out two years ago."

"Two years ago? Well 'ow time flies. It only seems like yesterday that she was forever dashin' up and down yer garden path without so much as a hello. No time for folks round 'ere I reckon. So she's gone an' she left you all alone 'as she?"

"Sort of. She's having a baby. And now she and her fiancé are moving to Surrey."

"They all go to Surrey..." Babs nodded sagely, staring wistfully at my weed pile. "To be honest with yer, darlin', she looked the type. Couldn't see 'er livin' in South East London for long. A girl like that belongs in Surrey. Friends, eh? Some say that friends is the family you choose yerself, but I say that's a big pile of shit 'cause friends are no more than people yer meet what stick around."

"She was my family." I sighed, now in danger of unloading my heartache on Babs. But I did want to talk about it to someone...

"That your boyfriend, is it?" Babs cut into my thoughts, nodding in the direction of the road and I turned to see the black-haired artist from Eustace Fox's soirée, standing at my gate.

POW!

There were fireworks exploding in all sorts of places. I managed to control myself and affect some kind of composure.

"No," I wobbled, "he's not my boyfriend. I don't even know his name."

But Babs had gone, sensing that she wasn't needed

now that Milk Tray man had arrived. I turned to the gate and my handsome visitor.

"I love what you've done here," he enthused in a voice that was pure chocolate. He strode into my front garden, surveyed the wreckage and then looked up and held me in a green-eyed grip.

I bit my lip. "Hi."

"Guy. Guy Newhouse. I saw you at Eust's party the other week."

Did he? Did *he* see *me*? I shook the outstretched hand. Even his handshake was handsome.

"Hi."

Handsome Guy Newhouse, Milk Tray man, looked around at the devastation again. "Are you doing some sort of archaeological excavation here? Are you going back to the pre-Roman?"

I laughed. "No. I'm going minimalist on the planting."

"I'd say *barren* is a better description."

"Well it's got potential." I said, loving the fact he was standing before me, hating the fact I was sans-make-up and sweaty and still carrying a hatchet.

"You sound like Eustace in full Estate Agent mode when you talk about potential," Guy clapped a hand on his head, squashing the bouncy black curls. "Talking of whom, I have come on business."

It took a moment for his words to register with me. And when they did my heart dropped. "You're here on business from Eustace Fox?"

"The man himself," Guy was inspecting the weed mountain. "You know these aren't all—"

"I know."

He strode around the mound. "I was going to ask to take some of these for my garden – they're expensive plants – but they're hacked to pieces. What the hell happened here? Did you have some kind of fit?"

"Sort of." There had been a frenzied element to the last three hours but Babs had been right – it *was* cathartic. Beth could walk down the road right now, married, with four screaming children in tow and I wouldn't even raise an eyebrow in a Roger-Moore style. I was at one. I was relaxed. I had soothed my inner anger.

"Nice skip by the way," Guy indicated over the hedge to my supersized window box opposite. "I see Da Notorious Baron has left his mark on it."

Did *everyone* know about the skip? "He has?" I peered over the newly savaged hedge. "Oh!"

It was true: one side of the skip was now sprayed with a stencil of a woman in a bikini and stilettos holding up a giant daisy with the 'artist's' name sprayed beneath. But like all Da Notorious Baron's work it was completely rubbish: the woman's legs were buckled and her breasts were freakily huge. Even the daisy didn't look quite right.

"Is that supposed to be a picture of you?" Guy asked. "Are you a muse for Brockley's answer to Banksy? Did Da Baron get you to pose mid-gardening?"

I laughed it off and then said, "How can you get a *daisy* wrong?"

"Well it's hardly a surprise that Da Notorious Baron can get a daisy wrong: the man could get a straight line wrong. Are you angry at him for defacing your skip garden?"

I thought for a moment. "No. Not really. Actually I'm quite honoured that Da Notorious Baron has come up with a stencil just for me and my skip. Someone's paid a tribute to what I've done."

"A bad tribute." Guy considered the artwork, frowning. "I don't know why the man doesn't just give up. I mean, it's downright shameful. Did you see the tiger he sprayed up by the station a few months ago? It was just awful. Mangled." He turned back to me and my hacked garden. "So what made you do it?"

"Do what?" My train of thought had derailed when Guy had made the comment about me being a muse for Da Baron. Did he really think I looked like *that* in a bikini and high heels? And had I ever worn a bikini and high heels at the same time?

"What made you garden the skip?" he said.

"Frustration?" I offered.

"Wow." Guy looked impressed. "The talk of a true artist: driven by frustration and the need to create. You know, I think you and I have a lot in common, Edda. You're obviously a very hot-blooded woman." He looked at the ripped and plundered garden and back at me, all sparkling eyes and loaded eyebrows. "Someone who isn't afraid to let go. Someone, Edda, with a passion. I'm a painter so I live for passion like that – I understand your need to express your inner being."

"Yes." *What?*

"Anyway, back to business," he perched attractively on

56

a stone bench I'd found under some plants and fixed me again with his green eyes. "You left Eust's party too soon."

"I know but my friend's pregnant. She was tired." I hovered in front of the bench. Should I sit next to him? He was very flirty with me but it wouldn't really be on if I was flirty with him would it? Would it? *Would it?* No – it would be fine. I perched on the bench beside him.

"Your best friend is pregnant? Well, another one bites the dust." Guy eloquently summed the situation up. "So this would be a perfect time for you to come to one of our gigs and get to know some new people. What do you think?" His eyes shone.

My heart was beating so loudly I was sure he would be able to hear it. "What gig?"

"Eust didn't tell you?"

"No. Are you in a band?"

"Not that sort of a gig." He laughed. "I thought Eustace had had the chance to explain who we were at the party. You really *did* leave early, didn't you?"

"Who are you then?" I asked. This was all getting a bit Doctor Who. I just *knew* he was too handsome to be real. I was on the brink of being abducted by gorgeous aliens and taken back to a dying planet of handsomeness.

"Eust told you nothing about us... Nothing at all?"

"No."

"OK then," he leant back and took in the weed pile again. "Well ... Eust wants you to join our secret society." He said the words quietly, with an eye towards Babs' house next door.

Aliens. Space ships. Dying planets. It was all coming true, in my front garden in glamourless South East London. "What sort of *secret* society?"

"I know. Completely melodramatic isn't it? We call ourselves," he leant close in to me, coming over all confidential and covert, "The Brockley Spades." He looked to see the meaning dawn on me but it failed. "We're guerrilla gardeners." He added.

"Oh." I sat and stared straight ahead, trying to remember what the hell a guerrilla gardener actually was. Some militant branch of the Royal Horticultural Society? Clearly Guy could read my expression because he added, "Guerrilla gardening … as in your skip planting," he nudged me gently with his shoulder. "It's at the very heart of what we do. It's undercover gentrification. We're a group of like-minded individuals stealing out under cover of darkness planting bulbs and beautifying lost corners of Brockley. Come along and see what it's all about. A week next Thursday night, at nine, the Working Men's Club on the Lewisham High Road. What do you think?"

It must have been what Peter Shaw had been alluding to at the office when he invited me to the soirée: the yarnstorming must go hand in hand with the guerrilla gardening. It was all making a vague hazy sense.

"Erm." I had no idea whether I should accept his offer or not. None whatsoever. On the one hand *stealing*, *working men's clubs* and *guerrilla* instantly made me think *NO* but on the other hand, what better offer would I have for a Thursday night? For any night? Ever again in my long and barren life. And the offer itself was put to me by a handsome stranger. Of course I'd do it…

Or would I? Damn. Where was my Beth when I needed her?

"Actually, I'm not sure. I mean I really flipped out when I decided to garden the skip. I'm not really usually quite so … you know … I'm not sure if I really am so like-minded as you think."

"Come on, Edda, can I expect to see you on Thursday night?"

"You mean can Eustace expect to see me?" I asked, keeping it real. After all he was in my garden because Eustace Fox had asked him to be.

"No. I mean can *I* expect to see you?"

"Maybe." I marvelled at how cool I sounded.

"Is that all you'll commit to? *Maybe*?"

"It is." I simply didn't trust myself to make a sensible decision without a huge amount of thought going into it. Without my Beth on hand to guide me – boss me – I would have to stand on my own two feet and work things out for myself, and that required time. And possibly a pen and an Excel spreadsheet.

Guy stood up from the bench and I followed suit. "I like this." He made a broad sweep with his arm, taking in the hacked wasteland around us, the hatchet, the shears, the weed pile. "It shows passionate spirit and untamed anger. You're a fiery woman Edda, with your fine red hair, '*behold those amber flames that lick the ice white ivory of your neck*'. Beneath that cool exterior I think there's an inferno burning."

Just in time I remembered to close my mouth and not gape at him as he said the words.

Yes! I was passionate. I was driven. I had an inner fire burning ... within me. Without thinking I responded with words straight from the heart, "Oh, right, thanks."

"I'll be expecting you a week next Thursday, Edda." He said my name and my stomach went hot. Strolling to the gate he paused, "I know you won't disappoint me, Edda Mackenzie." I wasn't sure, but he might have winked.

"Oh darling that's fab!" Beth hugged me tightly and I could feel the unfamiliar press of the emerging baby bump in between us so I pulled back in case I flattened its head. I couldn't even hug her now.

"The man is beautiful, even in daylight." I panted, still trying to get my breath back from the sprint I'd just executed between my house and Beth's flat the minute Guy had walked out of view in the opposite direction. "But I looked like this – can you believe I didn't even have mascara on? And he still flirted with me. He said I was like an artist! He said something about having an inferno inside me and something else about flames licking my hair."

"*Licking your hair*?" Beth looked disgusted.

"No it was nice. Something about auburn locks or something. It might have been poetry, now that I think of it. You know, I reckon he imagines I'm a really passionate spirit because I have red hair and once guerrilla gardened the skip, and then hacked my front garden to pieces."

"You hacked what?" Beth said.

"Excuse me! Coming through!" Jack was upon us from out of nowhere, staggering down the hallway with an enormous pink inflatable ball.

We stood aside to let him pass. "Are you going somewhere?" I asked as Jack squeezed the ball into the boot of his car.

"Antenatal classes." Beth said, checking her watch. I noticed with a stab of joy that she still wore the A-Ha watch that I bought her for her seventeenth birthday. "Crap. We're late. We couldn't find the goddamn ball but then I remembered we'd put it in the shed at the bottom of the garden. Jack's totally angry with me, but then he can't really blame me: it's all baby's fault, isn't it my tiny little darling?" she stroked her stomach. "I've gone completely ditzy you know, with the pregnancy. Look, sorry Eds, we really have to dash." She pulled the front door closed behind her and I was left with nothing else to do but follow her as she walked down her path to the waiting car.

"It's great that the artist thinks you're hot!" she said.

"But do you think I'm selling him a puppy?"

"No! Eds you're—"

"I mean," I continued, trying to ignore Jack's impatient tapping of the steering wheel, "do you think that he'll realise that I'm not a passionate militant gardener sort and then be completely disappointed that I'm just … me. Someone with red hair that once gardened a skip. And hacked her front garden to pieces."

"Darling!" through the open window Beth put a hand on my hand, "He'll be totally smitten with you just as you are."

"We are very, VERY late." Jack said through gritted teeth.

"I'll call you shall I? We're in Guildford at Jack's parents until Sunday but maybe the night after? Will you be in?"

"Yes." I said in a small voice. I was always in. "But Beth, before you go, do you think I should go to this secret society meeting?"

Jack laughed. "Of course you should go!" He turned the key in the ignition. "Sounds amazing. Bye, Edda!"

"I think you should go as well," Beth said as the car began to reverse away. "But then it's your decision."

"I know. I know." I clung to the car door. "He said I had an inner fire! He said he thought I was a passionate woman!"

"I'm sorry, honey, we really do have to get going right now."

"Of course, of course." I stood back and waved them off, watching as they disappeared down Manor Avenue and onto the High Road. Off and away to baby classes.

How quickly euphoria could turn into wretchedness. My inner fire had been extinguished: I was nothing more than an abandoned, sweaty, soil-covered red-head. Without having the benefit of a sombrero for cover, I kept my head down as I trudged back to my house so that Babs sitting splay-legged on her front step wouldn't be able to see the tears. My hands were clenched into fists at my side, my chin trembling but set in resolve: I would move on from this. I would do something with my life. I would not let this get me down.

Six

"What the heck is this?" I put down the free ads paper I had been scanning through and picked up the copy of *Mature Woman* that was lying on my desk at work when I got in. *The magazine for women who still have that get up and go!* There was a picture of just such a woman in her sixties on the front cover, holding a skipping rope and laughing.

What was making her so freakily happy?

Had she just carried out an assisted suicide on her not-so-active husband?

"I think Amanda bought you that." My boss looked up briefly from her PC.

"Really?" I shifted from being insulted to being moved at the thought of Amanda leafing through magazines and picking one out for me: touched that she'd thought of me.

Someone had thought of me.

Someone had cared enough to spend – I flipped back to the front cover – one pound seventy on me.

I was perilously close to needing my sombrero again. Instead, I pulled myself together and focused on the fact that it was *Mature Woman* – for God's sake – and then flicked through it, eventually reading an article: "Why women in their sixties are having more sex than ever before." How much of a kick in the teeth was that?

Well, at least I had all my own teeth…

"Hey there!" In bounced Amanda, a shimmying display of short white skirt, black high heels and long bare legs. "Like the mag?"

"Yes. Thank you Amanda. I'm touched."

"Well it had an article on loneliness: look…" She rifled through its denture-packed pages. "Loneliness: discover the new you in solitude." It's all about learning to be confident with who you are and how to meet people when you do want company."

"So … great. Thank you."

She perched on a clutter-free corner of my desk.

It was a yellow pants day. Lovely.

"What's this?" She picked up the free ads paper I'd just bought. "Are you looking for love? Oh my God you know like murderers and rapists and stuff lure their prey by advertising in papers like this? You could be totally in trouble with lonely hearts columns."

"Well, actually I thought I'd give the lodger idea a go." I repositioned myself so as to minimise my exposure to Amanda's underwear.

"Hey, that's what I said you should do! You're thinking about moving on! How cool is that? So have you had any calls about the room yet?"

"Loads!" I groaned and opened a note pad full of scrawled names and times for interviews.

Amanda took it and scanned down the list of names.

"Girls and boys! How many people have you booked in to see it?"

"Thirty-six."

"*Thirty-six?* You're going to interview thirty six people for just one room?"

"I know; that's too many isn't it?" I looked back at the long, long list. "But I didn't want to turn anyone away. What if the thirty-sixth person was *the* person and I turned them away because I thought I had too many to interview already?"

"Couldn't you have, like, checked them on the phone? Didn't some sound too weird so you just said the room was, like, gone or something?"

I tried to remember. "Only one person. He said God told him to call me about the room and that he knew the room was his by divine right. So I did tell *him* that the room had gone."

"Like *wow!* And what did he say to you when you said that?"

"He said that God moved in mysterious ways and he'd have to move to Vauxhall instead. But apart from that … I'm not very good at vetting. Actually, I'm not very good on the phone."

"Are you any good at interviewing?"

"Probably not, no." I had a sudden flash back to Guy the artist in my garden admiring my passion and my red hair and what the person he thought I was might do in this circumstance. Should I be trying to act more passionate and red-headed?

"When are you interviewing?" Amanda asked.

"Next weekend."

"Do you want help?"

"You'd help? You'd really come over?" I felt the beginnings of a lump in the back of my throat – wasn't it true that in a time of need friends came out of the woodwork? Didn't one of Amanda's other magazines say something about that in an article on karma?

"Of course I'll help! I, like, totally love this sort of thing: who stays, who goes. Like, oh my God, the power! You know? It's, like, *so* my destiny to be a celebrity talent-show judge. I could come to yours for practice, for when I get well famous. Can I?"

I was lost for words but Amanda quite happily ploughed on. "I read that it's, like, really important that once you've been dumped, you—"

"Can we not use the word *dumped*."

"Fine then. Once you've been…" she looked to me expectantly, "The victim of a friend's pregnancy…"

"Better."

"OK, so once you've been a victim," she said, "you deal with it right there and then. And this article, I think it was in *Marie Claire* or something, it said you should look at all aspects of your life, not just one, and reassess them or something. You know? And it's, like, you're totally doing that. You're, like, being committed to moving on."

"And that's not all of it—" I began, buoyed up with her image of me, and before I had time to think it through I was telling her about the skip. When I saw her look impressed, I told her about the party that I'd been to with the stuffed bear and the police signs. And then, caught up in my eagerness to impress her I found myself blurting out about Guy (*You go girl. You are, like, so over that divorce and everything.*) and the invitation to the secret society in the basement of the Working Men's Club.

"Bugger."

"What?" Amanda said. "It sounds great! I'd, like, so give my Mac make-up collection to spend an evening with a handsome artist. Even if it is in a working men's club on the Lewisham High Road. Is your secret society thing *this* Thursday?"

"Next Thursday. Amanda, you must not say anything." I overcame the urge to grip her by the arm as I implored her. "Please. I forgot it was a secret. I shouldn't have told anyone. I got carried away with all the excitement."

"Oh my God, don't worry about me or anything!" Amanda jumped off the table in a flash of lemon yellow. "You see Magda, from Lifelong Learning, over the other side of the office?" She pointed to the heavy-set woman with the permanent frown. "The things she told me about her and her husband's sex life. I mean, like, oh my God, you would not *believe*! So your secret is safe with me."

"That's great Amanda, because you haven't disclosed Magda's secret to me in any way."

"Exactly!" A stranger to irony Amanda tapped the side of her nose. "Your secret is, like, so safe. Anyway it's about gardening – I mean how exciting is that? Unless you're middle-aged or something. Who wants to hear a secret about *gardening*?"

Seven

I staggered out of the door with four filled bin liners: the first stage of my cleaning up in preparation for the new lodger. I was almost overcome by the amount of cleaning that had to be done, but at least I had made a start. Phase One in my Moving On Plan: not that there was actually a plan…

"Awright there, darlin'." Babs stubbed out her fag on our garden wall and put down the large white sheets of plastic she'd been cutting.

"Evening, Babs. What are you doing?" I pointed to the cuttings.

"Nothin'!" she said sharply. "Just somethin' for me grandson and nothin' for you to go lookin' at. Anyhow," she softened no doubt having seen the effect of her outburst on my expression, "I've not seen yer man round 'ere the last few days. Lovers tiff is it?"

"No, Babs." I heaved the bags down the path. "He's not my boyfriend."

"Aw and the way you two were lookin' at each other that day you went mental in yer front garden. There's summat there, you mark my words." She peered over the wall to see what I was hefting down my path. "Clear out is it darlin'?"

"Charity shop." I said. "Old clothes. Things I'm not going to wear anymore." Because I was never, ever going to go out anymore.

"Never say never darlin'," and in the blink of an eye the old woman sped down her garden path, up mine and stood beside me opening up the bags. "You don't mind, do yer love? If it's going to the charity shop I might as well have first look, eh? Charity begins at 'ome don't it? And if not, next door to yer 'ome." There was a whirl of clothes, mostly going-out clothes or clothes I'd worn when I was twenty and couldn't wear now I was almost thirty without risking a serious mutton/lamb combo. Each piece that Babs pulled out and examined had a particular memory either of when I bought it – with Beth – or when I last wore it out – with Beth.

The clear out had been a painful experience. But one of Amanda's magazine articles – "Why Clutter Causes Heartache" – had been very firm about the need to clean as a first step to moving on.

"You look all in. Everythin' all right with you?" Babs said, clutching a never-worn cherry-coloured basque that Beth had persuaded me into buying. Babs walked over the bared earth of my front garden and up to my bay window to admire herself in the reflection.

"Oh. Yes. Fine. Everything's fine thanks," I said, trying my best not to look horrified at Babs-in-a-basque.

She eyed me suspiciously. "Yer not in trouble are yer?"

"No!" I felt pretty confident that the kind of trouble Babs knew of in her world was something I would never experience in my own.

"Is it that friend of yours what got knocked up?"

"Any news this week?" I decided diversion was the best course of action as usual.

"It's been a quiet one, this week." She pulled out a sequined mini skirt and put it on one side with the basque. "Man threw himself under a train at the station at New Cross Gate yesterday. Selfish bastard."

"Did he die?"

"Course he bleedin' died, Edda! Not many people live after the London to Brighton's run over their noggin! Apart from that, it's been quiet. Oh I like this! I do like this! What is it love?"

"It's a belly dancing costume."

"An' are these real coins?"

"I think they're fakes."

"You do this belly dancin' then do yer?"

"I used to. With my friend. With Beth."

"Well I'll 'ave that an' all. Reckon me boyfriend will love that!"

She put it on the side and I fought hard to keep my head clear of any possible Babs/belly dancing images that were threatening to appear.

"So, how's it going with the room to let?"

I stared at her. "How do you know about that? How on earth could you possibly know that the room was advertised now? I only told you I was thinking about it."

"Oh, I never reveals me sources."

I shivered. It was all very well learning things about other people, about the death and sex and drugs in SE4 but now that I was the focus of such gossip – in my super mundane way – I didn't like it at all. How did Babs know everything? It felt as though she was in my head.

Did she know about the secret society? She could well do – after all she'd seen Guy in the garden with me… Though she'd never come clean on what she knew or didn't know about Eustace Fox.

"The lodger search is going fine thanks, Babs. I'm interviewing next week."

"You be careful, young Edda." Babs shook a gold lamé blouse at me. "There's bad people out there."

"Yes, but I'll interview them and—"

"Some of 'em," Babs continued, "looks as nice as pie. Butter wouldn't melt in their mouths. But thems the ones you 'ave to watch for. Evil people, Edda, believe me, *evil*."

"OK then."

"Heard a bloke, Deptford way," Babs paused to light a fag, "took a lodger what he'd never met. Lodger was a dodgy lookin' geezer from Bermondsey, need I say more? Anyhow, 'is neighbour 'ears screaming in the night. No one sees the bloke for a few days, lodger acting all cagey and stuff. Turns out 'e's gone an' killed the bloke 'cause 'e wouldn't watch *Grand Designs* on the telly. Killed 'im 'cause of the TV! And then to get rid of the evidence and what not 'e cuts the body up an' cooks it. Sick bastard. Mark my words, Edda, it ain't always a good idea. Anyway, I'll 'ave these clothes ta. Charity shop ain't gonna miss what it never 'ad is it?"

I had lost the ability to speak.

Babs twirled the ash off her fag. "Edda…"

I took a deep breath. "Yes, Babs?"

"Why was you askin' last week about Fox Estates?"

"I don't know," I said and at that point I really didn't know. The tenant-baking-the-landlord story had knocked me sideways and I couldn't think of anything except for the fact that I was willingly taking myself down a road that ended in me being covered in pie crust.

"I'll tell you what that man Eustace Fox is," Babs said in a low voice and I focused back on the here and now: she was ready to tell me what she knew! "He's a *homosexualist!*"

"Really?" I pretended to look surprised.

Babs was nodding. "Not that that's anything these days. Takes all sorts. Specially round 'ere. Anyhow" he's having it away with this bloke who's 'igh up in the Council – *bastardsthelotofem*," she added, cementing my firm commitment *never* to tell Babs what I did for a living. "My friend lives in a flat opposite 'im. She sees everything. That bloke 'e's with comes and goes at all times. Drives one of them fancy red covetable cars, Mercedes Benz it is – sports car with one of them roofs what go down an' up again. An' I'll tell you another thing," she was into her stride now, "he collects them police signs."

"I know!" I checked the door behind me and took a step towards Babs, "I know!" I was so relieved that someone else knew this.

Babs looked surprised. "How d'you know? You ain't seen him? My friend she sees him. Sees him creepin' out at night and takin' 'em back to 'is 'ouse."

"Well, when I went to a party at his house..." I

enjoyed the look of surprise on Babs' face for once. This was something Babs didn't know... "I saw them all stacked in his understairs cupboard. Lots of them. Fifty or more."

"Well I never did," Babs lit a thoughtful fag.

"Why do you think he hoards them?" I said.

"I reckon 'cause it's crimes 'e's committed." Babs gave it the full weighty tone, "It's written reminders of what 'e's done. Souvenirs, innit."

"My friend, Beth, thinks it's because he doesn't want the bad publicity for Brockley: it could put people off buying property in the neighbourhood. She's probably right – why would a successful business man in his sixties snatch bags and car jack?"

"Why does me neighbour on the other side eat dogs? I don't know. There ain't no logic in the world, Edda. But what I will say is," she put a cold bony hand on my arm, "You be careful, young girl. I don't like 'im."

It struck me that a lot of people around me were warning me to be careful. Was I really living so dangerously by joining a secret *gardening* society and getting a lodger in? Was I sleepwalking my way into peril or was it simply that I had surrounded myself with people who fretted too much?

"Babs I know you mean well but, to be honest, you do tend to see the worst in people sometimes. Well, most times. Really. Maybe your radar might be a little – skewed?"

"I tell yer what. Friend of mine, another one, tried to sell 'er flat with that Fox Estates business of 'is. West

Indian woman she is. Nothing wrong with that. But he – he wouldn't 'ave nothin' to do with her. Apparently," Babs stood close beside me and I gained the full benefit of the decades of chain-smoking cheap fags and PG-Tips on her breath, "he couldn't bring himself to stay more than a few minutes there. Said it wasn't his sort of flat. Wouldn't have anything to do with her. Racialist. That's what he is."

"Was there a problem with your friend's flat?"

"Only that it was 'ers and she was Jamaican. You look at 'is shop up there on the Brockley Road. You look at them fancy 'ouses and posh flats in 'is window. There ain't a single one there for the likes of you an' me. They're for *aspirating folks* aren't they? Folks what work in that Canary Wharf an' the City an' earn a thousand pound a month."

"As much as that?"

"Some of 'em. So next time you're passin' you just take a look. You think about it."

"I will. Thank you, Babs."

"'e don't want us." Babs picked up the clothes she wanted and made to leave. "'e don't want the likes o' me and my lot in Brockley."

I went back into my house, sat down, and spent a long time pondering and staring at the phone across the other side of the room. *Was* I mixing with the wrong sorts? Was I going to be made into Landlady Pie? If ever there was a time to call Beth it was now. But she would be busy – she was always busy these days – and even if she was at home and had time to talk to me she wouldn't properly listen to what I had to say. She was well and truly on Planet Pregnant.

I got up and made myself a cup of tea. I would not call Beth. I would be fine without Beth. I could manage on my own without Beth for goodness sake…

Beth walked back into the lounge and flopped beside Jack on their old Habitat sofa. They were watching TV. The room was dimly lit by Beth's Ikea floor lamps and the blue light of the TV flickered on their faces. They looked very content: very *sufficient*.

But Beth looked tired. My heart went out to her: there were dark smudges beneath her eyes and her hair was wild and bouffant, just like it always got when she ran her hands through it too much. Today had obviously been a difficult day for her.

Half an hour earlier I had cast caution to the wind and walked over to see Beth. I had to: I needed to talk to her about the secret society and the lodger and everything that was on my mind. It was ridiculous sitting at home worrying whether or not I should call her – she was my oldest friend. We shared *everything*. Of course I should go and see her. But I'd only made it as far as the path to her front door. Because seeing Beth and Jack cosied up in their front room in the early evening I realised that I couldn't intrude. Because I wasn't intruding on two people I was intruding on three. On a family.

Things weren't the same any more.

I was still dithering – wondering whether I should

pluck up the courage to ring their bell and impose on them with my petty babyless worries – when I heard a noise from down the street. There had been very few cars passing at that time in the evening and there had been no pedestrians at all, so the noise put me on full alert and I stepped back into the cover of dense fir trees that ran along the side of Beth's path.

Maybe it was just a dog-walker. Or a jogger. Stranger things had happened in the borough of Lewisham. But nevertheless it paid to be careful: after all there had been a cupboardful load of police signs in Eustace Fox's house.

I peered out between the heavy branches and up towards the main road. Under the orange pools of the streetlights I could just make out that the noise had come from a lone man, with no dog and no running shoes, and he was walking in my direction. More ominous than the lack of dog and trainers was the fact that the man was dressed in a long dark trench coat that skimmed the pavement, topped off with a wide-brimmed black hat pushed low on his head. A man in disguise: a man who wanted to blend in to the night. A man who wanted to look like a villain in a graphic novel.

I lowered an overhanging branch and drew back further into the tree, sitting as far back on the wall as I dared to go without risking falling off and into Beth's front garden. No one would see me now unless they specifically ruffled the branches to look for me. And who went about ruffling branches late at night?

Men in long black trench coats and wide-brimmed hats…

WOMAN FOUND DEAD: BROCKLEY RUFFLER SUSPECTED! "I just can't believe she was outside my flat when it happened," said Bethan Smedley, 28, of Manor Avenue, Brockley. "I'm just so glad to be moving out of Brockley and into the safe, semi-detached-off-road-parking-suburbia of Surrey to raise my child…"

Hardly daring to breathe I waited as the soft tread of the Brockley Ruffler came nearer. And nearer. He had crossed over and was walking on my side of the road.

I listened hard for sounds of ruffling.

And then there was silence. He had stopped walking. I sensed he was very close, I could hear his breathing and then – cutting through the silence of the night – the loud grate of metal on pavement. *What the bloody hell was that? Was that the sound of a weapon?*

I gripped the tree. There was more silence. Could he see me? Was he watching me? The hairs on the back of my neck rose. What was the metallic noise and why was he silent now? Suppose the man had watched me hide in the tree and knew I was here? Suppose he had been watching me all the time I had been staring into Beth's flat. Suppose he had been biding his time…

In the silence I heard him take a deep breath and then begin walking again. And then I saw him. He was straight in front of me. If I wanted to I could reach out and touch him. But I didn't want to. And then, thank God, he walked past. He was gone, his footsteps padding, heavily now, down the road.

I let out a long, measured, silent breath. He hadn't noticed me. I had escaped unruffled.

My legs tingled from cramp, my hands were sore with the effort of tightly gripping the tree trunk and I had two hamster-sized slugs on my thighs. I leant forward, still making sure I was well hidden by the foliage. The man had crossed the pavement and in a few seconds he would be gone from view, but before he disappeared he passed beneath the last street light on Manor Avenue. In a flash the streetlight illuminated a large metal police sign tucked under his arm. *That* was what had caused the metallic scrape. The fact that the man was carrying the enormous sign had meant his footsteps had been laboured since he'd passed me. It was Eustace Fox! I recognised him now, his gait, his build. It was so *obvious*, of course it was Eustace Fox. And when I recognised who it was I felt enormous overwhelming relief. Yes it was odd – creepy even – that he was going out at night and taking police signs off the streets in the area, but he was only doing it to protect the good image of Brockley.

Probably.

It was strange, I thought as I watched him disappear around the corner with his sign, this whole new secret Brockley that was opening up. It was as though I had been sleepwalking my first few years in the area when I'd been with Beth. All our going-out and the nights-in we'd had were so introverted that I'd never got to properly know the area or its people at all – and Beth probably less so than me: she would never talk to Babs and avoided the Mini Mart and Launderette: "in case I catch South

79

London disease and there isn't a cure". But the more I was looking around at the place I lived in, the more it fascinated me. There were sign-stealing toffs and handsome guerrilla gardeners and, of course, there was Babs' criminal underworld…

I so wanted to tell Beth about all the things I was finding out. And about the fact that I'd just seen Eustace Fox out and about stealing police signs in the dead of night. Because, however much Beth found South London distasteful, she would *love* to know more about it. As long as she wasn't immersed in it, as long as she had her get-out clause of Surrey. But how could I tell her what I had just seen? I could hardly knock on the front door now and say, 'Hey, Beth, I was just hanging outside your flat when you'll never guess what I saw…'

So, feeling rather sheepish, there was no option but to slip off the wall dispose of the monster slugs and, with dead legs, stagger back home as quickly as the pins and needles would let me, looking not unlike a cowboy who had spent far too long on a very wide horse.

Eight

With new determination I tried to focus on the forthcoming lodger situation, and the imminent interviews that would take place next week. Only after I had concentrated my energy on preparing for the lodger could I think about the secret society meeting, because, as Amanda's magazines advised, it was important not to take on too much at once when in an emotionally fragile state. Piling on the activities would end up with a visit to a nice padded hospital where the nurses spoke softly and carried tasers.

So the secret society and Guy the artist and Eustace the sign-hoarder were pushed to the back of my mind and the new lodger situation took over.

In preparation for the lodger, every evening after work, like a modern day Cinderella, I got into my rags and trudged up the stairs to the top floor to clean. But, unlike my distant hazy childhood dream of being Cinderella, there was no fairy godmother hanging around on the landing and waiting to bibbity bobbity boo me into a Vera Wang dress and a blacked-out stretch limo. There was just Finley, watching disdainfully from the threshold as I sweated on my hands and knees in the bedroom and bathroom that were going to earn me nothing more romantic than £500 a month. Less tax.

So – far from becoming my childhood dream I had become, instead, another character from my distant past. Now I was the hungry caterpillar of cleaning. On Monday I filled seven bin bags with rubbish, but the top floor still looked messy. On Tuesday I vacuumed for three hours after a hard day at work, but the top floor still looked messy. On Wednesday I dusted every surface and filled another bag with clutter, but it still looked messy. On Thursday I moved the furniture, changed the linen, put up new curtains, moved the rug and blacked the fireplace, but it still looked messy. On Friday I assembled all my cleaning products on my kitchen table, rejected them all, and instead gave two fingers to cleaning, opened a bottle of wine and watched TV. And it still looked messy.

On Saturday I took firmer steps towards my cleaning regime.

"What I need," I said to Mr Iqbal as we walked around his topsy-turvey Mini Mart, "is a cleaning product so powerful it carries a health warning."

Mr Iqbal considered me for a moment. I knew he would have the solution to my grime. Mr Iqbal's Mini Mart might look cluttered and small but it was the depository for every single item that I ever needed to live my life. And in my quest for a cleaner house it was my last port of call. I'd rejected the supermarket shelves full of environmentally friendly products which would *softly cleanse* dirt and *gently target* filth. They didn't sound effective enough, given that my inner Havisham had allowed real honest grime to accumulate over the last few years. What the house needed was the indoor equivalent of what I'd done in the garden with my hatchet. The house needed a complete annihilation of the dust of history: cleaning on a mind-blowing scale.

"Come here, young Edna," we walked past the yams and dented tins of chick peas and cheap toilet paper to a shelf of cleaning products. "Here you are." Mr Iqbal picked up a bright violet bottle with day-glo pink lettering. FILTHY EXTERMINATOR.

"Looks good, Mr Iqbal." I turned it over to read the instructions which were reassuringly badly translated: it boded well for an effective cleaning product as everything manufactured in the UK seemed too environmentally responsible and mild.

This our Filthy Exterminator range will slash through grime using MOST POTENT chemicals licensed for within household use! NOT LICENCED FOR USE IN FRANCE, GERMANY, USA, CANADA, BELGIUM, ISLE OF WIGHT. DO NOT MIX WITH OTHER CLEANING PRODUCT made China.

"Great – I'll take it!" I said. "And the toilet cleaner and the window cleaner."

"I get them from a friend in India," Mr Iqbal said, gingerly taking the products off the shelf as if they were made of gelignite and walking them to the counter for me. "Now then young Edna," he tapped the knackeredy stool beside the knackeredy counter. "Sit yourself down for a moment. I think there are a few things we need to read in the small print." And then he put on two pairs of glasses: one stacked on the other which he'd explained to me before were just as effective as varifocals. I sat on the stool and prepared to be lectured at – in the nicest possible way. A quick trip to the Mini Mart was never a quick trip: invariably Mr Iqbal would want to discuss the purchases. Beth would never go to the Mini Mart, unfairly saying it was dirty and tatty, which was a shame because if she could have overcome her inner snob she would have enjoyed the experience. I did. But then sometimes it wasn't the best choice of shop. I once made the mistake of trying to buy a pack of Marlboro Lights at 3am during a party and Mr Iqbal sat me down and explained exactly what they would do to my health with diagrams of cancerous lungs drawn on a paper bag.

" 'Warning'," Mr Iqbal intoned, " 'Use of Filthy Exterminator range may cause breathing difficulties, blindness, deafness, hair loss, tooth decay—' "

"*Tooth decay?*"

Mr Iqbal held a hand out, "Be serious for once, young Edna. Now … 'shaking, vomiting, palpitationing, dropsy, gout and the palsy."

He put the bottle down on the counter and folded his arms.

"My house is quite dirty," I admitted in a small voice.

He raised his twice-spectacled eyes at me. "I think what you're buying might be dangerous. How about you buy chemical resistant gloves – here – and as my most charming customer I give you a BOGOF – you buy one pair and I give you a pair for free." He slapped a second pair on the old counter.

"Thank you, Mr Iqbal!" I beamed, and then realised that it was probably just a line. "You put on the charm for all the ladies, don't you?" I said.

"There are not many ladies in Brockley, Edna. But those that make it into Iqbal's Mini Mart are assured of the very best service. Now then, can I interest you in fly paper? A mango? Basmati rice?"

Dressed in my oldest and least-loved clothes, and donning my chemical resistant gloves I started my cleaning by tackling the skirting boards and floorboards with FILTHY EXTERMINATOR X-TREME LAVENDER FLOR POLISH (for flors and dors) that stripped off a layer of varnish taking the boards back so they shone as brightly as the day the tree was felled by the Victorian woodsman. Except that now the wood was impregnated with the nose-singeing smell of Extreme Lavender and not its original pine. To disguise the smell, or at least compete with it, I arranged expensive vanilla potpourri in the newly black-leaded fireplace.

I stepped back and sniffed. It was a full on nasal assault.

When I recovered, spluttering and clinging on to the doorframe, I saw that at least the room looked clean and fresh and well worth the five hundred pounds I was going to be asking for it. I opened a window: after all I didn't want to kill anyone and Mr Iqbal had been very concerned about safety.

There was a small bathroom to the right of the bedroom and I moved on to tackle that, throwing away my first pair of chemical resistant gloves, which had almost burnt through. This time I used the bottle of FILTHY EXTERMINATOR BATH ROOM SPARKELGEL (*ensure room well ventillationed*), until the tiles shone and the taps glistened and wisps of blue and orange smoke came up from the plug hole. I found a sea-blue rug in one of the stored boxes and put that on the floor, and unwrapped a bar of soap in the shape of a dolphin and put it by the wash basin.

I stood back and admired my week's work, knocking back rosé straight from the bottle: there was no point messing around with dainty glasses when I was on my own.

I caught a glimpse of myself in the floor length mirror. Filthy. Sweaty. Dirty clothes and rubber gloves, drinking from the bottle.

Oh God.

The reflected me did not look good.

I really needed company. Had I left the interview too late? Would I be too far gone by next weekend? At least I had the secret society to look forward to in the meantime and get me used to being with people again.

Nine

Never before had a cat so plainly communicated the word *GO*.

I stared into Finley's narrowed green eyes, ogled at what he was doing to me, and then grabbed my coat.

I would go.

For the past half hour I had been wandering the house, wringing my hands and talking my situation through with Finley: S*hould I go to the secret society thing, Fin? Eustace seems like a nice man – he is a nice man, Beth says he donates to charity and he has rosy cheeks and he's really friendly and has a big house – but is guerrilla gardening legal? Should I get involved? Beth thinks I should and what she says usually goes – it must be OK if Beth says it is, she knows these things. But should I always do what Beth makes me do? Isn't that the whole problem? That I'm too caught up in Beth and now she's divorcing me – she's not divorcing me is she Fin? – just moving on, should I do my own thing. What should I do Fin? Should I go or should I stay here with you? What do you think?*

Really it had been quite freaky the way the cat had put the word *go* into my head.

The Finley effect only lasted as far as Beth's flat on Manor Road. It looked so cosy and inviting that I had an almost uncontrollable urge to ring the bell: I could have a quick drink and a pep talk from Beth to calm my nerves before continuing on to the secret society meeting. No more hanging out with the slugs in her fir trees: now I *really* needed her. And Beth would be OK about it. I wouldn't be intruding…

I checked my watch. Dammit I was already five minutes late. There was no time for a quick drink and pep talk. I dragged myself past her flat and continued on to Lewisham High Road. By the time I'd reached the shabby Working Men's Club all commitment to the cause had disappeared. I would much rather have gone back to Beth's for a drink. Or home to the TV and a glass of wine. But then both of those options carried a heavy price: having to explain myself to Beth, or to the cat. It was probably better to summon up the courage to actually go into the grotty club house: after all how bad could it be? I'd actually enjoyed guerrilla gardening the skip.

The Working Men's Club was a squat seventies building, covered in graffiti and – how ironic – weeds, with loops of razor wire and boarded windows that made it look derelict. It was not the sort of place I would have expected a man like Eustace Fox to choose as his secret society headquarters. It had a distinct lack of parapets and sash windows. What had the working men been thinking?

Had I got the venue wrong? Was there somewhere else, somewhere splendid, that I should have gone to instead? Dammit, had I been caught up in a Mesmer stare with the beautiful artist and not listened to where I should be going? I hung back from the dilapidated club house, loitering by the window of the South London Fried Chicken Parlour, pretending to read the menu (*eight thighs in a special Deep-South-London Sauce)* but surreptitiously watching the semi-derelict unlit building on the opposite side of the road.

I *must* have got the place wrong. I should go home. Or to Beth's. This was ridiculous. I had been dreaming of adventure but standing on the Lewisham High Road, surrounded by the smell of greasy poultry, I was distinctly lacking in the Famous Five spirit. There was surely no adventure to be had here.

A few fried-chicken minutes passed as I floundered. And just as I was on the brink of turning on my heels an enormous BMW, something dark and sleek, pulled up in a screech of tyres. A tailored, coiffured woman sprang out, threw a pashmina around her shoulders and disappeared behind the filthy boundary wall of the Working Men's Club. In an instant the car had executed a swift U-turn to avoid Lewisham town centre and sped back in the direction of Brockley.

Oh.

Maybe I *had* got the right place. *There* had been someone who was Eustace Fox's sort. And if the pashmina woman could go into that filthy derelict building, surely so could I?

I made my way across the road and into clean, chicken-free air. Taking a deep breath I headed through the gate and followed a walkway running the length of the grimy wall, the gloom deepening as I left the orange glow of the street lights. It looked as derelict from the side as it was from the road: the windows were boarded and those that weren't boarded were blackened with filth. It was silent, too, the only sound was my breath which was coming in nervous fluttery gasps.

Where was pashmina lady? What had happened to her?

A few steps further and I came to a boarded door. It was the end of the path. In the dark I could just make out that it was slightly ajar, the faintest crack of light coming from the side. With shaky hands I pushed and it creaked heavily, opening inwards and into a lit room. I walked in to a narrow cloakroom lined in filthy 1970s hessian wallpaper and there, in the centre, lit by a flickering striplight, was Peter Shaw, Head of Planning: affability itself in a pink cashmere turtleneck and chinos. The contrast between his clean-shaven M&Sness and the dilapidation around him was bizarre. He put down the copy of the *Telegraph* he'd been reading and took a step towards me.

"Nice to see you again, Edda."

"Hi," I managed, completely weirded out, as Amanda might put it, to be seeing a work colleague – of sorts – in a place like this. It was like seeing Prince Charles in head-to-toe Spandex throwing shapes on a Shoreditch dancefloor.

"Just follow the stairs behind you and head down to the dungeons," Peter said.

"The dungeons?"

"The basement!" he laughed. "No need to fret. Just the basement."

"Great. Thanks." *Comedian.*

Now I had no alternative but to look lively and head down the filthy, dark staircase in the knowledge that if the ground-level was revolting surely the basement would be even worse. What sort of secret society had a place like this as their headquarters? What the hell was I doing?

Thinking *inner fire* and *handsome artist* I gripped the stair rail with a clammy hand. What was waiting for me at the bottom? Did I really have to be doing this? Weren't there other less extraordinary ways in which I could fill the Beth-shaped void in my life? Like Pilates? Religion? Baking cupcakes?

The vision of Milk Tray man helped me on my path. Guy would be at the meeting in a room at the bottom of these steps…

Five steps down and I was deep in an impenetrable gloom. And something unnerving was happening. The thick wooden rail beneath my hands had given way to a thinner handrail that was cool and glass-like to the touch. The staircase, too, had changed: the shallow metal-edged steps at the top of the flight were now steeper and sounded wooden underfoot. A few steps further into the dark and I felt the staircase turn and, following a faint glow of a light somewhere ahead I began to pick out the way. In this new, lesser gloom, I could make out that the staircase *had* changed – from the chunky seventies one I'd started out on to a grand, old, wooden staircase with wrought iron balustrade. With every step the passageway widened until I reached enormous double doors. From behind them came the unmistakeable thrum of conversation. Grasping a crystal doorknob in each hand I took a deep breath and pushed open the great doors.

A golden brightness dazzled me. Still gripping the door knobs I squinted into what was a vast jewel-like ballroom. Overhead great chandeliers glittered and sparkled, reflected in floor to ceiling gilt mirrors. The room was cavernous. And it was in no way whatsoever connected with the Working Men's Club above it.

"Oh, I do so love it," Eustace Fox was before me, ruddy faced and loudly dressed, "When someone joins us for the first time!" He placed a martini in my hand. "My dear, magnificent isn't it? Do you like our Working Men's Club?"

"I…"

"You are inside," he put an arm around me and propelled me into the middle of the room, "the remains of Shardlow Hall, Brockley's most secret gem. German bombs took out the Hall itself but the basement ballroom remained. So – welcome to what used to be a store room for the working man's weak beer and pork scratchings."

"And now we keep our beer and scratchings upstairs and we socialise downstairs. Eust you've got it all wrong."

I instantly recognised the chocolate voice of Guy Newhouse and the hairs on the back of my neck stood on end. He had come over, come *right* over, and was standing so close to me that I could feel his arm against my arm. There was every chance my inner fire would actually catch and I was going to burn down to the ground.

"I don't believe we've got it wrong for an instant, Guy," Eustace said. "Edda, let me introduce you to our group."

At the far end of the ballroom everyone had assembled with drinks. Some of the faces I recognised from the brief time I'd spent at the party. The cool dreadlocked owner of the V-2 café was lounging against the bar with a beer: *Hey there Edda! How're you doing?* and his hippy dreadlocked wife, Anja. *Hey there!* There were about twenty others, including über-cool art students from Goldsmiths: *Yah, hi*; a man called Jake, who looked as though he were built entirely of muscle *Ngh*; an identically dressed couple called Roger and Bronwen: *Hey/Hi* and many others whose names became a blur. I smiled and answered their polite questions and sipped my martini and thought, *Thank God I didn't do the Havisham thing this evening*. This place was awesome. Beth was going to be so jealous...

"Now then," Eustace said, taking prime position along a 1920s mirrored bar, "let me show our new recruit a little of what we do." And he pulled out a copy of the *Lewisham Echo* from a blue leather Mulberry satchel. "If you wouldn't mind, Edda, please read it out."

I settled onto my barstool and spread the paper out in front of me.

"*It's A-Oaky on the A2*," I began.

"Now now!" Eustace held his hand up as the company groaned. "Let the poor girl continue. Have some compassion."

I continued, red-faced with embarrassment: it hadn't been my plan to be any sort of centre of attention. "*Last night twenty-eight substantially sized oak saplings appeared, planted at regular intervals along the verges of the A2, one of the most blighted highways in South London."*

"Media bastards," muttered a severe-looking man from the back, "calling our stretch of the A2 blighted! The stupid journo's obviously never seen the Seven Sisters Road."

"Hey don't diss the journalists," a tall man from the back of the group said quite sternly. "Not all of us are as bad as you think."

"Continue Edda, if you will." Eustace said, laying a placating hand on the angry man's shoulders. I bent down to the article again.

"The trees, some measuring up to two metres in height, were planted in the Brockley area and are believed to be the work of guerrilla gardeners known to operate in the area, but whose identity is kept a close secret. 'We applaud the London ethic of taking responsibility and acting for the good of the environment,' the London Mayor said, during a visit to the borough of Lewisham, 'it just shows that a few people with the right ideas can work wonders.' Since coming into office the Mayor has instigated the planting of an urban forest consisting of more than two hundred trees, although as many as one in three have been vandalised and—"

"That highlights an important fact!" Eustace cut in. "Thank you for reading, Edda, but I must say that we have to be vigilant! There are those who create and nurture, like ourselves, and there are those who would destroy it all. God help them and their worthless, petty lives."

There was loud agreement amongst the group and a dark and portentous grunt from Mr Muscle: a man who looked like he snacked on pebbles.

Eustace's expression had clouded over, bending down to the article. "I do so *loathe* the term *guerrilla gardener*," he said, tapping the newspaper article with a portly finger. "Why they have to call us that is beyond me. It sounds like we're involved in armed warfare: it's very third world."

"We should be armed!" a woman called Agatha said. "Do you remember that gang Eustace? The one when we were planting up—"

"That's quite enough." Eustace put a hand on Agatha's shoulder, and then quickly smiling he added, "We don't want to go frightening our newest recruit with ridiculous stories do we? Nothing happened, Edda, my dear. Lads shouting. We soon dealt with them."

"Yeah, we did!" Jake let out a deep and sinister laugh that sounded like a rock fall.

I looked at him from the corner of my eye.

Yikes. Did I really want to sign up for something that would involve me spending time with a man like Jake, in lonely places, late at night? And however jolly Eustace Fox was he *did* steal police signs and Babs – fount of all Brockley knowledge – distrusted the man, so there must be something about him to warrant her suspicion.

Just how much did I really want to do this? How much did I need to have something in my life to take away the ache of losing Beth to all-consuming motherhood? I looked over towards Guy who was looking straight at me with his deep green eyes. Straight into my very soul.

Ah... I wanted to be a part of this quite a lot.

I sat on a silver deco bar stool and the world of the Brockley Spades opened up before me. The glamour of the underground ballroom, the thrill of having an attentive and handsome artist at my side and the implicit adventure of imminent middle-class illegality was intoxicating. Surely if the Famous Five had been around now and in their thirties they would be guerrilla gardeners: George, scowling, hauling enormous trees down darkened streets, Dick scurrying after George and hauling smaller trees, Timmy being a look-out for crims on the High Road, Anne providing the Waitrose nibbles and fussing over the tapas, and Julian, surely, would be a slimmer, younger, blonder Eustace Fox.

"...and the grasses totalled four hundred pounds exactly." Eustace was cataloguing the last quarter's "Digs", as he called them, and summing up the use of plant stocks. It wasn't gripping stuff and I'd tuned out for most of it, preferring instead to surreptitiously watch Guy from beneath my fringe. My God he was gorgeous, slouched in a leather arm chair, dressed all in black with his black curly hair tumbling across his face. He was practically a one-man aftershave advert.

Eustace continued on and on and as he did so the sense of adventure began to wane in the face of minutes, budgets and lists. The Famous Five *never* minuted any of their meetings.

As the plant stocks were listed and their values calculated, I began to wonder just how all the money was raised to support their activities. There were fifty pound trees – thirty of them. Three hundred pounds worth of lavenders, eight hundred of turf and so on and so on. Thousands and thousands of pounds – which came from *where*?

A creeping suspicion entered my head that Eustace funded the society by bag snatching and car stealing just like the police signs had said. Perhaps Babs had been right after all and he was a bad sort: robbing the poor to pay for the peonies.

Or was I just being melodramatic? Was the secret society of guerrilla gardeners all financed by money from his own pocket – after all he was obviously a wealthy man. Nobody lived in an enormous villa like his, or wore such flamboyant trousers as he did, without being extremely wealthy.

Or perhaps the guerrilla gardening finances came from money siphoned off from the Fox Estates business? Maybe the scheme was a tax avoidance exercise?

Or, I felt a knot in my stomach, maybe the money was raised through its members i.e. Me. Moi.

Now that I was going to be a member would I be expected to pay into some sort of Ornamental Cabbage Fund every month to keep Brockley green? No one had mentioned this to me so far, but then no one had mentioned much at all to me, and it was hardly going to be the first thing that was said on the subject: *Hi, do you want to join our secret society and have the privilege of losing a hundred pounds every month from your bank account?*

I fuzzily sipped my third martini and remained silent. There was no way my new lodger money was going on ornamental cabbages. I had plans for that money. Shoe-shaped plans. And placating Mike the bank manager, of course.

"That's a good point," Eustace was saying and he turned to me, making me quickly refocus on what was being said. "A little while back, Edda, I set up a website which has all the information you need: digs, contacts, blogs. It's hidden on the Fox Estates site – here's my business card with the web address on. Once you're on the home page look for the icon of a spade. It's light grey and appears on the very top right of the screen: it's so faint you won't be able to see it if you're not looking for it. Click on it and you'll be asked for a password. It's 'Capability'.

"Because we're capable?"

Eustace let out a loud laugh. "It's after the great man himself, Lancelot 'Capability' Brown."

Everyone was looking at me, highly amused. "Ah, OK." I said.

"You do *know* who Capability Brown was don't you?"

"Of course…" I lied glibly. "Actually, no."

"Well tut, tut! The man was a landscape designer extraordinaire!" Eustace held his hand up in a flourish. "He landscaped the grounds of the country houses of the rich and famous up and down the country in the eighteenth century."

I nodded, sagely.

"The man was a genius," Eustace continued, "he single handedly redesigned the way we thought about landscape and what was considered beautiful. In fact in—"

"Well, you learn something every day," interrupted Guy. "But I do have to go in half an hour, so could we get back to business, Eust?"

Thank you. Thank you, handsome artist man.

"Now one more thing before we go," Eustace said, "This Notorious Baron chap."

"Oh he's a pain!" the woman called Agatha chipped in.

"He's sodding rubbish is what he is!" The journalist pounded the bar.

"The man is a blight!" Eustace cut in. "I'm all for a bit of street art – my God we can make Brockley edgy can't we, we're not Dulwich for Christ's sake – but what we want is some Banksy. We want some class and some damn *skill* here. The chap calling himself Da Baron is completely bloody useless. Did anyone see the clown with a detonator near the florists the other day?"

"I did," an old lady held her hand up, "but it did take me a while to work out what it was."

"He doesn't have a shred of talent," Eustace said.

"So you want us to widen the remit of the Spades to getting rid of graffit?" said a tired-sounding man from the back.

"My God no! I say lets make our own Banksy. Let's take this ruffian by his hoodie and let's do something with him. I want him identified, I want him sent to art college and I want him back on the streets doing something worth talking about. Who do we know with connections to the Brockley underground? How do we get to him?"

I studied my shoes while he looked around the group. Now was not the time to go bringing Babs into a conversation. Because Babs would probably know someone who knew someone who knew Da Notorious Baron.

"OK, Jim, I want you and your fourth estate friends to put out feelers. I want him. I want Da Baron. Guy – I need you to find appropriate courses. Something arty but streety too. Maybe give him more of an understanding into politics: that tired thing he does with the Houses of Parliament and the blood – can we have him a bit more politically savvy? Bansky is much broader ranging isn't he? Hey," he suddenly looked at Guy, "you don't know Banksy do you?"

"No."

"Shame. Anyway, do your best guys. Let's work with what we've got, yes?"

I sat silently and listened to the tirade, wondering with a heavy feeling in my stomach where the philanthropic gestures ended and the scary total-controlling began.

It was time to leave the chandeliers and the cocktails behind and I emerged with the others, through the grimy Working Men's Club, out onto Loampit Hill.

Everything was drab and flat and smelt of chicken.

"It's cool to meet you properly," the dreadlocked surf-dude Neil said as we ascended the staircase from the 1880s to the 1970s. "I must have seen you and your mate every weekend in V-2, yeah? And now at last I get to say 'hi'."

"You always look so busy," I said, emerging into the filthy lobby. "It seems wrong to take up more of your time for a chat: the café's always packed."

"Tell me about it," Anja said, coming up behind us. "It's a total nightmare from 8am to 6pm."

"But it's better than being stuck in an office." I thought about the beigey hell of working for the Council. "At least you're living the dream. I'd love to have my own café."

They laughed out loud and Peter, standing by the open door, shushed them. "Quiet now," he hissed. "There's still some activity on the High Road. We don't want to give ourselves away!"

"I'll walk you home, Edda." Guy appeared beside me, buttoning his coat.

I grinned in delight, completely unable to play it cool, or act – in fact – like a calm and elegant person with a fiery inner passion. I was aware that I just looked stupidly happy.

"Well, you do know where I live…" I said.

We said goodnight to Eustace who was preoccupied by making sure we all disappeared quickly and silently: a glut of middle-class types on Lewisham High Road near midnight might raise unanswerable questions and we were, Eustace insisted on repeating, *first and foremost a secret society.*

But the streets were deserted, save for us guerrilla gardeners heading back to our homes. Guy was in high spirits, chatting about a commission, "it's a portrait in blues and greys but the sitter is such a vibrant, lively personality. Really only a red palette could capture the essence of them, the life within them, you know, but my hands are tied. There's a struggle in me," at this point he pounded his chest, "between the artist and the practical business man who has to turn out a portrait conforming to the commission…"

But I was only half-listening. Because I was going to be a guerrilla gardener! Me! And I'd plucked up the courage to go along to the meeting *on my own* and it had been good. Except for the enormous great big question of funding – but apart from that…

Things were looking up.

"Here we are." We drew to a halt.

"Oh!" I said. We were at my garden gate already. I hadn't paid attention to where we were going at all. We would have walked straight passed Beth's flat and I hadn't even noticed. Surely that must be a good sign – a sign that I was moving on. Quite literally.

We paused at the front gate. "Your accent," he said. "I hear a hint of Scottish in it."

"Well, I lived up there a long time ago."

"Ahh but you can never tame the passionate red-head: I expect your ancestors were crofters were they? Hacking a desperate living on the barren Highland slopes against a slate grey sky. Dispossessed by brutal landowners. Forever burning with an inner anger."

"Erm. Maybe."

Guy looked deep into my eyes. "There must be a reason for that flame in your hazel eyes: a deep passion that fires you up. Goodnight, Edda. You will be coming to the next dig won't you?"

"Yes. I will." Eighty-five percent of me was certain it would be a *very good thing to do* but fifteen percent of me still had money/moral issues to come to terms with. But then Guy *was* very attractive…

"So, I'll see you on the fourth!" He had already backed away and was walking in the direction we'd just come. "I'll call for you on the way to the dig."

"Sure. OK. Thanks…" I stood in the garden and watched him go, melting into the night in his black garb with his inky black hair. With all the smouldering and arm-touching and inner-fire comments, I'd rather thought a kiss might have been on the cards. Instead I was alone in the dark beside an enormous pile of wilting plants with a hungry looking cat perched on top of it.

I turned to face the house, glancing quickly over towards Babs' house in case she was standing at her doorway listening in. If Babs had heard any of this the secret society would be secret no more: they would be talking about it from Catford Market to Peckham High Street. But from her open bedroom window I could hear panting and, just faintly, a regular jangle jangle jangle that could only be coming from my belly-dancing outfit.

"Oh, that is so wrong," I said to Finley as I collected him from atop the weed pile, "That a woman in her seventies ends her evening having her bells jangled and I end mine emptying your litter tray." I paused on way through the hallway to check my appearance in the mirror. But I couldn't see any fire, just eyes.

The following day at work I had an almost uncontrollable desire to stand on my chair and shout across the beige office to all the beige office people: *I have joined a secret society and we meet in an abandoned ballroom on the High Road!*

But I didn't. What I did do was stare blankly at my computer, a report and a memo, and attended a meeting where I stared blankly at the wall. Just another day at the office. The dispossessed crofter with a burning anger of injustice and a passion for hatchets was spending another day in beige civil service despondency.

However, my boss, unbelievably, noticed a difference in me. Rosemary usually spent her working day quietly at her desk avoiding people with her head down and trying to look busy. Which she never was. She pretended to work – apparently she'd spent the last twenty years pretending to work – and last week I'd caught her reading a paperback period romance, the book hidden in between the pages of a Council report on proposed traffic calming measures in the borough. *The Sea Captain's Passion* intrigued me and when she'd left her desk Amanda and I had managed to rifle through its pages to the juicy bits: apparently the eponymous Sea Captain's passion was aflame and uncontrollable. Briefly, around lunchtime, Rosemary looked up from her 'report' saying,

"You're very yawny today, Edda. You should get more sleep," before going back to the Sea Captain.

Yes Rosemary, that's because I've joined a Secret Society and was up all night. "Yes. A bit."

I felt like I was going mad.

My dull monotonous job was just about bearable when things were running along normally. But now that I was lusting after artists, joining underground societies and getting a lodger, my dull routine work had become completely undoable. I had no motivation to get the memo written or the tedious report actioned. And I couldn't even summon up enough interest to reply to the all-staff email about a night out at the local pub. I wanted to hot-foot it over to Planning and grab Peter Shaw by his M&S lapels and say, *That club house is so unbelievably amazing, what else have you secret society people got up your sleeves?*

When my boss slunked off for an inescapable meeting I opened up the internet and, checking around me in case I was being watched, typed in the address of Fox Estates. Work was impossible: instead I was going to check up on the secret society's secret website.

Welcome to Brockley! Welcome to a haven of tranquillity on the brink of Central London. Click to enter.

I clicked. I entered. And there before me was a picture of Eustace Fox, all loud golfing trousers and ruddy face. He was smiling magnificently at the photographer and shaking hands with the mayor of Lewisham, whose own smile was a little more tight and tired. The photograph had been taken in front of the Fox Estates office in Brockley. The chains, I noticed, had been removed from the bay trees for the day.

Brockley, SE4, was once an escape to the country for Victorian London's wealthier merchants and industrialists. Described by many as a hidden gem *(Baverstock) and* undiscovered idyll *(D B Hornby), Brockley — with its conservation area full of villas and coach houses, the early Victorian terraces and the many open spaces — is on the rise once more. Welcome to our website. We hope you find your dream home and will join the new merchants and industrialists of twenty-first century London, along with the burgeoning art and literature scene that has developed over the last thirty years. Fox Estates, Brockley's premier estate agency, looks forward to seeing you soon.*

Brockley
Like Broccoli
But not. You call to me
Call to me
With hushèd whispers down the
Elm-lined streets and stuccoed houses
A haven of London unspoilt ours is
So hold back you developers with your diggers of despair!
And discard your petty plans for cheap buildings everywhere!
For all should be wary of developing

Wary of ruining, wary of enveloping
Belovèd Brockley
Of destructing what's here the planners are warier
Thanks to our delineated
Conservation Area

Pippa Fortheringay (Tresillian Avenue, Brockley)
Click <u>here</u> for a link to Brockley Poetry Society

Even though there was the excitement of a secret society page buried on the website, the homeowner in me couldn't help but pause to take a look at the properties to see how much I could sell my house for. I navigated through the first few pages which were filled with examples of Eustace's grandiose turns of phrase: *this sceptred islet within London, this seat of architectural Majesty, this green and pleasant Transport Zone Two, this Brockley...*

The flats and houses were all at the upper end of the market and my house, for all its size, would probably be in the more 'homely' end of the market if it was for sale now. When I'd bought it from Fox Estates it had been given what looked like a hasty lick of paint and while it looked presentable it had never been in the category of these highly polished properties. I clicked through the property web pages: chandelier, chandelier, *chandelier in the bathroom* ... and then I saw Beth's flat and I froze.

For sale, excellent one bed ground floor flat with own section of garden. Would suit first time buyer or investor looking for a foothold in this up and coming neighbourhood.

And there on my computer screen at work was her living room, looking tidier than I'd ever seen it, except I could see her Jigsaw handbag peeking out from behind the Habitat sofa. The fireplace that we'd spent a weekend stripping and blacking. The kitchen, with the broken cabinets – looking straight for once. The bedroom spookily clothes-free. The bathroom retiled: when had she done that?

An excellent opportunity to purchase a flat of this nature: we are anticipating high demand and interested parties should act quickly.

I clicked on to the next property and was into the chandeliers again, and then I sat back in my chair and took deep breaths. My hands were shaking and my throat felt tight. How could she leave Brockley? How could my Beth leave me? A minute more and I'd calmed down enough to lessen the shaking and had decided that I had to pull myself together. Going to pieces over Beth's exile was not going to get me anywhere, so even if I didn't feel like I was coping, then I should pretend that I was coping and maybe that would kickstart me actually coping. Wasn't that what Amanda's latest magazine offering had said?

Heart now beating as if I really was on a Blyton online-style adventure … *Five go to Wikipedia* … I scanned the home page for the hidden grey icon that was a link to the secret society. The office strip-lights were dull and grey and the computer monitor was dirty. It took a lot of time positioning myself at various angles to try to identify where a hidden grey image might actually be hidden. And then I spotted it: a barely visible shaded icon of a trowel, slightly darker than the background of the web page. I would never have seen it if I wasn't specifically looking for it.

I clicked.

PASSWORD?

Capappab

Capabbil

Cpabailty

Captbilty

Damn it! My hands were shaking so much I could barely type. I took a deep breath and tried again.

Capability

Finally.

PERMISSION GRANTED. WELCOME.

I had reached the homepage for the Brockley Spades! Excitedly I scanned down the page.

Mission Statement.
Current Projects.
Past Projects.
Blog.

I clicked on *Mission Statement* once more slightly deflated that the secret society had such a thing: real adventures never started with a mission statement. "The Brockley Spades exists to materially improve the neighbourhood of Brockley, within the Borough of Lewisham, through planting and maintaining its open spaces." I clicked back to the home page.

The list of past projects was more interesting: as I scanned down the roll I realised that I'd noticed a lot of the society's work without knowing it. It had just sort of *happened*. One day the traffic island near the garage was a mess, the next day it was covered in rose bushes. The school had windowboxes, Brockley Cross had hanging baskets. At the time I'd barely given it another thought. But now...

The blog took all afternoon to read, which was fortunate as there was nothing else I wanted to do that day. It was full of messages like *awesome man* and *Gr8 work on the gardens!!!* Any blogs from Eustace were formal and grammatically correct without a LOL or WTF insight. There were a handful of messages posted from Guy, *including* I saw as I scrolled down *a message to me!*

"Edda – if you're checking the blog out – I'll call round at yours 11.45pm on the 4th for the station dig."

Guy had written to me! On a secret webpage. Belonging to a secret society I was now part of! Guy had posted a message just for me! I read his words and every atom of my being exploded with joy.

A man from Education looked up from his desk. Briefly.

Ten

"What *is* that smell?" Beth was wandering around my kitchen. It was the evening before my day of interviewing and she had come round to wish me good luck and "catch up on all your secret society gossip."

"It's Extreme Lavender. Do you want a coffee?" I said.

"Just a water, please, honey. It's very strong isn't it, that smell? Do you think it might harm Baby?" She put a concerned hand on her pastel-yellow-clad bump as if preventing it being sullied by the mere mention of harm.

"Probably," I muttered.

"It's amazing what you've done here," Beth continued, moving on into the living room. "You've completely transformed the place: it looks enormous! Why didn't you ever clean your house properly when I lived with you?"

I handed her the water. "I seem to remember we were too busy, too drunk, or too hung-over to pick up a duster. Biscuit?"

"Is it organic?"

"No," I said. "It says on the side of the packet that it's packed with synthetic chemicals that mutate babies' brains."

Beth shot me the look I deserved, eyeballed the biscuit tin with a look of longing but then moved away from it. "It's a shame that you didn't finish up the front garden before your interviewing. What *happened* out there? It reminds of a scene from *Terminator*."

I told her about my crazy session with the garden tools, "It was the same day that I ran over to see you – when you were off to your antenatal class with that big pink ball? Do you remember? Because straight after my gardening session Guy appeared at my garden gate and made the *inner fire* comment and invited me to join the secret society."

"Oh, OK. I remember. Sorry. We had to dash off didn't we? Anyway, it's a bit odd that you've cleaned up the house fit for royalty but the potential lodgers will still have to walk past that Matterhorn of dead stuff."

"But the skip still looks good at the front. So hopefully they'll just focus on that…"

"And let's hope they haven't read the local newspaper."

"Why?" I asked.

"Haven't you heard about the boy beaten up on the A2?"

"No." I said, wondering why Babs hadn't dropped it into a conversation.

"Well, apparently he wasn't badly hurt at all but he was tied up around one of the vandalised tree stumps, one of those that were planted along the A2 a few weeks ago. He couldn't escape – the police had to cut him free."

"Oh…" The memory of what Eustace had said at the secret underground meeting came back to me: "God help them and their petty lives." Surely the beaten-up boy wasn't connected with the vandalising of the oak trees…

"There was even a picture of him." Beth continued. "He was dressed up in an eight year old's public school uniform apparently, complete with cap and short trousers, so whoever did it was obviously out to humiliate him. And get this, right, his pockets were full of acorns. How weird is that? Do you think it's a drug thing? Are they making heroin out of acorns do you think?"

My stomach knotted. "Probably," I said.

Oh my God. Had Eustace really ordered a "hit" – or more like a "slap" by the sounds of it – on the yob that snapped down all the oak trees that the Spades had planted? Was it an eye for an eye? Was this a punishment?

"HEY!" Beth shouted and I leapt. "You've got rid of the horned helmets!"

Glad to be distracted from thoughts I followed her line of sight to the bare wall opposite the window where two horned helmets had once hung. "Not *got rid of*: just hidden in the loft." I said. "I thought they might freak out any prospective lodgers."

"Good plan, Eds. And the drinking horns?"

"Loft."

"Runic inscribed telephone?"

"That went years ago! Don't you remember you broke it that night we had the James Bond party? The number three stopped working so we could only phone the pizza place in New Cross, because the one in Brockley had loads of threes in the number?"

"But you've kept these..." Beth walked over to the photographs on the wall of a summer seventeen years ago. Me as an eleven-year-old with lank hair and braces on my teeth that caught the sun. I was baring my braces at the person holding the camera – dad – and I was dressed in my sheepskin gilet and hessian tunic, with mum behind me, her hands on my shoulders, laughing at something another Viking had said. And the others, who I knew as Auntie Barbara, Auntie Helen, Uncle Peter … all of them looking authentic and – in Shetland in the summer – borderline hypothermic.

"I did think about putting the photographs away," I walked over to where Beth was standing and put a hand up to a photo of my parents bent over a giant log, carving their beloved Viking longboat. "But I can't."

"Rightly so, honey." Beth said, and then laughed as she found the photograph of Auntie Jane and Uncle Henry in full warrior dress demonstrating how to use a shield against the driving Shetland rain. "Sometimes I forget you're not wholly Leicestershire." She said. "I mean I know you've still kept a bit of the Scottish accent but I don't really notice it any more – you're just you … I forget that you had a whole bizarre life before, well, before you moved down to Leicester and down to me."

"It wasn't that bizarre. Mostly, mum and dad were dentists and we lived in Edinburgh. It was just the holidays and weekends we went Viking."

Beth moved on to a group photograph taken in front of Ronas Hill on Shetland. "Do you still keep in contact with any of them?"

"No. Christmas cards: *pagan* Christmas Cards … you know. Nothing else."

"Do you miss—"

"Yes."

"OK!" She laughed and then turned to me and gave me a pregnant hug. "It must be very hard. Still."

"It is. Still." I said, loving the hug more than any single thing in the whole wide world. "It seems such a long time ago. It *was* a long time ago. Actually it feels like it all happened to another person and so it's wrong to feel bad about it because it doesn't affect me. Does that make sense?"

"No." Beth said, frowning in concentration. "Well, you're moving on and I think you're doing an amazing thing, Eds. I mean – the guerrilla gardening thing is cool and the lodger idea is great. Hey – maybe you'll be able to afford to leave your job and open that café you always talked about."

"Ha! Maybe." I said, knowing full well that I would always find an excuse to not do that: some things were just too scary to contemplate.

"Anyway," Beth sat down on the (sponged and vacuumed) sofa, "I know about Guy coming round and giving you the full Romeo, but what about the meeting itself? How did it go on the night? Tell me everything."

So I did. From the first chicken-filled moments of doubt to the chandeliers and silvered mirrors.

"You are so lucky," Beth said when I'd finished off my story with Guy walking me home. "I am actually jealous of you! Here you are on the brink of joining a secret society that meets in an abandoned ballroom. And you've got your first dig next week. Nervous?"

"Very."

"Well don't be. It's so cool! How cool are you going to be?" she grabbed my arm. "Don't be too cool will you, Edda? You won't forget me, will you, when you're out all night with the guerrilla gardening set?"

"Of course I won't forget you," I said, momentarily thrilled that right now Beth was afraid of being the abandoned one. Because, now, I also had something to look forward to.

"Oh sod it, I'm going in," Beth said and dived into the biscuit tin. "Oh! Chocolate malted milks! Edda… I can't remember the last time I had a chocolate malted milk! We used to eat these all the time didn't we?"

"Yeah, do you remember when—" but I didn't get the chance to finish: Beth had burst into tears.

I wrapped her up in a big hug and held her close, stroking her hair, loving the familiarity of her despite her increasingly unusual shape. I missed my Beth so much.

"You're squashing my malted milk," came the small voice from inside my hug.

"Oh," I pulled away. "I'm sorry."

"It's the pregnancy," Beth wiped her eyes and took some deep breaths. "It totally messes with my emotions." And she started crying again, big fat tears running down her cheeks. And I felt tears on my cheeks too. "I'm just…" she sniffed and nibbled her malted milk, "I'm just sad. Being here. Seeing the house all nice."

"I thought you were upset I didn't clean it like this for you."

"Well, that too." She sniffed. "But I miss this. I miss

us. I do." She shuffled closer and put a hand on my knee. "I know I go on and on about the baby."

"Yes, you do."

"I know. And you're really good about it. Except for the time when you kept kicking the skirting at Mothercare."

"I can't believe they got so upset about it."

Beth took a swig of water. "I've never been asked to leave a shop before. Anyway, apart from *that* you've been amazing, listening to me rattle on about motherhood. I'm sorry I've not been around much. It must be hard for you. And I do think about you, you know. All the time."

"It's OK. I'm coping OK." And I told her about Amanda and the divorce theory, which horrified Beth and caused more tears. "We're not getting *divorced!*" she wailed. "Don't ever say that!"

"But you are moving away. A long way away."

"A few miles…"

"Over an hour!"

"But I still love you! We're not getting a divorce, honey. There's the phone. We can call. Text. You can stay over at mine, anytime. Baby and I could even stay over here, now it's so clean." She managed a teary laugh.

"I know. Of course. And we will! Definitely. But I'm sad that what we had has gone." I cried onto a chocolate digestive. "And for the first time we're going different ways and of course we'll always be in touch— "

Beth lunged at me. "Don't ever think we won't!"

"But we won't have the same sort of things to talk about. I mean – you're going to want to talk about the baby. And that's great – but there are lots of things that I won't know about. And you'll have new friends who will want to talk about babies."

"Yes, but I want to talk about secret societies too. I wish we weren't moving to Surrey."

"But if you don't move to Surrey then your baby will be stolen and sold in Deptford Market."

"Oh don't be so silly." She said. "Greenwich market, surely. Anyway, the whole thing is Jack's doing really. He's the one who was pushing for us to run off to Surrey. I think South East London always scared him: he's not hard like us, Eds."

"I don't think you were ever completely sold on South East London, though, were you? Not entirely. But anyway, when I was cleaning I found a load of photographs from uni. Do you want to see them?"

"Yes!"

"Will you cry?"

"Of course. Go get! And bring more biscuits, Eds! Chop chop!"

I was sitting on the bench in my jumble of an overgrown back garden: as yet untouched by any gardening frenzy. It was ridiculously early on Saturday morning but, to make up for that, it was especially calm and beautiful: for once I didn't mind that I was up so early. There were no cars or trains rumbling past, the birds were singing and a fox had wandered about down at the bottom of the garden near the railway line without noticing me. It was like my garden but in another world. Even Babs and her boyfriend were silent.

My legs were tucked up beneath me and, blanket wrapped around me, I was sipping coffee from my favourite Up-Helly-Aa (Shetland, 1994) mug.

All in all, it wasn't the worst start to a day.

But there was a nagging, inescapable wretchedness. Last night had been great. But so sad too. Beth and I had got through all my chocolate biscuits, several photo albums and half a box of tissues. And now I was sitting in my back garden at six in the morning with puffed red eyes and emotionally spent and for the first time in my life nursing a chocolate biscuit hangover. It was almost like old times.

In a few hours Amanda and her pastel pants would be bouncing up the garden path and we would be interviewing forty-two candidates for the top floor bedroom and bathroom. This was the calm before the storm. And it would be a storm: because what was Amanda going to do? a) ask the prospective tenants if they were currently shacked up with anyone and what their star sign was and b) flash her knickers at them? I couldn't help thinking, now that it was too late to do anything, that Amanda was just a very bad advertisement for what was on offer at 189 Geoffrey Road. Wouldn't the male candidates get the wrong impression when they saw her? Wouldn't they be disappointed when they found out that actually Amanda and her pants were not going to be a part of the deal? And would the female candidates leave the house tutting and thinking *not my sort of thing thank you very much* when they got the inevitable eyeful of knicker? And would I want anyone who thought otherwise living with me?

I took another sip of coffee.

It should be Beth who was helping me today, not Amanda. Because Beth knew me better than anyone. She knew what I was like to live with and she knew who would work as a lodger and who wouldn't. Amanda was only interested in helping me out because she liked the idea of being on a celebrity judging panel.

"I don't know why you didn't ask *me* to help you out," Beth had said late last night, as she was bidding me goodnight on my doorstep. "You always say I boss you around and tell you how it is, so I'm going to live up to your expectations now and tell you something: *I* should be doing this for you, not some random work colleague. Why don't you tell this Amanda *thanks but no thanks* and I can come over and get you a nice lodger? Here – give me Amanda's number and I'll phone her if you don't want to do it yourself. It's the least I can do considering I'm abandoning you so badly. Here – give me her number," and she had whipped out her mobile.

"No. Honestly. It's fine."

"No, Eds, it's not. You need a firm hand and—"

"It's fine Beth! I'll muddle through with Amanda and anyway, there are going to be forty-two candidates: you're pregnant and will probably flop by the fourth. It's a full day of interviewing: think about it – it's probably not going to be good for baby is it?"

120

I had played my trump card and I could see it instantly had the desired effect. Beth had left, mollified but not entirely happy.

But it was done now. Beth was put off and Amanda would be on her way soon. And as I sat eyeballing the wild animals in the early morning, I realised that actually *I* needed Beth not to be with me today. I needed to do this without her domineering and taking over for once. I needed to take a small step out of her shadow and make my own decisions.

But for all the inner-strength and resolution I was feeling it was diminished by the realisation that choosing the wrong lodger would inevitably lead to being baked into an enormous – but very tasty – pie.

I don't know what I'd expected Amanda to wear when she came to help me interview prospective tenants, but *not that* would have been a really good start. She bounced into the house just after ten o'clock in the morning in a skin-tight magenta dress, unbelievably perky for someone who had been out until three in the morning.

"Did you go out in that dress last night?" I asked, remembering with a sudden fondness the times – so recently – that Beth and I had collapsed into V-2 following a heavy session the night before, still wearing the night before's clothes and make-up.

"Oh my God, no! I'd be like totally a granny if I wore this out. No I've got these just amazing hotpants…"

Of course. I smiled tightly. I made coffee. Tightly. I

felt like a suburban fifty-something housewife whose daughter had just discovered Rimmel.

"… so he came over to me in the club and it was like two in the morning at that point and he was, like, *I have this like really enormous thing in my pants for you* and I was, like, all *oh yeah* and then he said—"

"HERE'S YOUR COFFEE, THEN."

"Oh! Fab! Thanks, Edda!"

"Have you had any thoughts on what questions you're going to ask the candidates today?" I sat opposite her at the breakfast bar and sipped my own coffee. I was determined to keep complete control of the conversation from now right through to the end of the day.

Amanda looked thoughtful. "No. Not really. I thought I'd wing it. You know – follow your lead."

"Great. Sounds good."

"I love your house, by the way. It's, like, amazing and everything! And the whole thing is yours?"

"Every brick. It feels weird though – it's never been this clean. Even the cat's freaked out by how clean and tidy it is."

"Yeah. It's, like, really homely but also, like, a bit funky. I mean not way-out funky or anything like that. Sort of mature funky. You know?"

"I know." Any second now she was going to mention the word *sepia*. I braced myself.

"Yeah. Well. It's cool. And I love the garden. It's so … *posh*. Like a manor house or something."

"Well I went a bit mental with a hatchet recently," I said, "But I wouldn't say it's *posh*…"

"I mean, like, the sundial! It's totally mad! And the little hedge things in patterns. And get this, right, I actually *know* what that is! You've got a *knot garden*! Like, how clever am I? No, I'm not really. It's just that's like the *only* thing I remember from my history GCSE. Can you believe that? Like the single only thing! We did these studies of Elizabethans and stuff, you know those people who wore the ruffs around their necks? Anyway, they used to have knot gardens with the little hedges and the herbs. So did you go for the historical garden or something? That's, like, so weird to have a themed garden. Although I would just love a garden with a big fountain with these dolphins leaping out from it. I've seen it in magazines—" As she'd gabbled on I'd stared at her, my mouth opening wider and wider until, full gape, I walked to the front door, fumbled the catch with shaky hands and stepped out.

Into a perfect Elizabethan knot garden.

"My mud! My weed pile!" I looked around for something familiar to anchor myself to, to put what I was seeing into some sort of context. Was it really my garden?

"What's up?" Amanda bounded over beside me. "I think it looks kind of cool. Your garden makes the neighbours' gardens look well shabby, though."

Where yesterday there had been vast expanses of mud and rubble and the weed pile now there were neat clipped box hedges in curves and angles. In between the hedges the spaces were tightly packed with herbs and the paths between were perfectly filled with a purple-blue shale. And in the middle of it all sat the most enormous stone sundial.

I hung onto the door frame and stared at my *Country Living* front garden. I was shocked. Shocked that, between Beth leaving at eleven last night and Amanda arriving at ten this morning, someone had stolen into *my* garden and carted away *my* dead plants and done this. For *me*. It was them, wasn't it? It had to be. It *must* have been the Brockley Spades' work. Had Eustace been here: had he been among the gardeners? Guy? Had Guy been working in my garden last night? And how many of the people I'd met at the underground meeting had been repairing my damage while I slept just metres away from them? *Who had let themselves through my gate last night?* It was creepy to think that I'd been fast asleep just above them as they'd worked beneath. Did they do this for all their new members? Was this a perk of being a guerrilla gardener? And – more pertinently – did I like it? Did I like being the victim, if that was the right word, of guerrilla gardening? Did the fact that they felt the need to take over my garden imply I was in some way negligent or lacking in standards, horticulturally that is. Was Eustace worrying that my front garden, so near to Fox Estates, was bringing down the tone of Brockley? Which it was, of course. Even Babs had said as much…

"Hey look!" Amanda tugged my sleeve. "Do you think that's our first interviewee?" she pointed down the road to where a balding and horribly obese man was shuffling nearer.

"I shouldn't think so," I began, and then saw he was carrying the free ads paper I had placed the advertisement in.

"Urgh!" Amanda realised at the same time as me. "You should, like, totally have asked them if they were good looking when they phoned up."

"Well he's going to be an ideal opportunity to practise." I said, deciding to see the best in a bad situation (*Company* magazine, November). And besides, I needed a moment to pull myself together after the shock of finding my refurbished garden.

"Amanda?"

"Yes."

"Are you having fun?" I asked, with my head in my hands.

"No!" came the resolute response from Amanda across the table, also with her head in her hands. It was early evening and we'd spent the entire day interviewing for the room.

"It is so absolutely awful. It is really genuinely completely awful." I looked up and stared at the scrawled paper in between us. The names of the twenty-seven potential lodgers who had turned up on the day were written in the left hand column, the handwriting getting progressively messier as the list went on, then their phone number in the next column and in the third column there were scrawled notes on the interview and a mark out of ten. The first interviewee had scored a minus eight. The notes towards the end were illegible: as though a spider with ink boots had suffered a fit across the paper. By number twenty-seven Amanda and I had almost lost the will to live.

I rested my forehead onto the table top.

"Tired?" Amanda asked, yawning.

"Yes," I said and then quickly added, "But not because I'm old. Just because it's been a long day."

"I totally didn't say it was because you're old," Amanda said. "So who are you going to choose then? I liked the blonde bloke."

I leant forward to read her notes. "Blonde bloke … number twelve? Crispin from Bristol."

"That's him. The posh scriptwriter."

"No way. Too flimsy. And he was poor – how is a boy like him with no money going to pay the rent?"

"He could pay with his body in your bed."

"Amanda!"

"Well come on, the man was so cute! Who would *not* want to have a bit of that in their house? The way he sat there flirting with us and he had, like, just such enormous thighs … but I suppose he was like a bit young for you."

"Thanks for that." I savagely crossed the flirty blonde boy from the list. He was quite young, as it goes.

"I didn't like many of the girls much, did you? Except that one called Jane. Jane was OK." I said, trying to decipher my handwriting.

"Was she like the banker with that really amazing jacket that was, like, really expensive? Yeah she was OK but you wouldn't actually want to share with a girl would you?"

"Why? She was fine."

"Yeah, but that's like a waste of a go. Let's open the wine now!"

"Amanda are you only thinking of one thing?"

"For you! Not for me! I just think it's totally a good way for you to meet someone, because if you never go out—"

"I go out!"

"You do?"

"Yes I do! Remember the secret society thing I told you about. In strict confidence? Remember? And the artist called Guy who is an amazing Milk Tray type of man."

Amanda looked at me with a vague expression. "What's a *Milk Tray* man?"

Hmmm. "It was an advert that was on the TV before you were born. A swarthy James Bond-style man broke into a woman's house and left a box of chocolates in her bedroom and—"

"He broke into a woman's house?"

"Well yes—"

"And she didn't *mace* him? Man, the eighties were crazy! Oh my God was like breaking and entering acceptable in the olden days? Is that before locks were invented?"

My incredulity was cut short by a burst of knocking at the front door.

"Oh no. More!" I stayed motionless in my seat. "I thought Dan was the last one!" I rechecked the list. He was the last to be interviewed. It was gone six – that was it. We were supposed to be done for the day. I felt we had some legal right to be done for the day. "Maybe it's one of the no-shows," I said.

"Or maybe it's someone else. Not someone about the room?"

"Of course! It's Bethan!" I jumped up from my chair and flew to the door. She said that she'd try to come over in the evening to see how I'd got on. Bethan would know who I should choose!

"B— oh!"

"Hi!" There were two men standing in my mock-Elizabethan knot garden. Neither of them were Bethan.

"I'm sorry I'm so late," the younger, brown-haired man said, "I have an excuse but it's rubbish. Am I too late for the room? Has it gone?"

"I'm – ahh – " I looked from one to the other. I almost couldn't bear to ask the same old questions one more time and show an interest in the twenty-eighth person that day. I could just say the room had gone. It practically *had* gone, to the girl called Jane. And I could already hear Amanda fighting with the corkscrew in the kitchen behind me.

"I'm the reason he's late." The silver fox behind him stepped in. "I'm his father." He held out his hand. "Max Willoughby. Hi." I smiled and shook his hand, wondering where I'd seen him before. Did I know him? Was he something to do with the Council – his face looked very familiar.

Damn. Now I couldn't turn them away: not when I'd shaken his hand.

"*Max Willoughby*?" Amanda was beside me, suddenly. And now she was hanging on to the side of me. "Max? Max Willoughby?"

"Hi." The silver-fox father grinned and held out his hand to her as well. Maybe my new Elizabethan knot garden made everyone more formal. Now I had topiary I would start shaking hands with Babs and we would remark on the particularly clement weather for this time of year.

Amanda squeaked, "You're Max Willoughby!"

"He's Max Willoughby," the son said to me. "Does that have any bearing on whether I can still be interviewed for the room?"

"Oh my God, come in!" Amanda pushed me aside, literally throwing me against my door jamb, "I so think you're, like, amazing and everything! I want to be an actor too! I had this walk-on part in *East Enders* last year and I'm auditioning for a murder victim in a new series for BBC1 and, like … oh my God it's really you isn't it? Say a line!"

"Oh … well, where do I start…" Max followed her inside with a grin on his face and a wink at me.

The abandoned son and I stood in the knot garden and faced one another. "Hi."

"Hi."

"So … the room?" the son said.

"Yes! Yes, you can come and see the room." I stood aside and he came in.

"I'm Robert, by the way."

"Hi, Robert." I stood back to let him in. "Edda. And I'm sorry but you'll have to excuse the smell of lavender."

For the last twenty-seven candidates, Amanda and I had sat in the kitchen for the "Interview" before showing the interviewees the downstairs rooms and then up to the bedroom and bathroom on the top floor. For number twenty-eight – Robert – the routine had to change. Because Amanda was completely absorbed by Max Willoughby who, in turn, was utterly engrossed in her supercharged flirtation. He was saying witty things about the theatre and she was giggling and leaning in to him provocatively.

"So, you, like, do film as well?"

Max shrugged. "I recently had a small part in Harry Potter."

Robert and I looked at each other and laughed out loud. In fact I snorted, which was rather embarrassing. But Max and Amanda continued unabated.

"So," I pulled myself together, "Would you like a glass of wine Robert?" It seemed like the polite thing to do given Amanda has poured one for her and Max. "This is the hall by the way."

"It's very nice. No wine though, thanks. I'm driving."

"Oh, you have a car!" I refocused on the potential lodgerdom of Willoughby junior.

"Yes. Does that stand me in good stead? A famous father and a car?"

"It might do." I played it cool. "What sort of car is it?"

"It's an old VW beetle. It breaks down sometimes. But maybe I shouldn't tell you that."

"No … I think you've possibly damaged your chances a bit there. This is the lounge."

"Great. I like the shield above the fireplace. It's very … very *Viking*."

"Oh right. Yes. It's a replica of a … well … that's a bit boring really. Anyway, this is the dining room."

"OK."

There was a fit of giggles from the kitchen and Amanda's voice squeaking: *You just can't say things like that about Judi Dench.*

"And this is the back garden."

"Wow."

"What?"

"Well," Robert looked around the long, sprawling now fox-free garden which – I had to admit – looked very beautiful in the warm spring sunshine. "It's quite different to your front garden."

"Is it? Oh yes – yes it is. I keep forgetting."

Robert turned to me. "You forget how your front garden looks?"

"Mmm. Anyway, it's quite a nice neighbourhood. Mostly. Do you live nearby at the moment?"

"Greenwich."

"Oh. Very nice. Well it's not quite Greenwich, but it's getting there."

"It's convenience more than anything: I teach at a school in New Cross Gate. I wanted to move closer, so I could walk to work. So – have you had many people come to look at the room?"

"You're number twenty-eight." I said.

"Right." He looked deflated.

"Let's go inside." I led the way, feeling sorry for him. "Is your father really famous?"

"I think so. But if you're interested in the fame thing,

then I'm sorry but I've not followed in his footsteps; I teach history. But on the plus side remember I still have that car."

"The one that breaks down?"

"Only occasionally."

"So, if you did get the room, when would you be looking to move in?" I effortlessly slipped into my well-practised questioning routine.

"Whenever would suit you to be honest. I'm living with my dad but he's such, well, as you can see he's a real character and as much as I love him – I think I need my own space."

"You mean you're fed up of luvvie parties thrown by your dad?"

"Exactly! I get up early, he gets up late. I work days at school, he works evenings at the theatre. Our lives don't fit together very easily."

We were back in the kitchen and Max and Amanda looked up.

"Smashing place you've got here, Edda." Max said.

"Thanks. Look, Amanda, would you show Robert the rooms upstairs. I just have to – erm – do something. Excuse me a moment." And I dashed to my knot garden.

"Everythin' all right with yer darlin'?" Babs eyed me suspiciously over her fag. I was standing on her doorstep, on her territory, something I'd never done in the five years I'd lived in Geoffrey Road. "What happened to yer garden love? Shocked the bejeezus outta me when I had me first fag of the day."

"Oh. Just, you know, something I felt had to do last night, no time like the present... You know how it is. Anyway, I have to ask you a favour."

"Go on then. I ain't lendin' yer no money though, much as I like yer. Don't lend no one no money."

"That's fine. I don't want money. What I do want is for you to take a look at the two men leaving my house in the next few minutes and tell me … do you think, in your opinion that is, that the younger one is good lodger material? Basically do you think he's going to be the sort who will bake me into a pie if I don't let him watch *Grand Designs*?"

"You think I was jokin', but I wasn't." Babs intoned.

"Oh I'm sure it was true. I would like your opinion."

"All right then. You got one in mind 'ave yer darlin'? Yer've seen bleedin' loads today 'aven't yer?"

"Nearly thirty."

"Bloody 'ell. There's more people goin' in an' out of yer 'ouse than when it was a brothel. Don't know when I've seen so many people goin' up an' down that path. In daylight at least."

"Pardon … what?" I stood on her steps and gaped at her.

"Didn't they tell yer that then when yer bought the place? Knockin' shop it was. Everyone around here knew about it. Notorious place … Course the police brought an end to it didn't they? Raided it one night and arrested everyone, it were on the market a few days later. No one round 'ere could believe it sold so quickly, and at that price, given what it used to be."

"Oh … my … God." I leant heavily against her front door. A whole wave of memories came flooding back to me. "That explains why I used to get all those men knocking on the door late at night when I first moved in! *Eeeww*, Babs! They were looking for sex!"

"Ahh, they were 'armless enough men, most of 'em." Babs said wistfully. "Just lookin' for a bit of fun. One of 'em came 'ere once. Got the wrong address 'e did an' I didn't 'ave the heart to turn him away."

"You … what…?"

"That's how I met 'im, me boyfriend," she nodded in the direction of her house. "Stopped chargin' 'im after a week or so, of course. Weren't right." She laughed throatily. "'e couldn't afford it, the amount we was goin' for it!"

"I have to get back." I said shakily and started to walk down the steps. "But please, can you just have a look at the man when he comes out. The younger man. You don't have to say anything to him. Actually, please don't say anything to him. At all."

"All right but I gotta strain me parsnips in five minutes!" she called out behind me.

"You're so going to love it here," Amanda was saying to Robert and his father when I sped back into the ex-brothel I'd been calling home for the last five years, "And it's such a cool house. I can't believe Edda has the lot to herself, I mean how amazing is that? We should all get together when you move in and go out for lunch or something. We could show you round Brockley. Do you know it? It used to be, like, well drab and violent and stuff but now there's all these cafés and posh houses."

"Well, I'm sure Edda has a lot of thinking to do." Willoughby senior got up off his stool. "But I must say thank you for your hospitality and it's been great to meet you both. Personally, I hope Robert gets the room but I appreciate you must have a lot of good candidates."

He was shaking our hands again and, combined with the eager *go-on-tell-him-he-can-have-the-room* look Amanda was giving me, I felt under enormous pressure. But I refused to bow. I would be strong and make my own way in this world; abandoned divorcee that I was.

"I'll be in touch tomorrow if the room's yours." I fed Robert the same line I'd given to everyone that day, although it was given with more genuine feeling than most people had got. Together, Robert and I followed his father and Amanda out of the house.

"I am so sorry about my dad," he whispered to me as we headed through the hallway and out towards my stately garden. "If I'd have known he was going to be like this I would have installed him in the café round the corner. I think it's a mid-life crisis." And then he added hastily, "Not that your friend is... Not at all. But ... you know..." he petered out.

"I know," I laughed. "But thanks for bringing him. It's been ... memorable." I glanced to my left to see Babs, fag in, craning her neck to get a good look at Robert as we walked down the garden. Bless her.

"Well," we were at his car, "I'll maybe be in touch tomorrow."

"Good stuff." Robert got into the orange beetle, clunked the doors shut and manually wound down the windows.

"Yeah, she'll, like, so be in touch tomorrow morning!" shouted Amanda, over the roar of the tinny engine. Clearly it was a car that broke down quite often.

Robert and his famous father drove off towards Greenwich and, across the garden wall, Babs stubbed out her fag on her window sill and gave me the thumbs up.

Eleven

"Beth can you come round? You really have to come round to my place!" I was virtually shouting at the phone handset.

"Oh, honey, I can't," Beth was saying. "Is everything OK? Are you all right? How did the interviewing go?"

"It went really well and I've got a new lodger. And I've got a knot garden."

"A what? I can't hear you, sweetie. A knot garden?" I'd finally managed to reach her on her mobile but the reception was dreadful.

"Yes! Can't you come over? I have so much news! Where are you?"

"I don't know. Where are we Jack? Where? Burpham? We're in Burpham, Eds!"

"Burpham? Where the hell is Burpham? It sounds awful!"

"Jack says it's just north of Guildford. We're two miles north of Guildford. We're house hunting, my love. You should see Burpham though – I know it sounds disgusting but it's so pretty you'd absolutely love it here, I know you would. Can't afford a thing but it's fun pootling around. They have duck ponds in this area of Surrey, Eds! Duck ponds! And picket fences and village greens and—"

"They're taking our skip away Beth!" I broke into her speech. "It's happening right now! You really should be here!"

"Noooo!" the tinny voice on the mobile shrieked. And then, crossly, "Well, pull over then if I'm going to put you off driving." I could make out Jack muttering darkly in the background.

"I'm in my bay window," I continued, "and there's an enormous yellow council truck and they're picking up our skip! There are chains attached to the skip corners and the man's got into the cab and – yes – he's started to haul it up onto the back of the truck." I could feel a lump in the back of my throat. Our skip! Our last adventure together was being taken away and destroyed: the last memory of the two of us together.

"Oh, honey. Is it ready for taking away? The last time I came round to yours I didn't really notice it. I thought the plants were still OK."

"No. They're all dead. I didn't know how I was going to water it, without dragging a hose across the main road. And so they got dry and died. The geraniums were looking really bad. And actually that dead-dog smell was coming back."

"Oh well maybe it's not such a bad thing it's going then, honey, but I am sorry. It is sad that it's going." I could barely make out her words: Burpham may be posh but it sounded revolting and it had bad signal. Why would she want to move to Burpham? How bad was South East London that she felt the need to do that?

"OK! Our skip is on the lorry now!" I shouted into the phone.

"Are you all right? Not too sad?"

"Yes! No! Sort of!" I watched as the lorry began to slowly pull away, leaving a yawning big nothingness on the pavement directly opposite my house: a large expanse of pavement with a dusting of topsoil and a few geranium flowers. "It's gone now. Our skip has gone."

There was a crackly pause on the other end of the phone. "Well, at least you … skip removed. Which was what you've … *forever.*"

"But I like it now! It meant something!"

"I can't hear you! I'm sorry, love, the reception's … poor… Jack can you stop we're … signal! Pull over!"

"I have other news!" I shouted, moving away from the window now there was no reason to be there. "My house was a brothel!"

"A brothel? Did you say it was a brothel?"

"Yes! A brothel! Babs told me!"

"Bloody hell, Edda!" I could hear her laughing. "Is that why there was a pole in the cellar, Eds? Was … pole dancing?"

"Oh my God!" I shouted. "I thought that was scaffolding!"

We were both laughing now. "Tell me … lodger? Nice?"

"Yes! It's a man! He's called Robert! He's nice! You'd like him!"

"Handsome?"

"Not like Guy! But he's sort of handsome. He's nice!

139

He has floppy brown hair like that boy you went out with at school. He's nice!"

"Floppy what?"

"Hair! Floppy hair!"

She was laughing, cutting in and out of signal but I could hear the laughter and it made me laugh.

"…darling … was there! … free Sunday?"

"Beth? I can't hear you! What did you say?"

"Phone … shall I?"

"Yes! Call me when you can! I've got the dig tonight! Can you hear me? I'm really nervous! It's the dig tonight! I'm nervous!"

"Good luck! Good luck darling I … and in … is nervous!"

"Beth!"

"Can…"

"Beth? Beth!"

Twelve

I don't want to go I paced the floor of my bedroom at one in the morning. *I do want to go!*

It was exactly like the night of the Brockley Spades meeting, except this time Finley was staying out of my way. Which was a shame because I really needed him to be here and do the freaky Paul McKenna thing to me again. Perhaps it would be easier when Robert moved in next week and I could bounce ideas off my new lodger. But, obviously, without giving away the fact that I was in a secret society…

More than anything I wished that Beth was with me. She would tell me to get a bloody grip, girl, for God's sake, and stop dithering and – importantly – she would tell me what to wear on an illicit night-time guerrilla garden adventure. Yes, it was dark and no one would be able to see the subtleties of charcoal versus black but I did feel that – if I went – I ought to make every effort because Guy was, really, very handsome indeed and I didn't want to put him off by wearing grotty clothes.

Eventually at midnight I'd decided what I was going to wear without help from any pregnant or non-pregnant people or feline types but *all on my very own*. Obviously something dark, that much was certain so I'd laid out anything duller than magenta on the bed and considered the options. Anything flimsy or embroidered was out – I was after all going to be gardening. And anything too wintery was put away because the nights were getting warmer and no doubt I'd be getting hot and sweaty à la Front Garden Devastation With a Hatchet. The last cull of my clothing choice was the removal of anything that was too loved because it would probably get ruined. So I ended up with dark, attractive but basically expendable clothes: black jeans that were too tight and a black t-shirt with a picture of a man in a beret looking handsome and angsty that Beth had once given me but I'd never worn.

Wardrobe sorted I then had time on my hands to feel the awful doubt creep up on me again. *Did I really want to be doing this?* Think of the youth in the public school boy uniform with the pocket full of acorns. It *had* to be connected to the Brockley Spades: was I really going to be a part of a society that did something like that? Had Jake paid the youth a visit? But then I might be mistaken, and besides there were good reasons for going, too. I would make a list: a list would make it all much clearer.

Over the last few days Amanda with her magazine-page-wisdom had been teaching me to make lists of everything, from "What I want to achieve now my marriage is over" to "Moving on: a victim's guide to defining your three steps to happiness".

REASONS TO GO TONIGHT
Guy

New friends? (Neil & Anja from V-2 café, others)
Owe it to Eustace (knot garden/sundial)
Gets me out of the house/anti-Miss Havisham
Beth cross if don't go
Fin cross if don't go
Guy
Famous Five never passed up an opportunity
Guy

REASONS NOT TO GO TONIGHT
Acorn-boy/ getting into bad company?
It's illegal (or is it?)
Hard work late at night
Jake scary. Eustace bit weird (?)

The list seemed pretty conclusive. The reasons to go far outweighed the reasons to stay in and watch TV.

And just when I was thinking I ought to reconsider a few more elements on the list it was all decided for me. There was a soft knock at my front door. It would be Guy.

I trembled down the stairs and fumbled with the mortice lock.

"Guy. Hi," I managed to get it open and there he was, smouldering in the moonlight, leaning up against the wall. Any thoughts of not taking part tonight were instantly dismissed.

"Are you ready?" he said in a soft illicit-night-time-activity voice. "Sorry, I'm late."

"Ngh."

"Che Guevara." He pointed to my chest. "I knew you had the fighting spirit in you, Edda Mackenzie. You respect the legend too, do you?"

So *that's* who was on the front of my t-shirt. The name was definitely familiar but I still wasn't sure who he was exactly: definitely something to do with South America and guns. But apart from that … I resisted the urge to tell Guy that when Beth had bought the t-shirt for me I'd thought it was a picture of a cloth-capped Jesus. No point letting on I wasn't the inferno-burning guerrilla fighter he thought I was. After all, Alan Titchmarsh *himself* had said my use of colour had been "imaginative" so I had every right to take up the guerrilla gardening mantle.

"Thanks for the garden." I whispered as I quietly closed the door behind me and we headed out into the night. Fortunately Babs was indoors and hadn't witnessed us leave.

"Well, I'm glad you like it." I could see Guy grinning as we picked our way through the formal gardens. "It was Eust's idea, the Elizabethan theme. I wanted a Scottish wilderness to remind you of home and your ancestors but he wouldn't have it."

"Well it would be hard to recreate a Scottish wilderness in a small London front garden."

"Personally, I think your devastated wilderness was pretty good. But Eust would never allow that in Brockley."

I laughed. "Eustace wouldn't *allow it?*"

Guy raised his eyebrows, or at least I think he did in

the dim light. "Wait until you know him better and you'll get what I mean. Now hurry up or we'll be really late."

There was a black transit van parked in a darkened corner on the approach to Brockley Station. Behind it, as Guy and I walked to the site, I could make out that the dark grass slopes were crawling with black-clad guerrilla gardeners moving silently. In his all-night Mini Mart directly opposite, Mr Iqbal would be completely unaware that so many people were right outside and preparing to move into action.

We crossed the road and joined them, standing now beside the open van. "Right, Edda," Guy whispered to me, leaning in close, the curls of his long hair brushing my face, "First of all... "

And he said some things while I just stood and enjoyed the closeness of him, the brush of his hair, the smell of him, delighting in the fact he saw me as some sort of passionate heroine. Which of course I was...

" – so, good luck," he said and, winking, walked off to the slopes to take charge.

I stood on the pavement.

Right.

It was my first guerrilla garden and I hadn't listened to a thing. Nothing. Not my finest hour.

But how hard could it be? After all I *had* gardened a skip and won an invite to the secret society on merit. So surely this wasn't going to be so hard: get gloves, pull up weeds, plant non-weeds, kiss Guy. That was pretty much

145

what I had to do for the rest of the night to make it a success wasn't it?

Arming myself with gloves and a bag I headed for a space on the slopes and began my career as a proper, bona fide guerrilla gardener, greeting the people I'd met in the ballroom a few nights earlier. I was buoyed up with the same feeling I'd had on top of the skip that night, although this time my night gardening was without fags, cheap Cava and a pregnant friend to enjoy them with. And no one was wearing a sombrero for disguise.

It was difficult to see in the far-off street lights exactly what I was pulling up: weeds and grasses I presumed but, I cringed, dog mess was definitely in the mix. I dug gingerly at first, pulling up tuft of grass after tuft of grass but gradually I got more confident and started to throw myself into it. Soon the smell of the bared earth in the cold morning took over from the inner-city smell. It was rewarding, working my way to the boundaries of another gardener's clearings: bagging the litter, tearing up the weeds and clearing the way for the planting later.

Towards the top of the slope Jake – the man built like a double-fronted wardrobe – was wrenching up enormous weed bushes and saplings in the same way that I had pulled up clumps of grass. Nearer to me, Neil and his wife Anja, from V-2, were clearing brambles and moaning about how hard it was. I even saw the woman who I'd followed into the Working Men's Club, this time without her pashmina and dressed from head to foot in what looked like Cath Kidston gardening gear. She was daintily trowelling the earth and trying not to get her pinny too dirty, shuffling along the slope on a Liberty print knee pad.

If anyone spoke it was rarely and whatever was said was always whispered. For the most part the only sounds were the scraping of spades on stony soil, the soft ripping of roots and the rumble of the wheelie bins as they were filled and then loaded into the van.

"Hey, Edda," Guy came over to me and crouched beside me. "How's it going?" he whispered.

He was pleased with what I'd done, saying he'd been watching me – at which point I melted – and that I'd earned my stripes as a guerrilla gardener. "Most people flake out after the first hour. Gardening at three in the morning is harder than you would think."

"It's *three in the morning*?" I checked my watch, angling it towards the far off street light. How had two hours gone by?

"Come down to the van, Neil's got cakes and coffee." He took hold of my glove, whipped it off and held my newly bared hand. "Let's go," he pulled me down the slope with him.

What *was* it with this man? Had he gone to some School For The Especially Sexy where he'd learnt these moves? How could pulling off a gardening glove *do that* to me? And how could someone be so confident they could just hold your hand and know that you wouldn't pull away? OK so looking like an Adonis probably helped. No one could possibly pull their hand away from someone who looked like that.

"Glad you came?" Guy leant next to me as we waited

our turn near the van that was surrounded by famished and exhausted looking guerrilla gardeners.

"Oh I—" Not waiting for my answer he pulled me roughly to him and began kissing me, full on the mouth.

"Put her down, Newhouse." A man had come over and as Guy moved away I hastily tried to regain some composure. Which was a completely impossible task as I had the grown-up equivalent of an *It's Christmas!* expression on my face.

The crowd around the cakes dissipated and I took a paper cup of tea and an apple muffin while Guy had a chocolate slice.

"Anja is an amazing cook," Guy said with his mouth full of the evidence. "She's the reason V-2 does so well: no customer can resist her cooking."

"So it's not my charm then Guy?" Neil asked archly.

Before he could answer Guy was approached by another gardener who had dropped what looked like a bucket of rubble behind the van. "That's the last of the clearance, Guy. We're ready for compost, then planting, and you're needed over by the sacks. Sorry, can you spare him?" he said to me.

"Of course," I replied, magnanimously.

Guy made to go but halted and turned back. "Do you know what you're supposed to be doing now the clearance has finished, Edda?"

"Not as such." I said, determined this time actually to listen to what he had to say.

He strode off and returned with plans for the dig, which he spread on the bonnet of the van. Then, by the light of a torch I made out a long list of actions and the assigned individuals. All actions had times set against them: *ground clearance and preparation to 2.30am.* "We're behind schedule, aren't we?"

"We can make it up," Guy said. "There are more people working the site than we'd originally planned: planting time should be shorter. We just weren't prepared for the amount of clearance needed, but that's the way it goes. OK, you're working with me putting the oak saplings in at the back of the site."

Ten minutes later and I realised that they were *not* saplings. It took all my strength to heft just one of the things – the word *sapling* really did nothing to convey the huge, heavy-treeness of them. Guy, however, seemingly effortlessly managed two in one go. I dragged mine artlessly up the slope, stumbling as it whipped me in the face with its branches. I tried to peer through the leaves to see how Guy was carrying his – there must be some sort of technique that I definitely hadn't mastered – but even when I attempted to copy what he was doing it was impossible to negotiate the slope, carry the tree *and* check out Guy. So I concentrated on doing the first two as well as I could. At the top where the slope got steeper, I nearly toppled backwards as a branch slapped me hard across the forehead and I lost my footing.

"Got you!" Guy encircled me and pulled me upright, stopping me tumbling to a messy end on a Brockley pavement.

"Thanks."

"Any time." He shot me a grin and slowly, teasingly

slowly, withdrew his hand from my waist. I met his eyes and managed a smile before returning to my work. Outwardly cool, inwardly *burning up with lust and embarrassment and not knowing quite what the hell to do about it*. Hopefully, I thought, as I wobbled to the railings to prop up my tree, hopefully I just looked cool and unruffled.

If weeding and trowelling hurt, digging in saplings really hurt. My blistered hands bled, my arms were scratched and I was constantly getting hit in the face by unseen twiggy branches because it was so damn dark. Any pleasure I might have had from working with Guy was ruined by the sheer hell of the task in hand. By 4am I hated almost everything: the trees, the soil, the slope and the complete impossibility of gardening in the dark. Digging a site with trees and giant shrubs was a completely different experience to messing around in a skip with geraniums, topsoil and cheap alcohol. Nevertheless when anyone asked how I was doing on my first dig I was *doing fine* and *really enjoying it*. It wouldn't do to moan.

Working in silence, Guy was engrossed in measuring, digging and planting, while I focused on not grunting while I hefted the trees and dug the holes. I was deep in the task when Guy leant over and hissed, "He's here."

I stood up, stretching and aching, and followed his line of sight, down to the pavement below. A giant seventies black limo had smoothly pulled up alongside the van.

Eustace Fox, in the familiar long black trench coat,

stepped out of the car, his ruddy round face turned orange from the distant street lights. However benevolent and philanthropic I knew him to be I couldn't help feeling a sense of dread at the sight of him in that get-up. He was standing with his back to the dig site and looking at Mr Iqbal's Mini Mart, pointing something out to Peter Shaw, the Head of Planning at the Council, who had also emerged from the car.

"What's Eustace doing?" I whispered to Guy. "Why is he so interested in the Mini Mart?"

"God only knows. Eust has his fingers in a number of pies."

I was going to ask more about the fingers in pies comment but decided against it, seeing Guy's face knotted in a frown. "Do you think he'll be happy with what he sees here?" I whispered to Guy who was now busy collecting up the empty tree pots to take down to the van.

"I'd better find out," he muttered, "I'm going down."

It was amazing, absolutely *amazing* what we had achieved in four hours. All the frustration and anger and general dissatisfaction over the dig had vanished and I stood looking up at the night's work with a feeling of awe and pride. In the lightening sky I could clearly make out that the former scraggy wasteland approaching Brockley Station had been transformed into a garden of greens and purples with rich black soil showing in-between. The station slope was *beautiful* and stylish and, for the first time ever, it was clean and litter free. The volunteers were packing away now, bringing back the spades and trowels and empty containers, while others quietly brushed the spilt soil from the pavement and lugged the sacks of waste into the van. One or two gardeners were litter picking down the road. I laid my tools in the cage inside the van.

"'ere!" Jake thrust a five litre watering can into my hands, "Water. We're off-site in ten."

"Where's Eustace?" I asked.

"'e's gone."

I waited for a moment to see if there was going to be any more of an explanation. But no, there was not. This was Jake, after all.

For what felt like the millionth time that night I headed up the slope to the oaks, stumbling under the weight of the watering can and stupefied by lack of sleep. Everyone around me was watering, the wet soil tang mixing with the scent of the lavender, which reminded me of home. My lovely home of Extreme Lavender with its lovely hot shower and lovely, lovely big bed.

"I have to go," Guy appeared at my side, one hand resting gently on the nape of my neck. "I'll see you soon, Edda."

This time there was no kiss from him and I didn't have the confidence to take the lead and kiss him. I'm sure Che Guevara would have had the confidence to – if he'd wanted to, that is – but at that time in the morning after hours of digging I was utterly numb and exhausted. Horribly disappointed, I watched Guy walk away from me, down the road, shaking hands with the gardeners as he passed and then disappearing down Geoffrey Road to wherever he lived.

I milled around dejectedly, wondering what the protocol was for leaving the site, but there didn't appear to be one. Everyone was drifting off and so, with a wave to Neil and Anja, I started my short, weary walk home down the empty street.

Thirteen

Beth and I had spent an hour in V-2 with very little baby-talk and a great deal of me talking about guerrilla gardening. For once, Beth acknowledged that my life was at least as interesting as hers: new secret society, new lodger, kissing artists … things were moving on in a glossy-magazine-approved manner. She was, however, still reeling from the fact that I hadn't asked her to help me choose my lodger and, for the moment, that was all she wanted to talk about.

"I cannot believe," said Beth, between mouthfuls of ciabatta, "that you even listened to this Amanda person when it came to finding a tenant. Honestly, she sounds absolutely dreadful. I know you said she'd be upset if you told her not to do it, but honestly my lovely, what kind of advice would someone like her be able to give? You really should have had me with you honey."

"That's unfair." I said, "Amanda's fine, really. I just painted a bad picture of her. Talking of painting pictures, Guy—"

"But, for goodness sake," Beth continued, unabated, "I thought you said this Amanda person always has her bra on show in the office. What kind of woman flaunts their bra at the office?" Beth was eating so eagerly I felt almost

154

disgusted watching her, as she spat out the bread in her bid to talk. To say she was eating for two was an understatement. "I mean what did she wear when she helped you interview? Tassels?"

"Well, the house is a former brothel." I said, "It would have been fitting."

Beth pushed a sausage roll into her mouth. "Do you still have the pole in your cellar? The one you thought was scaffolding?" She snorted flaky pastry over me and the table.

"Yes." I dusted myself down. "To be honest I just can't bear to touch it. I should have put it in the skip outside the front of the house while it was still there. We could have put some climbing roses up it."

"Anyway, getting back to the point, Eds, you made a big mistake using your teenage friend, in my opinion: I don't know what made you do it, darling. I could have helped you, but," she sighed, "you didn't want me." Her voice wobbled slightly and a very small part of me thought *HA!* Let her be the one left behind for a change. Let her know how it feels. But outwardly I did the dutiful friend thing and squeezed her knee.

"It's done now, anyway. And the bloke we chose seems fine. Really nice."

" 'Nice'?" Beth emptied the crisps into her mouth. "What does *nice* mean?"

"Nice. I don't know. Pleasant. And other people think so too – I got a second opinion."

"Good girl! Who from?"

"Babs."

"Who?" Beth said and then her face fell as it dawned on her. "Babs? *Babs!* You got the old hag from next door to give her opinion on your new lodger?"

"She's not a hag. Beth you're being really mean about my…"

Oh God.

Beth nearly choked. *"Are you about to say 'friends'?"* she gaped. "Were you going to say I was being mean *about your friends*?"

"No. Not at all. Nope. No."

But Beth wasn't to be convinced. "You are! You're friends with Miss Pants-on-Show Teenager and your White Trash Neighbour."

The red mist descended. "STOP BEING SO BLOODY MEAN!" several people looked up. Including Beth.

We stared at each other across the food-covered table.

"Sorry." Beth broke the silence. "You're absolutely right. But they're not your *real friends* are they?"

"No. No I just … I seem to be with them a lot more, now. And they're OK. Really. Babs makes me laugh – oh come on, she's harmless enough." I was on the brink of telling her about the belly dancing kit, but then decided not to: it wouldn't endear Babs to Beth.

"Well, it's good you're out and about meeting people," Beth said breezily, both of us ignoring the enormous elephant in the room that was her complete and utter abandonment of me. "Anyway, this Amanda person— "

"You could just call her *Amanda*," I said quietly.

"So she based the decision about who should be your tenant solely on the fact that this silver fox father of his is a famous actor?"

"He is quite famous. In fact, I'd say he's *very* famous."

"But my point is, Eds," more ciabatta came my way, "you're not going to be living with the famous father are you?"

"No. But look – there were loads of people we interviewed who would have been fine, so it was a relief just to get the decision made for me. There needed to be some grounds for a choice between all the fine people and Amanda just happened to make it on the basis of the really very handsome and famous father."

"But the son's not handsome?"

"No. But like I said on the phone – he's nice. He's fine. He'll pay the bills and keep the house tidy, probably, and that's what I want."

"Sounds like a marriage of convenience."

"Well I'm not marrying him, am I? I'm hardly going to want some Heathcliffe-style fiery, passionate and broody lodger. I'll save that for my boyfriend."

Beth looked at me. "Have you?" she said. "Have you *got* a boyfriend? Are you seeing that guy from the secret society then?"

"He's called Guy."

"I know that. Are you and he … are you?" She was so shocked she'd actually paused in her eating.

"No. Well, I don't know what we are. We're something. I think." And then I took her through what had happened so far. She listened in, hungrily, only breaking in to ask questions such as, "What sort of a kiss?" or "What sort of an artist is he? Is he any good?"

Beth looked appalled at my answer. "You mean you haven't Googled him? Edda! Like how 1990 are you? If he's a famous artist he'll be all over the web."

"What do you mean 'How 1990 am I?' Now you sound like Amanda. Like *that* Amanda."

"Well, she seems like a perfectly sensible person then if that's the kind of thing she would say. Do you want me to be more like her? Would that make you love me more? Would you invite me to interview your lodgers if I was more like her?" she said, with a hint of a smile.

I shrugged and played along. "Maybe. Maybe I would love you more if you were like Amanda."

"So do you want me to get my enormous mummy knickers out like that Amanda gets her knickers out?" she was struggling to suppress her grin. "Is that what I should do to be your best friend now? I warn you they're beige and elasticated every which way."

I said no, she should definitely *not* get her knickers out.

But she did anyway.

There was a billow of maternity dress, the table rocked and the couple next to us gasped as I squealed out, "Jesus Christ, Beth, they're *enormous!*"

And in a flash I had my old best friend back again, just for a minute.

"Oh my God!" she rearranged her clothes and wiped the tears out of her eyes. "Oh, Eds! I shouldn't be laughing so much! It can harm the baby." And my old best friend left as soon as she'd arrived.

We walked from V-2, past Fox Estates and on towards Beth's flat – I was going to walk her home just in case she went into labour on the streets of Brockley. Very early.

"Oh, bloody hell!" Beth said. We had stopped outside my house and I had opened the gate into the year 1588. "What the fuck, Edda?" she said and then put her hands on either side of her bump to shield the baby's ears from the expletive. She walked the gravel path and then took a seat on the stone bench that had so recently been taken up with the handsome artist. "This isn't new though, is it?" she said, running a hand along its freshly cleaned surface. "Don't I remember this bench? Didn't I … didn't I fall asleep once and spend an entire night stretched out on it after the party in Blackheath when we first moved into London?"

"That's the one! I found it under brambles when I cut the garden down."

"Hmm. You know Eds it's a bit freaky isn't it, this guerrilla gardening thing. Breaking into front gardens and imposing your own style onto someone else. I mean OK so your garden was dreadful, but I guess some people might not like what it is now …"

"We don't go into gardens. We do shared areas like the approach to the station that I showed you before we went to V-2."

"Ye-es. It was beautiful and I guess that's good." She

mused. "But *this*. This is a bit freaky. Do you actually like this, hon?"

"I don't know. I think so. I mean it's very kind of them to have done it for me. It was done with the best intentions. Do I like it?"

"I don't think you do, hon. And I'm not convinced either," Beth said. "I'm actually thinking it's quite wrong. I mean – who tells the guerrilla gardeners what the people of Brockley actually want? Do you go out there and do covert market research before you lift the trowel? Do you hand out questionnaires asking for shrub preference and overall satisfaction with the borders?"

"Oh come on you're as bad as Babs, with all the doom and gloom mongering," I said, quietly, just in case the lady herself was listening.

"Babs knows about the secret society?" Beth whispered, also looking over at Babs' house.

"No. But she talks to me about Eustace Fox: you know she rates him as quite the criminal. She says the suited ones are the ones you have to worry about."

"Pah!" Beth waved it away, "The old biddy only says that because her family form the entire criminal underclass of South East London. Is her son – grandson – still in prison? What's his name?"

"Tyrone? No – he's out now." I said. "But maybe I should be a bit more wary of the secret society: if you think it's dodgy and Babs thinks its leader is crooked."

"Well don't take our words for it," Beth stood up, "Why not get another opinion from your pal Amanda? What does she think?"

"Meany." I followed her to the gate. "Can't I convince you to stay for dinner?"

"Nope. Sorry darling. Out with parents-to-be friends later. Café Rouge over in Greenwich: should be fun. Bye, darling." She leant over her bump and plonked a kiss on my cheek. I could feel her suddenly tense as she pulled away. And then I realised why.

"Hi," she mumbled across the garden.

"All right?" Babs gave her a curt nod from her raised doorstep.

What a witch, Beth mouthed to me when Babs turned and headed indoors. "Look Eds, as much as I hate to agree with the old hag next door but yes maybe you ought to take care. Maybe she is on to something with Eustace Fox."

"Enjoy Café Rouge!" I shooed her out of the gate. "And as we're dishing out warnings and cautions, you be careful with the blue cheese and the alcohol. And laughing too much. And using coarse language."

"I will! And hey – good luck with your lodger. Is it tomorrow he arrives?"

"Yup. Do you want me to be careful about him too? Babs thinks there's a chance that lodgers can get angry and bake their landladies into pies."

"No, darling, I'm sure you, Amanda and Babs chose a good one. Byee!"

189 Geoffrey Road was now home to three: me, Fin and Robert Willoughby. It was moving in day and Babs and I had been philosophising over the garden wall for the

last half hour while Robert and and his famous father Max moved boxes in.

"Don't get me wrong," Babs pointed a thoughtful fag in the direction of my sundial, "I like what you've got going on 'ere. It's better than that bleedin' mess you made before. But what I don't know is how yer did it."

"Oh, you know," I said, "I just got the urge one night and sorted it all out."

"All them weeds! I thought it were too much for one person to clear that lot! An' what's with the tiny maze then? Is it for kids or somethin'?"

I managed to conjure up an excuse about a long held love for Elizabethan knot gardens and that it seemed the perfect use of space to make my own version.

"I don't get the sundial either love I 'ave to say."

"Oh. Well. I've always liked sundials," I said, lamely.

"Don't get no sun in the front garden though do we darlin'? Not until June, and then only after four o'clock."

There was no answer to that.

We paused the conversation, to my relief, as Robert and his silver fox dad walked past with boxes. I smiled at them and Babs raised a friendly fag. Every time they staggered past me with Robert's belongings I felt a stab of guilt at not helping. I'd offered of course. Many times. But the boxes were heavy and they said they were fine as they were. It didn't stop me feeling immensely guilty though, standing around watching them.

The trouble was I had no idea of landlady/lodger etiquette. What was I supposed to do when a lodger moved in? I'd asked Amanda and Beth. Both of them had said I should definitely be in the house, rather than leaving him to get settled in on his own, and that I should offer to help. So far, so good. Beth had said the best thing I could do was to make tea and just *be nice*. Amanda said I should suggest lunch at a bar, probably in Greenwich, as a way to welcome him. So I spent the morning smiling, regularly offering to make tea (*no more just yet thanks*), and gearing up to ask them out to lunch. Which, in reality, boiled down to dithering around in the front garden and talking to Babs.

"'e shook me 'and." Babs said when Robert's dad walked past with a pot plant. "Max Willoughby actually shook me 'and." She stared at the hand with a look of awe. "I ain't never gonna wash it again."

"He seems like a nice chap. For someone who's famous," I said. "I mean – sometimes you hear of famous people being really up themselves."

"Ooh, if I were ten years younger…" Babs stared wistfully after Max Willoughby. "'e reminds me of me husband. God rest 'is soul."

"I didn't know you were widowed. I'm sorry." I added, because I thought that's what I ought to say.

"Don't be." Babs laughed phlegmily. "Shittin' bastard 'e was," she leant in so close I was practically smoking when I breathed in her breath. "He slipped an' fell on a bread knife 'e did. Terrible accident it was." And then she winked at me. "'specially as I was 'olding the bread knife at the bleedin' time! But that's between you an' me an' this wall right?"

Ngh.

"Yeah it's all well an' good lookin' all shocked about it Edda, but what you don't realise," she dipped her voice as Max and Robert appeared again, "what with your sheltered young life, is that some folks are proper fuckin' bastards. Bastards we're better off without. An' I were better off without me 'usband. I did miss the breadknife though – it was a good one: bone 'andled it was, proper expensive." She looked thoughtful for a moment, pondering the loss of the breadknife. "Anyways, I got a new one, eventually, down Deptford Market. And me boyfriend is the best thing that's 'appened to me since I had me veins done."

"Hi … hi!" Completely unexpectedly, Amanda bounced down the garden path, the most welcome vision I had ever seen in my entire life after Babs' revelations. "I didn't know you smoked, Edda!" she chirruped.

I stubbed the cigarette out on the wall. "I really felt like one," I said. News of Babs' killing her husband had sent me straight to the filterless fags.

"Well. I was just passing and, like, I wanted to see if anyone needed any help."

I felt my eyes narrowing. "You weren't just passing." I said, with the intuition of the most cunning of police detectives.

"Nope!" She bounced up towards me. "I see the van's parked outside, so I guess they're here, then? Is Max here, too? It *is* moving in day, isn't it? I have got it right haven't I?"

"Yes, he's inside. That's a nice dress, by the way."

164

"Ah thanks! You don't think it's, like, too short and everything?"

"Well actually…"

"It's not real leopard skin, though!" she laughed. "My old gran thought it was! Can you imagine! Like I'm some kinda Tarzan girl and stuff. Come on then, shall we go in?"

We sat in the back garden with coffees, making good use of the inspired biscuit selection Robert had produced from a box marked "kitchen". There were Jaffa Cakes, Party Rings and chocolate Malted Milks along with Jammy Dodgers and custard creams. Amanda had, without doubt, picked the right lodger for me.

"It's really such a charming house you've got," Max Willoughby said. "And I can see why you'd want to have a lodger: it's enormous. Is it four bedrooms, Edda?"

"Five. Well, six if you class the loft room."

"Six bedrooms!" Amanda gazed up at the house. "Like, you are so lucky! I know you lost your parents and stuff, but you have this amazing house and Brockley's really posh these days isn't it? You must be minted."

"So, have you had lodgers before?" Robert stepped in.

I hastily finished off a yellow Party Ring. "My best friend. We lived together for a few years until she moved in with her boyfriend. Just around the corner actually."

"Well it's such a nice spot here what with—"

"Yeah, but your friend's like moving really far away, isn't she?" Amanda added, and turning to Max, went on: "Poor Edda she's being *platonically divorced* from her best friend. It's, like, this really big deal for her 'cause, what was it, Edda, you were like sisters and stuff? Anyway, now this friend is moving away and getting married and having a baby, and all that, so Edda's just been left abandoned, haven't you Edda? It's really sad."

"It's fine!" I smiled my best smile. "Amanda's just exaggerating. I mean it's sad, but it's fine."

Max nodded. "Surrey is it?"

"Yes. How did you guess?"

"They all do the Surrey thing."

Robert looked vexed. "So why do people move out to Surrey? What happens if you raise a child in Brockley?"

"Terrible things would happen!" I said, trying to think of all the horrors that Beth was hoping to escape from. "Raising a child in Brockley would pretty much guarantee it would become a prostitute if it was a girl, or a drug addict gang member if it was a boy."

Robert and his dad laughed, but Amanda was wearing a horrified *Really, like, oh my God and everything* expression, despite the fact she'd been brought up in the borough without suffering such a fate.

"Well, thank God they're escaping to Surrey." Max said smoothly. "The only bad habit it will get into there is a weak tennis serve."

"Or a penchant for caviar," added Robert.

"Or a dependence on Waitrose." I laughed.

"Hello there," Beth was walking towards us. "I love Waitrose! Why are you talking about Waitrose?"

Oh. I stared at my best friend, open-mouthed.

This morning my house was like some terrible

166

theatrical comedy with people arriving unannounced Stage Left and Stage Right. Any second now my dead parents would stroll in, covered in seaweed: *But didn't you know darling, it was all an impossible, impossible mistake!*

"Sorry to walk in uninvited, Eds." Beth planted a kiss on my cheek, bending down slowly to accommodate the bump. "I did knock, but you didn't hear me. Hi!" She looked at the others around the table. "I'm Beth, Edda's best friend. And you must be Robert." She singled him out and shook his hand. "Hello. Welcome to Ed's place. I lived with her for years and it was great! And … Max Willoughby!" She lost it for a second in the aura of celebrity, but regained it just as quickly and shook his hand. "Yes. Well. Wow. I just thought you were in a TV soap or something." Max smiled politely and said something gracious about blooming.

"Ahh," Beth turned to Amanda giving her a lightning-quick up-and-down and taking in the tiny leopard skin dress and the four inch wedge sandals. "And you must be the Amanda I've been hearing so much about."

"And you must be the best friend *I've* been hearing so much about," Amanda retorted. The two met eye-to-eye in a silent tense standoff. I sat in my chair and wondered what the bloody hell was going on – it was like old-boyfriend meets new-boyfriend.

"Does anyone fancy going out for lunch?" I chipped in. "There's a new bar just opened up, near Hilly Fields, that I thought we could try…"

I sat on the edge of my bed staring out of the window at my skipless view. It had been an odd day. And now, downstairs, was my new lodger. I could hear him in the kitchen putting away the last of his food in the cupboards. My cupboards. It felt so strange after so long living on my own to know there was a man downstairs – a man with his own set of keys to my house – putting away his cereal boxes *in my cupboards*. I didn't even know if he had a middle name. Was that important? Probably not. The most important thing was that he didn't seem likely to put me in a pie, although there was bound to be something about him that Babs wouldn't like, given time.

I stared out of the bay window for a few more minutes. What I really wanted was a glass of water but I was already in my pyjamas and it didn't seem appropriate to go downstairs when Robert was down there. Stupid I knew, but nevertheless it didn't feel right. It was night-time: bed time. And not time to go swanning around with strange – if perfectly nice – men. Beth would have told me to pull myself together and go downstairs – goddamn it, Eds – and do it. Amanda would have persuaded me to ditch the pyjamas and do it.

It had been so strange to watch the two of them at lunch – a lunch which Max had insisted on picking up the tab for. After sizing-up Beth and engaging in spiky conversational warfare with her, Amanda pretty much only had eyes for Max. She sat beside him at the restaurant and spent the meal flirting outrageously: *Here, try some of mine*, feeding him with her cutlery, hanging on to every word he said, touching his shoulder, his arm. And Max Willoughby looked more than happy to oblige and had effortlessly adopted the role of mentor, explaining the size of wine glasses: *that's for white wine*, *that's for red, that's for water*, which completely blew her away.

And this left Robert, Beth and me to talk amongst ourselves: which had been surprisingly easy and enjoyable. Robert turned out to not be one of those men who get completely cowed by the disgusting and unknown wonder of pregnant women: the sort who daren't look at a baby bump for fear it would explode in their face like an atomic baby grenade.

"He's really nice, Eds," Beth had whispered to me as we all made our way back from the bar after lunch. "You've completely lucked out that the handsome famous father had a nice son."

"He does seem OK doesn't he?" I whispered back.

"Do you think – you know – that you might …" she raised her eyebrows at me.

"What? No! God, you're as bad as Amanda – she wanted me to get a lodger to shack up with. And anway, I told you about Guy didn't I? I mean I know it's casual. Very casual. And it might be nothing but, well, it's worth keeping the schedule clear if you know what I mean. I think I might be on to something with him."

"Yeah the artist sounds hot! What does Robert do for a job? I know you told me."

"He's a history teacher."

"Mmm. Historian or artist. Yeah – no contest really is there?" she'd said and linked her arm through mine as we walked back to 189 Geoffrey Road.

And now Robert the history teacher was making himself a drink in my kitchen before, probably, going to bed up the stairs that passed my room. It was all just too strange.

"How are you getting on with your new tenant?" Amanda bounced up to my desk and then bounced on to it. Peach.

"Very well." I said, "He cooked Sunday lunch for me yesterday."

"Very nice," Amanda said and then added. "His dad took me out for breakfast on Sunday morning."

It took a few seconds to register what she'd said. "Pardon? *Pardon?*"

"Oh come on, Mrs Prude." She slapped my arm. "We're all grown-ups."

"Yes but Amanda he's *really* grown-up. He must be forty years older than you."

"So? And it's thirty-two years actually. But, like, oh my God, can older men teach you a thing or two!"

Our boss looked up from her PC, frowned slightly and turned back to the report she was pretending to read. I squinted over to the open page and saw the words *caught in his throbbing ardour.* Crikey. The Sea Captain's passion was not abating.

"Anyway," Amanda continued in a slightly quieter voice that could now only be heard as far away as the lifts in Education (I knew this because all the middle-aged

170

women in Accounts were still looking at each other pointedly, while beyond the lifts they were straining to hear what was being said). "It was a totally cool breakfast. We went into Greenwich and I had Eggs Benedict, which I've never had in my life before but I *love*. You know what … he is just, like, so clever and everything. He knows everything. Eggs Benedict! Crazy!"

"I'm very pleased for you." I said. And I was. But also I was rather worried what effect Amanda's relationship with Max was going to have on mine with my new lodger. Would it make things awkward that my friend – friend? – was having it away with his dad? Or would it give us something to talk about? Or would it make no difference whatsoever? Although, obviously, there were going to be some subject areas that were going to be off limits: *Amanda said your Dad really knows his way around a woman's body. Can you pass the corn flakes please, Robert…*

"So, your mate Beth seemed a bit uptight and stuff." Amanda brought me out of my alarming thoughts.

"You think so?" I said. "I think she was probably just tired."

"I think she's jealous." Amanda crossed her legs with a peachy flash.

"Jealous? What on earth do you think she's jealous about?"

"I think she's like realising what she's leaving behind. " Amanda said. "I think she's going to miss you."

"You really think so?" I said, not unhappy to hear that another person had picked up on something I had considered, thus making it absolutely certain that Beth was now looking back at me and not just running thoughtlessly forward towards babydom.

"Yeah 'cause it's like I said, it's divorce isn't it – and she's gutted that you're, like, moving on already and so quickly and stuff. She's jealous of me. I, like, totally got that impression. She kept looking at me funny."

"Probably because you had a tiny leopard-skin dress on," I hazarded.

"Nah. Not the *way* she was looking at me. And I reckon she's going to be jealous of that Robert chap, too. Well, it's no good regretting where she's going is it? It's not a train from which she can disembark is it?" She clocked my expression and then added, "That's something Max said. He's got a real way with words, hasn't he? And with his hands, if you get my meaning!" She giggled.

"Yes. Thank you. Loud and clear. So, when are you seeing Max again?"

"Tonight!" she leapt off the desk and bounded round me. "Guess what? He's taking me to the theatre, Shaftesbury Avenue, to see some play about incest that his friends are acting in! And he's driving us there in his sports car! And then we're going for dinner after, somewhere on the Strand. How cool is that? Oh man, I am *so* glad I helped you get a tenant."

"Oooh," came a noise behind us and Rosemary snapped closed a thick report on *Economic Indicators: South London's Spatial Plan*. Red faced she stood up from her desk and wobbled away towards the lifts.

Amanda and I giggled. "Do you think she was enjoying the *stiff probing urgency* of Lewisham's regenerated town centre?" I said.

Amanda snorted and then, "Hey," she said, grabbing my arm, "talking of which, you should totally come and see my screen saver."

And there he was, Max Willoughby, giving the camera a sexy serious pose in his guise as Detective Calvados in a TV drama.

"Does he fight crime by pouting?" I said.

"Actually, Detective Calvados fights crime using detective skills honed from years on the beat." She was reciting it word for word again. "And using the psychic intuition passed on to him by his Romany gypsy mother. In one episode…" at which point I tuned out, preferring instead to daydream about Guy hard at work in front of an enormous canvas, stripped to the waist, sweating… Obviously working for the Council pushed a woman into living in a fantasy world if the third floor was anything to go by.

Fourteen

I made my way to the Mini Mart with a spring in my step.

Things were most definitely coming together. Robert was in and the weirdness of having a (paying) man about the place was receding slightly, much as it had probably done for Babs when her boyfriend got the wrong address... Beth was sad she was moving on from me (hurrah!) and I had become a secret, mysterious guerrilla gardener. But more than all that, the spring in my step was because of Guy and the way he'd kissed me on the dig that night at the station. The sexy gardener thought I was a passionate militant red-head from dispossessed Highland stock but hey – maybe I *was* and I'd simply not yet realised my full potential. Not long until the next dig and then, perhaps, if I put myself forward more, actually initiated a conversation... Maybe I should learn a bit about Che Guevara and then we could have meaningful conversations about him.

The sun was shining and Brockley was looking beautiful. There were fresh new leaves on the trees and not a cloud in the sky. I bounced passed Fox Estates and waved a jovial *hello* to Eustace who was polishing the brass and he stopped to salute me with a *Good morning to you, my dear*. I marvelled at the station planting, feeling a sharp stab of pride, and bounced right into Mr Iqbal's for emergency provisions. And then I did a double take.

"Good morning, young Edna." Mr Iqbal said from behind a glossy new counter.

"Hello…" I looked around – was I even in the right shop? It was the right owner talking to me, and it was next door to Gloria's Flowers, the new florist's shop, but apart from that everything was different. The clutter and the ethnic foods and the back-of-a-lorry-from-1989 stock had gone. As had the peeling lino tiles and the humming grey strip lights.

"You like my new shop, then, Edna?" Mr Iqbal beamed at me.

"How? Why? How?" There were wooden floors, light bulbs in etched glass shades, things in brown boxes and tall glass jars. There were no vats of ghee or *Filthy Exterminator* cleaning products.

"Organic cereals," Mr Iqbal swept a hand along a tidy wooden shelf, "Fairtrade sugars, tea and coffee – all organic of course – responsibly sourced chocolate, recycled tissues and paper. Biodegradable cleaning products – none of that nonsense I sold you last month, my dear. And did you like my awning?"

"Your what?" I followed where he was pointing to the outside of the shop. I must have completely missed it as I'd bounded in: a striped red and white awning over the door with strings of onions hanging from the supports. Underneath was an old-fashioned bicycle propped against a wooden pillar with a basket full of bread. Beside it was a chalkboard that read *fresh bread daily.*

And there were two bay trees.

"Eustace!"

"What was that, Edna?" Mr Iqbal joined me in the doorway.

"Nothing." I bit my lip.

"I think I heard you." He nodded wisely. "Eustace Fox isn't it? Well you're right," he leant against the door frame and nodded in the direction of Fox Estates, just around the corner.

"He made you do this?" I whispered. "All of this?"

Mr Iqbal laughed. "Of course not! What kind of a man do you think he is? No! He is very kind and good at business too. We sat down and talked about the business and about Brockley and how things were changing. And we came up with a *business plan*, so that I can survive in these new times. The old products are out and it is these new high-end products that people will be buying these days."

"But there are lots of people wanting the vats of ghee…"

"And that is what I said to Eustace Fox, but he convinced me otherwise. You see they take up so much space in my shop that could be used to sell more stock. And if I sold just two Mr Squirrel Organic Nut Bars then I would recoup the profit I would make from one whole vat of ghee."

"But people bought ghee!" I examined the nut bar. "No one will buy these; they're so expensive."

"They will." Mr Iqbal said. "Eustace said so. And I believe him, he is a very shrewd man. And he gave me the beautiful trees in the pots you see outside there. As a gift."

"I'm sure…" I said. "But didn't it cost a huge amount of money to renovate your shop and put entirely new stock in?"

"You must invest to survive," he said, in what sounded like a repeated mantra he'd no doubt heard from Eustace. "And now, what did you want to buy this morning Edna? Muesli bar? Ethically sourced cotton tea towels? Luxury free range pot pourri?"

I managed to find my sugar (fairtrade) and marmalade (organic) and bought a Mr Squirrel bar out of sympathy, but also to support my local business.

"Here, have one of our new bags," he put my purchases in a hessian bag with BROCKLEY PETIT MARCHÉ PURVEYORS OF CONVENIENCE SINCE 1974 printed on the side.

"All right there, Edda!" Babs' voice and fag smoke assaulted me on the street before I'd even turned in to my front garden. I looked up to see her sitting on her doorstep, legs apart, fag in, cutting something out of a giant square of thick card with enormous shears. The last time she'd been cutting out shapes I'd made the mistake of showing an interest and asking what she was doing. Not this time.

"Morning, Babs." I wandered through my knot garden, still in a post-Mini-Mart trance. "How are things with you?"

"Can't grumble," Babs said, and then added: "I've been

meanin' to say to yer that me boyfriend loves them clothes I got from yer, love. That belly dancin' thing – it's given 'im a new lease a' life in the bedroom." She laughed. "Turns out he were in the RAF over in Cyprus forty years ago. Got a taste for belly dancers while he was over there. Funny how these things work out, eh?"

"Oh I … I am glad."

"Ah, now I didn't mean ter make yer blush, darlin'." Babs looked amused at the sight of my face. "Ain't it supposed to be the job of the young 'uns to shock our generation?"

"I don't know." I leaned against the wall. "It's all mixed up for me at the moment. Did I tell you that my friend from work's seeing my lodger's father: Max Willoughby."

I had to remind her who Amanda was, but the instant I mentioned *leopard skin* she knew right away.

"An' what about you and that lodger o' yours. Fine bit o' man you got livin' with yer. Canny girl."

"Erm. It's going great. He made me a coffee this morning. It's all very civilised."

"Oh aye, darlin'. It is in the beginnin'…"

I sensed a pastry-themed comment coming and hastily averted it, "But I am seeing someone. It's very casual." *Why* was I telling Babs this? Why was I confiding in the local gossip? Maybe it was because I wanted to compete with her and her hot relationship and busy social life.

"That bloke what came here the other day. Leather jacket?"

"That's him. He's an artist."

"You ain't kiddin' darlin'." Babs lit a new fag with the stub of her old one. "Only an *artist* would have hair like that. Needed a bleedin' good wash it did, an' a pair a' scissors wouldn't go amiss. Still – if you like the broody sort. 'Ere, darlin', you ain't no good at art are yer?"

Babs' conversation veered off track again. "I'm OK. Why?"

"I'm supposed to be cuttin' these bleedin' stencils out for me grandson, Tyrone, an' I'm all to cock. It's the arms what I'm strugglin' with." She closed her legs – mercifully – stood up and walked up to the wall where I was standing.

"I'll come over." I put down my organic, fairly traded recycled bag and walked round.

"Here." She thrust the plastic-coated card at me.

"What is it?" I asked and then, "Oh my God, Babs!"

She laughed faggily. "That's what I say when I get a load of some of 'is work. But you know it's got a real beauty to it. An' 'Roney said it is art. It ain't smut." She checked that the road in front of our houses was empty and then held the giant stencil up for us both to see it. "The way that woman's doin' that thing to that other woman underneath. It's got real movement, ain't it? An' it's there that yer can see the artist's skill ain't it? But I can't be doin' with all these limbs and these high heeled shoes on this sillyette. I ain't got the sight no more, love."

When I recovered, I managed to look at the *work of art* without seeing lewd pornographic silhouettes and said, "You need a craft knife for this level of detail, Babs. You'll never get it if you use scissors."

Five minutes later we were in my kitchen at the table, me cutting out silhouettes of women's breasts while Babs looked around and passed comment. "Only saw it as a knockin' shop just the once," she said. "But fair play to yer, darlin', you'd never know to see it now would yer? There was a bar over there, and a big black and red chandelier hangin' just there and a statue of a man an' woman shaggin' – tasteful mind – where you've got yer fridge."

It crossed my mind that given her tastes and hobbies I should offer Babs the pole from the cellar: it would solve the problem of getting rid of it – of even touching it. But, then, did I really want to think of what Babs was doing with it, possibly in association with my belly dancing outfit?

"So, what do the teachers think of Tyrone's, erm, art."

"Oh 'e don't go to school!" Babs opened and shut my cupboard doors one by one, working her way around the kitchen. "Left at fourteen 'e did. Youth offending prison at fifteen, but he's past that now. My boy! Made me a Great-Nan, bless 'im at just sixteen!"

"So…" my craft knife hovered over an outstretched thigh, "If it's is not for school what is the stencil for?"

Babs swelled with pride. "My 'Roney – he's Da Notorious Baron."

With a shaky hand I put the knife down. "Your grandson is the Brockley graffiti artist?"

"One and the same," she said, examining my collection of tea towels. "An' I know some folks think what he does is wrong, but the lad's only tryin'. An' 'e's bringin' some colour to our grey old streets. That Banksy, 'e 'ad a whole museum taken over with 'is work, down Bristol way. Graffiti is the art of the people – that's what my Tyrone says."

But only if it's good.

I picked up the knife again – my hands had stopped trembling – and cut the outline of the breasts of the woman who was lying down. Tryone had made them vast and impossibly pert, with nipples almost touching her chin so I took some artistic liberty and reduced them from their comedy vastness and made their shape realistic.

"Babs you know that I'm not Eustace Fox's friend: I just know him." I said, conscious that I should be very, very careful over what I was about to say.

"You went to a party at 'is fancy pad."

"That's it. Well, the thing is, I know that Da Notorious Baron really gets underneath Eustace Fox's skin." And I told her about his rant, wanting to catch Da Notorious Baron and force him to art school.

Babs sat opposite me and laughed out loud. "Good! Snobs like 'im set themselves up for that kinda reaction. But it does stun me to hear yer say he wants graffiti of some sort. Thought 'e'd be dead against any type o' graffiti, but there you go. Shall I make us a tea darlin'? I'm standing 'ere parched."

"I'm sorry, Babs!" I got up but she insisted I keep cutting and instead, having carried out a complete survey of my kitchen, was able to make us both a drink.

"Now don't you ever go tellin' 'Roney about the

181

Banksy comment," she said as she mashed the tea bags. "'E can't stand 'im. Professional rivalry, ain't it? Well will yer look at that!" she moved round to my side of the table and watched as I finished off an ankle with the twist of a stilettoed foot. "You've got real flair for stencil cuttin', Edda. That's beautiful. I see what you've done – changing the angle of that leg an' makin' her tits better. Done summat with 'er chin an' all. It's good. The lad'll be over the moon with what you've done." She took the finished stencil from me and I put the cover on my craft knife.

"Hello, hello!" Robert bounded in from his jog, wet faced and damp, with swept back hair.

Babs sat at the table looking at him in awe. "All right darlin'?" She stared. "Nice run?"

"Smashing, Babs, thanks. How's things?"

"Can't complain. How's it goin' with that pupil what fancies you?"

I stared at Robert – this was news. Why hadn't he told me about the pupil that fancied him? Why had he told Babs and not me? "Oh she's moved on to her Maths teacher now, so I'm off the leash."

"There's lucky then darlin'," she winked at him.

Robert went over to the sink and poured himself a glass of water, before coming over to where I was sitting.

"So what's th—"

He'd picked up the stencil and froze.

"Shall I explain?" I said, laughing.

Robert continued to stare at the writhing women template. "Erm…"

"Your landlady's got a real talent ain't she?" Babs said, patting the stencil. "It's for me grandson. Secret, mind, so keep it under yer 'at yeah?" She stood up and took the stencil off the table. "Thanks for this love, bless yer. Tryone will be as 'appy as a pig in shit with this he will. I'll leave the two of you alone now, I reckon." She shot me a meaningful look. "Shower time, eh? Bye, darlin's!"

"But your tea!" I said.

"Don't want to intrude," she called from the hallway.

The front door closed and Robert flopped onto the chair opposite me.

We looked at each other for a moment and I was first to break the silence. "Babs' grandson is Da Notorious Baron."

"I thought I recognised his style." Robert said, playing with the cut-outs of the naked women. "And you're now helping him?"

"Once!" I said. "I helped Babs this once. Apparently Tyrone – that's Da Notorious Baron – gets her to do his cutting out."

"Well that explains part of the reason they are so bad, then. What on earth would your Surrey-bound friend say if she knew you were turning into a South London criminal?" he said.

"I am not! Oh God, am I? Am I? I am, aren't I? Oh no, you have to stop me turning all South London."

Robert held up his hands. "You could always move to Guildford. That seems to be a popular escape route. No one is going to press-gang you into being a graffiti artist's moll in Guildford, are they?"

"I don't know if I could move to Guildford. Beth says that they have picket fences in their gardens around there. I honestly don't think I could deal with picket fences."

Robert wrinkled his nose. "Well then, there's no option but for you to come to the Grand Theatre with me tonight. Dad's poncing around in some play with American famous types in it and I have free tickets. Theatre should purge the South London from your system: think of it as medicine."

"You mean instead of going to a cock fight or to see bare knuckle boxing?"

"Exactly. The theatre – are you free?"

"But do you think it will cure me?"

"I don't know, Edda." He looked me up and down critically, "But we could visit a very trendy wine bar just around the corner afterwards. That would probably sort you out."

"Jolly good. So long as they serve gin. Babs only drinks gin and only ever drinks it neat."

"You're on." He stood up and bounded up the stairs, peeling off his t-shirt as he went. "Shower time."

I sat at the table, amid the abandoned saucy cuttings, feeling odd all of sudden and rather confused.

It was Friday night.

"What are you—"

"Shh!" I snapped, and Robert flinched. "Sorry but I really want to hear this."

"OK." He took a seat on the opposite end of the sofa to hear what was so good it couldn't be interrupted.

See, here? The carrot fly is a pest you really have to get on top of, and fast…

Robert was staring at me.

I looked back at him. "What?"

"Do you really have nothing better to do on a Friday night than watch a programme about carrot fly?"

"Hey – *Gardener's Secrets* is good!" I defended my corner. "And we went to the theatre this week, so I've done my week's worth of socialising and highbrow art. I'm entitled to stay in. Look. Carrot Fly. It's important to know about these things. Gardening is very important."

"Oh. OK." Robert deigned to show an interest in my programme and Finley threw himself onto his lap, purring like a tractor.

"So, what are you doing instead, that's so exciting, on a Friday night?" I asked while the presenter demonstrated how to cull carrot fly.

"Marking."

"Ha! Give me carrot fly any day."

"I cannot believe," Robert settled himself into the sofa cushions, "that we are watching a gardening programme and my father is out in Fitzrovia partying with your young friend and colleague. It's not right."

"Ah yes," I said, "but you have misjudged the programme."

Together we watched Old Medieval Gardening Man as he moved effortlessly from carrot fly to cockchafers.

Robert snorted.

"Oh, come on!" I said. "How old are you? And anyway,

185

cockchafers are a real garden pest. Look – that lawn is in ruins."

"Yes but *cockchafers*! Who came up with that name? Oh, bloody hell, look at the thing!"

We both stared transfixed at the screen which showed, in high definition, a beast of a beetle, with a body that was half woodlouse, half horse, *with wings*. It had antennae with fronds and large beady eyes that looked straight out at us on the sofa and seemed to communicate: *I will kill you*.

"Fu-cking hell," Robert said.

"That's the last time I go in my garden, then."

"I have *never* seen anything as weird as that." Robert continued to stare. "That is just alarming. Are they really common in the UK? Are they here in London? Do you have them out there?"

Twenty minutes later and we were fully lost to the programme. Old Medieval Gardener had moved on to larger pests. Robert had brought in wine.

"*…and it's the root bore you have to pay particular attention to. Now, the wife and I planted a bed of potatoes earlier this year and what we now want to know is are we having roast potatoes with our joint of beef this weekend? So, let's see if our raised beds and egg-shells have done the trick…*"

There was a knock at the door.

"Oh … what?"

Neither of us moved. OMG's potato crop was on the very brink of being harvested, OMG's wife was hovering in the background, and no one knew if the crop was healthy. The anticipation was killing me. I looked at

Robert: he looked just as gripped as I was. Even Fin was watching the insects buzzing on screen.

"I would go and answer it," Robert said, not taking his eyes off the TV, "but it's your door. The chances are it's for you."

"Damnit. Tell me what happens to the potato crop then."

"Guy!"

"Hey," the delectable artist-cum-gardener smouldered in the night, barely more than a shadow leaning against the darkened wall. "Ready to come out and play?"

"I—," and suddenly he was kissing me, pulling me out into the night and then pushing me up against the wall with his body.

"Was it—? Oh. Yes. It was definitely for you." I heard Robert behind me and then the sound of the lounge door closing.

"And he is?" Guy pulled back slightly and ran his tongue slowly along my lower lip. "I'm not upsetting any boyfriends am I?"

"My lodger." I managed to croak.

"A-ha."

I took advantage of the break in being kissed to ask, "We're not gardening tonight, are we? I thought it was next week."

"We're not," he ran a hand down the small of my back. "But I've got Eust's 1971 Lincoln Continental parked out the front. And don't you think it's just the perfect night for a bombing raid?"

"Eustace lets you borrow this car?" I slid a hand along the length of its body. Even in the dead of night I could make out that the car was perfection itself. The black bodywork was gleaming, the chrome was perfect, as if the forty years since it left the production line hadn't touched it.

"Oh, he's an old pussy cat really." Guy opened the door for me. "He owes me a few favours so ... I asked Dad if I could borrow the car and he said yes."

"He's not...?"

"No. It was a turn of phrase."

"OK."

I climbed in, closed the heavy door shut behind me and was enveloped by the smell of wax polish and engine oil. Guy got into the driver's side and began fiddling with the old radio until he got a screeching wailing noise. While he tuned, I surreptitiously looked at his shock of springy black hair falling into waves around his shoulders: yes, perhaps Babs had been right, it could do with a wash. But it was so-o cool...

"Ahh, the genius Don Michaels," Guy paused to listen to the man on the radio. I had thought it was static in between the radio channels but actually when I listened hard I realised that it was actually someone fitting down a saxophone. "The greatest jazz musician of the sixties."

I sat back in the enormous stitched leather seat and *tried* to appreciate the noise but, tragically, all I could think was: *did Old Mr and Mrs Gardener from the TV have roast potatoes with their Sunday lunch?*

"This is the coolest car I have ever been in," I said

during a lull in the cacophony. And as soon as I'd said the words the realisation hit me. Since my parents had died, I'd actually been in very few cars. My aunt and uncle hadn't owned one. I hadn't needed one at university. I hadn't wanted one in London. None of my boyfriends had been well off enough to have owned one … in fact the only car I'd ever really been in was Beth and Jack's car.

I could feel my heart thundering in my chest. How strange, and also how maddening that the impact of losing my parents still had the ability to floor me. And that after fourteen years I still couldn't control it. It happened any time. Here I was sitting in the dark beside a drop dead gorgeous artist, in a 1971 Lincoln Continental, and I was on the brink of tears about my dead parents. How could I have no control over this, even now?

"Don Michaels is an amazing man. Simply amazing. Do you know he's never had a music lesson in his life? What you're hearing is all completely self-taught."

"No kidding?" I took a deep breath in and, shooting a glance at my companion, saw he hadn't noticed my mood change. Good. I hastily rubbed my eyes and put all thoughts of dead parents to the back of my mind. Bombing raid. Artist.

"What is a bombing raid?" I asked, not wanting to sound stupid but also wanting to know what the evening might hold, just in case he was more militant than I thought. Even though it seemed at the moment that I was immersing myself in a life of crime I didn't want to push it too far.

"Well," Guy peeled himself away from Don Michaels, "We wind down the windows and we throw seed bombs, or 'green grenades' as some people call them, at traffic islands and road sides. In six months' time there'll be miniature wildflower meadows all over Brockley. It's a New York thing: Eust wants us to branch out from straight night gardening."

He started up the car and it growled into life.

"This car," I said, as we cruised passed a gang of youths on a street corner who had all stopped to stare, "isn't it a bit too noticeable for a bombing raid? Wouldn't you be better running covert ops in something like a Mondeo?"

"I would rather die than drive a Mondeo."

"Right, yes … there is that."

Guy pulled up almost as soon as we'd set off. "Just look at that, Edda." We were outside Mr Iqbal's Petit Marché.

"I know! It's just so weird that the Mini Mart has become this French … style … you don't mean the shop do you?"

"No. This," Guy pointed out of the opposite window towards the beautifully gardened approach to the station. "Da Notorious Baron has been here."

"Has he?" I leant across him to see where he was pointing. The wall opposite the site had been graffitid and there it was – my two women stencil. I felt a stab of pride.

"Eust is livid."

"I can imagine," I slunk back into my seat and wiped the enormous smile off my face.

"He's got the painters coming first thing tomorrow before the commuters start. It's really hacked him off. But, I must say," Guy leant out of the window to get a better view, "it's showing a lot more promise than the previous works. In fact, if it wasn't for the fact that it was signed by Da Notorious Baron then I'd not attribute it to him. It's stylised but it's realistic."

"It does look very real. So is Eustace still trying to catch this Baron?"

"More than ever."

"Really? And he's going to push him through art school still?"

"I don't know. I think he's taken this pretty personally," Guy said, taking off the brake and pulling away. "I mean it takes the shine off the new station garden doesn't it?"

I bit my lip and said no more.

We slid through the empty South London streets in our giant black Lincoln Continental looking for all the world like bad gangsters, except that we had jazz on the radio and not *bangin' choonz*, which would have been far more appropriate. Guy was scoping the road-sides, looking for locations most in need of seed bombs. On his instruction I was doing the same, but mostly I was distracted by the lights in the houses, peering in to the curtainless front rooms to get a snapshot of the lives of South Londoners at ten on a Friday night. Watching TV. Dinner party. Row. Watching TV. Decorating.

And all the time the awful jazz.

From the open roads bordering Nunhead, where the

families lived in large semi-detached houses, we circled the narrow terraces of Crofton Park and then moved on to a series of rundown roads in Ladywell. There were a few youths on the streets: boys in baggy jeans and girls in thigh-high skirts screeching at each other and necking cans. All of them stopped as we drove by, whooping or shouting: *nice ride, man,* as if this was LA and not SE4.

And Guy loved it: dismissing them with a sneer or a throwaway comment but I could tell he was eating up their admiration.

It just would have been far cooler with Xfm on the radio.

Half an hour after we'd set off, Guy slid the car into an unlit side road and cut the engine. We were just off Wickham Road, a minute from Beth's place. Would the lights be on in her flat? What would she be doing now: watching TV? Reading? Talking to Jack or talking to her mother on the phone? Or missing me?

This was obviously a night for melancholy thoughts.

"Right, Edda, I've made up seventy five bombs." Guy reached down into my footwell, brushing my leg with his hand and looking up at me slyly as he bought the box up. "And, having sized-up the surrounding areas, I think we should aim to throw around twenty-five parcels of goodies on the Nunhead-Brockley borders, another twenty-five along the Crofton borders and the rest along the Ladywell border – I'll point out exactly where when we're nearer."

I peered into the box and pulled out a seed bomb. "They're condoms!"

Guy laughed. "Ah, so you haven't led a completely sheltered life then."

"I'll have you know that before my friend left me for her baby we were the life and soul of this city. There aren't many bars between here and Highgate we haven't stumbled or fallen out of."

"Very good," he said absentmindedly and reached into the box of condoms. "Now watch this."

He showed me how to untie the ends, being careful not to spill the seeds in the car and then he demonstrated a flinging technique. "Up," he said, "up with a flick of the wrist." He lobbed a seed bomb past me and through my open window. In the orange street light I could see the tiny seeds scattering onto the ground.

"So what happens to the condoms? We just leave them?"

"Yup. Eust has contacts at the Council and the litter patrol will pick them up in the next few days. I just have to list where we bombed and Eust will pass the info on. It's far more acceptable to see an official litter patrol in action during daylight, than guerrilla gardeners risking life and limb on road sides at dusk. In a few weeks the waste grounds surrounding Brockley will be covered in poppies and cornflowers and entire wild flower meadows. So – are you ready?"

"Absolutely."

"Then let's go."

"There is one thing," I said, putting a hand on his knee and stopping him reversing.

"And that is?" He looked over at me, saucily.

"Well, it's something that's been bugging me for a while. And … well… "

"Sounds ominous."

I took a deep breath. There was never going to be a good time to bring this up, but I did want to ask. "Well … it's about the youth that was found wrapped around one of the broken oaks on the A-2."

"Ahh." Guy killed the engine. "What about him?"

"Did Eustace do it?"

He laughed. "Christ no! Do you know, even in the dark your hair is flame red? Quite incredible."

Any other time and I would have melted, but right now I'd summoned up the courage to ask and I wanted an answer. "But even if you say Eustace didn't do it, it's connected to the tree planting isn't it? It's something to do with Eustace?"

Guy let my hair run through his fingers. "Yes," he said. "Eustace ordered one of his acquaintances to 'teach the lad a lesson': his words. But don't you worry about it: the vandal only got a slap on the hand, nothing more. It was more about the humiliation from what I can make out from Eust, to send out a signal: we've gone to all this effort with the tree planting, so don't do it again."

"But don't you think it's a bad thing? To have beaten up someone and left them unconscious wrapped around a tree." I looked at him, trying to read his expression in the dim light. How could he think it was acceptable to go around doing that to people?

"Eustace doesn't think it's acceptable. Not at all. And he had a word with the bloke who he asked to help him out.

194

All Eust was after was humiliation: the uniform and the acorns, tied up to one of the tree stumps that he damaged. But according to Eust's bloke the youth tried to fight back, there was self-defence involved and the youth ended up with a black eye because Eust's bloke had to knock him out. He didn't want to and Eust specifically said that wasn't what was wanted. It got out of hand. But then it's likely to when you're dealing with lowlifes, isn't it?" Guy put a hand on my shoulder. "Seriously, my Highland Beauty, don't spend any more time fretting about it. It wasn't how things were supposed to be. Eustace was as shocked as you are and I know that it won't happen again."

What could I say to argue against that? It was perfectly reasonable. Of course Eustace wasn't in the business of ordering *hits* on people. Why on earth would a middle-aged, loud-trouser-wearing man with a reputation to keep up do a thing like that? OK, so there was also the case of the hoarded police signs... No. I would have to let it go.

"And..." I said, "there is one more thing."

I leant across him and over to the dashboard.

"Wh— Edda what are you – you can't do that! What is that?"

"It's Xfm."

"But I was enjoying the jazz."

"And I wasn't. So, can we try something new, please?"

Guy looked genuinely thunderstruck. "Well. I suppose so. And what is this Xfm?" he asked, and then a moment later, "Oh dear God, Edda! Really? This is really better? But it's just noise!"

"No it's Kasabian. Now drive! Drive! I need to fling!"

It was good. Really good. The music was thumping, I'd lower the windows as we cruised by and *fling,* one wildflower meadow here, *fling,* another wildflower meadow there. I was a seed-filled-condom God of Creation. In Ladywell, we circled a run-down traffic island two, three, four times as I bombed it repeatedly, covering it with seeds and a meadow for the future, but leaving the more immediate impression that some sort of orgiastic romp had taken place in the middle of the Ladywell traffic system.

"Five left in the box!" I shouted above the music as the old Lincoln Continental pulled out of Ladywell.

"Lewisham, then." Guy screeched the car down the hill towards the town, slowing to merge in with other traffic. "You'll have to be careful, here, that you don't get caught throwing the green grenades. Look behind you before you throw."

"Head for the station, there's derelict land near there!" I shouted over the Chemical Brothers. The Lincoln Continental veered off towards St John's and Lewisham station.

"Police!" Guy was looking in his mirror. "I'll circle the roundabouts to let them pass."

Seed bombing in Lewisham was impossible. It was midnight, but there were people on the streets and cars and buses and bikes on the roads. It felt as if the whole of London had come to Lewisham that evening. "Now!" Guy lowered my window and I hurled out a bomb at a barren traffic island, quickly undoing the next bomb so that I was ready.

"Now!"

I was loving it but terrified of getting caught, knowing there were cars behind us and pedestrians beside us who must have seen me, but these were the last of the bombs and I didn't care. I hurled them across the carriageways and watched the tiny seeds scatter in a slow arc and the condom fall half emptied to the ground.

"Done!" I laughed, brushing my seed-covered hands out of the window and then I raised it, turning to look at Guy, who had been laughing too, caught up in the thrill of driving this beast of a car and the fear of getting caught throwing loaded condoms.

In a squeal of tyres we sped out of Lewisham up the Blackheath road, leaving the main route and taking a series of smaller and smaller roads until we pulled up on a rough track near the Heath behind a line of trees.

I still had the box on my knee, empty except for a scattering of seeds and, found at the bottom, three still-packeted condoms. I held them in the palm of my hand and looked up at my partner in crime.

"You haven't used these," I said.

"Not yet." Guy wrenched on the handbrake. "Onto the back seat with you."

I couldn't call Beth again could I?

Could I?

I looked at the phone on the table.

No. I couldn't.

I could!

I dialled her number. Her mobile was ringing without

going through to voicemail and I'd already left messages on her home phone.

Oh my God, Beth, it was amazing. Guy had me – had me in the back of a 1971 Lincoln Continental. OK, never mind the car, actually. Guy had me, he had me and it was amazing, call me, call me, call me, because I really need to— BEEP

OK, Beth, it's me again. What I was going to say was I went on this bombing raid around Brockley and it was awesome and I threw a green grenade into your garden so there'll be a wildflower meadow in six months, but you'll be gone anyway, but— BEEP

God, Beth, get your answerphone sorted out it keeps cutting out after a few seconds. Just call me, OK, I really, really want to talk to someone about Guy. Actually I need to talk to you, honey, oh please answer the goddamn phone will you? It was so amazing. OK, I'm going before the stupid— BEEP

Urgh. What was the good of it all if I had no one to talk to about it? Where was Beth when I needed her? She'd love to know about this: it was exactly the sort of thing we'd spend all day Saturday at V-2 talking about. Except this was so much more exciting than anything we had ever talked about at V-2 on a Saturday morning.

A door shut upstairs and I leapt off the bar stool, clutching my chest. And then I remembered: Robert! I'd completely forgotten that I'd got a lodger. How loud had my voice been when I'd left the messages for Beth? What had Robert heard?

"Hi," he padded down the stairs with Fin draped over his shoulder. "Have fun last night?"

"Yes!" I said, alarming him with the force of my response. "Yes," I added more calmly.

"Great. Look, I'm off to the supermarket. Do you need anything?"

Didn't he want to ask me about last night? Didn't he want to know anything about the mysterious man at the door, the one who had kissed me violently? Or why I was called out so late and where I went until three in the morning? Wasn't he at least curious? Couldn't he see I was positively *exploding* in my desire to tell someone all about it?

"Bran flakes?" I said, in my best woe-is-me voice.

I stood aside and let him pass. *Great* I thought as I paced the empty kitchen. I was being upstaged by J Sainsbury.

"ROBERT!" I pelted down the knot garden and threw myself at the windscreen of his Beetle. "Sorry! I forgot to ask, what happened to the potatoes? Did the gardener's wife get a full roast dinner?"

He grinned and started up the engine. "They had their roast potatoes."

"Well, thank God for that!" I stood back to let him go, suddenly deliriously happy for no good reason, waving him off down the road before walking back into the house.

"Ah, young love!" Babs sighed, phlegmily, from her doorway.

"Afternoon, Babs."

"Are yer free darlin'?"

"Ye-es...?"

"Fancy a cuppa?"

I did a double take. "Wh— in your house?"

Babs snorted. "Well we can 'ave it in the street if yer want to darlin'. But I'd like yer to meet someone." The last words were said in a hoarse whisper.

I glanced down the street towards Fox Estates, in case Eustace was buffing the silver chains on his bay trees and watching the goings on in Brockley with his beady eyes. There was no one about: the coast was clear. "Sure."

Babs led me to a front room that looked as though a chintz explosion had taken place: any surface that took fabric was covered in a vomit of florals. And, once my eyes had become accustomed to it all, I noticed a disaffected youth lounging with intent amid the blossoms on a squashy sofa. He licked the edge of a cigarette paper and completed what I presumed was an enormous spliff.

"Hi," I said, trying for cool but not getting even remotely close to it.

"'S up." He said and lit the spliff.

We looked at each other for a moment. I tried to conjure up my inner fire and militant personality so as to at least not feel completely square. "You must be Tyrone."

He gave a slight, disaffected, nod.

"Here we are, here we are," with a fag clamped between her lips Babs shuffled into the room carrying an Eternal Beau tray laden with a tea pot, cups, saucers and plates all in matching Eternal Beau. "So you've now met my 'Roney. My little Notorious Baron ain't yer? Tea, Edda? Milk? Sugar? Digested biscuit, darlin'?"

She gestured for me to take a seat on the rose-covered sofa opposite Da Notorious Baron.

What would Eustace Fox – just metres down the road in his office – give to sit where I was sitting right now, in front of Enemy Number One.

"So, 'Roney loved what yer did on the stencil, didn't yer darling?" she patted the knee of her drug-smoking grandson. "Thought it was the dog's bollocks that's what yer said, wasn't it?"

"It was all right. Yeah." He looked over to me. "You got trainin' in art and stuff?"

"No. Well A-level, you know. Not art school. Erm."

"It was good. Yeah." He flicked ash into an Eternal Beau ashtray. "It was still mine, though. It was still my work and, like, my ideas and shit but you gave it that edge. Y'know?"

"Yes. Absolutely." I nodded profusely.

"It was as good as anything *he* would—" Babs began.

"Nan! You know we ain't talkin' about 'im!"

"I was only sayin'," Babs held up a hand, "That it's as good as what *he* does." Tyrone glared at his nan and then relit his spliff. While he was occupied with the lighter Babs looked over to me, winked, and mouthed, *Banksy.*

The room was filling with the thin coils of smoke and I was starting to feel odd. "Well I'm glad you liked it," I said. "And it's really nice to meet you, Tyrone, but I ought to—"

"I've got more." Tyrone leant forward towards me, for the first time, looking straight at me. "An' I was wonderin' if you want to cut 'em? I ain't got no patience to cut 'em, and Nan ain't got no skill."

"Oh 'Roney!"

"Well you ain't, Nan," he said, and then added, "but yer make a good roast dinner."

"Ah, me boy." She patted his knee again. "Yer like yer roast beef an' all the trimmin's eh?"

"So, do yer wanna do it?" Tyrone looked at me, as did Babs.

Oh God. I sat on my floral sofa and squirmed. How do you turn down someone like Tyrone? And what would Babs say if I didn't agree to help her grandson? She'd assume I had gone over to the other side and was a close personal friend of Eustace Fox, even though I kept denying it. There would be frosty stares across the garden wall…

But then – as the thoughts raced around in my head – it occurred to me that maybe it wasn't such a very *terrible* thing to be doing after all. Da Notorious Baron's graffiti was going to be around Brockley whether I helped out or not. And it was very, very bad. But by helping out I might actually make it easier on the eye: didn't Eustace say he wasn't against graffiti per se, but wanted to improve it? So, really, if I did do this I would be helping Eustace out. In a very indirect, warped-logic sort of a way…

I left Babs and Tyrone with a muddled head and a handful of plastic-coated sheets of paper roughly drawn with future graffiti destined for the wider neighbourhood. Bolting around the front garden gates, in case Eustace was lurking, I dashed through my knot garden and into my house. If Eustace ever discovered I was connected to Da Notorious Baron, goodness knows what would happen. I put the sheets on the kitchen table and spread them out to see the tasks ahead. "Oh bloody hell." I sank down onto the bar stool, my head in my hands. Somehow I had craft-knifed my way into the criminal underworld.

Fifteen

"Oh my God and everything! This is *so* bad."

Amanda and I were in John Lewis and Amanda was cornered like a wild animal, trapped between a rail of pink tweed suits and a rail of lemon twin-sets. She tried to make a dash towards the Warehouse concession, but I grabbed her and pinned her to a rail of belted pea-green coats.

"OK," I said, soothingly, leading her out of the Jaeger section, "we might have got a bit lost, this isn't quite what we're looking for."

"Well thank *fuck* for that, then." She clung to me, still looking terrified by the mother-of-the-bride collections around her. "Like, at what point in your life do you start dressing like the Queen? *Bleurgh!*"

"Actually, I quite like that dress," I said, following her horrified expression. "But then I am very old."

"You're not as old as Max." She released her grip as we passed the Whistles rails. "He's fifty-four can you believe that? I can't believe I'm seeing a man who's fifty-four. But he's really fit. 'Cause I thought he'd be all wrinkled down there…" and so it went on, as it had been going on all morning in the office and now after work in the shops on Oxford Street. But I didn't mind:

not in the least, because Amanda was positively *glowing* with happiness. The last guy she'd dated had been a twenty-two year old joiner from Lewisham who had a tattoo of a urinating bulldog on his arm. He drank lager and punched people in the face late at night. Max, on the other hand, had taken her to see his friends acting at the Criterion, wined and dined her and introduced her to the art of *strolling through London parks on Sunday afternoons.*

"So, how does he want you to dress?" I asked her as we stopped at the Jigsaw rails. "What did he say?"

"Nothing." She looked slightly non-plussed by the question.

"Oh. So…"

"It's me. *I* want to look different."

"Why? Don't you think he likes you how you are?"

"Oh God, yeah! He's always saying how like amazing I look and stuff. But, like, all the people in the restaurants or in the cafés or wherever we are, they all look different to me and they look at me, like, *urgh* and everything and, if I have to be honest, I don't hate what they're wearing. Some of them. So, if I could just look a little bit less like *urgh* and a bit more classy then that might be good. But there is, like, no way I'm doing the full Buckingham-Palace and wearing pastel suits."

Two hours later, exhausted, we stumbled into Browns.

"Come on then, what star sign is he?" In between ordering and the food arriving Amanda had whipped out a handbag sized *Cosmo.*

"Who?"

"That artist bloke you're shagging! The one you've been telling me about."

"What, Guy? I have no idea what his star sign is."

"OK, so when's his birthday? We can like work his star sign out. Then we can see if you two are compatible."

"It's not that sort of relationship. It's not serious or anything. It's just a bit of fun."

"So it's, like, totally casual." She said, returning the magazine to her handbag with a look of disappointment.

"Very."

"And you're happy with that?"

"Ye-es…" Should I not be?

"Be careful of the rebound… Haven't you read any of the articles I left for you? I mean, like, at your age don't you need—"

"Excuse me," I held up a hand, "I don't think you are at all qualified to discuss age with me any more, seeing as you're dating someone who'll be almost a pensioner before you're my age."

"Max Willoughby!" She yelped and clapped her hands together. "Isn't it incredible? Anyway," she settled herself down and took another sip of her wine, "Let's focus on your bloke, because that sounds very exciting. You at least know his surname, yeah?"

"Newhouse."

"There then! You're like a proper married couple and everything. What's his job? Oh artist – yeah you've told me. Do you know where he lives?"

"No. Somewhere in Brockley."

"And you've not checked his address out on the Council database at work because…?"

"Because that's creepy and stalking," I said. And then added, "Actually it's because I didn't think of it."

"So no phone number either?"

"No."

"Email address?"

I considered it for a moment. "Sort of. I can get in touch with him online, but it's a forum that everyone can see."

"So how do you get in touch with him when you want some action?"

"It's not all about getting some action," I said. "We're part of a group, so I see him when I see them."

"Jeez that is, like, *totally* casual! Has he got a girlfriend already or something? Is there a reason he's keeping you at arm's length?"

"He's – he's not…"

Her words knocked the stuffing out of me. Maybe he had got a girlfriend! Here was I thinking that, hey, it was casual, but he was an artist and artists were like that. Probably. And besides that it was just the start of something much more. Wasn't it?

But now, being served my rocket and prosciutto pizza, I got the uncomfortable feeling that maybe *this was it*. I was a bit on the side. And there was someone else who had a relationship with him. So what we had – if *we* had anything – would never amount to more than this. Because I was just a bit on the side. The bastard. The next dig was in a week's time at Hilly Fields at the south end of Brockley. Guy was supposed to be calling for me: should I bring up the girlfriend subject then? Should I nip this thing in the bud straight away?

"So Robert's, like, totally happy living with you." Amanda blew on her forkful of lasagne. "You getting on OK, then?"

"Great. Smashing." I answered, and then forced myself to focus on what I was saying and not dwell on the thought of being nothing but Guy's bit on the side. "My cat Finley has adopted him. He doesn't want to know me any more."

"Shit. You keep getting abandoned don't you?" Amanda said absentmindedly.

"Yeah. Thanks."

"Oh, no I'm only joking! So does Robert mention me? Does he say anything about his dad?" she played it cool but I could tell she was dying of curiosity.

"To be honest, Amanda, it's sort of a subject we avoid. Sorry," I added, seeing her disappointment.

"OK. Well, it's probably, like, for the best and everything. Anyway, I bought this magazine because of you." She made room on the table and brought the magazine out again. "OK, so we don't know much more than like his name so we can't do star signs, but here's a quiz to see if you and your bloke are properly in love or not."

"Oh I *hate* those quizzes. They always tell me I'm a complete failure."

Amanda ploughed on regardless. "'What would you most like people to say about you both? A. you look great

208

together, B. you are great together, or C. you're so cool together.'"

"Well we're sort of secret. So we don't want anyone to know we're together. Is there an option for 'none of the above'?"

"Why don't you want anyone to know?"

"It's not that sort of circle of friends."

"Hmm. OK, next question: 'would you feel the same about him if he lost all his hair? A. it would be over, B. it wouldn't change a thing, C. what hair, he's bald and toothless and I love him.'"

"'A'. That's bad, isn't it?"

"You shouldn't be predicting the results. OK, next one, 'If he were to dump you tomorrow, would you A. feel cross that you'd wasted a chunk of your life dating him, B. go into mourning for the remembrance of him or C. pursue him relentlessly with every fibre of your being.'"

"Can we have a 'D' in there? I think I'm more of a D."

"There is no D, Edda."

"Well there is now. 'D, we're not official so it's easy come easy go. I'd be cool about it, I think.'"

"Yeah. Whatever. Next question, 'When you're together for a long amount of time, like a long weekend, do you A. drive each other nuts, B. enjoy every moment, C. get upset that it's going to come to an end?'"

"D. We aren't together for long periods of time."

"Edda, you cannot have D! There is no D!"

"I can. I am empowered and I create my own path. Look here," I snatched the magazine off her and held it aloft like a weighty tome, "Mostly D's: you're casual and in control of a hot one. He's definitely not seeing anyone else and you're both very happy. Well done."

"Max said, like, you're a comedian and everything." Amanda pointed her butter knife at me. "He said you look like someone who would seek solace in comedy, but that's not always the way out you know. You have to face up to things. You so have to be serious."

"Oh who cares about that? Here, smell my flower button-hole."

It was quarter to one in the morning and I didn't feel like seeking solace in comedy one bit. Because I was trapped. Trapped upstairs on the first floor of my house with no prospect of escape.

Dressed head to toe in black with a scruffy up-do and vampy smoky eyes I was all set to go but couldn't get to the front door. The way was blocked. I'd spent the entire evening fretting about Guy: did he have a girlfriend, was I just a bit on the side ... but now my bit-on-the-side fretting was being cast aside in favour of fretting that I wasn't actually going to make it out at all. Who cared if Guy already had a girlfriend? I was an enforced Miss Havisham on the first floor, unable to leave.

Crouched low on the landing floor I peered through the banisters, down towards the kitchen. Below me was my captor – Robert – keeping me captive *by making himself toast.*

Inching forward to the top stair I watched as he fumbled the loaf, made several attempts to post the slices into the toaster slots and then staggered round the kitchen in search of a spread. He had been out all evening at the pub with his mates and it showed.

I had to stop myself laughing, clamping a hand to my mouth, as I watched him wrench open the jar of malt and attempt to spread it on his blackened toast.

"What the *fuck...*" he stared at the goopy brown stuff dripping from his knife where he'd expected to see the firm paste of chocolate spread. He tried it. He liked it. Then he set about enthusiastically malting all the toast, his plate and the table before pulling up a chair and tucking in.

I checked my watch, angling the face of it to catch the light from the kitchen below. It was almost 1am. Guy would be here any minute. The thought of him sent my pulse racing, picturing him striding through the dark streets towards me, glossy black hair streaming from his handsome face. The twinkle in his eyes when he first catches sight of me, walking arm to arm, the feel of his body beside mine...

I had to get out! How was I going to get out of the house? Robert was between me and the front door. And the back door. There was no escape without passing through the kitchen and confronting him and what reason would I give for looking like I did and going out?

"You know," Robert called up from the kitchen, making me jump. "I may be the worse for wear, Edda, but I can see you hiding up there!" He hiccupped and looked straight at me, raising his dripping malty toast in a salute.

"Oh." I stood up and descended the stairs with as much dignity as I could muster. "I didn't want to surprise you."

Robert stopped mid-bite as I approached. "Oh my God, you look beautiful! *Sorry!* Sorry I'm drunk! Ignore me! You look *nice*. Just nice. Very nice. Have you been out? Did you decide to go out? Where did you go?" Red-faced he focused on his dripping toast.

"I thought I might go out now."

"Now?" he squinted at the clock. "Now? But it's – it's half – it's quarter half past, half to … it's *late*."

"I—"

There was a soft knock on the front door.

"I have to go," I threw on my coat and grabbed the front door key. "Don't wait up."

"You look good," Guy said as I closed the door behind me, "Good enough to eat. And I like the hair. Funky."

"Thanks," I said and *do you have a girlfriend … am I something on the side* hung in the air unsaid.

Any hopes I had, of a romantic tête-à-tête during our walk to the dig site at Hilly Fields, were destroyed by the fact that Guy was receiving endless text messages to which he was responding immediately. "It's Eustace," he said as he tapped in a reply, "he's remote managing as usual…"

I walked in silence beside him thinking deep thoughts. Guy had said I looked good enough to eat and Robert had said I looked beautiful! Robert thought I looked beautiful…

I smiled as I strode beside the texting Guy, down the near deserted streets towards Hilly Fields.

"Don't do that!" Guy said, grabbing my hand and pushing it down.

212

"I was only waving," I said. "And it was only to Mr Iqbal—"

"Well just don't look at him. Don't draw attention to us. We are a secret society for a reason."

"But I always wave to Mr Iqbal: he'd think it was odd if I walked past and didn't. He'd want to know why I blanked him. *That* would be drawing attention to us."

"Seriously, Edda: don't wave."

We continued down the High Road, Guy texting Eustace some sort of thesis.

"My friend's gaff," Guy looked up as we passed a grotty old pub that was in the process of being stripped out and renovated. "He's opening a bistro soon: something ultra funky for Brockley. I've been commissioned for the art work but I can't start it for another month yet – I'm just too successful, busy with my own commissions."

I did a double take. Did he really just say that? But then artists did have a reputation for being self-assured.

"Isn't that shop also new?" I pointed out a bookshop that had appeared where the kebab house had been as little as a month ago. "I liked that kebab house," I said, but to no one as Guy's phone had beeped once more and he was engrossed in replying. I stared at the new shop as we passed it. It had a very familiar look to it: was it a book shop chain? But then I realised why it was familiar: it looked almost exactly like the florist's beside Mr Iqbal's, and Mr Iqbal's too, now that it was a Mini Marché or whatever he'd called it. Because it was painted in a similar dark muted shade of grey and had the two bay trees out at the front. Did all the new businesses in Brockley have to put bay trees outside their premises? Was it a requirement from the Council? Was it a particular demand by Peter "Moses" Shaw that culinary foliage be on display?

We were leaving the shops behind and the road widened out with trees on either side. It was a mild night, still damp from earlier rain and the earthy smells struck me: the memory of the smell of the countryside: Leicestershire ... Beth ...We were almost at Hilly Fields. And now there were others on the street walking in the same direction. On a late night return from the pub I would be skirting the hoodies and yardies in an attempt to avoid having a yellow police sign experience, but tonight the pavements were overtaken by guerrilla gardeners: small gangs of the Boden-clad middle classes armed with Cath Kidston gardening equipment and Fat Face jumpers. There was no glint of a knife in the street light: tonight the only glints came off Rolex watches or designer glasses.

"Do you ever come across any violence on these digs?" I asked Guy, taking advantage of a text-free moment.

"What do you mean?" Guy looped his arm around my waist.

"Erm," the seriousness of the question was utterly ruined by the effect of an arm around my waist, "you know ... from the gangs."

"Any violence? Not really." He said distractedly and then pulled me closer, kissing me. But then came the now familiar beep of his phone which put paid to any conversation.

Not *really*? What did that mean? Did that mean there was moderate violence? Or there was occasional serious violence?

We walked further up the road, Guy busy texting and me silent – thoughts running amok in my head. I recalled the meeting beneath the Working Men's Club when one of the guerrilla gardeners had mentioned an *incident involving youths*. I remembered the reaction from heavy-man Jake – his ominous gravelly laugh – and then the way in which Eustace had rapidly changed the subject. Did this mean that there had actually been trouble with the South London gangs? That something had happened? Because the odds were on there being trouble for people hanging around this part of South London in the dead of night … it was a wonder we'd got away with it at the station dig. Or was Eustace taking care of that side of things…

"Look at that," Guy pointed to a post box, "Eust's not going to be overly impressed by that right next to a dig site."

"About wh—" and then I saw my kissing-women stencil and felt a sudden stab of pride. That was my work and it looked fantastic. Every detail of the stencil had come out perfectly and Da Notorious Baron had signed below with a flourish.

"Still," Guy paused to examine it, "the artist looks like he's improving. It's no Banksy but it's got merit."

"I think it's very good." I said. "Although I completely agree with Eustace, of course…"

We had arrived at Hilly fields and Guy didn't pursue

the conversation. The black van was there, the black-clad people were there, gathered together and in hushed conversation.

"Better go rally the troops," Guy said and was gone.

I was prepared for the dig this time: I'd read the blog and looked up the plans online and didn't have to rely on paying attention to Guy to know what to do. I was down on the plans to work with a man called Roger Wendell, renovating an old bench and bringing it back into use.

"Bloody stupid task for guerrilla gardeners," Roger moaned, after we'd pulled the bench out of thick brambles, cutting ourselves to ribbons. "The thing's practically *organic* it's so rotten." We dragged it clear and began to examine it properly in torchlight.

"I think it's going to be fine," I said. "It's got flaky paintwork and looks bad on the surface but it's sturdy enough underneath."

But Roger continued moaning, going on about *pointless bloody deployment* and Eustace *pushing the damn boundaries*, using phrases and words which made perfect sense when he told me, between moans, that he was a broadsheet journalist.

"I mean, how are we supposed to execute the stripping and painting of a bloody bench in the pitch dark? The task's illogicality itself. This isn't what I signed up for! I wanted to plant—"

"Well I'm sure it will make a difference," I cut him off. "Now, let's think this through…"

The dig at Hilly Fields was a variation on what we'd done before: *guerrilla market gardening* Guy called it. Eustace in full Victorian philanthropic mode wanted to educate the masses in the benefits of a healthy diet. "Some of them," he'd blogged, "only ever encounter potatoes in chipped form," and for that reason we were taking up half an acre of the sweep of Hilly Fields for tomatoes, potatoes, pumpkins, beans and on the far side redcurrants, blackcurrants, raspberries and strawberries. "We will combine the transformation of an area of simple grass into a potager of great beauty," his blog had continued, "with the practicality of providing nutrition to the masses. In this dig we will deliver to the people of Brockley on two levels."

So, watching the team begin cutting into the grass to create the fruit and vegetable patches why didn't I feel doubly enthusiastic? Perhaps I wasn't so convinced by this dig because it wasn't a tatty traffic island or weed-covered approach to the station. Hilly Fields was already beautiful, and the allotment, which is what it sounded like to me, was going to be an anomaly cut into the side of it. This was Eustace imposing himself on something that didn't need him, it was nice enough already: wasn't he going too far?

Suddenly the vast empty silence of Hilly Fields was filled with sharp rasping. All the gardeners had stopped to look at us.

"Shit!"

Roger had started sanding the bench then instantly stopped: "Well, no one bloody well thought that through," he threw down the sandpaper and block. "Stupid bloody idea!"

Guy was running over to us. "You can't do that any more."

"No shit, Sherlock," Roger said. "The whole scheme here isn't on, if you ask me, Guy. What the bloody hell was Eust thinking when—"

"Why don't we try and muffle the sanding?" I took the blanket we had been using to cover the ground from paint splashes and gingerly tried to sand with the blanket smothering it. It deadened the noise enough to not draw too much attention to us.

"Better. Good." Guy planted a kiss on my forehead and walked off.

After an hour of muted sanding followed by painting, Roger and I admired the end result.

"I know how you feel about renovating the bench," I said to Roger, not without a hint of sarcasm, "but I do think it's worthwhile bringing something like this back into use. It's beautiful: someone will enjoy using it."

"Someone did enjoy using it," Roger said as he pulled a screwdriver out of his pocket and ran it along the edge of a plaque fixed onto the bench back.

In memory of Paul Amos, who loved this park, 1911 – 1988.

"You're not really going to take that off are you?"

"This? Of course I'm going to! Nasty cheap thing," Roger said prising it free. "It's not even brass it's just plastic. Now, take a look here," he handed me a heavy brass disc that I angled to the far off street light. *Restored by The Brockley Spades, 2011.* "See? That's quality right there."

"But don't you think it's sacrilegious removing the old plaque?"

"Not at all. Eustace wants to leave a calling card and this is it. He's the boss…"

"But what about Paul Amos? His family must have paid for the bench."

"Then his family should have looked after the bench," Roger threw the plaque into a nearby bin. "And not been so bloody cheap with the plastic plaque. Now hurry up; let's get the second coat on before Neil cracks open the cake tin. I missed out on the bloody chocolate muffins on the last dig and it bloody well isn't going to happen again I can tell you." He re-opened the can of Farrow and Ball's Carriage Green and we painted in long smooth strokes, painting by sense in the dark, pretty much unable to make out where the first coat ended and the second coat began. Thankfully, we were working in silence, lost in our own thoughts at three in the morning: me dreaming about Guy, while Roger, no doubt, contemplated his God-given right to the muffins.

"Would you look at that! Just look at them going for the cake! Outrageous!" Roger thrust his brush angrily into the paint can. "Gannets. That's what they are. Bloody gannets!"

I followed his line of sight – Neil and Anja had set up the table of cakes and drinks and the gardeners working nearby had swarmed around them.

"You go," I said, gathering the tools together. "I'm not bothered about chocolate muffins."

"Selfish bloody gannets." Roger was already moving. "I'll save you one shall I?" He streaked across the grass in a blur of pent-up middle class rage.

I had to stop myself laughing out loud at the sight of him speed-walking to the muffins. God help the others if they'd run out of food by the time he'd made it over there.

Paul Amos's plaque was lying on top of the rubbish in the adjacent bin. Without thinking, I picked it up and slipped it in to my jacket pocket.

Traipsing over the dark field to the van, I could see Roger standing smug and superior with a chocolate muffin clamped in each hand. I ducked around the group to avoid him: an hour and a half in his company was more than enough. I crept over to the refreshment table from the other side.

"How's it going, babe?" Anja handed me a hot chocolate.

"OK. I'm exhausted though – and covered in Carriage Green. Has Eustace been round? I haven't seen him."

"Not tonight." Neil pressed a cake into my hands. "He's put Guy in charge of this one 'cause he's got some Council function to attend this evening. Eustace doesn't give up the social events: network, network, network!" Anja punched him in the ribs and he shut up. "Yeah. OK. Sorry. Forget that, man," he muttered. "Eustace is brilliant. Enjoy the fairy cake, yeah?"

"Hi," Guy was beside me and made me jump. "Enjoying the cakes?"

220

"I will do," I said, wrenching the paper off. Roger had a point: by three in the morning you *do* feel it's a God-given right to have cake for your trouble. I bit into it and it was beyond good. Moist and sweet and the perfect thing for a cold spring morning spent in hard physical labour.

"I saw your bench."

I had a mouth full of cake so all I could manage was, "Mmm. Nd?"

"It's excellent. You and Rog have done a good job."

"There is one thing actually," I said, when I'd swallowed the wedge of lemon icing.

"And that is?"

"Eustace is having us put a plaque on the bench."

Guy considered what I'd said. "I know."

"You do?"

"I do."

"And you know that the plaque names us as the Brockley Spades."

"Believe me, Edda," a weary sounding Guy said, "I've been over it many times before. This isn't the first time he's wanted to sign the artwork, if you see what I mean."

"But if he names us, then people will get to know of us and it's only a matter of time, surely, before our cover is blown."

Guy leant in, his mouth against my ear, whispering, "That's the problem with dealing with egotists like Eustace Fox," he said the last three words in nothing but a whisper, his lips brushing my ear. "But forget all that and come back to my place, my fiery red-head."

Sixteen

Beth's mother did it and my aunt did it: filling perfectly acceptable silences with inane chat. It was something Beth and I had vowed would never ever happen to us when we grew up, along with *making small talk with waiters* and *smiling at complete strangers in the street.* The last one was a guaranteed no-no: in South London smiling at a stranger would end up with becoming a statistic recorded in one of the yellow police signs that so irritated Eustace: *Smiling Woman Set Upon, any witnesses…*

But now, at four in the morning and with dawn breaking behind us Guy and I were striding back to his place with all the promise that that brought. And I was filling what would have been a deliciously charged silence with inane chat.

What the *hell* was wrong with me?

Probably, it was because I was so ecstatically happy that Guy was taking me back to his place and all that that meant. He really might not have a girlfriend after all … it was all I could do to stop myself skipping along beside him and bursting into song. Which would have been worse than inane chatter. But only just.

"Oh, just look at the beautiful colour of the sky," I gushed. "And the birds are waking up. It's amazing. Don't you think? Wow the sky is a sort of peachy colour isn't it what colour would you say it is?"

Guy shot me the look I so deserved.

But it *was* so beautiful that it just had to be talked about. How often was the sky the same colour as a perfect ripened nectarine? And I had never seen the streets and houses look so unreal as they did at that moment, like a dream sequence in a film. Maybe it was just nerves that were making me chatter on. I wasn't very comfortable with silences. Summoning up all my willpower I forced myself to shut the hell up and enjoy the walk in a dignified manner.

"This way," Guy said after a few minutes, reaching out for my hand and pulling me down a gravelled lane between two vast white villas. He kept hold of me, his fingers closed tight over my own. The lane turned to run behind the villas and on either side high yellow-brick walls closed us in, honeysuckles and jasmines tumbling over from the gardens behind.

"It's beautiful!" I said – I couldn't help myself – and Guy laughed, pulling me onwards.

The lane was widening and in a few more steps a group of buildings came into view – old coach houses huddled beneath oak trees like a miniature secret village. The world of guerrilla gardening was opening my eyes to a parallel Brockley: one that had existed side by side with my old mundane world and Babs' grittier version. Eustace Fox had been right: Brockley was a *gem*.

We had reached the nearest coach house. "This is my place." Guy bent down to a geranium pot and took a large iron key from beneath it. "Welcome to my home!" He unlocked the door and stood aside to let me in.

It was tiny: just one loft-style room with a kitchen at one end, and an old leather sofa on the opposite side in front of a giant wood burner. But it oozed cool: the walls were bare brick, the wood floor was waxed and right before us an old iron spiral staircase wound up to a mezzanine level.

Guy closed the door and I turned to face him. For a moment we stood before one another then he reached over and began to pop open the buttons on my jacket, one by one, easing it off my shoulders and letting it fall to the floor where it lay crumpled on the doormat.

He was asleep. Beautifully asleep. His black hair curled and twisted on the white pillow obscuring his face. I watched him, unmoving, for what seemed like an hour, running a finger over my stubble-chafed lips.

He really was completely and utterly beautiful and, asleep, there was a vulnerability beneath his artistic swagger: finally I had seen the man beneath the Milk Tray.

The change in him had been so sudden: one minute he was a black-eyed animal and now, a few hours later, he was just an innocent dark-haired boy asleep on his pillow.

I lay back down and stared up at the ceiling.

It was strung with fairy lights criss-crossing between the wooden beams. How many women, I wondered, had looked up and seen those fairy lights? How many women had watched this man sleep? I propped myself up. Guy stirred. I watched him again for a moment, hoping he would wake up. But no: he was fast asleep and no matter how beautiful he was there was only so long I could watch him. So I turned my attention to the room itself.

His bedroom was on the mezzanine level, overlooking the open plan living area downstairs. The bedroom extended as far as the iron bed and the large shaggy rug it stood on. After that the space narrowed to a long strip running against one wall which was his studio – benches lined the vast-windowed walls, cluttered with paint, brushes, rags. Silently, I swung my legs out of bed and padded over to the studio, naked. It was liberating, being naked in an artist's studio. And kind of appropriate too, after having slept with the artist. Having spent a night illegally gardening under the stars.

How my life was changing now that Beth had left me…

The first painting I saw was of a boy, grinning at the artist. It was painted in blocks of blues and whites. It was clever. Guy had captured the picture using only bold colour blocks. I placed it back down on the work bench and looked beside it. There was a photograph of the sitter. And attached to it was a letter.

Dear Sir
Please find enclosed a photograph of the subject – my son Jonnie. As requested, the walls and ceiling of the room in which we'd like to hang the picture are painted in F&B Dimity, Skylight and Lulworth Blue.

Please find also enclosed a cheque for two thousand pounds, as per your instructions.
Sincerely yours
Imogen Whitel.

I replaced it and moved on. A pared down painting of a family group in whites and greens, details picked out in a deep cherry red. I skimmed the letter that lay beside it.

Dear Mr Newhouse ...my brother in law's family ... anniversary present ... Zoffany Fennel, Chalk and Berry ... cheque for two thousand pounds ...

And on. Canvases started. Canvases yet to be finished. Drip laden pots of designer emulsion in every possible colour. And by each canvas and its paint pots was the corresponding photograph and the letter. *Please find a photograph of my son, my daughter, my wife, my family, my dogs.* And the lists of the colours of the rooms in which the painting would hang. And always the cheque. For two thousand pounds.

There was a noise behind me and I turned. Guy had stirred but was still asleep. Hastily, I put back the letters and photographs. Was this wrong? Was I snooping? Surely not. Snooping was going into drawers or opening books. All I was doing was seeing what was laid bare on the benches. I was *surface snooping* which really wasn't snooping at all: it was just *showing an interest.* Yes – if he woke up now I'd simply tell him I was showing an interest in his talent.

I'd reached the end of the bench and had come to a giant parcel wrapped in thick brown paper and string, addressed to a Mrs Sittinghurst in Norfolk. Someone's completed masterpiece ready to be despatched. Above it, pinned to the wall, was a two-page newspaper article from the *Guardian* a few months earlier. I leant closer to read it.

FARROW AND BALL PORTRAITURE by the *Guardian*'s Arts Editor Roger Wendell

When is a painting not a painting? When it's the interior decoration too – how London-based artist Guy Newhouse bridges the gap between art and décor and has become one of the hottest things in the art world.

Roger Wendell! I did a double-take: Roger Wendell was surely the irritable man I'd spent the evening with painting the bench up on Hilly Fields. I scanned Roger's article which had pictures of Guy's various *works of art*, one in yellows, one in greys, the other in blues. And there was a photograph of Guy, taken just where I was standing. He was working at an easel with an intense and brooding expression, his hair tied roughly back. I looked over my bare shoulder at the man still asleep.

"I don't feel I've sold out," Newhouse said, *"It's a new direction in art. I began my emulsion portraits for a celebrity friend who wanted art but didn't want to compromise the look of his lounge by introducing a new colour palette to the room. The commissions came from*

that. I enjoy working within the constraints of the medium: of only having usually between three to six colours to work with to bring out a portrait. Sometimes as an artist the world is too full of possibilities." You can join the rich and famous by having your own portrait painted. Contact Guy by email via guy@emulsion portraiture.co.uk.

"The making of my fortune."

"Oh!" I stepped back, shocked. I hadn't heard him get up. He was beside me, naked, pressing against my bare skin, his hands snaking around me.

I could feel myself blushing. "I—"

"It's a living," he said as he pulled me back towards the bed. "It's money and I like money a lot. Now come back to bed and do that thing you did one more time. I also like that a lot."

Dammit. I'd left my phone in the kitchen at Guy's. I realised I'd left it when I'd shut the front door behind me and had walked about five steps. Dithering, in the gravelled lane, I'd finally decided to not knock on the door and get it back, firstly because it gave him a reason to come over to my house and drop it off … *hey, as you're here why don't we grab a bite to eat …* and secondly because he was probably fast asleep and waking him up wouldn't endear me to him. It would take the shine off his impression of me as a Highland-Clearance Honey: "scatty" didn't sit overly well with the vision of a woman with an inner inferno. The sky was black and already

228

drizzle was falling: it wouldn't do to stay outside his house and dither.

I arrived back at Geoffrey Road in a downpour, Finley sheltering under the enormous sundial and making a dash for the front door when I got my key out.

"Hello, boy." I rammed the key in the lock.

"Good night last night was it, darlin'?" I was heckled over the garden wall, Babs' voice carrying over the deafening hiss of rain on pavement.

"Morning, Babs." She was standing under her porch with the habitual fag in.

"Funeral was it then, love?"

"Pardon?" I shouted.

"You love, dressed all in black! Someone died?"

"No. I was out last night!"

"Anywhere nice?"

"Nowhere special. I have to … I have to feed the cat!" I shouted and darted into the house. It was my only defence against spilling the beans: having a conversation with Babs was like playing a game of tennis. I'd deflect and deflect and deflect every question she fed me and then *wallop* she'd catch me unawares with an innocuous little enquiry and I'd have told her everything I knew about guerrilla gardening, my deceased parents' fatal hobby and what I had for breakfast. Better to run away and hide.

"Oh Fin!" I got as far as the kitchen and stared in horror at the surrounding devastation. "What's happened here Fin?" My first thought was burglars. But the door had been locked and all the windows looked to be intact.

Then I thought it must have been caused by Finley. But *then* I realised that, actually, it had been caused by none other than Robert. The sticky black-covered work top and appliances were from Robert's fight with the malt in the early hours. The breakfast stool had toppled over and – my heart sank – my precious Valhalla plate had been knocked off the shelf and smashed into an unmendable amount of pieces. Putting down my bag I lifted up the larger shards of the plate and stared at them, running a thumb along the familiar bumps and grooves of the plate my parents had given me at my first Viking festival up in the Shetlands. I had been eight. I'd hated the festival and I'd hated the plate which was grey and green and brown and not dayglo pink, which was the only colour I was interested in as an eight year old.

I liked it now though.

One more tie to the past cut free…

"Oh bloody hell, Fin," I squatted down and scooped up the biggest shard which had "Halla" across it, propping it up against the window. With a heavy heart I swept the rest into the bin before making a coffee, sitting at the breakfast bar and watching the rain streaming down the French windows. I was tired, from a mostly sleepless night, and in the mood for feeling maudlin. I stared at the remaining shard of the Valhalla plate. The Vikings seemed a long way away now: it felt as though that life had been someone else's, the hog roasts, the horrible itchy clothes, heavy weaponry, the canvas tents that leaked and the terrible Viking longboat.

"Hi." Robert was beside me. I jumped: I'd been so caught up in the memories that I hadn't heard him.

"Hi." My stomach knotted. I was going to have to act the landlady about the broken plate and the state of the kitchen, but what the hell was I supposed to say? Should I tell him off, or talk through my issues, or what? What would Beth do? What – in fact – had I said to Beth that time she'd broken the shower door after one of our more epic nights out? I struggled to remember and then it came to me: I'd hit her with my pillow. OK, so perhaps not the most appropriate way to mete out punishment in this case.

Robert sat beside me on the old bench. I looked at him. And then I laughed.

"What is it? Are you laughing at me?" Robert suddenly looked alarmed.

I clamped my hand over my mouth. "I am. I'm sorry. It's just your hair … it's completely mad."

"Oh, goddamn it." He tried in vain to push it down.

"Good night was it?" I said.

"Erm. Yes. You?"

"The best. Really excellent. Really very good indeed." *Go on – ask me.*

There was a pause and Robert said, "I am so sorry about the state of the kitchen. I was completely pissed last night … well you know what state I was in… and I'll replace that plate I broke. I'm so sorry. I did try to start tidying up, but I was just doing more damage so I stopped."

"It's fine…" I began.

"Robert?"

We both turned to the door where a petite blonde thing was standing, wearing Robert's favourite pyjamas: the red ones with the pink stripes.

"Oh," I said.

"Hi. Sorry to disturb you but, Robert, where's the bathroom?"

I stared up at the miniature beauty on my kitchen threshold.

Had Robert spent the night with her? Why was she in my house? Had he slept with her?

Of course he had. What was I – Victorian? She would hardly have arrived this morning and put his pyjamas on – so, in that case, where had she been when he came in last night? Had she been in the kitchen when I'd left and I'd not noticed her? Did he make the malted toast for her? Did he go back to his room for malty fun when I was out digging up Brockley?

Was the pretty little thing a *girlfriend*?

"Here, I'll show you." Robert got up and walked off with her.

I watched them go. She was so petite. And so pretty. Even despite his baggy pyjamas I could see she had a stunning figure and her blonde hair was bed ruffled, just as his had been.

Oh. Oh. I went back to staring at the rain running in crazy patterns down the windows, my head completely empty of any thoughts whatsoever. And I was feeling dreadful: I needed sleep…

And then there was a loud knocking at the front door.

Guy!

I dashed to the hallway, not thinking to check my appearance in the hall mirror or lose the baggy cardigan. He must have woken up soon after I'd left him asleep in the rumpled bed, and seen my mobile – he *was* keen! He *did* like me. We could spend a lazy day arm in arm around Greenwich, looking at the markets, having a long lunch in one of the cafés...

I wrenched open the door.

"Hi there, Edda." It was Neil from V-2, sheltering from the downpour underneath a giant Fox Estates golfing umbrella. He gave a short laugh. "Well! It's good to see I haven't lost my ability to disappoint women."

"Oh, no, not at all." I adjusted my expression from *total disappointment* to *polite interest*. "Come in, I'm sorry, come in, come in out of the rain."

"I can't," he hopped from foot to foot and now I saw that he was looking stressed beyond belief. Gardening all night and then running a café from seven o'clock the next morning must be some sort of hell. "The thing is," he ran a hand through his already manic blonde afro, "two of the girls are off ill today and Anja and I just can't cope." He dropped his voice. "Especially after last night. You know, man? We haven't slept more than a few hours. Anja's had to crash: she's whacked out. So, I know you said you were maybe interested, you know, in getting some work experience at a café? Well I don't suppose you want to do it today ... do you?"

No no no no no no no! In my head I'd begun planning the most fabulous day with Guy. He would be round

233

imminently with my phone and then after showing him how grateful I was to have it back we would walk to Greenwich. We'd have dinner in Blackheath and then go back to his…

"…and we'd be so grateful," Neil was saying. "Please Edda."

I bit my lip. "Of course," I said, "I've got nothing planned. What time do you want me?"

There was a pause. "Ten minutes ago?"

"Fine. Right." I said. "Give me fifteen minutes."

"You're a star, Edda! A big, shiny, wonderful star!"

He bounded off through the rain-soaked knot garden, back in the direction of V-2.

"Cappuccino and latte to table five!" Neil thrust a tray at me and I took it and wound my way through the café. It was the fiftieth tray that morning, the ninetieth latte and the millionth cappuccino. I'd guerrilla gardened for half the night and spent the other half getting to know Guy, and now I was waitressing to a packed café. I was full-on exhausted and I knew I looked it: a glance in the mirror behind the counter and I was horrified by the hag staring back at me.

But, however awful I must have looked, Neil looked worse. Pinned to the espresso machine he had spent the entire morning grinding, steaming, stirring and then knocking out the grinds before starting all over again. His dreadlocked hair had gone stratospheric and there was a touch of insanity about his wide staring eyes. He looked, in fact, like someone suffering from incredible stress, preceded by a night of manual labour and not enough sleep.

"Here's the order for table two," Neil pushed a tray towards me. "They just need a slice of fudge cake. Can you bung it on?"

"Sure," I reached into the cake counter.

"Enjoying yourself, Edda?"

"Ye-es?"

Neil laughed. "It's not usually as mad as this. It's the rain – no one's going into the parks in this weather but they want to get out of the house."

"So everyone from Brockley has come here?"

"Pretty much. And it's just you and me." Neil added. "I'm so grateful, Edda. Honestly. And you're doing a fab job."

"Ha! Right – table two…"

I picked my way through the narrow spaces with the tray held high, coffee cups clinking against one another and the cake perilously close to the edge of the plate.

It was hard work and my feet ached, my back was sore but it was a hundred times better than typing up the minutes of meetings at the Council. I reached the table and handed out the order, before heading back to Neil for the next one.

What was holding me back from trying to make it as a café owner? Apart from money, that is …

"Excuse me, could I have a cloth?" a woman caught my attention, and I looked down to see her tiny red-faced daughter, bawling, covered in chocolate milk.

"Don't worry, I'll clean it up," I managed a smile and headed to the back room for a mop and bucket.

"Edda!" a hand grabbed me as I emerged into the café with the mop.

I stopped in my tracks. "Beth!"

"Edda, what are you doing here?" she looked incredulous.

"Oh." I stared at her, mop in one hand bucket in the other. "Cleaning."

"Yes I can see that … have you changed jobs? Have you finally gone and left the Council?"

"No, no, I'm helping a friend out. Neil." I gestured over to the coffee machine. "I'd mentioned my café-dream to him and, well, he needed emergency help today, so here I am."

Beth stood silently before me. "I didn't know you were friends with the owner of our café."

I leant in and whispered to her, "Through the gardening."

She was thoughtful again. "I feel like I don't know you any more." Her voice was wobbly and indistinct. "I had no idea you worked in our café. Or were friends with the owner."

I leant in to her again. "And I spent the night with Guy last night! Can you believe it? I—" I stopped when I saw the look on Beth's face.

"Are you *punishing* me?" she said and there were tears running down her face. "Is that what this is? Are you punishing me for having this baby and you think I'm

236

splitting us up? Is it all about that divorce thing your stupid new friend was talking about?"

"No! God no, Beth! Everything's been manic the last few weeks and I've *tried* to talk to you. Didn't you get my messages on the phone – I left at least three. But you're always out house hunting or going to baby classes and you're so busy…"

"Yes but … oh I don't know." She wiped the tears away with the sleeve of her maternity dress.

"Look, Beth, I was thinking, my café dream isn't going to realise itself. Do you want to come property hunting with me soon? We can do a tour of South East London looking for places I could open a café of my own."

"Like Greenwich or Blackheath?" she said, brightening.

"Not really. I was thinking more like Lee, or Catford, or somewhere up and coming. I'd never be able to afford anywhere in Greenwich or Blackheath."

Beth was grimacing. "Catford? Really? So you're looking for the next Brockley I suppose." She smiled, still teary.

"I am. And you can help me find it. If you want to?"

"Sure," she said. "Hey – talking of up-and-coming Brockley have you seen the bookshop where Al's kebabs used to be?"

"I have! And did you see the place opposite where the grubby pub used to be? Guy's friend is opening a bistro there in the next few days apparently."

Beth raised her eyebrows. "So are you and Guy an item?"

"I think so," I said. "But it's not really clear cut, you know how it is."

"I think I can remember those days," Beth looked slightly gloomy. "Eds, have you noticed that Brockley's changing really rapidly?" She looked out of the window towards Fox Estates and the florist's. "Your house is going to be worth a fortune if all this regeneration keeps on going. Did you get my text about the Mini Mart? It's gone French – I half imagined Mr Iqbal to come out from behind the counter in a stripy shirt and droopy moustache and say *bonjour* to me. Do you know he tried to persuade me to buy chestnut mushrooms and a loaf of brioche?"

I was desperate to talk but I could still hear the milkshake covered child crying and I could see the mother looking at me desperately. So I had to resist the urge to tell Beth about Da Notorious Baron and my stencils and we quickly arranged a date. It was too big a news item to blurt out in a café when holding a mop and bucket, like some domestic Britannia.

"It's you who's too busy to talk to me, now!" Beth wiped away more tears when we'd arranged to see each other. "Oh, bloody hormones!" and she gave me a peck on the cheek and shuffled out.

At a quarter past five the last customer left the café: and not of his own volition if I had to be completely honest. I had hounded the poor man: he'd looked like he wanted to stay longer, settling into what used to be mine and Beth's sofa to enjoy a large cappuccino and the weekend papers but I shot him *I hate you, I hate you* looks from across the empty café and mercifully he took the hint. The second he'd walked out with me right behind him, like his shadow, I flipped the sign on the door and then I collapsed at a table, head in hands. I was tired beyond belief, everything ached and I felt horribly down because Guy hadn't turned up. And I really had thought he would turn up. I'd pinned a note for him to my front door just before I'd left, for when he dropped off the phone *Guy – at V-2 come see me.*

Neil, steamed out and exhausted, came over to me, pulling up a chair opposite. "Cigarette?"

"Are we allowed to?"

"And who will stop us?" he said, peering out of the window, through the neverending rain to Fox Estates opposite. Was he also convinced that Eustace was as omniscient as God and Babs?

I took a fag.

"So … did you enjoy your first ever day in a café then?" he said, lighting the cigarette for me. "Be honest now."

"Yes. But I am bloody tired."

"Bet Guy didn't let you get much sleep last night, did he?" Neil managed a grin despite his exhaustion, "Everyone saw you two sneak off early together."

"Bugger. Anyway, where's Anja, I haven't seen her all day? Is she really exhausted?"

Neil shifted on his seat and then, leaning forward, "Oh man! Don't tell anyone will you – least of all Eust," he said, laughing nervously and looking across the road to Fox Estates again, "But she's gone back to Pembrokeshire. Just to – you know – scout around. Talk to a few contacts back there. You know..."

I contemplated him for a moment from above my leftover chocolate croissant. "You're thinking of going back to Pembrokeshire? You're thinking of leaving London?"

"Shh!" Neil looked behind him, as though spies might be lurking behind the blackboard. "Nothing definite. Just to take a look." He sat back and yawned. "Man, I miss the sea and surf. And the grit of sand between my toes. I can't remember the feel of it any more, Edda: it's all pavement and road here. There's no escape in London, is there?" He was drumming his fingers on the wooden table. "Some days I feel like a zoo animal? You know what I mean, like I'm trapped and can only walk round and round the same small area. Man it's depressing."

I decided to ask the question that was on my lips, "I'm sorry, but why is it all hush-hush about you thinking you might go back? You don't have shareholders do you? You're not *obliged* to anyone are you? You could just sell up and— "

"I can't sell up," he said. "It's not mine to sell. I have a backer. Someone with a financial interest in the business and I'm contracted to work here for five years." He gave a sharp laugh. "I was stupid and fell in love with the apartment that came with the shop. Ridiculous I know, such a daft thing. But there are big penalties if we leave … *big* penalties."

"But couldn't you appoint someone else to take over from you?"

"Ha! No one would be as stupid as me and sign their life away to such a bad contract. It's a crap contract, man. A sentence really – seven days a week for five long years – and … well … I've said too much. Look, please, Edda, not a word, OK? Not one. I shouldn't have said what I said. Now, let's see … cakes! Do you want cakes? Everyone wants cakes! And I'll pay you for the work you've done today, thank you so much, man! You're such a star."

The instant I was out of the café I was soaked: the rain was horizontal and coming across hard. No wonder everyone had spent the day sheltering indoors. I hurtled across the road, pastry and muffin-filled carrier bags banging against my wet legs.

"Edda! Edda! Over here!" I turned and through the grey rain I could make out Eustace, standing in the shelter of the doorway of Fox Estates, holding the door open. "I have something for you!" he shouted over the rain.

I changed direction and ran into the shop, dripping guiltily on his plush burgundy carpet.

"Terrible weather, don't you think, Edda?" Eustace said as he closed the door behind me and I was suddenly overwhelmed by the smell of brass polish. "Still, it's very good for the gardens, so we might as well grin and bear it. Here – I thought you might like this," he handed me a red golfing umbrella. "It says Fox Estates on it but I'm sure you'll appreciate the shelter!"

"Oh," I said and took it from him. It weighed about the same as a Viking broad sword. "Thank you! But I only live a few doors down. As you know." I added. Of course he knew: I now realised that Eustace knew everything. Eustace Fox was the male, suited, fagless equivalent of Babs. Between the two of them they must know just about everything and everyone in the area. He was the Nouveau Brockley, she the Old.

And then it hit me: what did that make me then? I gardened for Eustace Fox and I cut graffiti stencils for Babs. Was I was Nouveau Brockley or was I Old Brockley? I had become caught between the two…

"Well, take the umbrella for another time, then," Eustace said, with an expansive gesture. "I've just had them made and I'm delighted with them. Waxed canvas with titanium spokes: top of the range, but then so is Fox Estates, so if one is going to promote one's business then one should do it well don't you think? So, anyway, tell me Edda, how was your day at the café?"

Eustace *was* Babs: he *did* know everything.

"It was fine." I said. "Tiring. You know – after the dig last night."

"Which I'm delighted with, by the by!" Eustace clapped me on the back. "Couldn't be better, it really couldn't. The bench you and Rog renovated just shines. Well done, top hole! I hear, by the way, that Roger was his usual complaining self, is that true? Did he moan all evening to you?"

How *did* he know? Had I mentioned Roger's moaning to Guy? I didn't think I had: Guy and I hadn't spent a great deal of the night in conversation…

"Oh, Roger was OK," I said, generously. It wouldn't do

to make any enemies amongst the Spades. After all, Eustace might really rate Roger, whatever he thought about the man's pessimistic outlook.

"Rog tends to feel rather superior to the rest of us, I'm afraid." Eustace sat on a mahogany desk and leant back. "Journalists, eh? Think their job gives them the right to look down on the rest of us mere mortals."

"I think he was frustrated at the task we had. It wasn't pure guerrilla gardening, was it? But it was fine," I hastily added, not wanting to cause offence to Eustace. Being polite and tactful was nigh on impossible when I was so physically and mentally exhausted.

"Well, between you and me, Roger owes me one or two favours," Eustace said with a confidential tone. "I gave Roger the heads up on a rather magnificent property down on Breakspears Road and we got it valued – well – lets just say Roger got a very, *very* good deal on it. But you see Edda you need good people on your side don't you? And journalists can be so very useful…"

I nodded, biting my lip nervously. Had Eustace just told me that he had sold an undervalued property to "buy" Roger Wendell's services as a journalist? Had I been bought too? Was my price the knot garden and the sundial? Is that how he had "bought" my co-operation?

I shivered.

"But of course, you're cold and wet!" Eustace stood up and clasped his hands together. "Whatever am I doing keeping you talking, you must be exhausted too! My dear, forgive me. I was so very keen to have a little conversation with you that I forgot all about propriety.

What must you think of me?"

I smiled politely. "Thank you so much for the umbrella."

"Of course. I actually wanted to ask you if you were enjoying being part of the Spades."

I assured him I was, with all the gusto I could manage after what felt like a lifetime of manual labour.

"Superb." He seemed satisfied. "And tell me, before I let you go, I'm always on the look-out for how we can improve what we're doing. And of course I bow to your excellent experience vis-à-vis the skip."

I laughed it off. "Oh. Well. I'll have a think then."

"Yes, do. I like the slightly off-the-wall approach you had. I'm more of a traditional man myself," he explained, as if the surrounding oils paintings, brass lights and mahogany furniture hadn't spelled that out already. "But I think a mix of both would be good. After all, Brockley's about vibrancy too. Well, well, I must let you get off." He opened the door for me and looked out into the rain before adding, "Next dig's bordering the A2: something that is going to push the boundaries just a little. Check it out on the website, but I can tell you it's in three weeks. *Ciao bella!*"

The rain hissed on the enormous Fox Estates umbrella as I sped home. It was deafening but, as I turned into my knot garden, it didn't drown out the, "Oh aye, darlin', what's that then?" from across the garden wall. I turned to see Babs, sheltering in her doorway with a damp fag on, looking straight at the umbrella.

Damn. Now she really would think I'd gone over to the other side. I was, quite literally, wearing Eustace Fox's colours.

"Babs!" I shouted above the torrential rain. "It was forced on me! What could I do?"

"It's nice!" she shouted back. "Posh! Would be though, wouldn't it, darlin'? You enjoy it!"

Seventeen

Safely installed in my hallway with the front door closed to the bad weather outside I fought to close the unwanted umbrella. And then, walking into the house, there were two items on the kitchen counter that caught my attention.

One made me smile, the other did not.

"Hello, Edda!" Robert handed me a beer. "Bad day?"

"Hi." I hurled the offending umbrella into the utility room and plonked the two wet bags of pastries down on the counter. "I'm exhausted. But it's all done now."

"I see you've noticed it," Robert gestured proudly to the Valhalla plate. "I rescued every single one of the pieces from the bin. I think I got all of them. There were two hundred and eight of them."

I walked over to the counter and ran a finger over its bumpy mended surface. Stupidly, I was near to tears to see my old plate again. "It's great." I said with a lump in my throat. "It's sort of *distressed* looking."

He laughed and then, looking suddenly solemn, "I am really sorry that I broke it. Really."

"It's fine," I said. "Accidents happen. Especially when you're pissed out of your skull."

"I was that man," Robert conceded, and then added:

246

"cheers," and he touched his bottle against mine. "Hair of the dog."

I reached over and picked up my mobile phone. It was the second item I had seen on the kitchen counter and the one that *had not* made me smile.

"Oh yes, and that is from your boyfriend. He dropped it off this afternoon."

I flipped it open. There were no messages for me.

"He's not my boyfriend."

"Oh. Right. I thought he—"

"No. He's not. Did he say anything when he dropped it off? Was there a message?"

"Nope. I told him you were working at the café. And he saw the note on the door. But he asked me to give it to you."

"Right." The lump was back in my throat. Guy had not even bothered to cross the road to personally deliver my phone to me. What had I been thinking when I'd fantasised about the day Guy and I would spend in Greenwich getting to know each other? How stupid was that? We'd shagged. That was it. He'd flirted and I let him and we shagged – twice (well, more than twice, but on two separate occasions). Everyone did it. So what? It was de rigueur wasn't it?

"Almond croissant! Pain au chocolat!" Robert had his head in the pastry bags. "Who are these for? For us? Really? All of them? Ho, ho, ho, ho, ho!" he rubbed his hands together and went to get plates.

"Is your girlfriend not here, then?" I said, as lightly as I could manage. Since I'd got back from the café I'd been

247

shooting quick glances up the staircase, to see if the petite blonde thing would emerge in another pair of colourful pyjamas.

"Oh … Greta? No. She's not my girlfriend. Well, you know," he broke off, "early days. I'm going to Greenwich with her next weekend. She's a friend of a friend. Oh lovely, lovely, jammy doughnuts! Oh, Edda, well done girl!"

I sank down onto a chair and drank my beer, smiling despite my disappointment. It was good to be home.

"Are you even looking out of the car window, Eds?" Beth shouted at me and woke me from my daydream. I sat up straighter in the passenger seat of her car.

"Of course I am." I said.

"What's wrong with you today?" Beth pulled over and turned off the engine. "You've hardly said a word since I picked you up. Have you changed your mind about looking for a place to open a café?"

"Well, I had a bit of a late night last night," I mumbled, a flashback of an entire table covered in cakes and biscuits, beer bottles and the hazy memory of a bottle of whisky…

"Was it your gardening activity?" Beth said. "Or working at the café?"

"No. That was the night before. Last night was just spent at home with my lodger."

"goddamn it, Eds, you don't need to rub in just how mundane my life is: gadding about with one man and then another."

"I didn't gad about," I said. "I stayed at home. Robert was at home too. There was no gadding. There were just lots of doughnuts and much too much alcohol..." Even saying the word made me feel ill. "Look Beth shall we go into that café. I think I ought to eat something. And I really do appreciate you driving me around the place."

"Much good it did."

"No it did. I *was* looking out of the window."

"Well let's hope you perk up when you eat something," Beth said crossly. "Did you mean you want us to go into this café? Are you sure you want to go *here*?"

"You *slept* with *Robert*?" Beth yelped.

"Beth! Shush!"

We were in the Greasy Finger café, on Catford High Street, and it was the nearest to Hell I ever wanted to get. The grease wasn't restricted to the finger: the table and chairs were greasy, the people serving were greasy and even the customers were greasy. And, right now, all of them were looking in our direction and not in a friendly way. I sipped my greasy tea and tried to look nonchalant. "You slept with your lodger and you're seeing Guy on the side! Edda! What kind of a dissolute life are you leading? You complete and utter slapper!" she said. Then added, "Mind you, I don't blame you. My sex life is over for ever. At twenty-eight. Urgh."

"Shhhhh!" I hissed, "And to be correct I slept near him! Not *with* him!" I hoped she'd take the hint on the volume. The pregnancy thing had been really affecting her on the occasional times that I'd actually seen her in the last few weeks. Now she reminded me of a character in an eighties drama that only operated on exaggerated moods of Tearful, Appalled and Thrilled. And all three emotional states were conducted at high volume.

"So, what does 'near him' mean?" Beth leant in, dutifully dropping her voice. "Does that mean you didn't go all the way? Did you share a bed? Were you naked?"

Almost imperceptibly the greasy Sarf Londoners leant in towards us, putting down their mugs of milky tea and five sugars.

"Yes it means I didn't go all the way!" I hissed back. "You have completely got the wrong end of the stick. I was saying that I fell asleep beside him. *Beside*."

"Dressed?"

"Yes! Look, Beth, the point I was trying to make was that we're getting on really well and talked so late that we fell asleep. And when I woke up he'd got a blanket and covered me up. That was the point. He's sweet. He's nice."

"'k." Beth stirred her water. "So what does Guy think of Mr Sweet? Is your loverboy jealous?"

"Of Robert? Of course not. He's only met him once and he didn't see him as any kind of threat. Why should he?"

"But do you talk about Robert to Guy? Does Guy get at all suspicious by how much you talk about Robert? You talk about Robert all the time to me: you've hardly mentioned the Romeo lover today: it's been Robert, Robert, Robert."

"That's silly. I just see more of Robert because he lives with me," I said. "And besides, he's got a girlfriend."

"Oh-ho." Beth looked up from her water stirring. "And the girlfriend is…?"

"A complete ditzy blonde." I chewed my fried bread. "Actually that's not fair. She's probably really nice."

"So you don't like Robert's girlfriend. Interesting … very interesting."

"What do you mean by that?"

"I mean," Beth said, "I mean you're in love with Robert, Edda!"

"Oh, come on!"

She looked at me pointedly.

"That's just crap," I continued. "Can we change the subject please? I spend the night in bed with a sexy artist and just because the following evening I happen to fall asleep on the floor with my lodger you straight away think—"

"On the *floor*?"

"So the café idea, then," I said. "Thoughts?"

"OK, fine then." Beth held her hands up in submission. "Let's ignore your *completely blind* sense of self for a moment. If you don't want to talk about Robert—"

"Which I don't."

"Or about how little you talk about Guy—"

"No."

"Then we'd better talk about the café idea. Otherwise we'll just sit here and stare at each other for half an hour."

I wiped my greasy hands. "Sounds good to me."

"Well, talking about the café, I'm really pleased for you, honey." Her hand was suddenly on my hand, across the table. "I really thought you'd – well that you'd struggle once I was having this baby. But you're not are you? You're thinking seriously – finally – about your café idea. You've got a lodger, you're meeting blokes and sleeping around and—"

"You know, it's probably illegal to hit a pregnant woman," I said, "but I am willing to try."

"Well, joking aside, I do think it's good that you're doing your own thing… Am I patronising you enough?"

"Pretty much." I said. "But thank you."

"I don't mean to patronise you. I'm sorry, honey. So, the café idea, well, to be honest with you, I think it's been utterly depressing this morning."

"It has hasn't it?" I said. We'd driven round all the areas that surrounded Brockley: Catford, Lee, Hither Green, Forest Hill, Ladywell, Nunhead, Charlton, St Johns and Woolwich looking for the next up and coming place. But not one of them had looked up and coming; all of them had looked utterly depressing.

"You're still adamant you don't want to set up in Greenwich or Blackheath?" Beth said through a mouthful of congealing sausage. "Why can't you want to open a café somewhere nice – somewhere that people actually want to spend their leisure time? You seem set on the grimmest areas."

"Shh! Beth, keep your voice down, you're going to get us lynched! Anyway, I can't afford Greenwich or Blackheath and besides, they're already packed full of cafés. What I need to do is what Neil did with V-2: I need to find the new Brockley."

Beth leant in. "Well, it's not Catford."

"I *so* know that."

"Can't you set up in competition with Neil? Open a café on the High Road?" There's enough people living in Brockley to support two cafés.

"Nope. Eustace mentioned at the secret society meeting that Starbucks has just applied for planning permission for a double shop there. Three cafés might be overkill."

"Bugger."

"I just wish I'd been more proactive and not spent the last five years dithering around and saying I wanted to open a café but not actually doing it. Then I could have opened up in Brockley and caught the wave and now I'd be happily serving cappuccinos."

"Yes but what would your friend Babs think if you ran a café in Brockley? *I don't have nothin' to do with no poncy types servin' three quid hot chocolates.*" Beth mimicked Babs perfectly.

I threw a greasy grilled mushroom at her. And then darted round the table and picked it up off the floor when the owner shot me a look across the counter that suggested he wanted to nut me. It was definitely time to be leaving.

Eighteen

It was the weekend but, rather than feel a sense of dread at the Bethlessness of it, I now looked forward to my weekends again: time to chat to Robert, Babs, Neil and Anja and time to clean and get my house in order. My inner Miss Havisham had been banished for good now that I shared my house with a lodger. Today I'd set myself the task of focusing on my front garden: although it was out of a sense of guilt rather than any more noble intention.

Maintaining an Elizabethan knot garden was back-breaking work. For three hours I had been on my knees clipping the low box hedging into its original shape. My knees were sore from the shale and my back ached. I could understand now why the style didn't endure. But I didn't feel I could very well leave the box hedging to go rampant, since Eustace and the guerrilla gardeners had spent what must have been a considerable amount of time and money on it. And especially as Fox Estates was so close to my garden – Eustace would no doubt be keeping an eye on its maintenance and I didn't want to be told off for not keeping it neat and tidy – would he throw me out of the secret society? Cut me off, socially, from Nouveau Brockley society? Would he convince Neil not to keep slipping me a free doughnut every time I bought a coffee at V-2? While I shuffled forward and debated how little gardening I could get away with, I became aware of wafts of cheap cigarette smoke blowing my way.

"Funny 'ow things turn out ain't it?" Babs called out.

Grateful for the opportunity to get up off my hands and knees, I staggered over to her on my bloodless legs. "What's funny Babs?"

And suddenly there were two Babs' standing by my wall.

"Me daughter." Babs nodded towards the slightly younger version. "Jan."

"Alrigh', darlin'?" Jan said. "'eard a lot about yer, Edda. Nice garden yer got 'ere. Right posh ain't it ma? Don't get none o' that down Woolwich Arsenal way."

"Well we're on the up, ain't we, Edda, eh?" Babs lit her daughter's fag in a tender mother-daughter moment.

"Your mother's convinced that Old Brockley is being pushed out," I said, to Jan, by way of explanation.

"Yeah, I just saw yer Mini Mart," Jan said, "Pett-it Marsh now, ain't it? I mean fuckin' 'ell there was a bleedin' bike outside with strings o' bleedin' onions 'angin' from it. What's that Indian bloke tryin' to do?"

"It ain't 'im," Babs said, looking straight at me. "In't that right, Edda, eh? We know who's behind the Mini Mart: who's puttin' pressure on old Iqbal."

"Who?" Jan said.

"It's that Eustace Fox what's tellin' 'im what to do," Babs said.

"Well, if it helps improve Mr Iqbal's business—" I began and then abruptly closed my mouth. Babs and Babs II were not impressed by my pro-Fox stance.

"Friend o' Eustace," Babs said to her daughter, pointing at me.

"I'm not. Not at all. I just know him, that's all."

Babs raised her eyebrows.

"If I was a friend of Eustace Fox," I came closer to the wall, "then I wouldn't be helping Tyrone out with the stencils, would I? You know Eustace wants Da Notorious Baron strung up from the crossroads."

Babs and Babs II cackled.

"Nah – she's one of us, ain't yer, darlin'?" Babs winked at me.

Pub or bistro? V-2 or Greasy Finger? Mini Mart or Petit Marché? I didn't know whether I was Old Brockley or Nouveau Brockley. I couldn't answer her question. But as I was slightly afraid of Jan leaping over the wall and nutting me I gave a very firm, "Yes I Am."

I was cooking risotto while Robert was at the kitchen table ostensibly marking; in reality he was dividing his time between chatting to me and staring into space. Earlier that afternoon he had taken pity on me and come out to help me tackle the front garden, bless him, so I'd offered to cook us dinner by way of a thank you.

"Can I ask," he said after some moments of silence while I scrabbled around in a blind panic for the stock, "why you have that photograph of Vikings in a longboat right over your fireplace?" He got up and read the inscription beneath it.

"Oh. Well..." I left my pan and went over to the photograph. The quality of the photo was poor because it had been so enlarged: grainy Vikings in a freshly carved boat on an iron grey sea. "It was given to me by a friend of the family. He was a Viking re-enactor."

"Oh my God, I've heard of people like them!" Robert snorted. "They're a bit weird aren't they? They go about the Shetlands in animal … hides … and … and … erm…"

He stopped. He put his hand over his mouth. He looked, in fact, like a man who has just realised his landlady's house was stocked with an unusually high volume of Viking-style paraphernalia.

"And how bad do you feel right now?" I took the picture off the wall and perched next to him on the table, sitting on a short essay about Bonnie Prince Charlie and the battle of Prestonpans.

"Pretty bad." He said through his hand which was still clamped firmly to his mouth.

"It'll get worse. This is my mum," I pointed to a grainy female Viking near the front. "And this is my dad, sitting beside her. I can tell it's my dad because he only had one horn on his helmet: the other had broken off during a staged fight and he hadn't got round to mending it. Anyway, my parents had worked with all the people in the boat to carve it out, over a summer holiday, and this was its maiden voyage. They're off the coast of Shetland." I said. "We spent every summer in Shetland. And sometimes we wore animal hides."

"I am so sorry about what I said."

"Don't be. I agree with you: they were freaks."

"Oh, no. It's really quite normal isn't it? Re-enactors. It's just me being stupid…"

"No. It's mad. It was really mad. They were mad. But it was fun – I do remember that we all had a good time: we were close like one large family."

There was a long silence in which Robert's hand came down from his mouth and we both looked at the picture. I could just make out Mum's smile as she hefted the oar and I could make out that Dad was looking at her and grinning. Everyone was pulling hard at the oars but they were so happy: so proud of what they'd achieved. As was I: I had been allowed to paint the eye of the dragon on the front of the ship. It had taken me hours to get it right but I remember being over the moon with the end result: it looked angry and intimidating, which was exactly as it should be.

"Your parents are dead, aren't they?" Robert said.

I turned to face him. "Yes." And then, surprising myself I added, "This is when they died, seconds after the photograph was taken."

There was a silence from Robert: what else would there have been – applause? And then, without looking up from the photograph, I made the decision to tell Robert about my parents. This was usually the *They're dead! They're dead and gone!* moment and I was determined that this time I wasn't going to do that.

"You see, the boat in the picture was new and untested when they took it out to sea. And for its maiden voyage the local news were filming it – which is what this is; a still from the film footage. You can make out on the photograph that they had already breached the headland and just after this a massive wave smashed into the side of them. The boat split in two, a lifeboat was scrambled but they were all swept out to sea and every one of them died. Twelve adults and two teenagers. I wasn't old enough to go. I remember being really angry at them for not letting me in the boat. The last thing I did was shout at them about how unfair they were being to me."

Robert stared at the photograph. "I don't know what to say."

"That's fine. Neither do I. I've not told anyone for years. Well, I've not really told anyone. Most of the people who know about it knew about it when it happened. It doesn't tend to crop up in conversation these days."

"So is your name a Viking name?"

"It means *poem* in Old Norse."

"And do you have a middle name?"

"Yes."

Robert looked at me. "So, are you going to tell me it?"

"No."

"Fair enough."

We contemplated the photographs again.

"If you think about it," I began, "it's not too terrible what happened. If you're a Viking then what better way to go than to sail to Valhalla? Better that than die in a traffic accident, or wilting away in an old people's home with your dentures fallen onto your lap. That wouldn't be very Norse. At least they died like heroes. Sort of."

"And they left you at what age?"

"Fourteen." I said in a slightly mangled voice. I had a lump in my throat now. But apart from that I was enormously proud of myself for keeping it together while I told Robert.

"What… " Robert looked up. "What is that smell?"

"Oh SHIT! Shitty shit!" I leapt up and dashed to the cooker. "I've spent half an hour on this stupid dinner and it's completely ruined!"

"Come on," Robert stood up and grabbed his coat and mine from the rack. "Let's eat out. I don't much like risotto anyway."

"What?"

It had been a beautiful, if chilly, evening walk down into Greenwich. It had become a sightseeing expedition, me pointing out the Brockley places of interest: *this house belongs to Eustace Fox. He has a giant stuffed bear in his hallway,* and him taking me on a detour up Croom's Hill where his dad had a serious-looking Georgian town-house: *this house belongs to Max Willoughby. He has a giant picture of himself and Lawrence Olivier in his hallway.*

"This is where you lived? Where you grew up?"

"Yup." He pointed to the front. "Up there on the top floor is my bedroom. I could see all the way over to the City from my window – it's a beautiful view, especially at night."

"Robert?"

"Yes, Edda."

"When did you lose your mother?"

260

As with my parents there was never a good time to bring the subject up in a conversation. But as we'd talked about my parents it seemed like an ideal time to talk about something we both shared.

"When I was seventeen."

"Oh." We had turned and started to walk down the hill and into the centre of Greenwich.

"She died in a Norman conquest re-enactment when an arrow went through her eye."

"Really?" I gasped.

"No, not really! It was cancer."

I didn't know whether to punch him or sympathise with him. So I punched him.

"Oh come on – it would have been funny though, wouldn't it?"

"No!" But at least the heavy conversation topic had lightened again. "So, is your dad still loved up with Amanda do you think?"

"Completely! It's good to see him like this: he's been down in the dumps since … well, since he was widowed."

"There haven't been any other women after your mum?"

"God, yes! Don't you know what these actor types are like? I can't remember how many times some new woman tried to make polite conversation with me at the breakfast table when I was younger. And quite recently, too. But your friend seems to be a project for him. In the nicest sense of the word."

"I know what you mean. She bounces into the office

and tells me about the theatre or the history of the Strand or wine tasting … she's lapping it up."

"You see what advertising your room to rent has done."

"I know. I'm quite the fairy godmother."

We found our way to the Trafalgar, a Georgian riverside pub tucked away behind the dry-docked and charred remains of the Cutty Sark. We settled in a bar filled with rowdy rowers and a few beer-drinking locals and I bought the food: I still owed him for the gardening. We took a table in one of the bay windows, looking out through the old glass and onto the blue-white lights of Canary Wharf across the Thames.

I chose risotto – because I'd already got my head around it and was disappointed by my disaster in the kitchen. Robert had sausage and mash, *because I still don't like risotto*, and we shared a bottle of wine. By the time the sticky toffee puddings had arrived we had moved on to which of us Finley loved best.

"Well, me, obviously," Robert announced.

"Yes. I can't argue with that. But I can't help feeling horribly rejected: the minute you moved in to the house he switched his allegiance from me to you."

"Maybe he's gay."

I laughed. "My cat is not gay: I think you've bought his affection with expensive treats that I won't buy him: that's what it is."

"Ahh, you've worked it out."

He poured more wine into the glasses.

"I saw a Gourmet Cat Cuisine wrapper in the kitchen bin the other day."

He laughed and held up his hands. We sat for a moment in companiable silence, listening in to a loud conversation about a female rower who was caught naked in the club house with another female rower.

"You know," Robert fiddled with the stem of his glass when the story had finished, "you're full of surprises."

"Am I?" I said. "You mean surprises about my parents?"

"No." Robert toyed with his post-dinner pint. "Well, that as well I suppose. But I was actually thinking about the guerrilla gardening..."

"*Pardon?*" I couldn't have been more surprised if my wine glass caught fire.

"Guerrilla gardening," he said, and then added: "You are one of them, aren't you?"

Oh. I felt like my eight-year-old self at the point when my dad had caught me with my hand in the Jorvik Viking Centre biscuit tin. I was caught in the act and there was nowhere to hide.

"How do you know that?" I hissed, in barely above a whisper. "Who told you? Was it Babs? Does she know about it? Oh, pants, she doesn't know about it, does she?"

"Oh, come on!" He grinned, clearly pleased to have got the rise out of me that he'd been hoping for. "It's so obvious what you are."

"It is?" I surreptitiously checked my fingernails. Perhaps I hadn't been quite busy enough with the nail brush...

"Well, for starters you sneak out at night – *late* at night – and the next day somewhere in Brockley is beautifully gardened."

"Well that doesn't— "

"And there's the skip that sat opposite our house that was full of flowers. You said yourself that you did that. You told me when you interviewed me for the room."

"Well I…" I didn't know what to say. My head was reeling: he'd said *our house*. My stomach had unexplainably flipped when he'd said it.

"And your front garden looks like a National Trust garden: it's immaculate. I was talking to Babs—"

"Well, you shouldn't go listening to Babs! Honestly!"

"Oh come on, she's a treasure! Anyway, Babs said that one night your garden was a wasteland and then by the next morning it was completely transformed. Overnight: under cover of darkness. So you got the guerrilla gardeners to work for you too."

"Babs called my front garden a *wasteland*?"

"No." Robert sipped his wine. "If I remember rightly, I think she called your front garden *a disgrace*."

"Oh." I said. "Oh. Nice."

"Well? Am I right?" Robert looked at me expectantly.

"No you're not! It was just a bit overgrown that was all."

"I mean about the guerrilla gardening?"

"Yes, of course you're right." I sighed and tapped the table, irritated that I'd been so easy to read. I was rubbish at being in a secret society: I would have got thrown out

264

of the Famous Five by the first book. I wouldn't even have made it on to Kirrin Island...

"And you know your house used to be a brothel?" Robert added.

"Yes, yes, yes. I know." I said, giving in to irritation that someone like Babs had dissed my garden when her paintwork was *shocking*. And irritated that she told Robert about my house once being a brothel. When I'd asked her not to.

There was a hand on my hand. "Hey," Robert was leaning forward. "That's cool."

"It's—"

"It's cool. You're cool. You're a guerrilla gardener. Your house used to be knocking shop. How edgy are you?"

I gazed into my wine glass. "Maybe," I conceded. I was certainly closer to Robert's vision of me than the fiery militant Highlander vision of me that Guy imagined.

"No you are. You're very Brockley. You're posh yet you live in South London. Your house is great but it used to be a brothel. You guerrilla garden but you also," he leant right in to me, "assist Da Notoriously Bad Baron with his graffiti."

"It's getting better."

"It is. Definitely. Thanks to your dexterity with the craft knife."

"Well, yes, perhaps I am cool." I said, delighted at being thought of as cool. And then I added, "It's Ginnlaug Bryngerør by the way."

"What is?" Robert said. I stared at him pointedly until

he got it. "Bloody hell! Are they your middle names?" he laughed.

"Yup. So now who's cool and edgy?"

"Well Edda Ginnlaug Bryngerør is of course!" he raised his glass in a toast. "Who the hell wants to be a Jane?"

Yes I was edgy; yes it was cool that I lived in a former brothel. And yes I was a guerrilla gardener by night with a lover who was an artist. But I was having another bad-Beth day and everything that was even slightly positive stopped counting on a bad-Beth day.

On a bad-Beth Day everything was grey and crappy. I had thought that I was past this stage: I thought the shiny new life I was building for myself was enough to distract me from the fact I was losing – had lost – the best friend I ever had. But since the Trafalgar, a few lonely eventless days were enough to put me back in the doldrums once more.

I had started out the day with good intentions. I'd been cleaning because I had a lodger and now took pride in maintaining my house, goddamn it. It had all been going well until I had found a pair of shoes in the understairs cupboard. Ridiculous how a single pair of shoes could move me so much. They were banana-yellow wedges and Beth and I had each bought an identical pair, for the first time that we'd gone to the Notting Hill Carnival, when we'd just moved down to London.

I have to phone her and tell her what I've just found! I must tell her she'll be amazed I've still got these. I kept returning to the thought but each time I stopped myself from picking up the phone. Because I knew that, unlike me, Beth wasn't looking backwards. She was looking forwards to her new and baby-filled life. Why would she want to come over to reminisce about an old pair of shoes for God's sake? Of what interest would an old pair of shoes be to her now? That was then – the baby was now.

I cradled the shoes in my hand and cried *because they were interesting to me still*: they were still interesting to the one who was left behind. And as I sat on the edge of my bed and bawled my eyes out – pathetically clinging on to what was a really bad pair of yellow wedges – I hated myself for being so completely Mostly Ds – *girl you seem to be unable to move on – you're an out and out disaster!*

"Going out?" Robert accosted me in the hallway.

"Just going to get milk." I trembled. After much patheticness I had decided to *get a bloody grip* and go over to Beth's flat to see her. I had the yellow wedges in a bag on my shoulder.

"Your eyes seem kind of strange."

"They're fine!" I chirruped in an *everything's great with me* voice.

"Is it hay fever? Are you OK?" I could feel his eyes boring in to me.

I fumbled with my boots, using my hair to hide my face like a twelve year old wearing her mother's make-up. "Sure. Fine. Want anything from the shop?" I dared to look up at him.

He clocked my swollen pink eyes and pursed his lips together. "No thanks."

I waited a split second.

Nothing.

Fine. Right. Of course he wasn't going to come over and hug me. Of course not. That wasn't what men did. And certainly not what lodgers did.

But I so wanted him to. I wanted him to say, "C'mere," and pull me to him in a big hug and tell me everything was going to be OK and go through all that 'how cool you are' stuff that he'd said in the Trafalgar the other night.

"Actually," he said, with a new found conviction, and I looked up at him again, "if you can get some cornflakes that would be great. Kelloggs – not the unbranded sort they taste crap. Do you want the money now?"

What a git.

"All right there young Edda!"

I leapt in the dark, steadying myself by clutching the stone wall. Christ! It was impossible to get a moment to myself. Suddenly fleeing wet-eyed down the darkened road to Beth's flat seemed a distant possibility what with people wanting cornflakes and fag-time chat. Modern life was completely getting in the way of good old-fashioned handwringing despair.

"Jumpy, ain't yer?" Babs waved her fag at me. "Sign o' guilt that is." She looked at me suspiciously. "Want one?" She offered the packet and, seduced by the freshly unwrapped white cigarettes inside, I took one.

"Here." She lit it for me across the garden wall.

"Bit nippy to be out this evenin', ain't it? Wish I could smoke in the 'ouse but me boyfriend only lets me smoke in the 'ouse after shaggin'," Babs said, lightly. "You OK, love? These fags do make yer choke don't they? Rough as a badger's arse these fags: kill yer faster than the gin these will. Anyways," she continued, "I wouldn't pass up watchin' the world go by, so I don't mind standin' out 'ere smokin'. Gets to talk to me neighbours, don't I? Not 'im though, the one on the other side what eats dogs. But you, love, I get to talk to you."

Still coughing, I was nevertheless touched by what she said. "So this is how you keep your finger on Brockley's pulse?" I said, when I finally recovered. "You watch the world from your doorstep."

Babs took her fag out and pointed it at me. "The bleedin' cheek of it! Like I 'ave nothin' better to do with me time than sit 'ere all bleedin' day an' night!"

"Oh I didn't—"

"I know yer didn't. Of course not. You're a nice un Edda. It may not look much like it but I do 'ave a full and stimulated social life. I mix with many people from Peckham right up ter Blackheath. Yes, I see yer expression. I mix with all sorts – even up the 'eath. Anyways, talkin' o' posh, 'ow's yer lodger gettin' on? Robert."

"Oh," I managed, recovering, "fine."

"Lovely arse on 'im," she said, matter-of-factly. "Nice boy an' all. You could do a lot worse than 'im."

"He's just a lodger. He pays me."

"An' didn't I tell yer that my bloke used to pay me for the first few weeks? Soon stops though: it don't feel right when yer enjoyin' it.."

"Anyway, how are you keeping Babs?"

"All right as it goes, love, thanks for askin'." She took a drag on her cigarette. "Just avoidin' 'im indoors if I 'ave to be honest with yer. Sex mad 'e is at the moment. It's that Fiona Bruce on *Antiques Roadshow*. Gets 'im right in the mood seein' 'er givin' it some round the porcelain. Somethin' about 'er arse."

"Right." I concentrated hard on my cigarette. Talking to Babs was the conversational equivalent of being hit in the face by a rounders bat.

"Well, I'll leave yer to it." Babs ground the end of her fag into the wall. "You 'ave a nice evenin', Edda. Don't do nothin' I wouldn't do."

Finally I was alone. No heartless lodgers or faggy neighbours, both of whom had stripped my evening of its melodrama.

The heartache over the banana coloured wedges had dissipated in the wake of the cornflakes and Fiona Bruce's arse. As I reached the front garden to Beth's flat I re-focused on the Keats-style heart-rendingly poignant moment.

SOLD, SUBJECT TO CONTRACT

The sign wasn't a surprise – she'd told me she'd got a buyer two weeks ago, but the finality of it still knocked me back.

I loitered outside the flat, staring hard at the sold sign,

trying to get closure. Trying to force myself to feel the despair I really thought I ought to be feeling to be able to move on.

But there was nothing.

What was I doing here? Did I really want to see Beth, and what would I say to her anyway. The banana wedges seemed rather ridiculous now.

I ought to get Robert's cornflakes.

Shit.

With a glance up and down the street to make sure Eustace wasn't on the prowl for police signs I headed back to Geoffrey Road. There was a litter bin half way down the street and I shoved the banana wedges into it. They'd been bloody awful shoes anyway…

And then my heart leapt.

There was a figure, up ahead. And this time it didn't look like Eustace.

This was it. This was my police-sign moment. Hastily I jammed my keys between the fingers of my fist, just in case. Beth would never need to do this in Surrey…

The person – a man – was walking in my direction on my side of the pavement and it was too late for me to turn and go back: Manor Road was a long straight road with no side-roads off it. I was trapped.

Head down I pounded forward, super-conscious of the feel of the keys between my fingers…

"Edda!"

I looked up at the ominous stranger and my heart leapt.

"Robert!"

"Edda!" He ran up to me, "Where were you? You've been gone ages: I was looking for you!"

"You were?" I felt an overwhelming happiness. So much so I unclenched my fist and let go of my keys.

"I thought you were going to the Mini Mart for cornflakes but Mr Iqbal said he hadn't seen you. And you were so upset when you left the house..."

"Oh. That. Well..."

"Are you OK?"

"Yes," I said. "I am."

"You seemed really upset."

"No," I said and then, clocking his expression, even in the dark. "Maybe a bit."

"About your friend?" he saw the sold sign outside Beth's flat.

"Yes. Is that tragic of me?"

"Not at all. Of course you're upset. Have you been to see her?"

"No." I looked down at the pavement. "I've just been hanging around. She'll be tired. Or busy doing baby things... I don't know."

"So you're not going to see her tonight?"

"I don't think so." I could feel tears prick the back of my eyes again.

"Shall we go to the Barge then? Have a pint?" Robert said.

I looked up. "Yes! That would be really good."

"Great. We can nip into the Mini Mart on the way there. I can pick up the cereal and tell Mr Iqbal you're OK. He's worried about you."

"Is he?"

"Yeah – when I went in to see if you'd been there and we didn't know where you were he said he could close up and come and help me look for you. He said you might have been murdered."

"Ahh, that's so sweet."

We walked back down Manor Road and on to Geoffrey Road again.

"Nice rats by the way."

"Eh?"

He pointed to the graffiti'd rats scampering along the bottom of a wall, chasing a terrified cat.

"Oh. Thanks. I only finished the stencil off for Tyrone two nights ago."

Robert looked sideways at me. "You just can't seem to shake off this South London thing can you?"

"It doesn't look like it." I said, slowly, because something was nagging me and I couldn't work out what it was.

"What's up?" Robert said. I had come to a stop and Robert stopped too.

"There's … just …" I walked backwards to my house, which we'd just passed on our way to the Barge. Yes – it *was* different. I could see there was something next to my front door. A lot of something.

"Ro-bert," I called him back. "Did you leave something by the door when you came out to find me?"

"No…"

I walked through the knot garden. In the dark I could

make out lots and lots of potted plants huddled together close to my wall.

"What are they?" Robert asked from behind me.

I leant down and read one of the tags on the plants. "Sweet peas," I said, still none the wiser as to why they were there.

"Is it to do with your secret thing," Robert said quietly, with one eye to Babs's house.

"It must be." I walked around the assembled plants: there must have been fifty pots of sweet peas huddled together by the steps leading to my front door. "A letter!"

We looked around in case the deliverer of the plants and the letter was still in the knot garden but they'd gone. "Let's go inside."

"You go in. I'll just run over to the Mini Mart to tell Mr Iqbal you're not dead."

"Don't forget your cornflakes!" I called out softly after him.

Once in the kitchen I slit open the expensive-looking envelope that had been sealed with a lump of red wax and – I noted – the imprint of a leaping fox. So it *was* connected to the Brockley Spades.

The first thing I took out of the envelope was a Farrow and Ball colour chart booklet of miniature painted samples. I opened it up, spreading it out along the kitchen counter. "Manufacturers of traditional papers and paint." There was a muted rainbow of expensive looking and terribly trendy samples of paint with names like Matchstick, Cord, Smoked Trout, London Stone, Radicchio and Babouche.

Behind me I heard Robert come in, panting from running, closing the front door and making a big fuss of Finley, who'd streaked across the kitchen to welcome him.

"Mr Iqbal says you should stop going out late at night on your own," Robert came into the kitchen, depositing a giant box of cornflakes in his cupboard before sinking down onto the bar stool opposite me. "He also said you might want an organic nut bar, seeing as you've had such a narrow escape from a terrible murder." He placed a Mr Squirrel Organic Raspberry, Fairtrade Chocolate and Responsibly Sourced Nut bar onto my colour chart.

"Brilliant. Thanks – do you want to go halves?"

"No need…" he said and opened a box of doughnuts.

"Doughnuts? I thought he'd stopped doing doughnuts? I thought they were not in keeping with the Marché any more?"

"Nope." Robert bit into the jammy sugary doughnut and sighed. "The doughnuts, bagels and basmati rice have made a comeback. Enjoy your healthy nut bar. Now then, what's this?" He peered at the colour chart. "These paints are crazy – why aren't any of them called Magnolia or Country Cream? You know," he polished off his first doughnut and reached out for another, "don't you think it's a bit creepy?"

"What? That I have all these plants? No. Why should it be creepy?"

"Well because someone was obviously watching our house." He said *our house* again and my stomach did its flip-thing again. He continued, "And in between me

275

going out and leaving it empty and both of us coming back the 'drop' took place."

"I hadn't really considered it," I said, biting thoughtfully on my nut bar.

"Well you should do. We've been watched. You left the house, I left the house and the plants were dumped. It's no coincidence."

"Oh stop freaking me out," I said.

Robert shrugged. "Go on then, what does your letter say?"

"It's from Eustace Fox. The head of the Brockley Spades. It says, 'Dearest Edda, I do so hope this letter finds you well?'"

"I didn't realise Eustace Fox came from 1840."

"He is a bit like that. He used the word *juxtaposition* the other day when he was talking to me, I had to look it up in the dictionary when I got home and I still don't know what it means. So, shall I carry on reading it out or are you not bothered?"

Robert clapped his hands together and sank onto a seat, "Please do so. You don't mind if I fix myself a sherry and loosen my cravat, do you?"

"So funny ... OK... 'I hope this letter finds you well. I sincerely hope that you don't mind accepting these few *Lathyrus odoratus*, which I believe would look superb planted up around the street lights along Geoffrey Road. I note many of the street lights have the paving slabs removed from around their base with the earth bared and it would be just marvellous to make use of these multifarious opportunities to create several miniature gardens along your beautiful road which is, dear Edda, at the very heart of our neighbourhood. Also left with you is a roll of twine and lengths of wire to enable the plants to climb. You will of course need to plant them soon (the weather is so fine for early June isn't it?) and you will need to water them every other day for the first fortnight. I'm sure Guy will be more than glad to help you out. I sincerely think you will make all the difference to Brockley."

"What a toss—?"

"Oh come on! He's just old-fashioned."

"He sounds like an idiot. He's seriously expecting you to plant up all those lathy odours or whatever they are?"

"He continues, 'Also enclosed, dear Edda, is a Farrow and Ball colour chart for your perusal'," Robert snorted and I paused in the reading to kick him. "'I note your facias and soffits are showing rather more wear than is strictly necessary and may I be so bold as to suggest French Grey (number 18) for both? I have appended the telephone numbers of two painters and decorators who – as very good friends of mine – will offer you excellent rates that I guarantee you won't find anywhere else: friends help each other out. Most sincerely yours, Eustace Fox, Esquire'."

"Esquire!"

"Oh, come on."

"So will you ask Guy to help you with the planting?" Robert said.

I put the letter down on the table top. "Maybe…"

But the truth was I didn't think that I would ask Guy.

I didn't want to presume on him in that way: our relationship – if indeed it was a relationship of any sort – was built on something that didn't feel sufficiently real or substantial to go asking him to help me out with some planting – even though it was for Eustace. Asking Guy to help me out was a shade too close to including him in real life: like asking him to do some plumbing or help me with the weekly shop. Guy was lust and excitement: he wasn't leaking taps and breakfast cereals.

Robert flicked the colour chart shut. "Do you want *me* to help you?"

"Would you?"

"Is it fun?"

"Ye-es," I said and then added: "sort of."

"It's hard work isn't it?"

"It can be."

"Well," Robert considered the situation, "you did bring all those amazing cakes home that day you worked at V-2. I do owe you … when do we have to do it? What did the letter say?"

"It just says 'soon' "

"Tomorrow, then? Are you doing anything tomorrow evening?"

"Nope." I said, ridiculously happy now that my problem was solved and my Friday night occupied. "I'll dig out the sombreros."

"The *what*?"

"Ah wait and see…"

"So this is absolutely necessary for a night of guerrilla

gardening, is it?" Robert said before he started another coughing fit. "Eurgh!"

We were sitting in my dimly lit kitchen, steeling ourselves for the night ahead in the only way I knew how.

"You get used to it," I said. "And actually this stuff is really hard to get hold of: I had to go to the depths of Penge to get this brand of Cava."

Robert refilled the glasses. "British Bulldog Cava?" he read the label. "BBC Drinks Company Ltd. Product of Erith, Greater London. Cava from South East London? Dear God, Edda, you could remove paint with this stuff. In fact you could probably remove the paint and the wood that was underneath the paint in the first place. This stuff is evil. Couldn't you have pushed the boat out and just gone for something crap instead?"

"Well it was the only brand that the Mini Mart used to stock, and when Beth and I were gardening the skip I wanted to have something special to celebrate what we were doing."

"It certainly is special. I suppose Umesh doesn't stock British Bulldog Cava any more, now the shop's a Petit Marché. It's all Tattinger and Krug I expect."

"Who?"

"Mr Iqbal – Umesh."

I stared at him across the dimly lit table. "*Umesh* Iqbal? You know Mr Iqbal's name? I've lived here for five years and I've never found out his name. Wow – you really are settling in here aren't you? You're becoming quite the South Londoner, too, aren't you? I bet Babs would like to give you an induction."

"She's certainly…" he searched for the right words, "keen."

"She says you're a fine specimen." I laughed. "She told me I'd done well getting a fine specimen of a man for a lodger."

"And I am." Robert downed another glass of BBC. "She told me the other day that I was just her sort of man."

"She told me you had a nice arse!"

"Edda! Don't tell me that!"

"Babs fancies you! And you must be young enough to be her son."

"Stranger things have happened." Robert shot me an enigmatic look and I choked on my drink.

"Would you?" I asked.

"No! Edda! What the hell is wrong with you? I was being ironic."

"I think you would, you know. Seriously, I think if you had enough of this BBC stuff, and Babs came over, you'd be willing…"

"Shall we start gardening now then?" Robert stood up, clearly keen to put an end to this conversation.

I, on the other hand, spent the next ten minutes laughing and winding him up. Which was surprisingly easy to do.

The first thing we did when we started our night of guerrilla gardening was to walk the length of Geoffrey Road to see how many mini street-light patches we had to plant. Robert then calculated that we had enough stock for four plants per street light with enough netting to wrap around all the lights if we limited the netting to 50cm per light. Clearly teachers made good guerrilla gardeners. We began the night at the top end of the street furthest from Brockley Cross, so that by the time we came to the last street lights it would be super late – or early – and there was less chance of people being around.

"Except for the really hardened gangsters out doing their business," Robert had helpfully clarified.

We had just got started and Robert had already begun moaning. "The sombreros really get in the way." He kept pushing his back off his head. "I keep hitting mine against the lamp posts when I'm bending over and digging."

"But they're necessary." I said. "So that no one recognises us. And besides, that's what we used when Beth and I gardened."

"But you don't wear them when you go on the proper digs do you?"

"No. But perhaps we should do tonight."

"I think I might take mine off if you don't mind."

Robert dug, I tapped out the plants from their pots and pushed them into the bared earth and covered them up while Robert lugged the water from the shopping trolley we'd commandeered.

"How long did that take?" Robert asked when the first of the sweet peas were in, the netting fixed to the first street light and the tallest sweet peas fixed to it with twine.

I checked my watch. "Twenty minutes."

He did a quick calculation. "Great. So by the time we finish up at Brockley Cross it should be nearly five in the morning."

"No-o…"

"Or we could speed up?"

"It's a plan!"

We worked rapidly, breaking only for the occasional and much needed beer.

"Why didn't you tell Eustace to sod off?" Robert asked when we had just celebrated the half way post. "I mean you shouldn't be doing solitary guerrilla gardening should you? The others probably don't and you already take part in the gardening for him, so why do all this extra stuff? You should have marched into Fox Estates and said no!"

"Well, firstly," I said, "because he gave me a knot garden with a sundial."

Robert considered the argument: "That's fair enough. And secondly?"

"Because I'd be afraid to, I suppose. I think Eustace Fox likes to be in control and he wouldn't take very kindly to someone messing with that. You need to keep on the right side of a man like Eustace Fox, I should think."

"Sounds ominous."

"Oh he's fine. Honestly."

"Babs doesn't think so," Robert said, draining the last of his beer.

"You and Babs! Are you two an item or something?"

"You're jealous," he said, returning to the hole he'd dug beside the street light.

"Yeah I'm jealous, that's it. So does your girlfriend know about Babs?"

"Plants please!"

It was half past three in the morning by the time we'd dug in our last much hated sweet pea and tied up the last despised tendril. We'd seen no one, thankfully, no muggers, rapists, gangsters, arsonists, bag snatchers and not even Babs. The minute the twine was tied on the last lamp post an exhausted Robert pushed the trolley back to the house while I collected up the remaining empty pots and followed him. Already the sky to the east was starting to lighten.

"Hey, Edda, take a look at this," Robert pushed the trolley to the old coal shed by the side of the house while I closed the garden gate behind me. "What is it?" I whispered.

He pointed to the front steps where the sweet peas had been and I walked up to investigate, still only half-able to see in the dim light. When I got nearer I could make out that there were two large cans of paint – Farrow and Ball Exterior Eggshell – with a card fixed to the top of the nearest one. "With thanks. E."

"Is the paint Farrow & Ball French Grey, by any chance?" I said.

"Do you need to even ask?" Robert looked at me. "Your friend really does like to be in control doesn't he? You weren't joking."

"Well, I think it's sweet."

"Sweet that he tells you to paint your woodwork?" Robert looked at me with what I could just make out as an incredulous expression. "Sweet that he tells you *what colour* to paint your woodwork? Or sweet that he gives you the paint just in case you show any free will whatsoever and disobey orders?"

"No?"

"So you mean it's sweet that he knows you did the guerrilla gardening tonight, that his spies were out there watching us and reporting back to him, or the big man himself was keeping an eye on you?"

"Are you trying to freak me out?"

"No. He does it all himself. I'm going to bed Edda. Goodnight." He headed up the stairs with Finley hugging his ankles as he went.

Nineteen

"I know it's, like, *so* amazing and everything!" Amanda was jiggling on my desk, but far from being a pantfest her presence was happily free from underwear thanks to a trouser suit bought on our joint shopping trip. It was actually quite odd to be talking to her and have *no idea whatsoever* what pants she was wearing. "I am just so completely excited!" she squeaked.

I sat on my beige Lewisham Council Posture Chair, torn between happiness for my friend but devastation at her news: Amanda had handed her notice in. Amanda was leaving. Me.

It was hard not to see this as another abandonment. Another person realising the dream and leaving me behind to trudge along, regardless. But I was really trying not to think solely how it affected me but to look outside myself and take pleasure in what others were feeling. *Red* magazine, February.

"So, I play this woman who has sex for money." Amanda was saying.

"You play a prostitute."

"Well, yeah. If you want to label it. But Max said she's not, like, a real prostitute because she's got seven children to feed so she's been forced into it. Anyway it's set like, a hundred and fifty years ago and I wear this really huge dress – like a tent or something – and I just lie there."

"You lie there?"

"'cause I'm dead."

"You play a dead prostitute."

"In a *film*!" Amanda looked at me incredulously. "In a *film*. With Matt Damon! He's like this man who's killed my pimp and he's also the father of my seventh child. Anyway, my role in the film is to lie there and Matt Damon cradles my head all sad and he cries and I lie there. And they're paying me, like, nine months' salary! For lying there dead and having Matt Damon hold my head! I mean, like – *hello* – how cool is that?"

"Well … that's great." I enthused, happy for her but, deep inside, also feeling the familiar selfish pain about how it was going to affect me. It looked like it was going to be Edda-no-mates all over again.

The realisation that everyone was doing great things with their lives and I wasn't was not easily ignored. No doubt Babs was on the verge of finding a cure for cancer and emigrating to the States to cash in on her discovery. And Robert would move out so that he could shack up with the pretty blonde thing and make beautiful children. And I would be back in the dusty dining room with the cobwebbed boxes of KFC and the rats…

"Max says it's the start of a really big thing for me." Amanda giggled, and launched into why that was the case. I would miss her. I needed her. She was airy and silly and spoke like a twelve year old West Coast American but she was great. Now all I was going to have for company was my racy-novel-reading boss and the admin staff of the third floor of Lewisham Borough Council, none of whom would win a 'most interesting person' contest, so far as I could tell. One man from Accounts wore a bow tie to work last year and it was the talk of the office for over a month.

"You know," she leant in to me, "I am so grateful to you. For having me help you choose a lodger. If you hadn't, then I would never have met Max and I would never have made it as an actress. I'd be trudging along in this dead-end place with these dead-end people for the rest of my life. I really owe you, Edda."

"O-oh," I managed. Amanda would have no problem in the theatre with the way her voice carried to the furthest walls. I could see the people in Housing Benefit, bristling at the dead-end people comment.

"And you know that Guy bloke you're seeing," she began.

"Well, it's not proper dating as you—"

"Yeah, like, exactly," she said. "So you're not like tied in or anything. Well, Max says that Robert really likes you. I mean like *really* likes you…"

"He does? Really?"

"Really." Amanda slid off the desk. "*Really*, really." She sauntered off, singing. Really, it was disgusting how happy she was.

For the rest of the day I checked out the Spades website, blogged reservedly, *Saw a tramp looking comfortable on my bench in Hilly Fields last week: job done!*

But mostly let my thoughts wander in a Robert-style direction.

Robert liked me. Robert really, *really* liked me.

I toyed with the scrap of paper on the kitchen counter.

"Greta & I gone to theatre – dad again! – C U Saturday. Good luck gardening. Rob."

Greta? *Greta?*

Of course: Greta was the French teacher at Robert's school. The 'friend of a friend'.

Greta was the blonde thing on the stairs in Robert's pyjamas. I'd heard about the kooky French teacher more than once and, now, I realised they were one and the same person.

The kooky French teacher had sat on my stairs.

The kooky French teacher had slept with my lodger in my house.

I scrunched up the paper and in a moment of drama hurled it across the room. It was fine. It was all fine. And anyway, didn't I have a gardening appointment to prepare for and a commercially successful and prominent artist to see? My Friday night beckoned.

Stupidly, ridiculously, I didn't know whether or not to go up to Guy when I arrived on site for the dig. He was deep in conversation with Neil's wife, Anja, who had obviously returned from her escape to Pembrokeshire. Why not go up to him? I'd spent the night at his place. We'd been around the borough of Lewisham seed-bombing: we were practically dating ... so why hover around on the sidelines until he noticed me? Where was that going to get me? If I wanted to *be* his girlfriend I should *act like* his girlfriend (*Cosmo*, July).

I strode up to them and only when it was too late to turn back did I catch the tone of the conversation between Guy and Anja and realise that, actually, if I'd have been able to make out their expressions then I would have seen that they needed to be left alone.

"...he's not going to be happy about it," Guy was saying.

"To be honest," Anja cut in sharply, "I don't think he gives a shit if Eust's happy or not. I think Neil's had enough. We both have."

"You told Eust you could do it. That was the deal. Come on, Anja, make Neil see sense." They both turned to me, me having rocked up right beside them.

"Hi..." I was now at the point of having to say something, so I said it and they both looked at me with what looked like relief. Clearly neither wanted the conversation to continue.

"Hey, Edda, how's it going?" Guy grabbed me savagely round the waist and kissed me. Out of the corner of my eye I saw Anja peel away, arms crossed and scowling.

"I've missed my little Scottish skip gardener," he said, taking me round the corner out of sight to show me just how much he'd missed me, doing things which I would imagine *never* happened to Miss Havisham, before or after the clocks stopped.

The dig got underway. We were spread out across a long stretch of verge that bordered the Lewisham High Road on the Brockley side. Below us the smart dolls' house terraces of St John's stretched down the hill towards Deptford and the moneyed lights of Canary Wharf blinked and glimmered.

We set to work clearing the dog mess and the litter and the weeds. We filled the rubbish bags and Jake the muscle silently dumped them all into the van. It was the worst stage of any guerrilla event, the stage before getting warmed up and really into the actual gardening. The tension caused by potentially being caught was still with me, and I didn't have the satisfaction of creating anything up to that point. I was just tidying.

"Hey, Edda…"

"Guy!"

I'd been crouched over a clump of weeds and had been so engrossed in the wrenching of the bloody things that I hadn't heard him approach. He stood close above me, obscenely close, the top of his thigh millimetres from my face. He looked down at me and winked.

"Is there something you want, Guy?"

"Of course there is." He crouched down beside me and kissed me. "But before that, Edda, would you mind helping out on the houses. I'll explain what's needed when we get there."

"Yes. Anything. Anything at all."

This was wrong. Very wrong. Lusted up I would have agreed to anything but now, sober and chilled in the early morning, this new variation on guerrilla warfare seemed completely and utterly the wrong thing to be doing.

As soon as Guy had walked me off the main battle site, Eustace's Lincoln Continental had drawn up. Eustace stepped onto a sheltered stone balustrade in the long narrow park and the troops had all gathered round expectantly. We were tasked, he informed us in his grandiose style, with taking the war *into the front gardens* of the houses that formed the outer boundary of Brockley and "…doing once more that which we did at Edda's property." He'd said the words with a nod to me. The gardeners looked my way. I tried to look grateful and suppress my horror at the thought of going into other people's gardens and guerrilla gardening their private property. It had been a shock when it was done to me and I was one of them. But now Eustace had brought up the fact that I had received such a treatment all my arguments and protestations left me: what could I possibly say – "Yes give me an Elizabethan knot garden but don't give anyone else the benefit of close-cut box hedging?" I had no option but to go along with it and be involved in it. The two cans of Farrow and Ball French Grey at home also made it fairly impossible to complain.

"Do yer want me ter get another of them sundials, then?" grunted Jake from the back of the group.

I shivered. So Jake *had* been in my garden the night it was knot-gardened. That threatening bag of muscle had lurked just under my bedroom window, a thin pane of glass away from where I had been sleeping.

"No Jake. No sundials this time. And no decorative

box hedging either, we're simplifying and neatening. What we have to achieve in the next two hours is a refurbishment in every single front garden: that's five teams of three gardeners doing two gardens each. Or one an hour per team. And that's asking a lot in terms of clearing out, turfing and rudimentary planting. I want a total clearout of all plastic furniture, gnomes, sun catchers *for God's sake*, breeze blocks, rubbish and litter. I've drawn up teams and property assignments which Guy is distributing to you now. My vision," Eustace swept his hands to encompass the whole of SE4 before us, "is to smarten this outwardly facing boundary of Brockley, so that those on the road to Greenwich and Blackheath stop and take note of our beautiful neighbourhood. To look at this well-maintained verge, and these neatly kept gardens, and think to themselves, *Yes, I could live here*. What we have here is the most public face of Brockley: it's most visible asset. We have early Victorian houses that have had their beauty hidden behind a bush for too long. So we must take it upon ourselves to right the wrongs. Yes," he said, looking down now from his skyline address and fixing on each of us, "it's difficult to go into someone's private property. And yes, some of you may feel uncomfortable. But just think of how those people will feel when they wake up tomorrow to see the splendour of their newly tended gardens below."

"Can I just ask, Eust," a Boden-male called Mark, piped up, "Why wasn't this aspect of tonight's dig on the website? The only info you had up there was about the park running on the A2: not about people's houses."

"A jolly good question," Eustace said in a voice loud enough to have the desired effect but quiet enough to not be heard beyond the group assembled around him. "I knew that if it was publicised then some of you wouldn't turn up tonight. Because, however daring you think you are, you aren't perhaps fully ready to truly push the boundaries of what we're doing. But I can tell you that you are. What you are about to embark on tonight is going to transform the face of Brockley – more than Hilly Fields, more than the station, more than the cemetery, the school, the roundabouts and Brockley Cross. All of it. Tonight we are performing essential surgery on the face of SE4."

It was an impassioned speech and if Churchill had been a middle class guerrilla gardener I'm sure he would have put it in a similar way.

Straight after the rhetoric we went into our teams, picked up our bags and set to work. But while everyone else appeared to retain the WWII-style enthusiasm, it waned in me and I stood, bag in hand, in what was obviously the front garden of an elderly person – there were grab rails by the front door – and felt like a burglar. OK so all I was stealing was a bag load of weeds and a really freaky plastic gnome that, bizarrely, resembled Winston Churchill, but still … I felt very, very bad. But who was I to say this elderly person wouldn't want someone to do his/her garden for free? To plant some cheerful flowers and green up the shabby patch of turf?

I tried to focus on the positives as a way of coping with doing something that I felt was wrong. Because it *was* wrong – of sorts – but it wasn't completely and totally wrong like stealing from children or tripping up pensioners for laughs. It was like the plaque on the bench, the 'recommendations' to Mr Iqbal and the ominous 'can we get to him' comments about Da Notorious Baron: none of it was wrong per se it just didn't feel right. Or *was* it wrong and I was just in so deep I couldn't tell any more? Perhaps, I wondered as I silently dug up the dead turf of the first house on the road, perhaps I ought to talk to Robert about it. He knew about the Spades now, he knew me – sort of.

My hand hovered over a dead rose bush.

How odd.

How very odd that I hadn't thought of turning to Beth first.

Neil, Anja and I cleared the garden within half an hour. Scraggy sweet peas, roses, geraniums – all of it went in the bin, because it didn't match Eustace's vision for a grander Brockley. Once it was all bagged Jake emptied an enormous sack full of topsoil over the cleared ground and then brought a wheelbarrow full of rolled turf, perennials and shrubs that had been assigned to this property: delphiniums, lavenders, blue and white alliums.

Completed, we stepped back and examined the finished garden.

"It's good." Neil whispered.

"It's wrong." Anja muttered.

But there was no opportunity to discuss it any further. For once Eustace was staying to watch this dig and we couldn't be seen talking and wasting time. Already he had despatched Jake to get bins for our next garden– careless talk costs lives.

We moved next door.

As we set to work again I saw with relief that Eustace had moved off to watch another team who now looked decidedly more stressed than they had done two minutes earlier when they weren't being watched.

I was consumed by the need to ask Anja what she'd been talking about with Guy. Were Neil and Anja trying to leave the Spades but Eustace wouldn't let them?

I couldn't bring the subject up: neither of them spoke much beyond 'pass the spade, would you' or 'is it delphiniums here or alliums?'

It took us longer with the second garden: it was a student house so the rubbish clearance alone took nearly half an hour. Besides, we were all tired and wanting to be anywhere else but in someone else's property cleaning up in the early hours of a Saturday morning.

Eustace was hovering, far enough away to not disturb us but near enough to be clearly visible.

"Bastard," Anja said into her alliums. "He's trying to intimidate us into speeding up."

A few minutes later two more gardeners had come to help us out. If we were to meet the deadlines we had ten minutes left to lay the turf and plant the remaining shrubs: we were struggling.

And yet we had done it. At just before five in the morning Neil, Anja and I downed tools and joined the others on the road opposite, the sky lightening in the east over Greenwich – a state of affairs that probably irritated Eustace – and the traffic was starting up again on the A2. It was time for the guerrilla gardeners to go home.

Eustace's vision had been realised. Stripped of their clutter and weeds the row of houses were perfectly trimmed and co-ordinating with front gardens of green and white and blue. The public face of Brockley had undergone a face-lift.

"Good work chaps!" Eustace said and went round the dishevelled gardeners and patted backs.

I was so tired I didn't even realise that Guy was standing beside me and looking over at the completed vista.

"I understand how you feel," he said, reading my expression and putting an arm round me, "but you're wrong."

"So it would seem." I kissed him back. "So what are your plans for tonight ... this morning..."

"Well," he slung his arms around me and pulled me to him, "I have an exhibition opening at 9am in the cinema in Hoxton Square and I have to be there all morning, so I shall be getting some sleep." He checked his watch by angling it to the nearest street light. "Three hours should be enough. Roger wrangled the exhibition for me – you know Roger, from the *Guardian*? And the *Guardian* will be covering it, too, so it's big business potentially. Come on, I'll walk you home."

"Great."

Great... What a completely rubbish evening this had turned out to be. Pushing guerrilla gardening to its legal (illegal?) limits, and then being given the brush-off: not seeing Guy all evening and not even getting an invite to his exhibition tomorrow. Did he think that I wasn't interested in what he did? Did he even think about me at all?

"So, a friend of mine is opening a bistro in Brockley on Saturday night…"

Guy had been talking non-stop during the walk home but it was only at this point that I tuned in, his intonation implying that a response was going to be required.

"…that's tonight. Shit, gardening at night really messes with your head doesn't it?" he said. "Anyway, do you fancy coming along? Should be fun: free drinks and a sample menu."

"Sure," I said, half placated at not being invited to the exhibition.

"Great. Come to mine around four?"

"I thought you said it was at night."

"I did," he said, squeezing my bottom.

"Oh." I blushed.

"That's if you want to?" he pulled away slightly.

"Oh, yes. Yes I want to." I pulled him back. "Very much."

We kissed at the garden gate and before I'd even thought about it, I said, "Why don't you stay over here tonight," my mouth was still on his. "And I'll let you sleep. I promise."

"I can't, Edda." He pulled away properly now. "I need to sleep. I need to be on my own. Tomorrow's really important – I can't afford to mess it up."

"OK. That's fine. It was worth a try."

"So I'll see you at four?"

"It's a date."

"A date?" Guy was backing away. "That sounds serious, Edda."

"OK it's not a date. It's a liaison."

"Better! Until the afternoon then."

Once inside the house I marched through the hallway, resolutely *not* seeing the tiny red high heels neatly placed beside Robert's brogues.

Twenty

"Good gardening session last night?"

"Great. Really great. Fantastic, actually."

It was Saturday lunchtime and Greta was nowhere to be seen: the tiny red shoes had gone by the time I came down at eleven and Rob was downstairs doing something inept with paper and glue. I'd thought it was too rude to ask him what the construction was supposed to be, but after five minutes' observation I cracked and had to know.

"I'm teaching my Year Seven class about the English Civil War. So these will help."

These what? "Oh … right." I picked up one of his *pieces*. "And was it the Roundheads or the Cavaliers that went round wearing glued litter about their person?"

"They're Roundhead helmets, Edda!"

"They are?" I put the piece on my head and examined it in the mirror, saying something polite about it looking quite helmety.

And then he picked up a cushion and hit me over the head with it, helmet and all.

"You are so rude!" he said, taking aim again. "These took me ages to make and they're historically accurate."

I quickly recovered and grabbed my own cushion.

"Well, they're *technically* rubbish!" I took a step back, just in case. "It didn't even stay on my head! No wonder the Cavaliers won!"

"They lost, you idiot! And for your information the helmet didn't stay on your head because your head is misshapen!" He took a swing at me.

"It is not!" I dodged the hit and got him in the chest with a tasselled pink cushion.

The fight took us up and over the sofa, round the coffee table and then out into the hall, panting and laughing, whacking each other whenever we could, holding our sides and gasping for breath when we got the chance.

"Peace!" I managed, half way up the stairs. "No more!"

"So, you give up then?" Robert sank onto the bottom step, red faced.

"Only for your sake. You look like you're going to collapse."

"You should look in a mirror," he panted, "you're not exactly box-fresh yourself."

We sprawled on the staircase.

"So, where's Greta?" I asked.

"Shopping with girlfriends," he said. "I think she does that a lot."

"Well I enjoyed our little 're-enactment'," I said. "Which battle did we just re-enact exactly?"

"I think it was Naseby." Robert laughed. "Why don't you come into school and pillow fight me a couple of key battles? What do you think?"

"I think you're one of those mad young teachers they make films about."

"Oh come on you'd love it... Come out for dinner with me tonight, then."

Oh.

The words seemed to have tumbled out of his mouth and we both sat in silence, he looking stunned at where they might have come from and me not knowing what to say: dinner would be good, great, but did he really mean to invite me? So should I say no? Or yes. And then I remembered...

"I can't!"

"OK."

"I'm meeting Guy later this afternoon. We're going to his friend's bistro opening."

"Sounds posh," Robert said, flatly.

"It won't be. Not at all. Look I can call and ... well, actually, I can't call because I don't have his number. But—"

"You don't have your boyfriend's number?" Robert looked up now.

"No. Well. He's not my *boyfriend...*"

"Really? I thought–"

"It's very casual."

"Oh. Right. There you go then."

The words hung in the air. *There you go then.* I didn't like what he seemed to be insinuating.

"And what does that mean?" I asked. Just because he was cosying up with the kooky French teacher didn't mean everyone should be doing the full-on boyfriend/girlfriend commitment thing. "Don't judge me."

"I'm not judging you." He snapped back. "You want a

casual relationship then good luck to you. I just thought you were the type of person who wouldn't have gone for something like that. The way you talk about him…"

"Just because you're cosily girlfriended up with the Happy Shopper doesn't mean—"

"And she's not my girlfriend," he cut in. "So now who's making judgements?"

"Whatever," I said. Because the word had worked when I was fourteen years old and why shouldn't it work now? I dumped my cushion on the floor and stormed up the stairs to get ready to go out and I heard Robert slam the front door.

When I went downstairs I was greeted by Finley who told me through narrowed green eyes, *Well, that was a complete fucking mess wasn't it.*

"Whatever."

I had better things to do than pander after a moody lodger and a judgemental cat. I had lovers to meet and bistros to party at. I deliberately walked past his empty bowl and out of the door. Let his beloved new master fill it up.

I pulled the duvet up to my shoulders and lay back on the pillows, arms behind my head, watching Guy. He was lounging at the foot of the iron bed, naked, strumming on an old guitar. *Afterwards,* I was coming to realise, he would sit there, strumming and muttering random clichéd lines of song: *so so blue … where the mountains close up to the sky … and the old man he looked me in the eye, yeah…*

And I would lie there and watch him. Because it felt as though that was what was wanted of me.

But not this evening. The bust up with Robert had put me on edge: I was in no mood to loll around and humour Guy's crappy chord-strumming. I wanted to get up, get dressed and go out – as promised. The last thing I'd eaten was a bowl of Cheerios, and that had been before the pillow fight. Like Roger Wendell with the chocolate muffins, all I could think of was my absolute right to free food. We were an hour late for the start of the opening of the bistro and I was beginning to panic that the sample menu would run out before we arrived. Then what? We could always pop home for a round of toast...

Home.

My heart sank at the thought of it. Going home would mean facing Robert and I didn't want to face Robert: not until I'd got my head around what I was going to say to him. Something along the lines of *I'm really sorry Robert* was probably going to be the gist of it. But the actual wording I hadn't worked out yet.

"Guy... I'm really hungry."

He fluffed a chord but kept the intent, artistic, earnest look. "Mmm ... so you don't want another tussle under the sheets then, my auburn-haired beauty?" He shot me his devilish smile.

"No."

He missed another chord.

"I thought we were going to your friend's bistro party." I said.

303

"The night is young, Edda," he picked up the tune he'd been playing with and started it up again, *Oh you river, winding your wet, wet secrets, yeah...*

I threw off the duvet and picked up my clothes from the floor. "Can I use your shower?"

"Sure," he said, strumming.

The pounding of the hot water felt good and I managed to wash away some of the mood I was in. Upstairs when I returned, cleaned, Guy was still where I'd left him.

"Oo-oh my Scottish beauty ... flammable passion, yeah ... oh, Edda ... red headed crofter, yeah, Che Guevara dreamer, oh...."

I stood and looked at him.

Finally he put down the guitar. "I'm sensing anger."

"Well," I buttoned up my shirt, "there's anger because there's hunger. I haven't eaten for hours."

He strode over to me, kissed me sluttily and asked was I *sure* I didn't want to do that— No. No I did not.

"Fine, fine. I'll shower and then we can go. Mix yourself a drink or something. I'll have a JD and coke if it's going."

Guy bounded down the spiral staircase to the tiny shower room below leaving me alone on the mezzanine. A door shut and a few seconds later I could hear the shower running.

I turned to the studio. The pull of it was irresistible.

This time I walked further into it than I had before, beyond the stacked canvases and the pots of emulsion and on to a more cluttered area that I hadn't reached on my first foray. Behind an old paint-splattered photocopier there was an enormous purple folder labelled *Carbon Paper A1*. Checking in case Guy had come up the stairs I lifted the lid of the photocopier and turned over the paper inside. It was a client's photograph, with the giant blown-up photocopied version lying on the table, a letter paper-clipped to it: *please find enclosed a photograph of my daughter and her fiancé* …Guy had enlarged the photograph to the canvas size using the photocopier.

Fascinated I followed the paper trail, ducking and stretching and walking the length of the table to uncover more. It began with the photograph of the subject, along with a cheque for two thousand pounds. The photograph was put onto the photocopier and enlarged to the appropriate size. Then I could see that the outline of the subject and key features were traced from the photograph onto a canvas using carbon paper. Once the traced image from the photo was transferred, the paints – already chosen by the customer, depending on the décor of the chosen room the picture would hang in – were applied in blocks of flat colour. I stared at the table in disbelief. All of this was just painting by numbers. But without the numbers.

Guy was not an artist! The pouting, dark-eyed artist who *had to be consumed by his muse* and *feel the white-hot wave of his inspiration wash over him* was a fraud, a sham, a cheap fake who was making a lot of money out of a gimmick. Guy painted by numbers!

I returned to the newspaper pinned to the wall that I'd read the first time I'd stayed over at his house.

FARROW AND BALL PORTRAITURE by Arts Editor, Roger Wendell

"*... one of the hottest things in the art world ... a big favourite with celebrities.*"

So Guy's attitude towards his art was a complete fraud – his work was a production line of coloured-in copies and nothing more. But what if ... what if the fraud didn't stop there? What if the fraud extended to how Guy was promoted and publicised? Because Roger as the Arts Editor of a national newspaper was promoting Guy in the paper and the paper had sponsored Guy's exhibition, which had taken place that morning. What if Roger did it not because Guy was an up and coming artist – but because he *owed* Eustace (and Eustace's friends) a favour. Such as being given the opportunity to buy a house in Brockley at an unbelievably cheap price. Eustace had told me the arrangement the day I had worked at V-2. He'd told me that it was a good idea to get a journalist on his side as journalists were important.

So Eustace gave Roger a deal on a house, Roger gave Guy publicity, Eustace gave me a knot garden, I helped out with the guerrilla gardeners. Everyone was indebted to everyone else and that was where Eustace's power came from. That is how he manipulated everyone, by managing the debts.

I was sitting on the edge of the crumpled bed, staring at the studio. And the shower had stopped.

Shaking with something like excitement and maybe a little fear I scurried down the stairs to mix drinks.

Unmasking Guy as an artistic fraud had instantly broken the spell he had over me. Guy didn't come from another more glamorous world than me – he came from the same world as me: he was just another guitar-strumming, emotionally distant bloke. And he had a particularly skewed version of himself: *I have to wait days, weeks, for the inspiration to capture me before I start a commission.*

What complete crap. The only waiting he had to do was for the photocopier to warm up.

And what an idiot I had been, believing all the things he had fed me.

What I wanted to do more than anything was to rush back to my house and say, "Hey, Robert, guess what *I found out!*" but after our big barney, rushing back home to him wasn't the most appealing option. Better to let the dust settle. And anyway, there was no way I was going to give up the opportunity to eat, and for free. Better to go along with the plan tonight and get fed. And tomorrow I would apologise to Robert, apologise to Finley and then reveal Guy's big secret and – most importantly of all – the other purpose of Eustace's secret society.

"How do you know the owner of the bistro?"

Guy and I were walking past my house and I was overcome with the desire to look *happy and carefree* just in case Robert was looking out of the window. I wanted him to see how unbothered I was that we had rowed.

"Claude? He's a friend of Eust's."

"He's not a gardener?"

"He's helped out a couple of times. But he's not one of us per se. You know you really shouldn't—"

"Yes. I know. I'm sorry."

"So your lodger's still at your house, then." He leant in and nibbled my ear. "What is he – a tax collector or something?"

"No!" I batted him away, irritated. "He's a teacher. A history teacher."

"Ha!"

"What?"

"I don't know which is worse: tax collector or dusty old history teacher."

We walked on, past Fox Estates, the Petit Marché, the launderette.

"Pardon?" Guy leant in to me. "Did you say something?"

"I said *a tax collector*. It's worse to be a tax collector than a history teacher."

"You're still thinking about what I said about your lodger?" He laughed.

"Yes."

"So, in your opinion, it's better to be a regurgitator of tired old history facts to kids who only want to go out and make out?" he said.

Oh.

My fists balled in my pockets and my heart was racing. How dare he be so superior when all he did was paint by numbers and get his commissions from dishonest promotions? As if he were somehow better

308

than Robert who worked hard at what he did and didn't go on about his *talent* all the time.

We walked down the Brockley Road in silence: or rather me in silence and him quietly and huskily murmuring the threads of songs like a tracheotomy patient trying out karaoke. Now that I'd seen him for the fraud he was this vagueness and disconnected attitude was really irritating. Just how good was a free sample menu? How many vol au vents would make up for having to spend more time with Guy tonight? There should be more to a man than a pretty face, a great body and a mews house, after all. We walked past the Chinese takeaway and I felt the urge to veer into it to take something home instead of going out to the bistro. But no – I was dressed up and ready for the free food. And at least, after the opening party tonight, I would have something to discuss with Babs over the garden wall. When I'd mentioned the event earlier in the week she'd told me many tales of the former pub that the bistro had replaced and if the party spilled out around the back of the bistro I was definitely going to look out for the line of bullet holes in the brickwork where members of an infamous South London gang had been lined up and shot in the 1960s. Maybe the New Brockley owners had made a feature of it and underlit it with Heals spotlights.

"Doesn't it strike you as odd," I said, having decided to interrupt Guy's stream of conscious tunefulness, "that all the shops and bistros and cafés that have opened in the last few months all look the same?"

Guy thought for a moment. "I don't see how the deli

looks like the bookshop... Sausages. Dictionaries. Very different."

"I mean how every single one of the new businesses have bay trees outside them. The deli, the bookshop, Fox Estates, the beauty salon, V-2. They all have the trees chained in tubs outside. And even Mr Iqbal was given bay trees by Eustace as part of his shop's facelift."

"So?" Guy looked slightly cagey.

"And all the new shops are painted the same set of colours."

"Oh, come on, Edda," Guy stood before me, bringing me to a halt, steps away from the bistro and the free sample menu. It was a dangerous tactic to come between me and my food. "The shops are new and they're on-trend. Of course they're going to choose currently fashionable palettes. And I can tell you that on-trend right now is Charleston Grey, Pelt, Shaded White … and the bistro here is done out in Brinjal and Oval Room Blue." He laughed, seeing my expression. "I work in Farrow and Ball, Edda. I *know* Farrow and Ball."

"Of course you do."

"So let's…" but he trailed off. He was staring at something across the road and I followed his line of sight. He crossed the road and I followed, intrigued by what had caught his attention.

It was one of my stencils: a woman in a wedding dress and the suggestion of a billowing veil blowing in the wind, holding aloft a giant AK-47 and weeping. Sprayed in black and white there was a pool of crimson blood at her feet and spattering the hem of the wedding dress.

"Now that really is quite good." Guy traced my stencil with a finger, "The movement, the feel of despair. Look at that gun, Edda, it's so realistic, just picked out with one or two highlights, but it's enough to be realistic."

"Probably drawn from real life," I said, remembering with a smile a bizarre afternoon sitting at Babs' house with one of Tyrone's AK-47s laid out on a lace covered side table beside a plate of bourbon biscuits on a doily. "You know these South London gangs."

But Guy wasn't listening to me. "Finally Da Notorious Baron is producing something of merit."

"Great. Does this mean Eustace isn't going to pursue him and drag him to art college?"

"God, no. Graffiti's a powerful weapon and Eust will no doubt want to control it, you know what he's like. He said to me the other day that he wants gentler themes that aren't going to upset the gentry moving in with their children. I mean, for all this artistic merit you can see here you've still got firearms and blood. That's not going to sit very well with the Middle Class Young Family is it?"

"You really think it has artistic merit?"

"No doubt about it. Why are you looking so pleased?"

"Oh I'm not. No. I'm just pleased for Brockley. That we've got our own Banksy..." I petered out.

"Come on in." He grabbed my hand, kissed the palm, and led me across the road, up the steps of Bistro Brockley, passing the suspiciously fairy-lit bay trees in their chained-down wooden tubs.

Twenty-one

Bistro Brockley was stifling, crammed with glittery, sequined people. Guy led me through the masses and towards the bar, holding my hand through the crowds in case I got lost. The décor was dark: exposed brick and charcoal-painted walls lit by orange pendant lights hung from a concrete ceiling. *Who the bleedin' 'ell would eat in a place what looks like the workin' class pub it was in the sixties? All that brick an' cement: looks like a doss 'ouse. The bloke's a bleedin' nutter.* Babs had been her usual eloquent self when discussing the décor earlier in the week.

"Come and meet Claude." Guy looped his arm around my waist and I felt a sudden gladness that I was there with him and he was taking care of me. It was very overwhelming, so many people and no one I'd seen that I knew.

I was dragged further across the room, towards a wall of red-lit champagne bottles where Claude, the chef-patron, was talking animatedly to a journalist. He had to be a journalist: he was holding a Dictaphone one millimetre away from Claude's mouth. I prided myself on my perception.

"Edda, Edda, Edda! *Buona sera!* It is nice to meet you!" The tanned and perfectly presented Claude shook my hand energetically. He tried to put a hand on my shoulder but, as he was probably just shy of five feet, he gave up.

"Thank you for inviting me."

"But not at all! A friend of Guy's is a friend of mine! We are all in it together, yes? Yes? Have you eaten? Have you tried the figs they are divine! I say it myself but—" he stopped. A fraught cry from the kitchens caught his attention. "I go! Enjoy! Eat! Drink!" he backed away to the crisis, winking at Guy.

"He's Italian," Guy said, nonchalantly as he helped himself to a platter of meats. "Third generation. There's loads of them in Lewisham. Did you know that? They all came over a century ago when things got tough in Italy or whatever the country was called in those days. I have no idea about that history shit: I'm no dull as dishwater history teacher am I?" He looked pleased at the joke. "But they're *good* foreigners, if you see what I mean."

"Pardon?" Had I heard him straight? Had he just said they were 'good' foreigners?

"You know," he waved his glass in front of me, "they don't cause trouble like the— "

"Guy!" A blonde woman fell into his arms and planted a kiss on his stubbled cheek. "Darling!"

"Hello you," he put an arm around her lazily and kissed her. "How's things?"

"Oh, God, frantic…" And she launched into why her life was frantic, still with his arm around her waist, and, I noticed, her thighs resting between his thighs as he leant against the bar. Neither of them noticed me.

The Italian immigrants don't cause trouble like the what? What had Guy been on the brink of saying before this woman with the thighs had thrown herself between us?

I stood for a few more moments, wondering whether Guy would surface and introduce me: *Hey blonde-thing, this is my girlfriend Edda/ this is my lover Edda/ this is Edda...* whatever I was to him and he to me, but Guy was completely lost in the blonde and, like the meat platter, I had been forgotten.

I turned my back on them and walked away. There was no point standing there like a lemon.

I was niggled but not upset. And that didn't surprise me... Because I wanted to get home. I wanted to speak to Robert and say a whole series of things including *I'm sorry* and *I'm really sorry.*

"Canapé?"

"Oh, God, yes!" I gave in to my famished Red-Cross-package feeling and scooped up an obscene quantity of canapés and set to work on them.

"Edda! Edda, my absolute saviour and favourite person in the world!"

"Neil!" Before I could put down my prawn toasts I was caught up in a bear hug with the beads of his dreads slapping my head. He smelt of coffee.

"Thank you so much for helping me out the other day."

"It's fine. Honestly." I took a champagne flute from a passing waitress. I was now going to be an official freeloader. "Have the staff returned to help you out?"

"No. I'm only allowed to pay minimum wage and

314

they've got better jobs. It's fucking shit." Neil ran a hand through his dreadlocked plaits. "My life is *over*, I tell you. I thought it would be this great way of life but all I ever do is grind beans and foam milk." He stared with glazed eyes into the crowd behind us.

"What about Pembrokeshire?" I whispered to him.

Neil shot a panicked look around. "I don't know, man. We've got, like, no money. How are we going to set up in Pembrokeshire with no money? You've got to have money, man. When we came here and Eustace offered me this café deal, well I nearly bit his hand to get it. But there's not going to be any deal if I move back to Pembrokeshire. That's it, man. It's here or nowhere."

"So why don't you just tell Eustace that you don't want it any more? He'll find someone else." I even had, in the back of my head, thought that I might step into his shoes. Hadn't I always wanted to work in a café and here, possibly, was an opportunity waiting to be grasped? But then by taking up the V-2 I would be putting myself entirely in the hands of Eustace Fox – and the prospect of luxury accommodation would not work on me.

Neil grabbed another glass of champagne from a passing waiter.

"But presumably you pay rent to Eustace. He didn't just *give* you the café and the flat." I said.

"Oh he takes everything. All of it! I get to live rent free and in return I put in eleven hours a day seven days a week and get pocket money: hardly anything. I'm a fool, I know I am, for making us do this in the first place. Anja and I work like dogs and he's got me by the short and curlies, because how would I live any better elsewhere? I couldn't even dream of opening up my own café. Not in a credit crunch, and definitely not in London." He looked at the floor and wavered. "I didn't read the small print, Edda. Don't they always tell you to read the small print? I just saw the fancy apartment with its chandeliers and wet rooms and I was seduced."

"Champagne? Orange juice?" The waiter came over and broke Neil out of his dark thoughts: the free spirit obviously didn't like being owned by the man in the sharp suit across the road. The leash around his neck must have felt very tight.

"I'll just take two," Neil winked at the waiter – or rather he thought he did, he was so drunk he actually closed both eyes, "in case I miss you when you do your rounds again."

The waiter smiled sarcastically and looked like he'd heard the same excuse for freeloading a hundred times already that night. The look he gave Neil irritated me, so I took two drinks as well.

"Where is Anja, tonight?" I asked.

"She wouldn't come." Neil downed a glass in one gulp. "She won't go anywhere near Eustace now if she can help it." He gave an intoxicated laugh. "She just wants us to go back. Even though we've got no money – she says that doesn't matter. Says we'll muddle through. Go back to our knackered old caravan and make do until we find our feet again. I just don't know if I can go back…"

There was a sudden roar of voices and Neil and I looked up. Eustace Fox had walked in and people were clapping. As he entered a camera flashed and he shielded his eyes, "No! No photographs! Please! Claude! Claude this is fabulous!" he ducked out of the way of the cameraman, but not before he shot the man a dark look. I found myself frowning as I watched him. Why didn't Eustace Fox want to be photographed? Surely he was the master of socialising and networking: wouldn't having it evidenced in the papers be right up his street?

I watched as he was received into the room like a celebrity, shaking hands and kissing the cheeks of everyone assembled: a word here and laugh and slap on the back there. I looked to see how Neil had taken the arrival of his boss/owner. He looked crushed.

"This is a nice place," I said in an effort to bring my friend back from the unhappy place I'd put him in by talking about the café. Maybe if I hadn't pried so deeply then he wouldn't be so intent on drowning in bubbly.

"Yeah," Neil looked about blearily, "yeah it's l-lovely. It's goddamn lovely." He held on to the bar. "And good for Claude that's what I say! He's wanted to do this for so bloody long, and now he's finally got the chance."

"What did he used to do before opening the bistro?" I asked, hoping I wasn't putting my foot in it again. Tonight there seemed such a fine line between taking an interest and mortally wounding Neil.

"The man was a policeman! Would you believe. Lucky the minimum height thingy was relaxed 'cause he's such a shortarse. Don't know how he ever caught the crims. Probably bit their kneecaps or something." His hand slipped from the bar and he staggered down.

"Look, Neil, maybe I should walk you home."

"I bet," he pulled himself back upright, "I bet Claude managed to nego … neg … " he tried the word out before slowing down to pronounce it properly, "Net-o-tiate a better deal with Eustash Foxsh than I got. What do you think? Do you think he'll get to keep the profits from this place? You can't fuck a p-policeman around can you? Wonder what Eustch got in return? Why doesh he want to do Claude? It'll be the police connection won't it? Yeah. Eust wants the p-police connection."

"Why?" I cut into his mumblings and he slapped a hand on his mouth.

"No. Don't say. Don't say anything will you? All hush. All hush hush!"

"Oh my God," I said, as much to myself as Neil. "It really is all Eustace isn't it?"

Neil frowned at me and tried to put a finger to his lips.

"I mean I had a suspicion that he was involved in some way. It's the bay trees – they're like a calling card for him aren't they? They're a sign!"

"Edda, I—"

"I thought he was a controlling man with the gardening: changing things on the surface of Brockley but actually, *actually* he's imposing himself onto the neighbourhood isn't he? Does he own all these new businesses around here?"

"Really Edda. D-don't." Neil scooped a handful of canapés off a passing tray.

318

"But I'm on to something aren't I? I am aren't I? Admit it."

"Yes," he muttered, shooting a nervous look across the room at the man himself. "That's estate agents for you," he hiccupped, looking like a man on the brink of changing his mind and talking at last. "The place becomes vacant, or should I say *vacated* eh? Eh?" He made to tap his nose but missed. "And Eustace is in like a shot. I mean. He only wants the best doesn't he? For Brockley. He wantsh it to be Greenwich. He's always going on. About Greenwich. You know. Greenwich thish, Greenwich that. Sometimes, you know, I think he really hatesh Greenwich. Has this enormous chip. On his shoulder. You know. Eust grew up in Brockley didn't he? Went to this p-posh school in Greenwich or was it Blackheath? Anyway, one of the two. So, I bet the posh kids, man, I bet they slated him for coming from Brockley; I bet it was a right shithole in those days."

I thought about Babs and what she would have said to Neil about that.

Nothing, probably. She just would have socked him.

"So you think Eustace is trying to make Brockley into Greenwich by guerrilla gardening?"

"Fuck yeah!" he wobbled and clutched onto the bar again. "And the rest."

"You mean by buying up all the shops he can lay his hands on and making them into Greenwich-style businesses?"

Neil threw his head back, "A ha! A ha ha ha ha! You've got it there haven't you? Buying. Taking. Buying. Take

319

take take. Clever old Eust eh?" He laughed again and then leapt skywards as Eustace clamped a heavy hand on his shoulder.

I hadn't seen him make his was across the room either and I felt my heart race at the sight of him. How much of what Neil had said had Eustace heard?

"Having fun?" he asked lightly. "It's a splendid venue don't you think? So imaginatively decked out; it's exactly how I'd wanted it to be. A friend of mine did it. And he did the bookshop over the road. Have you been in yet, Edda?"

"No. No, I haven't." I said into my glass. The cold sobriety of Eustace was in sharp contrast to Neil's ruddy cheeked drunkenness.

"Oh you should. It's lovely, like a bijou version of Waterstones. Anyway, I won't keep you – you were obviously deep in conversation. I'll pop round to V-2, perhaps tomorrow Neil – maybe get a mid-morning cappuccino, what do you say?"

"Great," Neil nodded, looking down at the floor and swaying.

"And Anja? Is she well?"

"Yesh."

"Such a shame that she couldn't be here tonight. Well, then, see you later, Edda." Eustace leant over and slowly planted a kiss on my cheek before disappearing through the crowd to the other side of the room.

"I have to go!" Neil scrabbled for his coat that had slid off a bar stool and was being trampled into the floor.

"No!"

"Yes. Sorry. Edda. See you around."

I watched as he clumsily tried to stuff his hands into the balled up arms of his coat and jigged to work them free.

"Here let me help you…"

"'s fine." Neil pushed violently against the sleeves. "There I'm free." And he was gone.

I looked across the room and saw Eustace with a hint of a smile on his lips, head turned to the door and watching Neil's exit.

Vacant and *vacated. Buying and taking.*

There was a significant difference between the two words that Neil had used.

Eustace was obviously behind the estate agency and the transformation of the Petit Marché, but tonight Neil had let slip that Eustace was also behind the V-2 café and the Bistro. Now I was realising there were all the other businesses too: all the Farrow and Ball painted bay-tree touting shops had been acquired through him. Legitimately and otherwise.

I turned away from watching Eustace. *Vacant* meant the premises were empty and the new business was free to move in. *Vacated* – did that mean the old business was forced out to make way for the new business? Is that was Neil was implying? All these bistros and cafés and book shops, all these bay trees and Farrow and Ball painted signs, had there been a wholesale pushing-out of the old businesses?

What *were* the old businesses? I'd been in Brockley a few years, surely I'd remember.

I pushed my way through the spangled crowd until I was standing by the steamed windows. With my sleeve pulled over my hand I rubbed a circle in the steamed up glass and peered out into the darkened South London street.

The book shop opposite had been a kebab shop. The bistro I was in had been a rough pub, the florist's on the corner had been a tatty convenience store, Fox Estates had been a betting shop and Booze Busters off-licence was now an antiques shop. I craned my head left and then right. I could count twelve bay trees in twelve identical pots chained with identical chain two to the front of each of the six premises.

Was Eustace really behind all of this? My fingers froze on the steamed panes of glass. Was this what Babs knew about Eustace: was this why she was so hesitant to talk about him? Not because he was a snob that wouldn't sell her friend's flat and didn't want to know her sort of London, but because he was cold-bloodedly wiping old Brockley off the map and replacing it with his own cosmetically enhanced rival to Greenwich.

Hadn't Babs said that the gangs in suits were more frightening than the gangs in hoodies?

My hand was shaking on the pane of glass.

"I hear Neil was off his muffin." I felt Guy's arm slip in around my waist. "Did you ply him with champagne, Edda? Tut, tut, the boy can't take it you know! These beach bums are more spliff heads."

"Guy," I turned to face him, wiggling to free my waist from his arm.

"Having fun?" he said.

I looked at him, the worse for wear, tousled and, I noticed, red-plumped kissed lips no doubt from the blonde with the thighs.

I smiled.

But I didn't care one jot, not even a very small jot. In fact… "Guy, you remember you told me that you have to wait for the inspiration to come to you in order to paint?"

"Ye-es," he looked at me from the top of his champagne glass.

"And that you have to search for the muse?"

"Mm-hmm."

"Well do you need the muse to embrace you while you enlarge family snaps on a photocopier?"

"Wh—"

"Does the mood have to be right before you trace the image onto canvas using carbon paper? I was just wondering, because the painting by numbers thing you've got going doesn't seem to tally with all that crap that you spout about being a true artist."

"What are you trying to say, Edda?" Guy struck a pose.

"Well, I'm trying to say what I'm trying to say. You're not an artist are you? You convert photographs into paintings by enlarging them and copying their outlines. That's not the same as interpretation and inspiration is it?"

"There's a lot more to it," he downed his drink in a single draft, "than someone not of an artistic bent could ever understand."

"Like how to remember if number 3 was Cooking Apple Green or Lulworth Blue? You don't even get to choose the colours do you? That's decided for you by your client. It's hardly Rosetti or Millais is it?"

"What's wrong with you, tonight, Edda?" he said through tight lips.

"Nothing." I grabbed my coat from the bar stool, heart pounding but completely ecstatic. "Goodbye, Guy."

And I fled, champagne-headed and with heart pounding, running through the empty Brockley streets, one less convert to the Eustace Fox cause.

"ROBERT!"

An amorphous shape spasmed on the bed. "What the—" Robert thrashed around, fighting in the dark with the duvet.

"I'm sorry! Don't be scared it's me! Look I'm going to turn on the light."

"What? No! Don't *argh!* Bloody hell, Edda, what the bloody hell are you – what time is it?" Robert, hair all over the place, leant over to his watch and stared at it blearily. "It's one in the morning, Edda!"

"I know. I'm sorry." I perched on the edge of the bed. "Can we talk?"

He fell back onto the pillow, tousled and pyjamad and – the feeling hit me *walloped me* in the stomach – more desirable to me than Guy would ever be. And then came the realisation that I was acting like a complete prostitute, spending the afternoon in bed with one man and then lusting after another, full of canapés

324

and champagne sitting on his bed at one in the morning.

Oh well… Now was not the time for fretting about moral niceties.

"Robert, listen, Eustace Fox is running Brockley! He's got this whole empire thing going on around us!"

Robert groaned and sat up. "You're not going to go away, are you?"

"No! You *have* to hear this."

"I don't have to hear it, Edda."

"Oh, please." I flopped down beside him, breaking every landlady rule in the book.

"Edda, can we talk tomorrow?"

I turned to face him on the pillow. "It is tomorrow."

"Later," he said, a touch ominously.

"That was very ominous."

"I'm very tired."

"OK," I propped myself up, "But can I just say that I'm sorry. I'm really sorry for being such an idiot earlier."

He ran a hand over his eyes and yawned. "Look, Edda, can we talk about it tomorrow morning?"

"Yes. Let's. Let's talk tomorrow." And then I leant over and kissed him on the mouth. And fled out of the room, turning out the light before I could see Robert's expression.

"Oh bugger!" I whispered to Finley, a few minutes later, slopping out Forest Friends Meaty Pieces into his bowl. "Bugger, bugger, bugger. Fin: I've really messed up."

Twenty-two

We had a good routine to Sundays. Robert would be up at around nine. He'd go out to Mr Iqbal's, to pick up the Sunday papers, and then on returning he'd put a pot of coffee on and settle down at the breakfast bar. At which point I'd emerge from my bedroom, barmy-haired and dressing-gowned, and help him read the papers and assist in the drinking of the coffee. Sometimes on those Sunday mornings we hardly talked – just grunted a *hello* and then sitting side by side we buried ourselves in the papers. Other times we'd discuss the news, although we didn't always see eye to eye on what we classed as news... *I cannot believe the Government's bringing in the new legislation on pensions/Yes but look at these plastic pink jodhpurs do you think I should buy plastic pink jodhpurs?* As a rule he liked the bits of the papers that were large and had pictures of graphs and cross looking middle-aged men in them. While I liked any bits that were on glossy paper and had pretty pictures in them, mostly of shiny things to buy. We argued over the property section.

But today I was up at six in the morning. By seven I was showered, coiffed and made up, dressed casually yet attractively, perched neatly at the breakfast bar with the

Sunday papers that *I'd been out to buy myself*. I was pleased to note that enormous vats of ghee had appeared in the Petit Marché again along with some of the exotic Caribbean and Eastern European foods that had always formed a staple of the Brockley Mini Mart. Cracks had started to appear in Eustace's carefully managed world.

"Edna, it is very early for you. Robert is ill?" Mr Iqbal asked with concern as I'd handed over a small fortune: the last time I had bought the Sunday papers they had been about seventy pence.

"I thought I might get the Sunday papers this week."

"Well, I am sure he will like the rest. He is working too hard at the moment isn't he?"

Was he? How rubbish was I that I didn't even know. I made a mental note to ask him about his work: as soon as I'd told him my news of course ... "Yes he is working hard," I said.

"And would you like to buy this organic muesli bar, young Edna? It says it's packed full of free range nuts and wholegrain."

When I got home I divided the papers into two piles: dry news and glossy fluff. I straightened the piles and pushed Robert's pile in front of his stool and mine in front of my stool. I made a pot of coffee. I poured it away and made a better pot of coffee. I drank a mug of it, then another mug of it, ate my organic muesli bar and felt rather ill. I flicked through my glossy fluff magazines. I checked my hair. I ate the second muesli bar. I made another pot of coffee and I wondered:

where was Robert? Why wasn't Robert coming down? I checked my watch. It wasn't even eight o'clock. Urgh. There was still an hour to go before it was his usual time to get up.

I stared at my reconstructed Valhalla plate and my heart sank as I remembered kissing Robert last night. Why had I done that? What good would that have done? I still hadn't worked out what I was going to say when he came down and I so wanted to tell him my news. I wanted to jump on his bed and scream, *Wake up! I want to talk to you about Eustace Fox!* but I didn't dare to go into his room again. Because maybe, since the incident late last night, he'd dug out his old cricket bat and was now sleeping with it under his pillow in the event that I launched myself on him again.

And I didn't want to call Beth. Because she was so out of touch with what was going on it would take half an hour to bring her up to speed, by which time she'd have lost interest or have something she had to do. Like give birth.

"Oh, bloody hell!" I threw down the stupid magazines, chucked the bad coffee down the sink and stormed outside, grabbing my hatchet and gardening gloves. I had an inner anger that was making my hands shake and hacking away at the back garden was the only way I could think of working it off. Because hey – it'd worked for the front garden.

I stood in the morning light, panting slightly, still angry, but determined not to ravage the wilderness at the back of the house to the same extent that I'd ravaged what had been the wilderness at the front. I could vent my anger by taming, trimming, cutting. There would be no hacking this time. No slashing.

"Crikey, Edda..."

"Robert!" I threw the hatchet down onto the heap of cuttings. "Hi!"

"What have you *done*?"

"I've been gardening."

"Edda, you've completely decimated the back garden."

"Have I? Have I really?" I turned to look back on my early morning's work with fresh eyes. "Oh, crap, I have haven't I? Damnit. I didn't mean to."

"What happened to the Rowan tree?"

I peered round the garden. "It's there. By the heap of hedge cuttings."

"You hacked down the *rowan tree*? That thing was a beast."

I shrugged. "I had a lot of coffee this morning. And I had things to think about. Anyway," I turned back to him, "how are you? Are you OK?"

"I'm fine. You have stuff in your hair, you know. Clippings. Twigs."

"Oh. Pants!" I reached up and pulled vegetation from my hair. I had been so immaculate at seven that morning and now, I checked my watch, at a quarter to ten I was dishevelled and tramp-like. "Look, Robert," I said, flinging the twigs from my up-do, "I'm really sorry about last night."

He looked at me slightly askew. "Which bit?"

"What do you mean?" I said, coyly. Perhaps he couldn't actually remember the last bit …

"Well I mean are you sorry for the shouty bit early on, or the bit where you kissed me."

"Oh. Well. Both. Both, I think. I'm really sorry for shouting at you. I didn't mean to shout at you at all. Not in any way. But there you go – I did and I'm sorry. And as for later on, well, I'm sorry for that too. That was wrong. I mean, I wasn't invited…"

"All right there, me darlin's?" Babs' voice carried over the garden wall along with the smoke from the first fag of the day. "Nice mornin' for it, Edda, love! Another one of them posh Nationwide Trust gardens is it? Got more o' that box hedgin' comin''ave yer?"

"Morning, Babs," Robert and I said simultaneously said and then looked at each other and laughed. And the tension was broken.

"Come on inside," I whispered, grabbing him by the arm. "I have some big news."

"Edda, is your big news that you went out to buy the Sunday papers all by yourself?" Robert perched on his side of the breakfast bar and looked at me askance. I liked his askance look: it was sort of sexy, but also sort of had-a-fight-with-the-pillow. I gripped the edge of the kitchen counter. I would *not* lean over and kiss him. He really would take a cricket bat to me if I tried to do that. And I would have to go through the whole interview process again for a new lodger and Finley would no doubt have to go into feline therapy now that the great love of his life was moving out…

"It's real news." I cleared my head and pulled up my stool beside his. "Just listen to this."

Ten minutes later Robert closed his mouth.

"Oh," he said.

I leant in to him. "So is that news, or is that news?"

"Yes. That's news." He toyed with the empty coffee mug I'd put out for him two hours earlier. "Do you know it *had* crossed my mind that it was a bit odd that there were so many of those clipped bushes on sticks all over the place. But I thought that some mad nurseryman had come to Brockley with a job lot going cheap. But, as you say, the signs are all painted in the same sorts of paint and the shops have this sameyness *thing* about them haven't they?"

"Eustace said as much to me, when I spoke to him last night. I don't think he'd really thought about the words he was using: that the bistro was *exactly how I wanted it to be*. So that suggests he did have a say in the set-up."

"But you're not basing your assumptions purely on that, are you?" Suddenly Robert looked doubtful.

"No! There's what Neil's told me, too."

"Neil who could barely stand upright, according to you…"

"Yes, but that's beside the point."

"Well, if he could barely stand, isn't there the smallest possibility that he might have been either not telling the truth or putting something across in not quite the most coherent way? Oh come on, Eds!" He saw the deflated

331

look on my face. "You're probably right, you know. I'm just playing devil's advocate."

"Maybe you're right, though," I said sullenly. "Maybe I am making it all up."

"Or maybe not. Come on, grab your coat and let's go exploring Brockley. You never know we might find something out if we go looking for it."

"Oh!" I almost trembled with excitement. "That is so Julian!"

"Meaning?"

"Julian, from the Famous Five! Taking charge! Going on an adventure!"

"Fine, fine." Robert aka Julian laced his trainers and held open the front door.

"Can Finley be Timmy the dog?" I said.

"Yes. And you're Dick."

"Thanks for that." I grabbed my Farrow and Ball colour chart booklet and dashed out after him. The adventure was afoot!

"Your rats have gone," Robert whispered to me as we passed the wall that ran next to Fox Estates.

"Well that's one element of his control," I whispered back, head down as we passed the vast polished windows of the estate agency. "Eustace's partner is the Head of Planning at the Council and Guy told me that he arranges for Council graffiti patrols to clear up the art work, if not on the day then the day after it was sprayed up. Apparently, Eustace employs what he calls his *street walker* to walk every street in the neighbourhood every day to monitor graffiti."

"OK, that's weird thing number one: the man employs surveillance across the neighbourhood."

"And don't forget that he's trying to 'get to' Da Notorious Baron, to send him to art school. He wants control over the graffiti."

"Weird thing number two." He jotted it down on a pad.

We were outside the Petit Marché with its bike and onions, chalkboard and stripy awning.

"Three." We said in unison and, waving to Mr Iqbal we continued on our quest.

"V-2." I said. "Owned and managed by Eustace Fox. And," I whipped out my colour chart, "painted in Citron, with woodwork in Mouse's Back."

Robert looked from chart to café and back to the chart again. "It's Dead Salmon."

"Bay trees?"

"Two. Check."

"Chalk board?"

"Chalked A-board. Check."

Past the station garden (Weird Thing Number Four) we were on the High Road.

"So the florist's..." Robert paused outside it. "Gloria's Flowers."

"Farrow and Ball ... Downpipe and Borrowed Light."

"Bay trees?"

"Two. Check."

"Chalk board?"

"Check."

"And what was it before?"

I thought hard. "A tatty convenience store. Do you think we should go inside and ask them something as part of our investigation?"

Robert considered it. "Like 'did you illegally take over the tatty convenience store and are you owned by Eustace Fox?' "

I shot him a look and we continued down the road, noting down the shops, what they used to be and what shade of Farrow and Ball they were now painted in. And each had bay trees at the front: some with ribbons some without. Some with fairy lights, some without.

"There appear to be nine shops in the Eustace Fox Monopoly set." Robert went down the list. "Convenience store to florist, kebab shop to book shop, off-licence to antique shop, video shop to clothes boutique, pub to bistro, newsagent to café, appliance repair shop to deli, chip shop to stationer, and of course Mini Mart to Petit Marché."

"So, what do we do now?" I asked. "We've listed out what they are and were. They're all painted in Farrow and Ball and they all have bay trees. What next? That's no proof of anything is it? Maybe all newly opened shops look like that these days: if we went into Putney High Street we'd see just the same thing and Eustace can't own Putney High Street can he?"

"We-ell." Robert put down his pad and surveyed the street. "What about the old businesses that are still here? We could go and ask the owners if they know what's going on with the shops around them? They must have some idea. And we can be pretty sure that the people inside aren't connected to Eustace Fox in any way, so we won't get into trouble asking about him."

"Will you do the talking?" I said, trying to look as doe-eyed as I could.

"No."

"Oh, come on! I'm?"

"It's your research, Edda, you do the talking. I'll do the running if there's trouble."

"OK, so who shall we go and see. Oh, I know, let's go see Reg at the launderette. I like Reg. He used to give me garibaldi biscuits when I used the launderette. That was before Beth made me get my own washing machine and stop being common."

"I don't reckon I'll be still in business in six months or so." Amid the folded piles of laundered clothes, Reg lit a cigarette and contemplated us. "Everyone's got a washing machine these days, haven't they? Time was a machine was a luxury, not now though. All my customers these days are students and them on the dole."

"You could go into dry cleaning," Robert suggested.

Reg snorted. "If it ain't wet it ain't cleaned. I ain't going into that chemical business: waste of bloody money. Nah – I've had letters anyway."

"Letters?" I leant forward.

"From the Council. Telling me I've had complaints about the business. Noise pollution. Water pollution. I ask you – forty years I've been here and it's never bothered anyone, and now – apparently – I'm causing untold misery to everyone within five miles of my shop."

"So what do the letters say? What do they want you to do?"

"Close down!" He laughed and then added, "It's not spelled out, of course. They're just threatening me with the environmental people. And they talk about increasing the Council Tax to take into account this and that. It'll be the end of me."

"Do you know who actually complained about your business?" Robert asked.

"The letters didn't say," Reg looked thoughtful. "They just said *people* have complained: people what don't want to be identified. Anyway, I'm now waiting to hear what the Council have to say about my 'working practices', as they call them, and then I'll know where I stand."

Robert and I exchanged knowing looks.

"Tell you what, though," Reg shuffled up and turned off a machine that had finished its cycle. "It's not all bad. I've had an offer on the place. Not a good one, not by any stretch, but given all the complaints I've had and this action from the Council, and the fact that no one's using laundrettes any more – well, I've got a mind to take it up. Right timely it was, coming when it did. The wife definitely has it in mind for me to take it up."

"Who is the offer from?" Robert asked lightly.

"Wouldn't say. But it was made to me by that fancy estate agent round the corner."

"FOX ESTATES!?" I said in a voice that made Reg leap out of his cardigan.

"Steady, love! That's the one; the fancy gaff run by that bloke with the loud trousers and the yawping voice. Anyhow, the bloke said they would handle the sale for me 'on behalf of an anonymous purchaser' or something like that. Time was a buyer would come and slap an inch of notes down on the table and you'd shake hands and the deal was done. Things change though don't they: business is all secretive now."

"Not always." I tapped my pad. "Reg, when did the appliance shop next to you close down?"

"Now that's an odd thing, right there," Reg sat forward. "Old Tony and I went way back, thirty years we've been neighbours on the High Road. And then one morning Tony, and his shop, was gone without so much as a goodbye and by midday there were workmen all over the place turning it into a delicatessen. I ask you – the place is full of things I can't afford and even if I could afford them I wouldn't know what to do with them. The wife went in the other day and felt very out of place. Not our sort are they?"

"So why do you think your neighbour left? Was business bad for him?"

Reg considered the question. "I don't think so. He always had his customers did Tony. Regulars. Tradesmen. So it was odd that he went so sudden, but then look at the street now – we're the ones that are out of place, what with all these funny new places opening up. I tell you what, though, if you're asking…" he leant forward, as did we.

"What?" Robert and I said.

"Old Dino, in the kebab shop over the road, well the book shop *as was* a kebab shop, he didn't want to go. Got pushed out he did."

"No way!" I gripped my pencil in excitement.

"I'm telling you! There were letters from the Council telling him he'd had all these complaints about health and safety."

"Like you had with the noise pollution."

"Just like me. And letters from goodness knows what other department telling him about 200 per cent rises in his rates on the place. And then this man comes from the Council and advises him that his business is going to be closed down, without so much as an inspection, and then this other bloke comes out of the blue and offers him a sum of money for the place and out he went. He loved that shop did Dino. And he'd only just had it retiled inside, all posh it was But now he's looking at starting all over again, opening up somewhere in Forest Hill, but it ain't the same, not when you're Brockley born and bred."

"The man who came to tell him the place was closing, what did he look like, do you remember?"

"I didn't see him." Reg shrugged. "Drove up in a fancy red car, though."

"A red sports car? Convertible?"

"That's the one! You know the bloke?"

"Peter Shaw," I said.

We had got what we needed.

"So what was all that about?" Robert and I were walking back to the house. "Who is Peter Shaw?"

"Eustace's partner," I leant over and whispered to him, "Works at the Council and heads up the Planning Department."

"OK, so there's a link to the big man," Robert said, "but surely he's only doing his job, isn't he?"

"Going round to businesses and telling them they're going to be shut down on health and safety grounds without any inspections whatsoever? That's not his job: Peter Shaw is office-based and never goes out into the streets. He has teams to do that for him. No – he wasn't doing his Council duties, he was doing his boyfriend duties."

"Boyfriend duties! Now there is a marvellous concept, eh?" came a voice behind us.

"Eustace!" My heart stopped beating and Robert and I turned to see the man himself, poised outside the door to the estate agency that we'd just walked past, a bottle of Brasso and a duster in his hands. "Edda, Edda, Edda! And how are you, my dear? I'm sorry I hardly had the time to speak to you at the bistro opening last night, it was quite hectic wasn't it? But such a good evening don't you think? But, you know, Guy is very low."

"He is?"

"He is. Slunk off soon after you left. Have you two had a bit of a run-in, eh? Ah, young love is so full of passion and drama isn't it? I think he may call you today. And who is your friend here?" He turned to Robert who was looking at me in an odd way.

"Oh. Sorry. Yes. This is Robert. Robert – Eustace Fox."

The two men shook hands and Eustace made small talk while I tried to look at him and see him for the criminal he was: the man who was forcing out established local businesses, gardening the mess, cleaning up the graffiti. A man, in fact, who was trying to run Brockley as his own private empire. But he looked too round and jolly to be the runner of an evil empire. And his trousers – orange and green tweed today – did nothing to advance any suggestion of evilness. Really he should be walking with a stick, have only one eye, a heavy foreign accent and sport an evil black moustache.

He should be a Bond villain, in fact.

"Claude will no doubt do very well with the bistro," he was saying to us. "And it was a very good night, last night. But I'd imagine some of us will have sore heads this morning, eh? Your friend Neil, for example."

"Yes. Yes, I expect so." I said, itching to get away and at the very least to hide the notepad scribbled with all our findings from the investigations. Investigations into him and his businesses…

"Yes, Neil seemed pretty blotto for most of the time. Was he even talking sense?"

I could see that Eustace was looking at me, hungry for information: he was steering the conversation in a direction that I did not want it to go because I didn't want to get Neil or myself into trouble.

"No. Not much." I bit my lip.

Eustace nodded. "Neil seemed quite animated while he was talking to you."

"That was just the drink, I'm sure." I glanced around, desperately trying to think of a way to get out of this situation.

"Well, yes, but he clearly had some points to make. What was he getting so het up about?"

He'd come out and said it. I'd have to be careful.

"This and that…" I struggled.

And then I felt an arm around my waist. "I'm so sorry," Robert said in a cool and measured, teacherly voice, "but Edda and I really have to get back, don't we, darling? Nice to meet you Mr Fox."

"Likewise…" Eustace frowned.

Still with a hand around my waist Robert propelled me down the street.

"Keep walking, Edda," Robert was saying, "he'll probably be watching us. Don't let him see your nerves."

"How can you tell I'm nervous?"

"You're shaking."

"And I feel sick," I admitted.

"Well, for God's sake don't hurl on his beloved Brockley pavements. Then he really will flip out."

Despite how I felt I laughed and he squeezed me even closer.

I held my head up and tried my best to walk normally. And focus on Robert holding me tightly. He hadn't let go yet. Which was … promising. And not completely necessary, now that we were out of the view of Fox Estates.

We were home. Home to the paint-peeling gate, the knot garden and my beloved cat, who I could see bobbing up the path to greet us. I bent down to pick him up but he sidestepped me and threw himself at Robert.

"Bloody cat."

"She's not picking up." There was a note of desperation as I put the phone down. For the last quarter of an hour I'd been trying Beth's new Surrey home number and then her mobile. There was no answer on each. "Maybe she's in Burpham…"

"Well she's missing out," he said. We faced the back garden devastation in silence, sipping our coffees.

"Bethan always knows what to do," I said, "I wish she'd pick up. Beth always comes up with the best plans."

"Like the skip?" Robert looked at me.

"No. No that was my idea."

"There you go then," he said, "she doesn't come up with *all* the best plans. And what about getting me in as a lodger?"

"OK. That was Amanda."

"See?"

"Yes, but the skip was my idea and look where it led! I ended up fraternising with a South London criminal empire and knee deep in illegal activities."

"You mean like producing stencils for graffiti artists to deface the neighbourhood?" Robert looked at me, eyebrows raised.

"Fine, OK, that was all my doing! Damnit will you stop pulling me up on everything."

"I'm only saying … you should give yourself some credit for having a brain all of your very own. *You* came up with the skip idea. *You* made the final decision on me as a lodger and so Amanda and my dad ended up together. *You* improved on Da Notorious Baron's graffiti and ended up permanently helping him out. Seriously, Edda, you should give yourself a break."

"Fine. I'm a genius." I said sarcastically. But, inwardly, I felt a little bit better about myself.

"So…" Robert ran a hand along the edge of the bench, "Eustace said something about your boyfriend Guy being upset?"

"He was never my boyfriend," I said. "And yes, I finished with him. But as he wasn't my boyfriend, that doesn't mean much."

"It just means you gave him the brush off and you don't want to see him again," Robert said.

"Something like that."

For a moment we sat and looked straight ahead at the garden.

"So you finished with the poncy artist?"

"He wasn't an artist," I said. "That's one of the things I was trying to tell you last night."

"When you jumped me and started kissing me."

I pursed my lips together. "When I sat on the edge of your bed and gave you a goodnight peck on the cheek."

"Funny," Robert was still absorbed in bench-examining, "I remember it quite differently."

"You must have been dreaming."

He looked up at me and he was smiling.

"Anyway," I said, hideously embarrassed, "it doesn't help us to work out what we should do."

Robert shrugged. "Why should we do anything at all?"

"Oh. I just thought we should do *something*. We can't not do anything can we?" The idea of uncovering what we had about Eustace's Brockley empire and then *just leaving it* had never occurred to me. Why should it, the Famous Five never left the treasure on Kirrin Island just for jollies…

"What good would it do to act on what we know?" Robert said.

"Well, because if we do nothing then Reg is going to be thrown out of his launderette, because he thinks he's in trouble with the Council, and because Eustace's deal is going to look unavoidable. He'll be pushed out of Brockley just like Dino has been from his kebab shop…"

"Maybe."

"Yes, maybe. But also Brockley would be overrun with bay trees."

"So?" Robert said.

"And unsuspecting residents would have their front gardens dramatically altered."

"Again: so?"

"And Babs' grandson would be forced through art college," I said. "So many people are caught up in Eustace's neighbourhood empire, including me. I'm forced to garden for him and I've been given a garden and paints as a sweetener. I can't very easily duck out now that I have so much in terms of an obligation to him."

"True enough." Robert now agreed. "So what are you going to do about Eustace Fox?" He leant back on the bench and took a sip of coffee.

I stared at the desolate back garden for inspiration. "I don't know. That's why I need Beth. Can't I wait for Beth to return my call and then she can tell me what I should do?"

"Edda, Beth is going to take about four-and-a-half hours just listening to all the messages you left her. If we wait for her we'll be waiting forever."

"Urgh. OK then, we could go to the police," I said, throwing my hands in the air.

"And how do you know they would believe you?"

"We could tell them that we interviewed Reg from the launderette. And I could take along this Farrow and Ball colour chart to explain about all the shops being the same…"

"Edda you'd end up blabbing and you'd tell them about you being in the guerrilla gardening group wouldn't you? And then they'd nick you."

"No. Yes. Probably. Oh pants, I couldn't go to the police could I? I'd probably tell them about the stencils and Da Notorious Baron. And then they'd throw away the key."

We sat in more contemplative silence.

"What about," Robert finally said, "what about we tell the police about Eustace Fox's evil empire, but do so *indirectly*. So we grass him up, but we don't get ourselves into trouble."

"You mean we write the police an anonymous letter?"

"No. We tip the police off South London-style." He said the words in a flourish of pride.

"We mug them?"

"Edda, you're an idiot."

"And you're being obtuse!"

Robert stood up. "You don't even know what obtuse means."

I stood up. "Yes I do. It means 'fat'."

He tried to respond but he was laughing too much, so I just affected a superior look and besides, the conversation had to come to an end: Babs was hanging on the garden wall and watching us.

"All right there, me darlin's?"

"Babs!" Robert wiped his eyes and pulled himself together. "Babs you are just the person I wanted to see right now! Can Edda and I come over to your place?"

The newly lit fag fell out of her open mouth: Babs' Christmases had come all at once.

"'e's on 'is way." Babs came back into her kitchen and put the phone on the cradle. "'e's bin working down Deptford way, so I'd give 'im ten minutes. Now then, darlin's, tea is it or shall we go for somethin' stronger? What time is it? Ah it's nearly midday ain't it? What about a gin?"

Babs' kitchen looked like something frozen in time from the 1970s. Robert and I were seated on an orange plastic banquette surrounded by orange and brown wall tiles. The floor was beige, the melamine kitchen units were beige and the walls were beige. The only decoration was the enormous collection of wall-mounted plates commemorating the Royal Family. And, above a giant gold-edged plate of Charles and Diana was mounted the

346

biggest and most frightening machine gun I had ever seen. It was attention-grabbingly huge: matt black with an ominously long silencer that stretched out towards a plate of Prince Andrew and Sarah Ferguson.

"'s a Mac10. Got it from the Peckham Reds last year when we took 'em down."

I whirled round to see who had just spoken. In my anxious state I hadn't noticed the shaven-headed Tyrone at the kitchen door.

"Roney! You're back quick." Babs flew across the room and planted a kiss on her grandson's cheek.

"Jason nicked a BMW last night, we've bin ridin' round in that."

"Oh my boy!" She patted him on the chest, "An' how's little L'Oreal?"

"She's doin' fine, Nan. She 'ad her first chip last night."

Babs clapped her hands together in delight. "You bring your little girl round 'ere this weekend. I'll put on a nice roast. Get some more chips in for 'er if she likes 'em. Bless 'er!"

"'s'up wiv you?" Tyrone dragged an orange bench seat to join us in on the banquette, yanking his crotch pretty much in my face before he sat down, beneath a plate of Prince Philip looking confused.

"I'm fine, thanks. And we're here because Robert has a proposition for you." I said, coming over all Joanna Lumley.

"You what?"

"Custard cream, darlin's?" Babs passed the biscuits round on an Eternal Beau plate.

Robert took a deep breath. "Well, Edda's got herself into some trouble."

"Who da *fuck* is hurtin' you?" Tyrone instantly switched to 'angry' and bit savagely into his custard cream. "'Cause no one ain't gonna hurt none of my friends." He finished the biscuit and then got out an enormous flick-knife from the pocket of his baggy jeans and started to clean his nails with it.

A little part of me felt completely charmed by Tyrone's sentiment and I had the fight the urge to put a hand on his knee and say, "Awww, thanks." But the fear of being stabbed managed to stop me.

"Well," Robert had captured Babs' and Tyrone's attention – and mine too, he still hadn't told me what his plan was – and he played it for all it was worth. Slowly he slid apart his biscuit and ate the cream filling. There was no option but to kick him under the table and mouth: *bloody well hurry up.*

"OK. It's like this, Edda has fallen in – through no fault of her own – with Eustace Fox?"

"Edda!" Babs was horrified. "I thought you said you was no friend of that man."

Robert held up a hand. "He approached her and she thought she was doing the right thing."

"But I wasn't," I added helpfully. "I'll tell you how I got into this mess with Eustace Fox, shall I? And then you can tell us all about your big plan that you still haven't told me about," I said, pointedly, and Robert nodded in agreement.

Babs shuffled onto the banquette with us. "Go on then, darlin', knock us all out."

"Fuck me!" Babs said when I told her about the chandelier-lit basement of the Working Men's Club. *"Bastard!"* as I came to the part about the hoarding of police signs. *"Arsehole,"* she muttered, lighting another fag, as I came to the part about Eustace's boyfriend being employed as the Head of Planning at Lewisham Council. And then, when Robert took over and revealed what we'd found out about the pushing out of Brockley businesses the expletives tumbled from her like water from a waterfall.

Even Tyrone had put down his knife.

"I knew it!" Babs spluttered. "I knew it was organised, all that closin' of shops and businesses an' the openin' of them posh new places with them fancy dwarf trees out front and the same sort o' feel about 'em! I knew it was linked! An' it's 'im: that Eustace Fox. So bleedin' obvious now, ain't it?"

Tryone went back to cleaning out his nails with the knife blade. "This bloke," he said, after a moment's silence, looking up straight at me, "What do you *want* to 'appen to 'im?"

"Pardon?" I looked at Robert who had the answer, apparently. But before Robert could answer Tyrone continued.

"I mean, like, you was talkin' 'bout this man what puts acorns in the pockets of 'is enemies an' maybe he oughta see what that's like. To 'ave it done to 'im."

"Erm..."

"But we ain't got no acorns and I don't know where

we're gonna get acorns from. They don't 'ave no acorns down on no market that I ever saw. Do you 'ave acorns?"

"Erm. No. No I don't have acorns. And I don't really want acorns in his pockets. Although … I do have something." I suddenly remembered something and fished in my pocket, leaning over to Tyrone. "You could put this in his pocket."

"Edda that's not part of my great and splendid plan…!" Robert interrupted.

"Who da fuck is Paul Amos?" Tyrone, very slowly, read the plaque. "'In memory of Paul Amos?' Did Eustace Fox ice this Paul Amos bloke?"

"No – not as such," I said. "Well, he sort of did. In a way. He iced the *memory* of Paul Amos."

"*Fuck dat!*" Tyrone nearly fell of his chair. "How'd he do that? Is he some kinda scientist bloke? Ain't no one gonna ice my memory, no way man. No fuckin' way right there."

"OK." I held my hand out and took back the plaque. "I think perhaps no icing of people…"

"I can get him. I can stab the bastard, I could?"

"No. Really. Thank you," I said. "It's really so nice that you're offering to kill this man for me and I'm really touched that you'd do it, but I don't think that's the answer."

"Fuckin' right dat's de answer! Da Fox guy needs fuckin' *icing!* He needs a fuckin' bullet in his fuckin' *head*. Sorry, Nan."

"Can I butt in?" Robert interrupted the circus. "I do have a plan."

We fell silent.

"OK, well, I think we should basically *out* Eustace Fox. I think we should tell the police?"

"Fuck dat!"

"Ty-rone!"

"Indirectly – we should tell the police *indirectly*," Robert soldiered on, "using the skills of the people around this table." And then, seeing we were still non-plussed, "Using Da Notorious Baron and Da Notorious Sidekick, here." He gestured to me.

"Go on then, darlin'." Babs pushed the Eternal Beau his way. "Knock us all out. What's yer big idea? What do you want us to do?"

Once Robert had told us exactly what his Big Plan entailed, and Babs, Tyrone and I had enthused about it, it took us all afternoon to bring it about. At five Babs put a dinner on for all three of us: *egg an' chips good for all a yer, darlin's?* While around the table Tyrone, Robert and I wordlessly set to work on the sheets of card. Da Notorious Baron had roughed out sketches based on ideas we'd discussed from Robert's Big Plan and, using my craft knife and Tyrone's flick-knife, Robert and I cut out, and improved, the stencils. When any of us spoke it was to work ideas, discuss the drawings and amendments to them. Robert and Tyrone side by side, me opposite and Babs flitting around: *oh that's good darlin', I like 'er, that bloke's just like real life, ain't it clever what you do?*

Every so often, to have a break from the fine knifework, I would look up at my colleagues, absorbed in the shared task. Tyrone with a roll-up, bent over the Formica table and lost to his drawings. And Robert, deep in concentration, flicking his brown hair from his eyes, cutting surprisingly good stencils, slowly and methodically, unlike me with my speedy slices. And the strangest thing, as the four of us passed the impromptu afternoon together, was that it didn't matter that Tyrone was a teenage gangster and Robert and I were … not. Because we were all together in the cause. Tyrone deferred to me for advice, Robert and I discussed cutting techniques. Babs came up with ideas and ogled Robert. For one afternoon we were a team: brought together by criminal activities. Really it was quite beautiful.

"Who is dis geezer?" Tyrone took my t-shirt off the table from where I'd been tracing out around it for a stencil.

"It's Che Guevara." I said.

Tyrone contemplated the print. "He looks cool. What does he do?"

"He's dead. But he was an Argentinian Marxist revolutionary who played a significant role in the Cuban Revolution," I said. When Robert stopped cutting to stare at me I added, "And since his death, his heavily stylised image has become a symbol of anti-establishment and counter-culture."

Now they were all looking at me: Robert paused in his cutting, Tyrone temporarily stopping his sketches and Babs holding the frying pan of eggs.

"And I thought he was a cloth-capped Jesus until someone told me who he was." I added.

352

"Now I can believe that." Robert went back to his cutting. "Edda thought that the Cavaliers won the Civil War."

"Da fuck man?" Tyrone picked up his sheet of card again. "You guys is talkin' fuckin' crazy talk."

"'Roney!"

"Sorry, Nan."

"Where ish thish place?" Robert wheeled round and round and I made a grab for him so that he didn't fall over. I missed him and toppled headfirst into a sharp and prickly shrub.

"Is it? Is it? Is it one of thosh little model villages?" Robert was saying as I picked myself up. "Look atta tiny tiny hedges. Look! Look at the tiny doll hedges! Where ish thish place? Issit a model village? Tiny hedges ahh."

"Issh fron' garden." I staggered towards our front door. "Hhome!"

"Is it? Is it? Is it?" he careered round the knot garden in the dark. I stumbled over to him, managed to grab him by the hand – after a few attempts – and hauled him towards what I hoped was the direction of the front door, based on hazy memory.

"Whassa time?" he squinted at the clock in the super bright hallway.

I shielded my eyes and tried to read the Dali-like clock face where all the numbers were bouncing into each other. "Eight? Eight? I think iss eight." I leant against the wall. "Oh, God."

"Gin!" Robert staggered up to me. "Gin! Babs Gin! Gin!"

It was a while after I woke up that I opened my eyes. There was something pressing down on my feet. I managed, squinting, to look down the end of the bed.

"Fin!" The cat was asleep on my legs. He hadn't slept on my bed for months – he always spent the night with Robert.

Unaccountably delighted to have my old friend back on the bed with me I gently lowered my head onto the pillow and pulled my watch off the bedside table. It was ten in the morning.

"Stop moving," Robert said from somewhere near my shoulder. He threw an arm around me.

Robert was in bed with me.

Oh.

I was in bed with Robert. This was Robert's room. Finley was on the bed because this was Robert's bed.

And … I gingerly lifted up the duvet. Ah. I didn't have any clothes on.

I lay perfectly still for a few seconds. And then I lifted the duvet again.

Neither did Robert.

Golly.

I lifted it a bit higher.

Golly!

"Edda!" The hand moved from my waist and he pulled the duvet down again.

"Sorry."

354

I stared up at the ceiling for a few more moments, then I turned towards Robert and snuggled up to him, naked body against naked body, and fell asleep again.

"Morning."

"Hi."

Blinking the sleep from my eyes, I looked across at the tousle haired lodger.

"What time is it?" he asked.

I checked my watch. "Midday."

"Wow!" he said, impressed. "So..." He smiled from the pillow. "Gin then?"

I could feel myself blushing. "Yes. Gin. Can you remind me what happened? I can't quite..."

"Well we spent the day cutting stencils."

"I remember that."

"And Babs made us dinner."

"I mean what happened after all that."

"Well Tyrone left us after dinner."

"OK..."

"And Babs got the gin out."

"I remember that."

"And we drank."

"Did Babs drink?"

"Don't you remember?"

"No! Remember what?"

"Don't you remember what Babs did?"

"No! What did Babs do?"

"Well her boyfriend came home."

"Oh yes I do remember that. He was very young wasn't he?"

"And you said that you had a pole in the cellar."

"Oh… I didn't did I? Did I tell her about the dancing pole?"

"You did. And her boyfriend and I went to get it."

"Ye-es." I said, the memory coming back to me now.

"And then he and Babs went upstairs. With the pole."

There was a silence in the bed, the only sound was Finley slightly snoring at our feet.

"And we…"

"We carried on drinking in her kitchen."

"While they were upstairs?" I asked.

"Yes."

"With the pole?"

"Yes."

"Oh, God."

"And then we came home."

"Yes."

"And then we came up here."

"A-ha."

"And then…"

"We talked?" I said.

"No Edda. We didn't talk."

"Did we?"

"Did we what?"

"You know…"

"No. We didn't."

"Oh." I lay there, looking at him across the pillow.

"You have a very nice body," he said in a hoarse voice.

"So have you."

"Thank you." And then he reached over and pulled the two together.

I staggered out of the bedroom, pulling my dress on in a bid to exhibit at least some modesty. I clutched the banister as I hurtled down stairs on legs that refused to work properly. Reality seemed rather blurry. I ran into the kitchen and grabbed the phone. It had been ringing almost constantly for the last ten minutes and we'd done our best to ignore it, but clearly somebody somewhere very much wanted to speak to one of us.

"Edda!"

It took a moment for me to place the voice. "Beth!"

"Where have you been?"

It took me a split second to decide that I shouldn't answer that question directly. Where I had been required a long and detailed conversation delivered in person. "What time is it?" I said.

"It's three o'clock!" Beth sounded slightly breathless.

"Is it?" I started laughing. "Is it really?" And then I sobered up in an instant. "Are you OK? Is the baby coming?"

"I'm fine. Why were you laughing – what's going on today?"

"Oh. Nothing. Well. No – I'll tell you when I see you. When are you next coming over to?"

"Eds! Eds do you know your road is on the *national news*?"

"What?" I sobered up in a flash. Robert was coming

down the stairs, deliciously bed-headed and rumple-shirted.

"Eds, I've been watching Geoffrey Road on the BBC news for the last ten minutes. I even saw your house when the presenter was walking past it! Something really big has happened in Brockley."

Oh God. Things were starting to slip into place. Yesterday at Babs'. Tyrone. Robert's Big Plan…

"The police have sealed all the streets off around Brockley Cross. The radio said there are no trains or buses stopping there all day. The local news called Brockley a *lock down*."

"What's happened Beth?"

"Edda, how the bloody hell should I know? I am calling you on your home phone aren't I? How can you be at home and not know that something's going on?"

"Hmmm," I said, realising that yes, actually, I could hear strange noises outside and the sound of at least two helicopters fairly nearby.

"The people on the news aren't able to say anything yet. They're just calling it a *significant incident*, but that there hasn't been any loss of life."

Of course not. Loss of life hadn't been in Robert's Big Plan.

"How come you don't know about it?"

"I?"

"Oh God, Eds! You're not loved up with that artist bloke are you?" she said. "You're not doing that all-day-in-bed thing are you? Oh I hate you! I hate you!"

"Right idea, wrong man." I whispered as Robert left the kitchen.

"What? *What*? Damn your eyes!" Beth said on the other end of the phone. "Call me back when you're free to talk. But in the meantime put some knickers on and get dressed. Find out what the big deal is with Brockley!"

She hung up and I put the phone back on the kitchen shelf.

"It's done?" Robert said, sitting on the bottom stair.

"Sounds like it," I said. "Beth told me it's all over the news."

He was laughing and, joining him on the staircase I couldn't help but laugh along with him. "Oh, bloody hell," I said, "bloody hell."

"Shall we go and investigate?"

It was obvious that something major had happened the minute we stepped out of the knot garden. A police riot van was mounted half on the pavement opposite my house where the skip had once been, and towards Brockley Cross there were policemen *everywhere*. And the noise … crowds talking, people shouting, sirens, car horns on blocked roads further away. It was mayhem.

Dazed, Robert and I walked out into the street, his hand finding mine and making me feel fizzier than a Sherbet Dip Dab.

"No Babs, I see." Robert said and I looked up to her house. The curtains were closed and the front door shut.

"Sleeping it off," I said.

"Or keeping a low profile."

Robert closed the gate behind us. "It's the plan isn't it? All these people and all this police presence. Tyrone must have carried out the plan last night."

"Oh God."

"Are you ready to see our work?"

"I think so." I bit my lip. "There's no turning back now is there?"

"No. Come on."

My heart was pounding in my chest as we walked, hand in hand, down towards Brockley Cross, threading our way through the curious locals: *one more of them gangs' work ain't it,* and frightened newcomers: *I just worry that it's going to bring down our asking price.*

"Look at V-2," I pulled Robert to the café. There were four police officers standing at the front of the café, one of whom was talking to one of the new girls who worked there. She looked terrified. As we drew nearer I could see a note pinned to the window: *Gone to beach. Back (no time) soon.*

"So he's gone…" I said, feeling relief that they'd got out before all this hit. Neil had escaped at last.

"Edda!" Robert pointed to the other window. There was the first of them: a stencil of fox in a pinstriped suit and smoking an enormous cigar with one paw squashing down a rabbit's head. The rabbit was splayed out beneath the fox and in one paw it had a crumpled and spilt coffee cup. FORCED 2 WORK was sprayed across the window.

A woman beside us leant in to me. "I don't see why everyone's going so crazy about it. There's graffiti all over

360

London. Why they have to close down Brockley because of this is a mystery. I mean it's good and all, the fox is brilliant, but it's not a Banksy is it? Or is it?"

"You really think it's brilliant?" I asked, swelling with pride. "You think the fox is brilliant?"

"Come on, you." Robert put a hand behind my back and propelled me away.

"It ain't the quality," a man in a cloth cap piped up, "it's the quantity ain't it? There's loads of the bleedin' stuff all over the place, on them posh shops." He had a bull terrier with him, tied on a piece of blue nylon rope at his side.

"*Edda, stop staring at him.*" Robert hissed in my ear.

"God. Sorry. But he has a cloth cap and a dog *on a string.*"

"Look at this, then," Robert took me by the arm and led me to Fox Estates where two policemen were standing on either side of the doorway and inside were more policemen and what must have been detectives going through paperwork.

And across the spotlessly clean plate glass window was sprayed X MARKS DE SPOT.

"Oh my God."

"Hey it came out really well." Robert nodded to the stencil of a fox standing upright, tailored in a pin-striped suit, fanning himself with a paw full of bank notes. And, poking out of the back of his stripy suit jacket – a thick, arched tail. "I didn't think the pinstripes would come out because they were so fine. It's a good job you had that craft knife, I'd never be able to have done it with Tyrone's blade. He did a good job spraying them on."

"Or you could shut up." I said, jabbing him in the ribs. At least one person had overheard what he'd said and was looking curiously in our direction.

"Can you see Eustace?" I whispered, craning my neck over the crowds on the street and looking into the busy estate agency. There must have been ten policemen in the building.

"No. Is there a back room or an upstairs? If they're questioning him on-site they'll probably do it away from all these people." Robert turned to me. "How are you feeling?"

"Scared," I said. "And excited. Does that make sense?"

"Yes. Come on, let's see what else there is."

On a mission, now, Robert and I sped on, through denser crowds and round the corner to the Petit Marché. A pool of brilliant red paint was puddled on the pavement with a thin trickle running from the door of Mr Iqbal's shop. In the same vibrant red but spray-painted onto the window was the word *VICTIM* with two bikini-clad Miss-World types stencilled either side, posing in a mock-shocked attitude, mouths open and hands on foreheads.

"Yours?" Robert asked.

"Yup. Well, Tyrone's, of course, but modified by me."

"It's very good. I didn't see that you'd done that one."

"Edna and Robert!" Mr Iqbal emerged from the store. "Here, have a nut bar, my dear customers! Well what a very exciting day this is, don't you think so? What a day for Brockley!"

"Thanks." Robert took the nut bar and immediately

362

tucked in. I looked at him, horrified. He obviously wasn't *sufficiently* scared and unnerved by what was going on for his appetite to be suppressed. I, on the other hand, felt so nauseous that I would never be able to eat again in my entire life. Everyone around us – the police, the people, the TV crews – was here because of something I had done, because of an idea that the man beside me had come up with. It seemed incredible that we could pass through the crowds completely unnoticed because – to me – it felt as though there was an enormous red flashing arrow above my head with the word *GUILTY* above it.

"And take a look, here, at my window." Mr Iqbal pointed, proudly, at the stencil we had cut for him.

"It'll wash off." I said to Mr Iqbal. "You haven't got any paint on the woodwork so it should all go."

"Oh I like it, Edna." He turned to the bikini women. "I've had so much interest in it. I gave an interview to the BBC and to Channel 4 and a lovely woman from a newspaper. I gave her a nut bar too, she was very polite. I think it's very good and I've sold so much stock today it's incredible." As we stood talking to him I noticed that the basket on the front of the old bike now contained imported tins of coconut milk and packs of rice. "I don't know why my window has the word 'victim' on it though. Perhaps it is because my beautiful trees have been set alight. For that I am very sorry, because they were such a kind gift. But then all the little trees have been set on fire so we are all victims today in Brockley. Do you know what is going on? I really have not one idea."

"No," I said. "Is there more round the corner?"

"Go and see," he said. "And you will think I have escaped lightly, yes?"

He went back into his shop and I turned to face the approach to the station. It was easy to cross the road now that the traffic had been banned: we walked up to the gardens that I had helped dig what seemed like a lifetime ago.

"Of all of the stencils we did," I said, admiring our work, "this was this one that I thought was least likely to work. But it looks great doesn't it?"

A King-Kong style gorilla with a trowel was standing astride the wall, roaring.

"That is so cool," Robert said. "You are a guerrilla gorilla graffiti genius!"

To draw the gorilla gardener I'd gone back home to get my Child's Picture Book with its double page picture of King Kong, which Tyrone copied and I had embellished with his help: *no that won't work sprayed up, you need more fur here…*

I'd wondered, while I cut out the gorilla, just what my parents would have thought if they had known how the book was going to be used: "To Edda," said the inscription on the front page, "Happy Christmas 1982, love Mummy and Daddy xxx". The surprising thing had been that I hadn't felt sad when I'd seen it: far from it I'd felt happy, happy that in some silly small way my parents were still a part of my life now, thanks to the purchase of a book so many years ago. It was because of them that I had a picture that I could use. Somehow, stupid I know, they were with me.

We left the gorilla and some students taking photographs of it and walked down the road, past Reg's launderette and on to the deli: I FORCED DA SHOP OUT slashed across the window, a fox bounding along the window with red paws, red paint dripping like blood down the window and pooling again on the pavement. Again at the bistro: PUB LICENZ REJECTED 4 ME, the antique shop: DIS PLACE RENT FREE and on. Foxes running on the windows, leaping on doorways with their bloodied paws and the occasional fox paw print trail in blood red paint on the pavements. Robert had traced them from the same Child's Picture Book. And everywhere there were burnt bay trees, kicked over into the pavements with their soil scattered and their chains cut from the walls.

"Hi there," a policeman was suddenly beside me. "Sorry to make you jump," he opened his pad. "Do you mind if I ask you a couple of questions? We're asking everyone round here."

"Sure. Fine. Absolutely." I tried a smile.

"What's your name, love?"

"Edda Mackenzie."

"And you live locally?"

"189 Geoffrey Road." He noted it all down in an official notebook. Robert put an arm around me and held me tight. Which was good as I was shaking so much my voice was starting to go funny.

"And where were you last night?"

"I was at home."

"Alone?"

"No. With my erm…" I looked to Robert.

"Live-in lover," he said, absolutely straight-faced.

The policeman didn't even blink. "I'll put partner if you don't object, sir."

"That's fine."

"And did you and your *partner* see anything or hear anything suspicious in the night? Anything at all?"

"No. We're pretty heavy sleepers," Robert said, "aren't we darling?" He turned to face me.

I could have punched him. "Yes. Yes we are."

The policeman asked Robert's name and while he was answering I could see Claude being led out of his bistro and taken to the back of a waiting police car, escorted by two officers.

"Do you have any leads at all?" I asked the policeman. "Do you know anything about what's behind all this?"

"We're following up a number of avenues," he said and then asked us to get in touch if we could think of anything.

We left and wandered back to Fox Estates, where a TV crew were setting up for a transmission.

"I don't think he's in there," I said.

"Do you want to see his house?" Robert said suddenly. "Da Baron might have gone there too."

"We didn't talk about that, did we?"

"No, but he might have gone off-plan and decided to do something on his own."

We turned and walked briskly beyond *our* house – still no Babs next door – and down towards Eustace's grand villa.

"What do you think Tyrone will have done?" I asked as we walked. "Used more of the fox stencils on Eustace's house? What good would that do?"

"I have an idea…" Robert said. "It was the way he looked at you when you told him about that soirée you went to at Eustace's house."

"What about it?" I asked, but it was too late. We were in Tresillian Road.

"He *has* been here." I said. There were more police cars but there were fewer spectators this far away from the main scene of the crime in Brockley Cross.

I couldn't help laughing. "Oh my God, Robert!" We walked slowly up to Eustace's house – or as near to it as we were allowed to get what with the police tape rolled out around it.

"That boy," Robert was laughing, "is a genius! I like Da Notorious Baron's style!"

I got my phone out and took a picture of the scene before me. "Beth is going to love this!" I looked at the photograph, laughed and then forwarded it on to Beth's phone.

Positioned in front of Eustace's house were all the police signs he had ever taken off the streets, listing all the crimes that had been committed in the area: the stabbings and snatchings and muggings.

"Tyrone must have broken in to Eustace's house last night, liberated and arranged them," I said. "Can you imagine what Eustace must be thinking right now? The horror at seeing his empire collapse?"

"And there is the man himself," Robert said and I

looked up to see Eustace, in handcuffs, being escorted down the beautiful mosaic-tiled path that I'd walked up seemingly so long ago.

He was scowling hard, and sweating profusely; even from across the road I could see the shine on his ruddy forehead. It took him and the policeman beside him a while to negotiate all the tightly packed police signs and as he did so Eustace looked up straight at us.

Even though I was feeling terrified I managed to summon up the courage to wave at him and Robert gave him the thumbs up. Eustace scowled and was then pushed down into the back of a waiting police car. The car started and it sped down the hill in the direction of Lewisham town centre.

My phone beeped and I read my text. It was from Beth. "ON MY WAY!"

Robert nudged me in the ribs. "Edda!"

"What?" I looked up and Robert was pointing to further down the road just beyond Eustace's house. "Oh! Guy!"

Guy was standing on the pavement at the entrance to the track leading to his mews house. He was taking in the sight of the police signs and the police cars and police tape. And then he looked up and saw me. His face fell – even from this distance I could exactly make out his expression: *'YOU!'*

I laughed when I saw his reaction.

"Tell me what it meant," Robert slunk an arm around me as Guy looked on. "Tell me why you had Tyrone spray that enormous stencil of Che Guevara up on the wall of Guy's house."

"Well, Guy noticed once that I wore that t-shirt with the picture of Che Guevara on and he imagined I was some sort of follower of the man. He used to call me his militant Edda, and say that I was a dispossessed Highlander or some such nonsense. So I got Tyrone to spray up that enormous image of Che Guevara and have *I AM DA NOTORIOUS BARON* written across it."

"So he'll definitely know it's you doing the graffiti?"

"I should think so." I was watching him, staring at Robert and me from down the road. "He said that he really rated Da Baron, and that the graffiti showed real artistic merit. So I wonder how he's feeling now that he knows that it was me who was at least partly responsible for it."

"I don't know about you," Robert said, "but I could really do with a drink."

"Gin?"

"No! Not gin. Never again in my life. I was thinking more along the lines of a beer."

"Well we can't go to the bar at the bistro or to V-2 café," I said. "How about the Barge?"

"Perfect." He slid his arm around me and, without a backward glance at Guy I walked with Robert back to the pub.

"I like your Big Plan," I said. "Do you think it will have worked?"

"Definitely. The police are bound to investigate what's behind the businesses aren't they."

"And you really don't think that Tyrone is going to get caught?"

"No. And anyway, he's doing the police a service isn't he? He's a copper's nark: even if they do work out who Da Notorious Baron is and catch him then they'll only want to know how he came by the information. He's working for the police on this one."

"*We're* working for the police," I said. "Anyway, if he's Da Notorious Baron and I'm Da Notorious Sidekick, what are you?"

"Da Notorious Planmeister," he said after a moment's thought.

We were on Geoffrey Road again and heading towards Brockley Cross.

"Beth's on her way," I said.

"Shall I get hold of dad and Amanda and ask if they can make it?" he asked. "We could properly celebrate the reclaiming of SE4. What do you think?"

"Definitely," I said as we walked past my house and on to the pub.

"All right there, me darlin's! Lovely day, ain't it, eh?"

Epilogue

[Extract from the *Guardian Weekend* Supplement]

THE JOY OF SE4 – Cleaned up in more ways than one

An elegant suburb on the doorstep of Central London, affordable properties and just a whiff of scandal makes SE4 well worth investigating *writes Derek Offshore*.

I start my visit to Brockley in the V-2 café near the station. On its walls are framed black and white photographs of devastation – a not-so-gentle reminder to those enjoying the freshly baked muffins and fine coffees that this part of South London suffered the infamous V-2 rocket attacks during the Second World War. "The old bomb sites are where you see the 1970s low-rise tower blocks," the owner of the café, Edda Mackenzie, tells me.

But it's not the tower blocks that are the pull to this area of South London: it's the stuff in between. The elegant early Victorian villas, the bijou coach houses and the sweeps of terraces almost all of which fall within a conservation area – put in place to stop more devastation in the eighties, this time not by the Germans but the town planners. "It's the most exciting place to be in

London," says Nigel Green, the sharp-suited owner of the new agency Brockley Estates that has opened up at Brockley Cross. "They say if there's a Starbucks in an area then you've already missed the boat in finding a gentrified area – house prices will already be high. I can tell you there isn't a Starbucks in Brockley yet, but a planning application has been granted for one in the south of the area, near Hilly Fields."

Nigel's words *Brockley* and *planning permission* were perhaps also a sly nod to the owner of a former local estate agency: Fox Estates. Fox hit the headlines nearly a year ago for operating a network designed to 'cleanse' Brockley of its South London roots, which the owner – one Eustace Fox – found personally distasteful.

"It's all in the past," Nigel Green is keen to tell me. "New businesses, *legitimate businesses*, have started up in the premises of the old businesses. What Eustace Fox started has taken off, but this time with more of a community spirit and everyone included. Brockley plays by the rules these days. It's a party and everyone's invited."

Edda from V-2 Café is less sure. "Brockley's never going to be totally straight, in the way that Greenwich or Blackheath are straight." To illustrate her point she gestures out of the window down towards Foxberry Avenue. In the last week a giant skip has been guerrilla gardened: painted a pillar box red and covered in turf the Skip Garden is dominated by a silver table and chairs which had been stolen from outside her café. "I don't mind." Edda tells me. "It's art. It's beautiful and it was created by a real artist."

I ask her who the artist is but she just shrugs and says nothing. There are still some secrets hanging around in SE4. On the subject of art, the now famous graffiti artist Da Notorious Baron hails from Brockley and was responsible for exposing Eustace Fox's fraudulent activities via street art, some of which has been preserved by a surprisingly open-minded Lewisham Council. "It's a positive contribution to the look and feel of the area," Greg Watson, the recently appointed Head of Planning at Lewisham Council informs me. "We have our own Banksy right here, fronting what is a burgeoning art scene." Da Notorious Baron had his own art exhibition at Lewisham Town Hall in February of this year – made even more public when fellow graffiti artist Banksy contributed to two of the pieces in his own signature style and spurred the infamous graffiti-off that stretched through London.

So, Brockley is on the up: it has the houses, it has the art scene, and it has an edge that the pipe-and-slippers neighbourhoods of Greenwich and Blackheath can only dream of.

Before I leave Brockley I pay the guerrilla gardened Skip Garden a visit. There's an empty bottle of Cava glued onto the table and two empty wine glasses stuck beside it. A toast to Brockley's future, perhaps…

More from Claire Peate

CLAIRE PEATE was born in Derby and lives in Cardiff with her husband and two children. She studied English Language & Linguistics at Sheffield University, and now works as an associate director in the market research industry. She has been a speaker at several festivals, including the *Guardian Hay Festival*.

Praise for Claire Peate

"More substance than your average chick lit" Big Issue

"The suspense and humour will keep you gripped"
Western Mail

"Very well written, wry and funny" dovegreyreader.co.uk

"A light-hearted and fun read" The Bookbag

"...will keep you turning the pages"
South Wales Evening Post

"Claire Peate writes with wit, affectionate humour and insight" www.gwales.com

Headhunters by Claire Peate

9781906784027
£7.99

A 'girl's own' adventure for grown-ups

Winchester's not the most happening of cathedral cities, but journalist Kate might find something juicy to dig up on the newly appointed Dean, Archie Cartwright. He's not so much socks and sandals as Converse All-Stars and Italian sports cars. A thief has just lifted the head of Canute out from under Archie's nose, his eye being caught by a rather tempting lady cleric.

Up in London, Edgar Thompson is having a hard time keeping a lid on the biggest archaeological find in British history – currently being exposed beneath Kings Cross' busiest platforms. Especially when the most important artefact of all – another famous ancient's skull – disappears overnight.

Where are the heads going? Will Kate, Archie and Edgar manage to find them before their own careers do a similar disappearing act? Not if Archie's Bishop, Kate's conniving colleagues and Edgar's over anxious father have anything to do with it...

All Honno titles can be ordered online at
www.honno.co.uk,
or by sending a cheque to Honno
with **free** p&p to all UK addresses.

Big Cats and Kitten Heels by Claire Peate

9781870206884
£6.99

Rachel's staring a Dull Life Crisis in the face... With a lifestyle that owes more to *TV Quick* than *Tatler* or *Wanderlust*, it's time to get up off the sofa and out into the wide open spaces before she loses any more of her best mates to the bony-bottomed, manipulative, but 'marvellous', Marcia and her dazzlingly awful zest for life.

Luckily, the very next weekend offers her best chance of excitement in months: she's booked on a hen weekend in the Brecon Beacons packed with horse-riding, hiking and lots, lots more.

And what with sheep torn in two, perma-tanned South African big game hunters and a devastatingly attractive Welsh farmer in waxed jacket and wellies, it turns out to be a much bigger adventure than even marvellous Marcia could have wished for.

All Honno titles can be ordered online at
www.honno.co.uk,
or by sending a cheque to Honno
with **free** p&p to all UK addresses.

The Floristry Commission by Claire Peate

9781870206747
£6.99

There are some things in life you'll never forget – or forgive – that mean flinging your plum suede kitten heels into a bag and leaving without a backward glance...and most of your wardrobe.

For Rosamund it was the sight of her erstwhile boyfriend making love to her swine of a sister in front of the fridge. She's nowhere to go but the Welsh Marches and her old schoolfriend Gloria – after all, she could hardly run home to Mum.

But if Roz thought the City was full of intrigue and betrayal, it's got nothing on Kings Newton. Before she knows it, she's up to her eyes in trouble with the testily pre-nuptial Gloria, planning floral subterfuge with a camp and gossipy colleague, and covering for all and sundry in a desperate attempt to survive the battle between the swoon-inducing lord of the manor and his unruly townsfolk.

All Honno titles can be ordered online at
www.honno.co.uk,
or by sending a cheque to Honno
with **free** p&p to all UK addresses.

ABOUT HONNO

Honno Welsh Women's Press was set up in 1986 by a group of women who felt strongly that women in Wales needed wider opportunities to see their writing in print and to become involved in the publishing process. Our aim is to develop the writing talents of women in Wales, give them new and exciting opportunities to see their work published and often to give them their first 'break' as a writer.

Honno is registered as a community co-operative. Any profit that Honno makes is invested in the publishing programme. Women from Wales and around the world have expressed their support for Honno by buying shares. Supporters liability is limited to the amount invested and each supporter has a vote at the Annual General Meeting.

To buy shares or to receive further information about forthcoming publications, please write to Honno at the address below, or visit our website: www.honno.co.uk.

Honno
Unit 14, Creative Units
Aberystwyth Arts Centre
Penglais Campus
Aberystwyth
Ceredigion
SY23 3GL